LOTTIE

LOTTIE

Jacqueline Jacques

HONNO MODERN FICTION

Published by Honno
'Ailsa Craig', Heol y Cawl, Dinas Powys
Bro Morgannwg CF64 4AH

First impression 1997
© Jacqueline Jacques

ISBN 1 870206 23 1

**Published with the financial support of the
Arts Council of Wales**

Cover design by Penni Bestic

Typeset and printed in Wales by Dinefwr Press, Llandybïe

For Peter,
whose love and support made this possible

9 September 1999

A door bangs, startling me. Was I asleep?

Feet scuff and it's the cleaner pushing his broom along the wide top step, solo performer on an empty stage. Round the pillars, sweep, sweep. He stops, grunting, to pick up empty packets and cans, dropping them in his bin-bag. He has his routine by heart. He starts down the gallery steps, left to right, then down and right to left. Soft. Shoe. Shuffle. Sweep, sweep, stop, grunt, clatter, to the next and the next. Towards the ninth step where I am sitting. Still.

I feel, I suppose, much as litter might feel. Guilty, redundant, out of place.

But I'm not. Not at all. The ninth step on the ninth of the ninth, ninety-nine. That was what we agreed. I'm here where I'm supposed to be. This is the one date you don't break, not if you know what's good for you.

He's coming. Hands twist in my lap, one trying to calm the other. Nails thick and ridged under two layers of lacquer. Age spots masquerading as freckles. It's all a masquerade now.

He whistles through his teeth until he reaches the step above mine, the tenth. Pauses. He cannot ignore me any longer.

'Stopping there all night, gel?'

He thinks I'm a bag-lady. Once he would have called me 'miss' or 'darling'. I tell him I'm meeting friends, and see my vowels unsettle him. Now he doesn't know what to make of me.

'At nine.' Why do I feel he has to approve? Has to understand?

'Yeah? You got a long wait.'

'Not much longer now.'

He chuckles, not getting the point. But how can he know I've been waiting here all day? Since the crack of dawn? Nine o'clock on the ninth. They'll laugh when I tell them. Because, of course, they didn't mean nine o'clock in the morning. Silly me.

'Fought you was finking of nicking the exhibits.'

'Sorry?'

He explains, 'Making off with a picture in your 'anbag.'

'Oh.' Whatever is he talking about? I have a shoulder-bag, a small shoulder-bag. And the only pictures are the postcards, bought when the gallery was closing, written and ready to post. Just in case.

He can't mean them? Unless he has found me out. Has he? Somehow? Fingers flutter over the fastener. Eyes mist, blood beats in my ears. He's watching. He's been watching all day. He knows ...

Then I realize, oh God, that, of course, he was joking.

I smile with difficulty.

He tells me, 'Funny place to meet someone, steps of the Tate. Dead and alive round 'ere after dark.'

True.

'We always meet here.'

I can tell he doesn't believe me.

'Every eleven years.'

'Oh, right.' He nods, clearly casting me as a silly old bat. Playing along, he says, 'Got something special on, have you?'

Only suicide.

His mood changes when I simply flash him another stiff smile.

'You going to let me do that step?'

I move so he can tut and whistle over my lonely heap of cigarette ends. Somehow it doesn't feel right up here. That wasn't the arrangement. When the cleaner has gone I go down to the street and count up again to nine.

*　　*　　*

Downriver, past Lambeth Bridge, past Hungerford Bridge, the millennium bandwagon has come to the South Bank. Finger-posts on Riverside Walk point discreetly to theatre, art and music to delight the connoisseur. But it is night-time now – everyone's gone home. A breeze has come up from the river to bowl a can along a deserted terrace, flip the festive banners with a careless rhythm.

And down among boxes and beer-farts, Bri snorts awake and opens an eye at the dark, fighting a full bladder without hope. Cursing, he crawls from his greasy quilt and lurches out to the terrace. You don't piss on your own doorstep, even here. Moonlight and floodlight focus on a single earring and piece together the tousled frame of a man, young in years only. A dog pads

2

after him, its claws clicking on the pavement. The youth yawns and scratches between his buttocks as he pisses off the embankment into the ebbing tide. The dog sniffs out its own spot at the entrance to the Festival Pier and lifts a leg briefly, then follows its nose along the railings until it reaches a gap and skitters down some narrow steps to the silted mud below, in search of adventure.

"Ere, boy,' whispers the youth, hoarsely, 'come back 'ere, yer bleeder!' When the dog fails to return, he shrugs and goes shuffling back to his filthy nest. But he is pulled up sharp by a din of barking that cleaves the skull. 'Fucking hell!' he mutters. 'Fucking shut your row, can't ya?' But the dog goes racketing on, excitement amplified to hysteria under the hollow bridge.

'I'll kill him!' Armed with loathing and an empty bottle from beside a bin, he steps down carefully into the dark, his hopes of sleep seeping like sump oil into the mud.

A girl in a blanket appears and leans over the rail, calling down unnecessarily, "E's under the bridge. Shut 'is row, for fuck's sake, Bri. He'll wake the bleeding dead. What's he got, anyway?'

'Dunno. Rat, prob'ly.'

'Aagh, Bri, I hate them things. Get it off him.'

'Have to get hold of him first,' says Bri, picking his way gingerly over reflections in the squelch. He is almost under the bridge and can see the dog's jigging dance spotlit by the full September moon. The cause of its frenzy seems to be nothing more than a pale heap of rags, washed through by the tide and left to dry on the mud-bank behind the concrete stanchion. Bri's echo says, 'Pawh! Bloody stinks under here ...' but the words are choked off by the dog's clamour and his own rising bile. For his stomach has already analysed what his eyes are still questioning and then he understands why the dog, a hard-bitten scavenger, is standing back.

When Bri emerges from the shadows at the thin end of the wedge he is dragging the dog by the collar, but it is not fury that propels him, pell-mell, over the stinking ooze; pell-mell and mindless of the sliming of his jeans and the filling of his shoes. His pallor is luminous, like an epileptic's in recovery, and his eyes are wide and white. 'Oh, fuck!' he gasps at the top of the steps. 'I'm gonna puke.'

* * *

3

No doubt about it: she was a dab hand at suicide. Neat, sure, almost practised. As you'd expect from one who had considered ways and means for over forty years. On Vauxhall Bridge, halfway across, there are dried dribbles of the blood that spurted from her throat. From the direction and shape of the stains, they figure she must have been perched up on the rail with her back to the river, so that, in dying, she would have done a frogman's tumble down off the bridge. Her shoes were lined up neatly, as if beside a hotel bed, left where she had removed them to aid her backward scrabble up the barrier. The heels of her tights had been snagged by rust and peeling paint. They never found the weapon but they think it must have been a scalpel or something equally sharp. There was a gill-like slit under her left jaw, the trial attempt, and then a strong, deep, gaping wound from ear to ear; the obscene toothless grin that had made a sick joke of Bri's supper.

Otherwise he might have had the wit to turn her over, search the shoulder-bag, slung securely across her body and buried beneath her, in the mud. He would have found money, both folding and plastic, among the sodden contents, and a 1999 diary. Just legible still, after a birthday reminder, the entry for Friday, 9 September, is ringed in red: '9 o'clock – Tate Gallery – Final Reunion.'

CHAPTER ONE

Rosie in May, 1954

It was too hot for chemistry. The windows beat solid slabs of sun into the work-benches, and mirages shimmered around the flames of fifteen bunsen burners.

Anna and I sweltered over ours in the back row, our skins gently poaching. Our test-tube was a distraction. Anna had had another letter from her 'big cheese', smelly Alan from Manchester. We'd met him on our Easter hostelling holiday. She had led him on and led him on and now he couldn't sleep for thinking about her.

'How pathetic,' said Fen, who knew a thing or two about boys.

So Anna was composing a reply, with our help, to dump him. It would hurt, we knew that, but you had to nip these things in the bud, as it were. It was kinder in the long run. And you couldn't get serious about blokes who worked in cheese factories. In Manchester.

She could hardly wait to get the letter in the post.

He would have it in the morning, which, I pointed out, would be the fourth of the fifth, fifty-four. A palindrome.

The test-tube clouded.

'A palin-whatta?' Jo looked up from the next burner, fine tendrils of red hair sticking to her forehead.

'Reads the same forwards as backwards, like Mum,' I said.

'Or Anna,' said Anna.

'Or Abracadabra,' said Jo.

'No,' said Anna.

'So, anyway,' said Jo, 'if tomorrow's a palin-thing, that makes it special, yeah? Like, lucky.'

The test-tube blackened.

'Auspicious,' I said.

'Portentous,' corrected Anna.

'Unlucky for him, though, poor guy. Was he really going to hitch-hike all the way from Manchester just to see you?'

'Pathetic ...'

The teacher was on the prowl, so I covered the letter with my book and wrote *Aim*, ruled beneath it twice, reverently, and the teacher moved away. The test-tube fizzled and the whiff of a notion wafted into my head. I pulled out another set of centre pages from my anorexic exercise book, wiped my sweaty palms on my blouse and wrote:

As it's a palindrome, we should do something to make tomorrow memorable – Luv Rosie

So I started it. Me.

If it had been a film they'd have had the music to go with it. Prokofiev in a minor key, to ensure that the audience did not miss the SIGNIFICANCE of the moment.

I watched with mild nausea as Smudge sucked the end of her pencil. It was chewed soft and wet and ragged. Sandra Mary Hodgekiss, puppy fat and eager, was partnering Jo, and her cheeks shone dirty pink as she wrote '*A party?*' beneath my fateful words.

The note came back to our end of the bench curling grey from sweaty fingers. It read:

A party! Grate idear! Rosy can bring her lot from chruch – Jo
Get your brother to come, Anna – Fen
Can you lend me your blue top Rosie? – Smudge
Time/Place?? – Maggie
How about Annas? – Jo
Sorry, folks – Maths, Latin and History homework tomorrow night. Parties are off. Anyway, my mum says she wants six months notice next time! – Anna. She'd drawn a picture of her portly mother, with electrified hair, and a round mouth going 'Eek!'

But we got to sellibrate tommorow must be a truning piont. Thats inportant. Jo's spelling was depressing.

Maggie had written a cryptic *Point of no return ... ???*

Maggie's little joke. She had a one-track mind, but we could all keep up with her. I wrote:

We're not talking IT, are we, Mags? – Who did you have in mind? – luv Rosie.

My little joke. Our encounters with boys had been the kiss and 'fend off' kind, apart from my brush with Geoff Singleton after Evensong last Sunday. I couldn't tell them how my hand had been shoved against a hard bulge in his trousers. If that was the shape of things to come you could keep it!

Anna added a caricature of a couple doing 'IT', each with some-what excessive equipment and smiley faces. There were bright

6

pornographic sparks erupting from their middles and the comment 'Bingo!'

The note came back with Jo's spelling mistakes corrected and a scrubbed-out scribble from Smudge, which had been overwritten with:

Someone come up with something sensible for God's sake. And what was the best that *she* could offer? *How about coming to school out of uniform? All for one and one for all – Smudge*

Boring! I wrote. *No, it's got to be something we'll remember all our lives.*

What, like arson?

Can't read your writing, Smudge. Arse what? – Maggie

Burn something. Games pavilion? The hockey sticks would make a lovely bonfire – Smudge

Why? – Fen and Maggie XX

I abhor and detest hockey – Smudge

I doant

Don't think so, Smudge. Where else would we meet? – Anna

My Dad's allotment shed? – Rosie

There followed an interval of deep prayerful thought, answered by Maggie and Fen's test-tube issuing forth black papal smoke and then bursting into poisonous shards. A snaggle of blood curled around Maggie's thumb and she dripped an impressive crimson trail along the floor of the classroom and out of the door.

Anna wrote: *It's a sign! We must do a blood pact. Swear eternal friendship, the six of us.*

Ow! – from Jo

Cut our thumbs with a razor? And she drew a diagram of a thumb, complete with arrows and dollops of blood.

Not how? Ow!

I abhor and detest pain – Smudge

Only a little scratch – won't hurt. Tomorrow morning, the fourth, before dawn, at Rosie's dad's allotment – Anna

My heart sank. Me and my big ideas! Perhaps it would rain.

Our test-tube went next, with a decisive *crack*! and Smudge sat on the note (girls had been expelled for less) while the teacher hurried to our bench with a dustpan and brush. She accused us of doing it on purpose. And apparently we should have produced some sort of crystal, not brown sludge. We all had to turn off the burners and admire Olive Bracknell's in the front row, and then wash up.

'So what time's "before dawn" then?' Smudge wanted to know.
'Dunno. Four?' I said.
'I'll never make it. They won't let me out at that time in the morning.'
'If you're not there we can't do it. We need everyone.' Anna was good at making you feel guilty.
'You can say you're 'elping me do the papers, if you like. Oh, look at that!' said Jo, having scrubbed her test-tube so hard that the brush came out of its bottom. 'Mi-i-iss!'
'What is this, a conspiracy?' snapped the teacher. 'Oh, put it in the bin, Josephine, for goodness' sake! And stop grinning, girl. Do you take me for a fool? The first test-tube might have been an accident, the second unlikely, but the third strikes me as something altogether more significant!'
We thought so, too. And not only because she made us promise to buy new ones. Three broken test-tubes were so meaningful. The blood pact was a must. And Smudge had to be there.

* * *

I could see why she was doubtful; Smudge's dad needed to know the ins and outs of a duck's behind, my dad said, when he didn't think I was listening. They taught in the same school. Derek Hodgekiss was a small, fussy ex-RAF navigator, with glasses and a moustache. She was a small, worried child, with glasses and inhibitions. Play, with little Sandra, had been hard work. She had needed props and prompting all the way. I'd be charging over deserts on the rocking-horse, creeping through dense forests, scaling glass mountains to do battle with the twin-headed ogre, and she'd be sitting there, simpering, in her Mum's old dance frock and silver sandals, waiting to be fed her next line.
Not like the adventures I had with Anna. We had rapport. With a look, it was understood that the only way to escape the sabre-toothed tiger was to climb the nearest tree. Too bad that I got the hem of my dress caught on a jagged branch. Without a word, we knew we had to roll over and over down giggling green hills to catch the Golden Bird of Memory. Too bad that a muddy swamp awaited us at the bottom. We could sit for hours in a hollow tree or a wardrobe or my Nan's cellar, sharing silent thoughts or talking fantasy. Too bad that they had been looking for us for tea, or shopping, or a clinic appointment. Together we

8

sat in the treatment room, reading nasally from *The Magic Faraway Tree* while rubber tubes, like elephant tusks, drained our catarrh into kidney dishes. Too bad they thought she was a bad influence.

I had known immediately who it was, when I was woken in the middle of the night by low voices at the front door.

'Treasure? What treasure?' Mum demanded of the little girl whose knocking had woken her. Anna was still in her nightie, cuddling her cat for company, with sticking-plaster over the lens of her pink National Health glasses to cure a lazy eye.

'In the cave under the floorboards.'

'Cave?'

'Under Rosie's bed. I've come to help her and ... and ...'

I dived under the bedclothes ...

Breakfast was a gentle inquisition. They thought my imagination a precious thing. They didn't call it lies, not then. I sort of remembered telling Anna about the treasure but I never, for one minute, thought she would take me up on it. Naturally I denied all knowledge and they believed me. They always believed me: 'Such a good girl!' Anna must have been having some sort of crazy dream.

'Mad Anna', my Mum called her. But she was neither mad nor bad, but God's sweetest gift to childhood. A gullible friend.

So there were three of us, for starters, on that first day in the grammar school. We huddled together for strength in our bulky green uniforms, two sizes too big (to allow for growth), and labelled to absurdity. Even our navy school knickers had our names on: Anna Turnbull, Rosemary Woodhouse and S. M. Hodgekiss, which was speedily diminished. She was clearly more Smudge than Sandy, with egg on her tie and accumulating ink stains and mud and grass and school milk and dinner by the minute. You wore your blouse for the week in those days, gym-slips for half a term, so you learned to be careful. Smudge was a slow learner.

It was during a maths lesson that we decided that Jo had possibilities, despite her lower-Walthamstow aspirates, lack of. Anna and Smudge and I were lower-Walthamstow, too, but our parents were upwardly striving and we were snobs.

'Miss,' piped up this redhead from the seat in front, 'I got these sums right and you marked 'em wrong!'

'Because you haven't put down your working-out, child. For all I know, you could have copied from the girl next to you.' Who was Smudge, who, no way, would have provided the right answers.

'I ain't no cheat, Miss.'

We all put down our pens and waited.

'No, I don't suppose you are. But working-out would be proof, do you see?'

'I don't need to do no workin'-out, Miss.'

'*Really*, Josephine ...'

'Give us a sum, Miss.'

'What?'

'Give us a sum. Make one up.'

Tight-lipped, Miss Watkins wrote on the board: *x squared = 3 (x + y) + 3*.

Jo looked at it for a moment and said, 'Six, *x* is six. And *y* is five.'

And when Miss Watkins had worked it out, she had to admit that Jo was right.

'Now tell us how you did it.'

'It just come to me, Miss.'

'An intuitive, how extraordinary! But I'm warning you child, you will never amount to anything unless you conform,' and turned back to the board.

'Hey, Ginger ...' whispered Anna at the freckled neck, eager to extend the hand of friendship to a fellow genius. The girl whirled on her, her silky pony-tail whipping spots of rage into her cheeks.

'Bugger off,' she snarled.

'The name is Jo,' she informed Anna at the next break, bouncing up and down on her stomach, fingers twined in coarse, tawny hair. 'What is it?'

'Ah! Ah! Ow, shit! Okay, okay! Jo, bloody Jo! How was I to know you were touchy about it? Bloody get off and let go my hair!'

'Just so's you know. I ain't "Coppernob" nor "Carrots" nor "Ginger" nor "Red" nor nothing, only Jo. Got it?'

That half-term we took her with us to the fair on Chingford Plain and we crashed around in the dodgems, two to a car. An extra-violent collision with Anna's older brother, Phil, had thrown Jo against the steering wheel and cracked out the corner of her big front tooth. Anyone else would have gone into a decline, but not Jo; she'd just crossed her eyes, grinned a Dennis the Menace grin, and paid for another ride. It gave her a piquancy, like a pirate with an eye-patch.

One lunch-time Jo, who had known Maggie at primary school, pulled her in for a game of 'Come to Coventry', and Maggie dragged Fen along. Fen and Maggie lived in the big houses near the forest. And now we were six. Others came and went over the years, but we remained the in-group. We worked together, played together, holidayed in twos and threes, and by the Fourth Form were a force to be reckoned with.

* * *

Maggie didn't emerge from Sick Bay until home-time and who could blame her? We filled her in on the plan after school. We were *all* going to say we were doing the paper round, including Anna, and Jo would make up some tale about a puncture to explain why she was late. Buoyed with the idea of the blood pact we sailed down the hill to see Fen and Maggie onto their bus. They would have to get the night bus back to the 'lottie', or walk. Somehow I couldn't see them making it, but that didn't matter.

Propping up the pillar-box on the corner of the High Street was a crowd of teddy-boys, crêpe-soled creeps whose heads emerged tortoise-like from their padded shoulders as we sauntered by, directing their usual barbs of wit at our puke-green backs. 'Fancy a shag, darlin'?' To which you didn't reply, didn't indicate by the twitch of a hair that you had heard. Girls like us had nothing, *nothing*, to do with drape-coats, velvet collars and haircuts with rude names. So we hurried on by, praying that they wouldn't notice, wouldn't think, wouldn't remark like last time:

'Cor, nice tits! Look at the bum on that, ba-boom, ba-boom!' and that another wouldn't join in:

'Bum, tit-tit, bum, tit-tit. Come over 'ere, darlin'. Give us a feel!'

This time it was worse.

'Oi, Ginge! You got them freckles all the way down?'

She stiffened and slowly, slowly turned to face him.

'You talkin' to me, pig-face?'

Well, there was only one of us with freckles, whose brown eyes were, by this time, sparking hot.

11

('Leave it, Jo, he's not worth it.')

But she ignored whoever was tugging at her arm and, with her head on one side, silently studied the youth who began to shift his ground, a weak grin playing around his lips as he looked to his mates, in vain, for guidance.

'Yeah,' he replied, uncertainly.

'Least I ain't got gallopin' *acne*. Them blackheads and pimples, like you got all over your face ... you got them all the way down, 'ave you? All over your bum, all over your dick, 'ave you? Must look like a dollop of red porridge, your dick! Least I ain't got nothing catching!'

'Jo-o!'

'Come on, Jo, they'll think we're interested.'

'Interested!' she squeaked, rolling her eyes, 'Who'd be interested in them? Rentokil? They'll 'ave all the drains up, looking for the stink, and it'll be B.O. Incorporated!'

And then we had to run for it. One thing about drape coats and beetle-crushers, they do slow you down, and chasing after mouthy girls doesn't do much for your image, or your DA. So we reached the bus stop intact, though Maggie and Fen were wetting themselves laughing. They were great gigglers, particularly when there were boys about.

'Rats,' said Anna, 'I never posted Alan's letter.'

'You still can. We're going back that way,' I said.

'We are *not!*' said Anna. She tore it up and put it in the bin.

'He can whistle,' she said.

* * *

I tolerated Fen for Maggie's sake but she was always a puzzle to me. She never wore twice-darned socks, like the rest of us, or home-made blouses, the collars of which never quite lay straight. Her cardigans (she had at least two) were the expensive sort, from the school suppliers, not hand-knitted in two shades of bottle green with a line to show where the first frugal purchase of wool had run out. She wore a clean blouse every day and smart white socks. Her hair was thick honey and cut iron-straight by experts, not home-permed by her mum, like mine. She was the only child of doting, rich parents. And she had no sense of loyalty.

* * *

'Anna Turnbull, Margaret Willis, come out from behind the rockery!'

The deputy head's bark rang around the open air theatre, the pride of Walthamstow High, and ricocheted off the Greek pillars downstage. Birds beat out of the hawthorns with a squawk and a flurry of petals, and headed for cover. I could see the joy draining from Anna's already pale face, as the shock of discovery froze her nerve. At twelve, she wasn't yet the prettiest of us. The classical bones were there, just, and the Pre-Raphaelite colouring, but her pale blue eyes were dim behind her specs and right now she had a sheepish look, especially when her jaw sagged in dismay. She moved clumsily, on flat feet, caught between flight and standing her ground. You need your wits about you to be graceful in a crisis.

'Who else do we have? Ah, Josephine Carter. I thought you wouldn't be far behind. A regular nest of naughty girls. How many times do you need to be told? And that other girl who thinks I haven't spotted her behind the rockery. Miss Swinton is it? Yes, come and join us, Fenella. I'm sure your mother will be most interested to know how blatantly you break the school rules. And Sandra Hodgekiss, too. Wonderful, I do believe we have bagged the entire gang. One, two, three ... No, no. We are missing Rosemary Woodhouse, are we not? Don't tell me she has finally seen the error of her ways?'

No, but I had seen hers. I had a perfect view, from ten feet above Mrs Mountjoy's head, in the oak tree. Not daring to breathe, I clung tight to the branch above. Not one of them looked up and I showered my undying gratitude upon their loyal heads, Jo's tousled red, threaded with bits of twig, Maggie's cap of black, sleek and well-behaved, Anna's proud and tawny mane, Smudge's fraying chestnut plaits, even Fen's perfect page-boy, and all were sprinkled with may blossom, like confetti.

She stamped and raged across the stage, empress at the games, loving every minute of their suspense. Her black curls shook in righteous wrath and I, in my tree, saw the silver parting and sweat beading on her upper lip, as first Smudge, then Maggie, began to cry. And still she railed. Thumbs down, thumbs down. No pity.

At last she herded them away, Christians to the slaughter. As they dragged themselves down the great steps, across the stone-slabbed auditorium and up the other side, they hugged to themselves a tiny scrap of triumph. That, in the end, the joke was on her. They had saved me from discovery, at least.

They were leaving the theatre. Fen was last, her square shoulders drooping with disgrace. I dared to bend trembling knees ready to climb down, to unclench numb fingers, to take a lungful of breath.

And then Fen looked back.

I don't suppose Lot's wife meant to do it. I expect she'd have kicked herself if she could. I could have kicked Fen. Right in her neatly braced teeth. What a dingaling! Maggot brain! Twit! Because, of course, Mountjoy's eagle eye followed her gaze.

And I was punished along with the rest, only more so because I had been climbing trees and should have known better: I was a trusty. They took away my prefect's badge.

Fen never apologized for her part in my downfall, or even owned up to it, though she must have known. And I never mentioned to her, or to anyone else, that glance over her shoulder, which could not have been a mistake. She knew and I knew the truth. It had been a Judas kiss.

* * *

I patted my pocket to make sure the keys were still there. I'd never been up this early before and something, either lack of sleep or excitement, lodged in my stomach like undigested food. Lamps lit up the sleeping street as I clutched my cardigan close to my chest. I hadn't expected it to be cold.

'Rosie!' The whisper caught on the silence, and the squeal of Jo's brake-blocks startled a cat from under a privet hedge. Smudge, on the saddle, legs dangling, smiled myopically as Jo hopped along the kerb to a standstill. I helped hold the bike and steady Smudge as she staggered off and we all crossed the road together. On the path that ran down to the allotments, between back gardens and a brambly wild place that was the grounds of the new Town Hall, we met Anna, wheeling *her* bike. She only lived down the road, but the bike added credence to the paper-round story.

'Wotcher,' she said. 'Got away all right, then, Smudge?'

'No trouble. No trouble at all. They think I'm being very, well, very responsible, really, getting myself up and out to do the papers. Be a different, a different story when I have to report it's just one more thing I'm no, I'm no good at.'

'Mmm. Me too,' though she was just being kind; Anna never failed. Skilfully she turned the conversation. 'Killed me getting up this early. Don't know how you do it every day, Jo.'

'It's a bit early for *me*, this. 'Alf-past-five I get up usually but my lot ain't awake then neither. They dunno what time I go. Or care, truth be told.'

Smudge pressed her lips together. We all had our problems, I thought. Some parents believed in the bootstrap principle and left you to get on with it, and some smothered you to within an inch of your life. I guessed Smudge's mum had seen her off at the door or even walked down to the corner with her to meet Jo. They meant well, Derek and Liz, they always meant well. They'd meant well when they'd coached her through the eleven-plus, and then could only nag when they found their darling, hopping about helpless in academic mud like a frog at the bottom of a well. She wasn't the only misfit, by a long chalk.

Waiting for us at the gate was a small, lonely figure, whose will-o'-the-wisp face shone porcelain white and whose big green eyes blinked in the beam from Anna's bike lamp.

'It's Maggie!' we told each other in low voices.

'What, no Fen?' I whispered, trying to keep the hope out of my voice. 'She was supposed to be coming with you.'

'You're not going to believe this ...' said Maggie.

'O-oh, *what*?' It was too dark to see Jo's face but her irritation was plain.

Anna was guessing: 'She missed the bus?'

'Nah. She's told her Mum and Dad, ain't she? Stupid cow. Bet they made a stink and stopped 'er coming.'

Maggie shook her head, a strange smile on her lips. 'She'll be here soon.'

Smudge wiped her wet nose on her palm and looked up, gloomily. 'I bet, I bet she's getting her dad to bring, to bring her in the car.'

Anna looked at me and raised an eyebrow. It spoke volumes.

'What's the matter wiv 'er, eh?'

'She's ... she's thick, that's what.' Though even as she said it I could see Smudge thinking that perhaps that wasn't all there was to it. There was thick and *thick*.

'Oh won't he love that?' I said, heavy on the sarcasm, 'Childish pranks, what a hoot!'

It occurred to me that if Mrs Swinton, queen of the Teachers'

Centre, did her usual trick of passing on 'a word to the wise', our dawn escapade would be dinging down the educational grapevine to my dad in no time flat. She'd got Smudge and me into trouble before. Smudge started chewing her nails.

Maggie was beginning to look worried, too. This was all getting far too heavy. 'Not really!' she blurted out. 'She's only having a wee, behind the bush!' and she tittered nervously.

'You ... you ...' I think Smudge would have hit her if Jo's bike hadn't been in the way.

'Sshh,' hissed Anna. 'They'll do us for trespass if they catch us out here.'

Fenella emerged, giggling. 'Got you going there!', quite undaunted by the vote of no confidence and Anna's terse, 'Shut it, Fenella.' Fen had a thick, if pampered skin. She wasn't beautiful, at least not by my standards; she didn't have Anna's Greek goddess looks, or Jo's fiery splendour. She wasn't even 'striking', which is what people called me, for want of something kind to say. Fen had the vacuous look of a dazed kitten, if you can imagine a kitten pouting. She even had a go at dimples once, sticking knitting needles in her cheeks for hours on end. But she remained flat-faced and plain as an empty canvas. Until she got busy with her paints.

It was cheating, I always thought. 'Mr Max Factor of Hollywood' should have used her in a 'Before and After' advertisement, because cosmetically, she was stunning.

Her body, on the other hand, was all her own! At fifteen she was slim and satiny, a sun-bleached blonde with a streamlined figure on long legs. Like a golden palomino – and a whinny to match, in my opinion.

And Maggie, sweet, simple Maggie, was everything I wasn't: good-natured and generous. *She* wouldn't have thought ill of her 'friend' or wished that she *had* overslept or, better still, had met with a nasty accident and thus been prevented from sharing our tryst.

It was dark in Dad's shed, and the light from our torches cast shadows of rakes and hoes around the walls to spook us. We sat in a circle, on the mud-clodded floor, on sacks, and left the door open so we could see the sun when it rose. It wasn't cold now but we all felt shivery, knowing this would confirm our specialness. But Fen kept on nattering. The problem with her was that everything was a game.

And this wasn't about playing games; this was, as Jo had put it, 'a truning piont'. We would not be the same afterwards. The omens in the date could not be denied; four, five, five, four. There were even lucky nines if you looked for them, if you were on the right wavelength. And the significance of the date, the cut thumb, the three broken test-tubes couldn't be denied.

Or *was* this a childish fancy? See-sawing between girl and woman, I could see the sense in it and the nonsense. Anna read my mind.

'Look, the date and the other things aren't important,' she said. 'Do you want to swear a pact of friendship or not? If not, go home, tuck yourself back into bed and forget all about it.'

'All right, I will if you don't want me,' I flounced. 'But you can jolly well go and find somewhere else for your mumbo-jumbo.' I sounded petulant, even to my own ears.

'Oh, don't be like that, Rosie.' Maggie put her arm round me. "Course we want you.'

'Yeah, don't be a twerp.'

'Do you know what a twerp is, Jo?' Fen piped up. 'A pregnant fish!' And she and Maggie squealed. Ignore them, said Anna's eyes, and I sat down again.

I wasn't the only one with qualms. Jo, the intuitive, felt there were ends to be neatened. 'I'm all for promising to be friends for life, yeah, but say you don't, say you lose touch or you fall out with someone. What you got coming to you?'

Anna shrugged. She didn't see the problem. She might have been pretty sharp academically and fizzing with imagination but in practical matters even I had to admit she could be vague to the point of clumsiness. That was part of her charm.

'See, it's not just a promise, is it? It's an oath.' Anna still looked blank. I tried again, 'It's like you're saying, I promise such and such to so and so and if I don't deliver then I give something outside of the two of us, some supernatural something, permission to send down a load of "woe betide".'

'No, it's not!' said Anna.

'It is!' said everybody else.

Anna said she didn't believe in the supernatural. I said, in that case, blood pacts were a load of hooey and we might as well all go home.

'Good,' said Maggie. 'All this talk about the supernatural is putting the wind up me.'

'God's supernatural,' I said.

Anna snorted, 'God puts the wind up me. No, not God. The people that thought Him up. The weirdos at your church, Rosie!'

'They're no more weird than we are,' I said. 'Like I said, you don't make an oath to nobody. We don't know what's out there listening in. If it's not God, what is it?'

Fen lowered her voice dramatically. 'The genie of the "lottie". Just waiting for young girls to make oaths so's he can think up some nasty woe to betide us with. He's outside and in, all around us, in those shadows, listening and rubbing his hands. Can't you see his yellow, staring eyes and crooked fingers reaching out ...?'

Maggie squealed and clutched my arm, infecting me with her fear.

'Fen! For God's sake! You're such a dumb ... Oh, Christ, Maggie, you're hurting!' But she wouldn't let go; her bony knees dug into my side as she whimpered like a puppy and attempted to climb into my lap. 'Get the hell off, Mags!'

In the end Jo had to get up and waggle the torch beam around the dark corner and take the sack off the hook to show Maggie that there was nothing hidden beneath it.

'Sorry, Rosie.' Maggie unclamped her fingers from my arm.

'It's okay. Wasn't your fault.'

'You could, you could send yourself mad like that,' Smudge observed.

'And everyone else,' I said, rubbing my bruises. 'I think I prefer to stick to God.'

'Ah, but which god?' Anna was looking very smug.

'Does it, does it matter?' asked Smudge. 'One god's woe must be pretty much, pretty much like another's.'

'You two are asking for a thunderbolt!'

'But there never is a thunderbolt, is there, Rosie?'

I glared at her. This argument had whiskers on it. The one about if God wanted people to believe in Him, why was He so coy? Why not communicate more overtly, give us signs etcetera, etcetera?

Smudge looked from me to Anna and decided she wasn't going to hang around for another deep debate. She 'abhorred and detested' deep debates. 'Wait, wait a tick,' she said, slipping outside. For a minute or two, she was lost in darkness. Then her silhouette formed dumpy black against the bean-frame and a pink-tinged sky and we saw that she was ripping out plants from the next allotment.

'Hey,' I whispered hoarsely, 'he'll kill us!' But it was too late. Smudge returned, loaded with tall stems of Solomon's Seal which she dropped on the floor. 'For crowns,' she said, 'add a bit of, add a bit of glamour to the proceedings. It's good stuff. Cures spots.'

'Yeah?'

So when we'd twisted the stems into delicate wreaths and put them on, the greenish-white flowers hanging down over our foreheads from upright pointed leaves, we rubbed what was left onto our faces, streaking them an impressive green.

'You know what,' observed Fen, 'if we're going to do this thing properly we ought to strip off. You can't go greeting the dawn in school uniform.'

'God, Fen, any excuse ...' I said. 'And suppose someone comes?'

'We'd've had it, anyway.' Anna was already taking off her shoes. 'Come on, Rosie. No one can see into the "lotties" – the trees'll screen us.'

'You sure?'

'Oh get a move on, I want, I want my breakfast.' By now Smudge was down to her slip and bra.

What the hell, I thought. I wasn't bothered by nudity; we pranced around in the school showers after swimming and games like baby seals. So I unbuttoned, unfastened and stepped out of my clothes, hanging them on handy spade handles and rakes, and wriggling my toes in the dirt. There was a lot of shivering and fidgeting. No one knew quite what to do with her hands.

Then I doled out the new lino cutters I'd stolen from Dad's drawer. It wasn't really stealing as they were educational supplies. Fringe benefits. They were still wrapped in waxed paper and looked lethal, all different-shaped blades and every one razor sharp. Lino cuts were Dad's last term's class project. He'd printed dozens of Christmas cards, lengths of material, lampshades, you name it, far keener than any of his pupils who'd kept gouging lumps out of themselves instead of their slippery squares of hard lino. This term they were doing batik. He wouldn't miss the knives for years.

'The sky's getting lighter,' Anna said. 'If I should slice off my

19

thumb and bleed to death, give us a decent burial, won't you? Aagh, Maggie, don't take your bandage off! That's revolting. You don't *have* to do the same thumb, you know.'

'It's cleaner than the other one, look.' She held out two tiny thumbs, one neon white with a thin red wound curling around it, and one brown with dirt. We examined our own hands.

'Smudge, *your* hands are filthy!'

'Are they?'

'Ugh, Smudge,' said Jo, 'I ain't doing it with you; I'll cetch sun-thing!'

'Nobody's very clean,' observed Maggie. 'I suppose we ought to wash, really ...' So she and Smudge fetched a bucket of water from the well next to Dad's plot. They'd been longing to play with it since we arrived. But water from fifteen feet under the ground is icy. Gasps and muted shrieks accompanied a rather cursory dipping in of hands.

Jo was finished first. 'Ready? I'll do it, shall I? Countdown begins. Wait for it, wait for it ...'

Our eyes strained across the allotments, our ears pumping with silence, our hands poised. Between the bean frame and the well there was a thin paring of light and, for some reason, as the torch-beams faded, I found myself blinking back tears.

The land bled pink and the first blackbird began to warble. Jo said, 'Three, two, one, go!' We stuck our thumbs with the lino-cutters and cried out in pain.

'Hush,' I told Anna.

'Oh, blimey, I'm gonna faint!' said Jo, beginning to sway.

'Head down, head down!' Smudge grabbed for the red head like an all-in wrestler. 'Don't, don't suck it! You'll have to do it again!'

'You're breaking my bloody neck, woman! Uhhh! C-Christ, S-Smudge, don't splash us. That's not fair!' Jo yelped, skipped away, came back and splashed our podgy friend, whose smothered squeals vied with the thin whistles of waking starlings.

'Oi, you two, come on,' said Fen, 'we'd better do the pact thing before it all dries up.'

'Quick, mingle the blood.' And with cries of 'Mingle, mingle!' and 'Cheers!' and 'One for all!' we pressed the six dripping wounds together.

'Undying friendship,' said Anna, and ran her bloody thumb in a straight line from my forehead to my navel, and smiled strangely as I did it to her. Over the heroic brow, straight down the Grecian nose, over the narrow lips and the stubborn chin, that lifted to show me her throat. As I was tracing between her breasts I saw her tongue reach out to taste my blood.

'Now,' she said, huskily, turning to the others, who were daubing and hugging each other and giggling, 'we must make our pact. What'll we say? I'll do it, yeah, and you join in? Um ... By this blood that is spilt on the Earth ...'

'I haven't, haven't spilt any ...'

'Go on, then, squeeze a bit out!'

'Oh, shit!'

'I ain't got none left!'

Eventually we had all expressed our blood and our devotion to each other and were sitting round in a rather queasy circle on the wide grass path that ran through the middle of the allotments.

'Was that, was that okay?'

'Bit quick, weren't it?'

'What else can we do?' Maggie looked to others for a lead.

'We could arrange to meet up once in a while.' Fen with a bright idea! Whatever next?

'For a booster-jab?'

'Oh please, Anna,' laughed Maggie. 'I've done enough blood-letting to last a lifetime.'

'Well, just a meeting then. To confirm the pact. Say, the same time next year? Fourth of the fifth fifty-five?'

'Make it the fifth and I might, I might remember it.'

'Smudge, that's it!' I said. 'Five o'clock, five, five, fifty-five. And then six o'clock on the sixth of the sixth, sixty-six. Every eleven years.'

We agreed that we couldn't count on the allotments still being around in twelve years. People wouldn't want to grow their own vegetables in 1966. The meeting place ought to be more central. And because we'd all been to the Tate Gallery on an Easter trip with the Art Club, of which we were the core, we decided that that should be the place.

Fen said it would be impossible trying to get up to London for five in the morning and I had to agree with her, reluctantly. Five in the evening was far more practical and wouldn't spoil the lovely symmetry of our reunions.

'And what if we can't make it?'

'You double-booked then, Jo?'

'What if sun-thing turns up? The tube breaks down or we're ill or sun-thing? What's the penalty? More woe?'

'Mmm.' There had to be something to enforce the pact. I looked at Anna. She was rolling up her eyes and tutting.

'Just better turn up, then,' said Fen. 'Mustn't tempt Fate.'

'Oh, come on,' said Smudge, her round cheeks shining, 'all for, all for one ...' and her stubby fingers took Jo's across the circle. Anna grasped mine and Maggie took Fen's. Then six hands were intertwined. We were in it together, for better or worse.

Cue for more atmospheric music.

Afterwards we bathed in the dew, hopefully, that we might be beautiful, according to legend, and disgracefully, rolling in the grass and horsing around, singing Johnny Ray's 'If You Believe', like clumsy and irreverent nyads. Pivoting, twirling. Nothing could touch us now. Breathless, we lay along the path like fresh-picked marrows to dry in the rising sun, still garlanded with Solomon's Seal, and Maggie picked mint and lemon balm and sweet herbs and sprinkled them over us.

'Here's rosemary for you, Rosemary,' she told me. 'Rosemary for remembrance.'

'And sage for you, Maggie,' I said, feeling prophetic.

'I can just see us,' said Anna, lazily, when we were dressed again and sleepy, 'in two thousand and ten, two thousand and twenty-one, still toddling along to Pimlico.' She stood up and doddered over to me, nodding and smiling in a vacuous, senile way. 'Come on, Rosie, old girl, you can do it.' Her voice cracked with age. 'Just a little bit further. Ooh, me aching back, ooh, me wooden leg! Don't think ... I'm going to manage these, gasp, gasp, steps ...' And she expired in a heap on top of me. A dead weight. Even as I giggled and rolled about with her, a shiver ran through me. Because, yes, that's how it could be.

'I'm not going to, going to get old,' said Smudge, firmly.

'Not much you can do about it.'

'Oh, yes ... yes, there is,' she said, darkly. 'Sixty's my limit.'

'Don't you want to see in the year two thousand?'

'What for? I'll be, I'll be too old to enjoy it. My Nan was sixty when she, when she died,' said Smudge.

I remembered her. She had always been old, a spent force, thin, colourless, sometimes there in the corner of the room with Gregory on her lap, stroking his pale hair while he slept.

'No,' I said, 'I don't want to get old, either.'

'I'll do you in when it's, when it's your sixtieth birthday,' said Smudge, 'and you can do, you can do me on mine.'

'Your birthday's after mine!' I laughed.

Maggie said, 'We could all go together ...'

'At the date with Fate in 1999. Mass suicide!'

Who said that? I've a horrible feeling it was me.

Fen wasn't persuaded. 'While there's life there's hope,' she said, confidently. 'They'll have a cure for most things by that time.'

'Or euthanasia will be legal,' said Anna, without much hope.

'Never!' said Jo, whose mother had been tempted by a bottle of aspirin when Jo's grandfather had had a stroke. He was now in a home, she said, a mumbling vegetable, and Mrs Carter cursed herself for missing her chance of putting him out of his misery. 'This suicide thing puts us in charge, don't it? We get a choice when to die.'

'And where and how.'

'What if you fall under a bus ...?'

'We could, Fen, we could decide to fall under a bus, together,' said Anna, deliberately misunderstanding her, 'or off a bridge, or any number of quick deaths but at least we won't have to die of old age.'

'So we're, so we're all agreed, yeah?'

'I'm not doing it,' said Fen. She always had to be difficult. 'It's a horrible idea,' she said, flouncing off down the path, and turned. 'Is that what friends are for? Force you to kill yourself?'

'Not now, dope: 1999. God,' and I felt so certain, 'the world will have ended by then.' Forty-five years was impossible to imagine. Even our parents hadn't lived that long and they were over the hill.

'Oh, come back 'ere, Fen, you great fairy!'

But she carried on, in what she obviously considered was high dudgeon, towards the gate. I looked at Jo, at Anna, at Smudge, and perhaps the exchange of blood gave us access to the others' thoughts. Perhaps that's what telepathy is.

Smudge shrugged and slowly took off her blouse again. Holding the two ends, she swung it over and over to make a thick wad. Then we broke into a run. As Jo and I grabbed Fen's arms, Smudge and Anna whipped the blouse over her head, over the mouth going 'Wha ...?' and tied it tight. Her eyes bulged in

23

shock and rolled around for help. Maggie seemed not to understand what was going on, but stood there, gawping like a fish. Until Fen began to kick and buck, and Smudge and Anna took a leg each; then she realized how she could help. She ran and took the cover off the well.

We only hung her in there for a second or two. Upside down, so her squeals and cries made dank echoes against the walls. She didn't dare struggle in case we dropped her. Maggie, kind soul, held Fen's skirt up over her knees. Small things plopped into the water: a button off her blouse, hair-grips.

We intended no hurt. Just a bit of horse-play. Smudge and Maggie had already begun to giggle nervously when we hauled her out and laid her gently in the leeks. She was very pale and her eyes were slits of hate. She slapped off our hands when we attempted to help her to her feet, and swore savagely. She never could take a joke!

We walked in silence to the gate, Jo and Anna wheeling their bikes in front, Fen last but one, Maggie bringing up the rear like a worried little sheep-dog. Our arms still ached with Fen's damaged pride.

Jo turned first. 'Sorry, Fen,' she muttered, and stood, sucking her wounded thumb dismally, as the rest of us grunted apologies. Maggie tried to put her arm around Fen.

All she said was 'Bugger off!'

CHAPTER TWO

Smudge in May, 1955

In the summertime, when hormones pop like lupin pods and sex drifts on the breeze like pollen, a sure way of keeping your sixteen-year-old daughter from straying is to give her GCEs. That's what Rosie said, anyway.

Not that I had a boyfriend yet, but it wouldn't be long, I felt sure, and I could hardly wait.

Who would it be? Who?

Malcolm? A good-looker, if a bit … well, if I'm honest, *decidedly* on the short side. And the shared interest in art did not extend to his description of the afternoon life class at the tech, which he described rather too intimately for comfort. I felt hot and squirmy, listening to words like 'nipples' from a boy, but you can't be rude, can you? That was something else for me to worry about, lying awake at night when Gregory was screaming. Greg was my brother. He was brain-damaged.

Keith was one of Rosie's rejects, a public-school 'chep' who made me conscious of my vowels. He had cornered me at her last party, and spent the entire evening trying to bring me to Jesus. I had to leave early to get away from him but he was dead keen. *Dead* keen. Arrived on our doorstep next day, Bible in hand, looking fervent. A Baptist minister's son, he seemed to have led an even more sheltered life than me. 'Born under a gooseberry bush' Daddy said. He thought brassières were what navvies warmed their hands on! I mean, really! A mutual initiation might have been nice but I didn't know what to do after the groping and I'm sure he didn't. No wonder Rosie dropped him.

And there was always David, next door. He was the brother I didn't really have, my respite from the battles at home. Mummy had an understanding with Auntie Kath that when things got bad, she could send me in next door to play and, when I was young, I'd listen to the racket through the walls. When he was five David told Auntie Kath, who'd told Mummy, who'd told me, aged four, that he was going to marry me. Honestly. He'd

25

not mentioned it again and nor had I but I guess I was always waiting for him to broach the subject. He was working in 1955, in insurance, so at least he could afford to treat me to the one and nines at the Granada now and again. I didn't think about him in bed at all. Well, not much, anyway.

Not a brilliant choice; no one to turn my knees to jelly, but it was early days, I kept telling myself.

The others had already made a start.

Anna's family had just moved to a new estate, a mile or so up the road towards the forest, and there in the High Road the Whistle-Stop, a new coffee bar, had opened its doors. Anna asked for a job. Evenings or weekends, she didn't mind. Great, they said, start Saturday. So now she was working two nights a week and some weekends. All she had to do was froth milk, pull espresso and look decorative. Great, she said. And when they were slack she would sit on her high stool and read *Lady Chatterley's Lover*. Great, she said, specially for breaking the ice with good-looking customers.

Rosie always said, 'Anna rushes in where fools fear to tread'. If it worked out, fine. If it didn't work out, equally fine. You learned from your mistakes.

My mother said Anna was bohemian, as if that wasn't quite nice. I thought it sounded dead romantic. But if ever I wanted to go anywhere, do anything, I never mentioned Anna. Never Anna. Rosie was the one. If Rosie was going along then it must be all right. Rosie was the steady, sensible one, according to Mummy. She wasn't, she got up to all sorts, but with her big spaniel eyes she had them all fooled.

The Whistle-Stop was a rich vein of untapped left-wing manhood, Anna said, plenty for all. Plenty. But the first night, when I saw how dark and empty it was on the other side of the bamboo curtain, I nearly scuttled back to the bus stop. Strange music was squealing from the juke-box and the place was foggy with cigarette smoke. A couple of boys in sideburns and chunky-knit sweaters were nodding to the beat over dirty cups and a heaped ashtray, their faces squeezed shut in concentration. When the music stopped they sighed, shaking their heads sadly. (They looked old enough to be sixth-formers. My heart went pit-a-pat.)

'The best, man.'

'Yeah, great!'

Anna introduced us. Monk and Bug. Monk and Bug? 'Monk' because of Thelonius Monk, and a flat haircut. 'Bug'? No idea. The glasses, maybe, the bunching jaws? Smoky eyes looked us up and down, approved and moved in for a deeper study. Views and opinions were demanded. What were our musical tastes? *Musical tastes?*

'Classical.' Rosie played the flute in the school orchestra, and actually listened to Brahms, when she and Anna got together.

'Bill Haley,' said Maggie. Yeah, that was a name I knew.

'What about jazz?' Jazz?

'Oh, yes, yes, goes without saying.' Rosie, you fraud, I thought.

'Trad, mainstream or modern?'

'Um ...' Anna was looking anxious. But we had been well primed. We recited the key words: Armstrong, Bechet, Charlie Parker, and that was all that was needed. I had the feeling, all along, that they were showing off, with their talk of sets and riffs and motifs. I had no idea what they were talking about. I didn't say much, I don't think, but I think they knew that I was impressed. Then 'God Bless the Child' came on the juke-box, (Billie Holiday?) and I couldn't get it out of my head. I started humming it and I suddenly realized they'd all stopped talking and were listening to me and nodding with their mouths turned down. That was approval. Anna stopped biting her nails and, when she caught my eye, smiled.

And then my heart sank. They were talking politics. What did we think of Labour's chances in the coming election? Our expressions said we were considering the matter from all angles. All except Fen's. She was doing a fair imitation of Bardot, pouting prettily and doing things with her eyelids.

Who would succeed Attlee when he retired? Attlee? Rosie looked thoughtful and mumbled something about it being a hard act to follow. Jo said there was only one serious contender, weren't there? *Wasn't* there? Leaving them to supply a name and smiling knowingly when they proposed Gaitskill. Fen was working hard on her dimples.

We were saved by a rattling of the bamboo curtain. Three more boys, in slacks and sweaters, broad-shouldered their way over to the table. Pete and Wiggy and a gorgeous young version of Tony Curtis called Roger. Couldn't stop, they apologized. They'd just come to pick up Monk and Bug for an ILP meeting down at the Baker's Arms. Did we want to come?

'No, no thanks,' I said wrinkling my nose. I wore my CND badge with pride; of course I was against nasty things like bombs and racial discrimination and inequality. I was against *anything* political. Dry, boring stuff. I could never follow it on the television.

Rosie, Jo and Maggie declined, too, regretfully. We didn't tell them we had a ten o'clock curfew. And the Baker's Arms was a *pub*! A *pub*!

'Yes,' said Fen. 'I think I will.'

I got up to put some money in the juke-box and was trampled in the stampede of male bodies fighting to escort Fen to the door. As the 'one, two, three o'clock, four o'clock' beat blasted them out of the door, she turned and waggled her fingers at us in a smug 'Bye ...' Roger turned and smiled, bewitchingly, catching Rosie's eye. 'See you ...' he said.

But they wouldn't see us. Nor would anyone, not for weeks. The exams were looming.

Those were the days when you had lessons to the bitter end. No study leave, no let up until the question paper was in front of you. You revised in the evenings, at weekends, when you could.

And it was such a farce. Mummy and Daddy nagging me ragged, even though they knew I didn't have a prayer. Daddy got this teacher from his school, Richard Skinner, to help with the Maths. Bad mistake. Oh, I suppose he did his best but, though I could do the mechanical stuff, given enough time, the words, the problems, made no sense at all. Like, if a train, at point A, is travelling at a speed of 120 mph and a rabbit, travelling at 0.25 mph, crosses the line at an angle of 57 degrees, 3.5 miles from A, does the rabbit have a prayer? Believe me, after a while, your attention starts to wander. So did his. Pretty soon he was taking every opportunity to hang over the back of my chair to point out mistakes, or to sit up close to give me reassuring squeezes and pats, to breathe hot halitosis down the neck of my French peasant blouse, somehow always managing to brush my breast with his arm as he described graphs and totted numbers. Now I may not be a raving beauty, but breasts I do have. Big ones. I felt my cheeks burn. Suppose it was an accident? Suppose it wasn't? I couldn't deal with it. My response, that electric zing through my nipple to some deep, hidden nerve-ending down between my legs, that was wrong. I was hot with guilt and shame. And stuttering like mad. Well, it's not really a stutter. I tend to, tend to repeat words. It gives me time to think.

28

Then came the breakthrough. In spite of the distractions, I finally, *finally* discovered the meaning of isosceles triangles. And in the excitement, this hairy paw landed on my knee, moved my skirt aside and crawled up my leg. Up my leg! I gasped, stiffened, but this was Mr Skinner, Daddy's friend, a teacher. Even so ... my leg! So I flicked the hand aside as you would any other summer pest. And it was strange, his face didn't alter in the slightest. Not a flicker of annoyance, anger, nothing. His fat finger, trembling only slightly, was pointing to the next line of text and his lips were moving with the words.

I consulted Fen, she being something of an authority. We were beating eggs in the D.S. room, rehearsing soufflés for the Cookery exam.

'Sounds like a D.O.M. to me. Only one thing to do with them.' And I watched, fascinated, as she took two more eggs from the box, weighed them carefully in one hand and then crunched them together, viciously. 'Oh dear,' she sighed, regarding the slimy mess, and ignoring my explosion of mirth, 'Mi-i-iss, I'm afraid there's been an accident!'

'Fenella Swinton!' squawked Miss Pitts, wattles flying. 'Eggs do not grow on trees!' And she should know, I thought. She strutted about, going, 'Waste!' and 'Carelessness!' and 'Young people's attitudes!' before coming to a decision. 'Oh, strain them into a bowl and put them in the fridge. The first-years can use them for cakes.'

When she came back, Fen said, 'Talking of D.O.M.s ... Remember last summer? I went with my parents to that farm in Devon?'

I did. We had been the year before and Daddy had recommended it to Mrs Swinton, Fen's mother, as a cheap, nutritious and educational holiday. I had a feeling I knew what she was going to tell me.

'You lot had gone youth-hostelling and I was feeling a bit fed up.'

'You, you could have come too.'

'No thank you! Jesus! Trudging round the country with rucksacks, sleeping in bunks? Not my thing, Smudge.'

'Rosie and Anna met those, those boys ...'

'Yeah. Healthy, outdoor types.' She shuddered. 'Anyway, I was still sore after the well thing.'

I was sieving flour into melted butter and couldn't look at her.

'I hated the farm on sight, dirty, smelly place. Gross animals

29

and grosser men, you should have warned me. Just some horrible twelve-year-old who was staying there, too, with his family. Though even he was starting to look good at the end of two weeks, I tell you. God, it was vile. Nothing to do in the evenings except play shove ha'penny. Or sing songs.'

'I wish we'd, I wish we'd sung songs.' I pictured the low-ceilinged farmhouse, dim with oil-lamps, and Mummy and Mrs Jessel chatting over their knitting while Daddy and I were out walking Greg along the country lanes. Even after a day on the beach my brother still, *still* had energy to burn. Walking was the only way we could get a decent night's sleep.

'The kid's dad had a ukelele,' Fen was saying. '"Leaning on a lamp-post", can you believe? Christ! I was thinking, "Let me die, *now*!" Then old Farmer Jessel brought out the scrumpy and we all got tight and the songs started to improve. Some quite tasty ones, "Foggy, foggy dew" and that. The parents quite surprised me; they knew them all! So, anyway, old Jessel was being very attentive but I thought no more about it. Next day he wanted to give me a ride on the back of his motorbike. Said he'd heard me telling the kid that I'd never ridden one. Well, thank God, the kid wanted to come, too, in the side-car, otherwise ...' She stopped to stare at my mixture. 'Why doesn't mine look like yours? It's gone all thick. Look, the spoon won't go round.'

'Oh, Fen, what've you done? You've put much too much flour in.'

'Eight ounces, it says; that's what I did.'

'*Two* ounces, dope! You haven't got ... You haven't ... Why don't you wear your glasses, Fen?'

'Bloody hell, Smudge, what do I do now?'

'Start again; I would. Go on, go on, I'll keep her busy. Give us the saucepan and get a clean one. A *clean* one. Only hurry up, mine's nearly, mine's nearly ready for the eggs.'

So I went to the sink, buried her stiff remains under a pile of crockery and turned on the tap full-pelt, wrenching it stuck. The water thudded onto the dirty spoons and dishes piled there, and sprayed back with the force of bullets, drenching the floor, the walls, the draining board and the girls working at the nearest table, who shrieked and jumped about.

'Turn it off, Sandra, turn it off!' screamed Miss Pitts. But I couldn't, could I, poor helpless little me? So she had to come and show me how, and was immediately soaked. 'Oh!' she gasped, flapping her wings. Not me, I'd kept well clear. Well clear. She showed me where the mop and bucket were kept and then went off to find something dry to put on. Fen had reached the flour stage again by the time I got back.

'Thanks, Smudge,' she whispered.

'What, what're friends for? Hey, where's my, where's my soufflé?'

'In the oven. I put the eggs in.'

'What a little treasure!'

'What are friends for?' she smiled.

'So what happened then? With the, with the farmer?'

'Well, he stopped off in this field and pulled me down into the grass. Barry thought it was a hoot.'

'Barry?'

'The kid. He sat there watching. Very educational. So anyway, there's this disgusting old codger lying on top of me poking away.'

'He didn't!'

'No, he didn't. I don't know what he was playing at. Well, I do. But he didn't. He just talked about it. What he'd like to do to me if Barry hadn't been there. God.'

'And you didn't, didn't do anything?'

'I couldn't move, Smudge. He weighed a ton.'

'Weren't you, weren't you, you know ... scared?'

'I don't think so. Not like I was down the well.'

I blinked at the taboo word, embarrassed for her. For me. I'd have died if that had happened to me. Not the farmer thing. The well. Well, not *died*. But I wouldn't have mentioned it. Brought it up like that in conversation. I'd have had some consideration ... Not Fen, though. She liked to rub it in. Liked to see us squirm. I still didn't understand how it had happened. What had come over us?

'No,' she went on, 'I felt very calm, if anything. What's the word? Detached. Sort of looking down at the people in the grass as if they had nothing to do with me. And I knew that nothing would happen. Somehow I just knew. After a while we got up and went back to the farm. Now does that look better?' She held up the soufflé like an offering.

'Fine.'

'Is there an oven free?'

31

'Put it in with mine.'

'You don't want yours to collapse when I open the door.'

'That one, then; Marion's just, just this minute put hers in.'

And Fen went off to kick open the oven door, yelling, 'Okay for me to share your oven, Marion?' and closing it very carefully shut.

When she came back I told her.

'He, he tried it on with me, you know.'

'Who, Jessel?'

I nodded.

'You might have said.'

I shrugged. 'Didn't seem important.'

'Tch,' she said, 'didn't you tell *anyone*?'

'Nope. Did you?'

'Not at the time ...' She waited. 'So? Go on, then!'

'Nothing much to tell. He'd finished milking. I'd been watching. He pushed, pushed me onto a pile of hay in the corner of the cowshed.'

'Smudge!' She made a face. 'The cowshed! Ugh, it stinks in there!'

'Anyway, nothing happened. Nothing. He'd just, just got to putting his hand down my bra when the gong, the gong went for tea. And I sort of, sort of rolled away.'

'Ugh, Smudge! God, those horrible red fingers, like sausages.'

'He must try it, must try it on with every girl that goes there.'

'He must. When we got home I had a letter from Barry. Silly little twerp couldn't get it out of his mind. Anyway, my mother read it! Can you believe how embarrassing that was? Well, I had to tell them the whole story, of course, and they were hopping mad. My father told the Devon police and they told Mrs Jessel. Seems she knew all about it. He'd been at it for ages. No harm in him, she said. Still, they took away their licence or whatever you have to have to take paying guests. I felt a bit guilty, really.'

'So do you, do you think I ought to tell my dad about Skinner?'

'Maybe. He might be messing about with the kids at school.'

'They're boys!'

'So?'

But Daddy seemed to find it funny. *Funny*. 'Poor old Skinner,' he chuckled. 'Doesn't often get a chance to snuggle up to a shapely wench. All right, all right, I'll have a word with him, but you're going to have to learn to deal with it yourself, Sandra. You're growing up and men are going to find it hard to ignore you.'

And there was Daddy, back-slapping, *back-slapping* Skinner out of the door, hearty man-to-man stuff, with a mild, 'Bit on the young side for you, old man. Still wet behind.' Hardly the outraged father.

I'd always known there were at least three sides to Daddy. There was his worldly-wise, all-chaps-together image, for the staff-room and round the pub. In all-male company I learned that he'd call Gregory 'the imbecile' and refer to Mummy as 'her ladyship' in order to get a laugh or a pat on the back. And, according to Rosie, who overheard her father telling her mother, the jokes he told were disgusting. When Auntie Pat said, 'Go on, then,' Uncle Mick had refused to enlighten her.

And I don't think they were all that, *all that* impressed by Daddy's setting himself up as the polished man of culture.

When I was small and Rosie's family came to see us, Daddy went over the top with his show of refinement, the Van Gogh prints on the walls, the leather-bound classics on the shelves, still in their protective cellophane. Sometimes we kids were let into the sitting-room to listen to the gramophone but we weren't trusted to put the records on in case we scratched them, so Daddy chose stuff for us: worthies like *Peter and the Wolf* or the Strauss Waltzes or Gilbert and Sullivan. Then, when I went to Rosie's and heard their selection, 'Mrs Buggins' Christmas Party' and 'Ivan Skavinsky Skavaar' and 'Sandy, the Dirt-Track Rider' I was shocked. Wow! I got Rosie to play them over and over. I'd gone home singing 'The Rich Maharajah of Magedor' and Dad had been horrified. He'd 'had a quiet word' with Uncle Mick, who had roared with laughter, according to Rosie. But from then on, Daddy had embarked on a campaign to educate the Woodhouses. We all had to go and see *The Bartered Bride*, which I don't remember as I fell asleep during the overture, and *Orpheus in the Underworld* which seemed very rumbustuous and quite mystifying. But not as mystifying as the nods and digs and winks and eyebrow-waggles that Daddy kept giving Uncle Mick, who fidgeted with his collar and looked hot. Hot and uncomfortable.

On the Saturday night when we heard Rosie and I had both passed the scholarship to the grammar school, he and Mummy invited the Woodhouses to celebrate by watching 'Café

Continental' on our television. (They didn't have a set until the Coronation.) And Daddy, who thought anything French was wonderful, went on all night about the 'Folies' and 'les girls' and went through the nudge and wink routine again. Mummy was pink and Uncle Mick and Auntie Pat just smiled. He was trying too hard. Way too hard. He'd got Mummy to continue the French theme by rubbing the salad plates with garlic, and there was crusty bread and some disgusting cubed vegetables in salad cream that he called 'mayonnaise', but it looked like sick and Rosie left hers. Greg threw his plate at the wall. Poor Daddy. Appearances mattered so much. Just like my passing the eleven-plus. So I couldn't keep up? I was a grammar school girl; that was enough.

With Skinner went my fragile hopes for a pass in Maths. Daddy tried to help, one Saturday afternoon, but he gave up in disgust. He may have been a wonderful metalwork teacher and adored by his boys, but he couldn't teach O-level Maths for toffee. *For toffee*! I believe I called him a 'useless bloody teacher' before I slammed upstairs and swamped the bathroom, swamped it, washing my hair.

Afterwards, in the garden, I could feel his hurt burning the back of my neck through the deckchair. I glared at my History notes where Bismarck and Garibaldi were darting about meaninglessly. And then, when he came out with a cold drink to make amends, I dissolved.

'It's, it's no good,' I wailed. 'You may as well face it, Daddy. I'm never going to learn all this stuff; all these facts and dates. I'm thick. Thick. I might as well pack it in now and get a job, get a job in a tea-shop.'

'Oh, cherie,' he sighed, 'don't give up. OK, so Maths is not your strong suit. I'm sure you could pass some of the others if you tried.'

'Like what?'

'English Lit. for a start. You've read the set books ...?' And raised his eyes to heaven as I shook my head. 'What the hell have you been doing all year, Sandra? Messing about with those friends of yours, chasing boys! Why you can't be like Rosemary, I don't know. Mick tells me she's been swotting for months. Months! Well, you've another three weeks. You can do it. Just need to get a line on the characters and plots and you're there. It's only a pass we want, nothing startling.'

I noted the 'we want'. That's what it was all about. We. Just so he could sound off in the staff-room. And as for me getting a pass in Lit … He really had no idea. No idea. *Sue Barton, District Nurse* was about my level. And I could lose myself in that one day and have forgotten it the next. Completely forgotten it. As for the set books, *Hamlet* could have been written in Icelandic for all the sense it made, and *Mansfield Park* sent me to sleep. Likewise History and Geography. I thought I might get Art without too much trouble, and Physiology and Hygiene, maybe. And Domestic Science, of course.

I'd done most of the cooking at home since I was about twelve. Mummy was always near to collapse after a day with Greg. Coll-apse! So I'd get him to cut up vegetables while she put her feet up and had a fag. And when she saw that I was coping all right, she'd maybe do some mending or write some letters. Greg and I had progressed, over the years, from beans on toast and fruit salad, through omelettes and baked rice pudding to things like stuffed haddock with garlic potatoes and a green side salad, followed by crème brulée. Working through the recipe books, I could make a fair attempt at all sorts of stews and sauces, puddings and pies. I had a light touch with pastry and I could cream eggs, butter and sugar so they didn't curdle. And while it was all cooking, and Greg was stuffing down the leftovers, I would set the table, with napkins and a vase of flowers, ready for Dad when he came in at six. He came to expect it as his due and, of course, never lifted a finger to help. 'Why keep a dog and bark yourself?' he'd say. A dog.

This was his third side.

There was a fourth, a very dark side indeed, which showed itself when Gregory played up. But I'd rather not talk about that.

'I'll only get three at the most, Daddy.'

'Oh, no,' he said, decisively. 'You need five, at least, to get into Trent Park. And a couple of 'A's.'

'Oh, come *on*! This is me, not Rosie Woodhouse. I'm never gonna get A-levels! And I don't want to be a teacher; I hate kids. Hate kids. Let me stick to cooking. I can make, make a success of that.'

But that wasn't what he wanted to hear. Anyone could cook.

'But if I'm, if I'm happy …?'

'You can be happy teaching, Sandra. You could even teach cookery, I suppose.'

Not on your life, I thought.

* * *

'What's up, Smudge?' asked Fen, when she found me chewing my lip in the library.

'They've only put our Practical on the, on the sixth, Fen. To get it out of the way. That's this Friday. Day after tomorrow.'

'Yeah?' She was examining her hair for split ends.

'So, what are we going to do?'

'How do you mean?'

'Fen, the meeting's on the fifth!'

'Meeting?'

I thought *I* was thick! 'At the Tate. We'll have to skip study period as it is, to be there for five. There'll be no time to get everything ready for the exam.'

'Like what?' she said.

'All the stuff set up in the D.S. room. The place settings and dishes and, and ingredients and that. Pitts wants it there ready for a nine o'clock, nine o'clock start.'

'Do it Friday morning.'

'That's cutting it a bit fine. I'll have to, have to do the shopping tonight and hope it doesn't go off!'

'Can't your Mum do it tomorrow?'

'Not with Greg. He's a menace in shops.'

'Give you a hand, if you like.'

'*Thanks*, Fen!' She was full of surprises. Then I thought, 'Won't you be doing yours, though?'

'I'll get mine after school tomorrow, while my mother's doing my table decoration. She's good at them.'

'The meeting ...' I reminded her.

'I'm not going, Smudge.'

'Not going? But I thought ...'

'Count Basie's at the Granada. Roger's taking me.'

'Fen, you don't, you don't even like jazz.'

'I like Roger, though.'

'I thought, I thought Rosie was keen on him ...'

She flung back her hair from her small hot eyes. 'Rosie didn't want to go.' There was a pause in which she stole a glance at my frowning face. She pouted, 'Oh, don't look like that. It's not my fault. He asked her and she said no, so he asked me.' And then she shrugged, 'And I really don't see the point of traipsing all the way up to town, just because Anna and Rosie say we have to. I mean we see each other practically every day.'

'But we agreed last summer ... the blood pact!'

'Stupid bloody nonsense. Especially when the fabulous Roger Trench has tickets for a concert.'

'If you, if you put it like that ...'

It was a mad rush, but at five to five on Thursday the fifth, I was galloping along Millbank, with devils gobbling at my heels. Devils. I could see the girls on the steps, jumping up and down and roaring me on. Strangers turned to watch, thinking perhaps that this was some crazy student stunt. I can't run. Can't. Well, I can, but not to win anything and in high heels it's total exposure. Total. The pavements shout your weight, pound for pound, and your bouncing bosom is so much mortifying flesh. I'm not one of your gazelles, more one of your purple, sweating, gasping baby elephants.

'So slow down,' crooned a seductive voice in my head. 'Slow down. It's not worth it!'

But I couldn't stop, couldn't be late. There was a sharp pricking pain in my side as the safety pin fastening my waistband sprang open. My hair snaked loose. And as I plunged across the road beside the gallery, my foot twisted and I yelped, cars screeching all round me. I stopped to pick up my dainty glass slipper which turned back into a scuffed size six, wide-fitting, and I limped the last few yards to rousing cheers and the bafflement of the dogs of hell. I fell up the steps, splitting my blouse finally, and flung myself into Rosie's arms.

'Made it!' I gasped, my face on fire, at one minute to five. There were no prizes but I knew, and the others did, too, that we had triumphed over something, simply by being there. And Fen? Fen had failed. When I'd got my breath back and repaired some of the damage, we took it in turns to take wobbly pictures with Maggie's box camera, until an American woman offered to snap us all. She was puzzled when we insisted on pressing our thumbs together but no one enlightened her.

'You English,' she purred, 'and your quaint old customs.'

As my colour faded I felt, for once, as beautiful as my friends.

37

Up-to-the-minute in pony-tails and lampshade skirts, scented as a summer breeze, we mounted the steps to the gallery like models on a catwalk. Fen would have been in her element. 'Tough,' said Rosie. Just 'Tough'.

Forty minutes before the gallery closed, but it was long enough to sigh over the languid blondes and sensual redheads of the Pre-Raphaelites. We knew there were finer artists, but none so, so romantic. Rosie stood for a long while before Windus's *Too Late*, a poor girl, dying of consumption, that's TB, whose lover, who has been away, returns to find her on her last legs.

'Use it or lose it,' she muttered gloomily. 'Reckon I've missed my chance now with Roger, don't you?'

I hadn't a scrap of comfort for her. What Fen wanted, Fen would get. Oh yes. 'But if he can't see that you're the better catch, he's not worth it anyway.' I did try.

Anna said, 'I don't see why you're making such a fuss, Rose. He's only a pretty face. No substance there.'

'Plenty more fish in the sea,' said Maggie.

Jo said nothing but gave her a rueful smile.

Rosie just shrugged.

There was the usual argument about Burne-Jones's *The Golden Stairs* as to who was who. To me, the faces of the troupe of girls descending the enigmatic staircase were almost identical. I reckoned the artist had used one model for the lot, two or three at the most, but Jo and Anna thought the one bending forward looked like Rosie, one further down playing a violin was the image of Mags, and a rather plump soul, at the top of the stairs and looking back, was me. Thanks. They all looked too sweet and innocent to be Jo or Anna or Fen. Specially Fen.

Before the guides began clearing the gallery we all gathered before everyone's favourite, *Ophelia*.

'When I was little I always thought it was a picture of Rosie,' said Anna, 'because that's what my brother, Phil, always said: "Here's rosemary ..." I didn't realize that it was Ophelia's speech.'

'Nothing like me,' said Rosie.

'No, I never thought so, either. Tell you who it is like, though,' said Anna.

'Fen!' We all spoke together and laughed.

'Just wants a touch more, a touch more mascara,' I said, 'and a peroxide rinse. Fen to a tee.'

'The cow,' said Rosie, mildly.

'Oh, come on, Rose,' said Anna, 'you practically offered him to her on a plate. What's she supposed to do?'

'Say, "No thank you," and come out with us, like I thought she would.'

'She'll be so-o-rry!' Maggie sang, though her eyes were crossing her fingers.

'Anyway,' I went on, 'she's not so lucky having to, having to listen to all that jazz. She can't stand that burbly-burbly sort.'

'Who can?' said Rosie. 'Give me Chris Barber, any time. You know that skinny boy at the Whistle-Stop? Whatsisname?'

'Monk,' I said, rather too quickly. Anna gave me a funny look.

'It's not really, it's Maurice,' Rosie went on. 'Did I tell you, *he* asked me to go?'

I stared at her in dismay. Not Monk as well? What had she got? What? I sighed. I'd have given the world to be her. Or Anna. Or Fen.

'Sent me a letter, didn't he, Anna? Anna's been playing go-between.'

'And?'

'Told him to get lost.'

Anna shrugged. 'And he's so keen on her,' she said. 'Says she's broken his heart.'

'Ah, he's such a drip! He's got those soft, sweaty hands and ...' She made a face. 'He's a slimy kisser. If any of you go out with him take a hanky. Yuck. Anyway, I couldn't go out tonight, could I? I'd have gone with Roger if I'd gone with anyone.'

I stared gloomily at *Ophelia*, thinking that slimy kisses, whatever they were, were preferable to none at all. And Monk wasn't so bad. He had nice eyes. Nice eyes. So what if his name was Maurice?

'She had to lie, for weeks, in a bath of cold water,' said Anna.

'Who?' I asked, thinking she meant Rosie and that maybe that had something to do with her objection to slime. Who and why?

She inclined her head. 'That woman, the model.'

'Oh.'

'She must've got out to go to the bog.' Jo was ever practical.

'Wonder if she blew off. You can't hide it in the bath.' Anna made trapped air-bubble noises.

We laughed so hard Maggie had to run out to the toilet.

'Wouldn't catch me doing it,' said Jo. 'Getting all crinkly.'

'Not even if you knew people would still be talking about you in a hundred years' time?'

'Nah. Wonder she never died of pneumonia.'

'She did,' said Rosie.

'Don't think she died. Well, not immediately,' said Anna.

'Ophelia did.'

'Died, died of pneumonia?'

'Of a broken heart. Loved Hamlet so much she went nuts and drowned herself because he'd rejected her. Don't you think it's romantic?'

'Bloody pathetic, if you ask me,' said Anna. 'Don't any of you go doing anything so wet.'

'*Anna*!'

'What? Oh, the play on words. Sorry. Well, if any of you feel like drowning yourselves, you can't. You have to wait until 1999. Then we'll all go together.'

I had a thought.

'Is this the same, the same, um ... Hamlet as the Shakespeare one?'

'Smudge!'

So as we walked along Millbank, they filled me in on the Hamlet story and quoted in chorus. We crossed the river, rehearsing the soliloquy and, by the time we reached County Hall, I was almost confident. We were going to the National Film Theatre to see *Great Expectations*. This was the only reason Mummy and Daddy had let me come out. There would have been no point in telling them about the date with Fate at the Tate; they'd never have understood. But a set book, now that was different. And if I was with Rosie ... Such a responsible girl!

Lavatory heels and pointy toes were not meant to tread London pavements. Anna and Maggie had blisters and I had laddered my stockings by the time we reached the Festival Hall. Jo had a stomach ache which threatened to be the onset of the curse. We all groaned. Jo's periods were phenomenal. She would turn green and faint, and was generally off school for a day or two. She said it hadn't got a good grip yet, that the walk had probably helped. While we were in the Ladies, all polished mahogany and roller towels, Rosie loaned her some tape and a Doc White's and the rest of us messed about putting on 'brown' make-up, the latest fashion fad, and backcombing each other's hair. I took off my stockings and binned them, peeled off my roll-on – oh joy! – stuffed it into my handbag. Anna washed her feet. By this time the other 'ladies', in their expensive hats and frocks and fox-furs, were tut-tutting and wrinkling their pink-powdered noses. Since she couldn't reach the towel with her feet Anna lay on the floor with her feet in the air and Rosie dried them for her.

There was plenty of time, before the film, for tea and cakes in the café. Maggie and I, sharing a meringue, made a bit of a mess, and picked up the crumbs with sticky fingers. Rosie's perfect lips sparkled with sugar from her doughnut and Anna was squishing her way through a cream slice, shaving the ooze with her blunt little finger and licking it clean, and Jo, who hadn't wanted anything to eat, was sipping her tea and aspirin quietly, two freckled hands clasped around the cup. We looked around the table at each other and smiled. No need for words.

I must have been back to the Festival Hall a hundred times, and always, always, as I push open the glass door, I am drawn to the café, to our table under the stairs, its clutter of spectral crumbs and dirty cups, with pamphlets of coming events, long gone, with plates daubed with ghostly cream and sugar. Shoes have been kicked off around the chairs, bags propped against table legs. And I smile again, remembering utter contentment. Food and good company is my idea of heaven.

There was as much unity in protest. As we wandered out into the sunshine, Rosie groaned.

'Bloody good, isn't it? The best time of the year, the *very* best time, and we're stuck indoors, revising.'

Except we weren't, were we? Guilt, guilt …

'Stuffin' our 'eads full of facts we won't never need again, long as we live.'

'All year they nag you for not getting enough exercise and fresh air and sun and that and just when it's all laid on, gratis, they shut you up with a dead language for company.'

Gratis? And what was a dead language? Anna was so wise.

'And tell you off for staring out of the window.'

Maggie, too?

'And for picking your spots,' I said.

They gave me a pitying look.

'Prob'ly shortens your life …' said Jo.

'What, picking spots?' You learn something every day. I was

leaning over the parapet to watch a motor launch go by. A couple of greasy deck-hands waved to us and I waved back.

'The feelin' of how am I supposed to learn all these formulae in three bloomin' weeks? I'd rather be up Clacton, or down Southend.'

'On the sands, with a nice boy,' said Maggie.

'Not nice, Mags,' laughed Anna, 'definitely not nice.'

'As long as he looks like Rock Hudson,' said Maggie.

'Dirk Bogarde,' said Rosie.

'Harry Belafonte!' said Anna.

Jo gazed after the launch with longing. 'Must be great to just get on a boat and go where you fancy.'

'France,' I said, 'I'd like to, I'd like to go to France.' No I wouldn't. Anywhere but. Anywhere but. Why had I said that?

'Not as far as that,' said Jo. 'Just to the coast'd do me, where you can breathe a bit, where there ain't no crowds, no rush, no having to get jobs and pass exams. That's what I'd like. Bit of sea and sky and a beach to walk on. Suit me fine.' As an afterthought she said, 'Don't know as I'd want Rock Hudson, neither. Or any bloke, come to that.'

'Not ever?'

'Nope. Not if I can 'elp it ... well, it's a bit scary, innit? All that sex and stuff?'

Anna looked surprised. 'Oh,' she said, 'it's not scary. I'm looking forward to it. I think about it all the time. Well, boys do, why shouldn't we? My brother has wet dreams every night.'

'What's that?'

'What do you think?'

'What, you mean he actually ... while he's asleep?'

'They all do, Mags. They can't help it. My Mum goes barmy. Keeps threatening to make him wash his own sheets out.'

Anna was a fount of knowledge. A fount. In her family they actually talked about sex, openly, around the tea-table, her parents and the two brothers and four sisters. Two years before, my mother had given me a delicately pink booklet published by the Dr White people, telling me, in delicately pink prose, about all the delicately pink changes I could expect to see taking place in my delicately pink body, and why. Better late than never; I'd been menstruating for a year. The book said nothing about wet dreams and all the other titbits that Anna passed on to us. Was it any wonder she was so, so popular?

42

She had closed her eyes to the river breeze.

'I shall save myself, of course, for the man I marry. I shall come to him on our wedding night, bathed and powdered, with my hair brushed down my back, like old Beata Beatrix and wearing something Greek and diaphanous, like that lot on *The Golden Stairs*, though I don't know why: he's only going to rip it off me in a frenzy of passion! Will he throw me on the bed? And take me, swooning?' She pressed the back of her hand to her forehead. 'And then, oh God!' she moaned, a deep-throated Sybil Thorndike. She blinked. 'I wonder if anyone's ever passed out with the excitement of it all and missed it?'

No one said a word. Not a word. We were still on the bed.

'And who will be the lucky man? That's another thing. Can't see it being anyone I know now, Pete or Wiggy. They're just mates. And you have to really love someone one hell of a lot to let him do *that* to you.' She paused and her eyes darkened to navy. 'Bug, now, he was a bit different, when he took me home the other night. Now he really can kiss. Phew! Couldn't think straight after that. I mean how're you supposed to concentrate on French verbs when you're still reeling from French kisses?'

'What are French kisses?' Maggie wanted to know, and was as appalled as I was when Anna told her.

'That's re-, that's revolting,' I said. 'God, I'd puke.'

'Oh, Smudge! Imagine, Smudge and David-next-door getting smoochy. Dave gets his tongue in and Smudge brings up her tea!' Jo made retching noises that echoed under the walkway, like ghosts. Not David, I thought, no fear! Breathless with giggles, we bundled through the door of the Film Theatre into the sweet smell of celluloid.

'I'm going to have to sit down,' said Jo, holding her side. So Anna and I joined her on the deep-pile carpet while Rosie and Maggie went to buy the tickets. 'They'll be doing revision themselves, won't they? Your blokes?' Jo asked Anna.

'Not tonight, they're all at Count Basie, aren't they? Time off from their A-levels. They must be hard at it: they've not been in the Whistle-Stop, not in donkey's ages, at least not on my nights.'

'Don't know how you can spare the time for that job.'

'Oh, it's only a few hours, six 'til ten, twice a week. I've cut out the overtime. I have to get out, Jo. I'd go mad stuck indoors with the same old faces. Rosie's the one. Miss Boffin. She said she crawled out from her books last Sunday, first time in ages, blinking at the sunshine like Mole, to go to church, but was so riddled with undigested revision and guilt it was no fun at all.'

'Like *who*?' Was this some new boy they'd not told me about?

'*Wind in the Willows.*' I was none the wiser.

'Few more weeks and it'll all be over,' said Jo.

'Then what? Back to the paper round?'

'Not 'til September. Got a job in the shop 'til then.'

'All summer? No wonder you sit and dream of the sea,' Anna said.

'What you doing then, Anna?'

'Rosie's mum and dad are taking us to a farm in Devon. Fen's mum gave them the address. It's where they went last year. Where Fen met that super bloke. You remember, she told us. Whatsisname? Barry?'

*   *   *

I was up early, collecting dishes and cutlery, Mum's cutwork tablecloth and napkins, and my ingredients.

I'd written the menu in twirly writing with Daddy's calligraphy set. He'd got me some pale green card from school and after several attempts, two with blots and one which Gregory ate, it looked all right: *Brill Soufflé with Mousseline Sauce, New Potatoes, French Beans, followed by French Apple Tart and Cream.*

Daddy had wanted to write it but I wouldn't let him. As it was, it looked so professional I was almost ashamed of it.

They were both there to help me load up and to wish me luck.

Mummy was flapping about the fish, which had been in the fridge for thirty-six hours.

'It smells all right, Sandra, but don't go eating any of it, will you? Just in case.'

Then she was off to fetch thrift from the garden for my table decoration.

She brought a daisy or two so Greg wouldn't feel left out. He snatched them from her and sat under the table shredding them.

'He loves me, he loves me not!' laughed Mummy.

Daddy even walked me to the bus. He was trying so hard, poor thing, desperate for me to do well. Desperate.

I was the first to arrive, hot and sweaty from lugging the heavy bags up from the bus stop. The tables were set up in the room next to the D.S. room. They were transformed from scrub-

44

bed wood to elegance with crisp table-linen, sparkling water-glasses and silverware and imposing centre pieces of freesia and tulips, fern and primroses. All but one, which had been left for me.

The fridge was bursting with meats and cheeses, pots of cream and bottles of milk. I took out a box of eggs, labelled 'Olive Bracknell' and poked in my brill. Eggs should be used at room temperature, anyway. *Any*-way. It was as I was finding a home for my butter that a saucer of something sticky shot out onto the floor. It didn't break but landed upside down, and the syrupy stuff soaked rapidly between the floor-boards. If I scooped it up it would be full of grit and splinters, so I mopped the place clean and refilled the saucer from the Tate and Lyle tin in the cupboard.

At last my table was set. Jo's dream of the sea had reminded me of a shoebox at the bottom of my wardrobe, stuffed with spoils from Devon. Last night, late off the train, I had untied the string and exhumed the contents. Now skeletal driftwood formed the basis of a seascape; pebbles and shells, pink and grey, from Ilfracombe were scattered in artless heaps and a broken bottle of sea-scoured glass, misty as memory, filled with thrift and sea-holly completed the table in anticipation of my fish dish.

Fen made it for registration. Just. She looked blotchy. Probably missed the bus and panicked, I thought. She'd tell me about it later, no doubt; right now we had an exam to do. Two hours to cook up a well-balanced, nutritious meal for two. We weren't allowed to speak, but she smiled wanly as I did my quaking-in-my-boots dumbshow. Not that I was really scared. Not really. I'd practised this meal for weeks. They were sick of fish soufflé at home.

It was strange, cooking in self-conscious quiet. It wasn't silence, of course. There were chopping and stirring sounds, metal chinking on china, wood softly thudding on dough, whisking eggs, banging tins, the hissing kiss of liquid and hot fat, but so quiet in between, you could tell the dusty flop of a spoonful of flour from the sea-surge of sugar. And the smells spoke a language of their own. Warm and buttery, pungent, spicy, floating on steamy promises of satisfaction.

I heard Fen slicing behind me, sneezing and sniffling, the smell of onions so strong, *my* eyes began to smart. And then her gasp

45

of pain. I was in time to see her staring, fascinated, as an invisible pencil drew a thin line of red across her thumb. The red beaded, bulged and dripped. Then the examiner was there, murmuring and wrapping plaster round the wound. There was nothing I could do. Nothing. And my apple purée was ready.

I had everything timed to the minute. Only when the flan was filled and glazed and the fish was flaked did I make a start on the soufflé. This way I could give it my full attention. As I stirred the yolks into the roux I became aware that things were not going well behind me. Not at all. A bang made me jump, a scuffle, a smell of burning sugar, but I couldn't look up. The soufflé was at a critical stage. The fish had to be folded in just so, and then the egg whites.

And I didn't dare breathe until I had shut the oven door on both soufflé and tart and set the timer for forty-five minutes. There was no time for washing up but I took the saucepans to the sink, to soak. And there I met Fen, looking hot and bothered, also filling a pan which was burnt black. Black. I made a face of sympathy. She raised her eyes to heaven and, with her finger, cut her throat.

I couldn't find her after the exam. Gone. The other girls were all-of-a-dramatic flutter, flushed and floury.

'I don't want to *see* another Crêpe Suzette as long as I live!'

'Well, nobody told *me* we were supposed to do *hot* soufflés. When I asked her if I could do a sweet one she said 'Fine'. She never said it had to be hot!'

'... Not a hint of ginger in that syrup, I don't understand it. That's the whole point of Chinese Pears; that they taste of ginger! Miss said I should have put it in a jar with a screw-top lid instead of a saucer. Leaving it uncovered in the fridge made it lose its flavour.'

I hurried out to look for Fen, and found her eventually sitting on a bench in the playground, snuffling into her handkerchief.

'Oh, Fen, was it horrible?'

'Don't want to talk about it,' she growled.

'Fine.' After a pause, I said, 'Tell me about the, about the concert, then. Was it good?'

But that seemed to upset her even more. She was sobbing in earnest now, weeping into my neck.

'Fen, Fen, it's not that bad surely?' But I knew it was. What could I say? My own meal had cooked beautifully; the new

46

potatoes shiny with parsley butter, the beans neatly bundled with a strip of crisp bacon, the soufflé risen to record heights, and the apple tart glistening beside the jug of cream. I hadn't knocked anything over or dripped anything onto the tablecloth. I had spatters of egg on my blouse and sticky apple in my hair but that didn't matter. I knew I had passed, no problem. We had all been shooed out of the room at eleven-thirty, leaving the examiner alone with her clipboard. And through the window, I had seen her purse her lips at Fen's sad offering.

I patted her shoulder for a while and, when she surfaced, offered her my hanky as hers was a tight, wet ball.

'Go on, blow hard, it'll help.'

Little by little she grew calmer and I began telling her about *Great Expectations*. How we'd all screeched when Magwitch had jumped out from behind the gravestones. Screeched. How they had told us off for making too much noise ...

'I've failed the Practical, Smudge. Nothing went right, bloody nothing, from the moment I cut my thumb. Did you hear me drop the damned potatoes on the floor? I never do that. Why me? Why today of all days? And while I'm cleaning up the mess, the bloody saucepan of caramel burns through, so my soufflé flops while I'm making some more. Then, when I carve the chicken, it's not cooked properly. All raw and bleeding inside, and the stuffing's all gloopy like wallpaper paste.'

'Oh, Fen.' I almost giggled, it was all so horrible. 'Maybe she'll let you do it again. Say you weren't well, or something. You looked, you looked awful when you came in. Like you hadn't slept. What, what was it, period or something?'

'Wish it was.' She looked at her shoes, splotchy with potato, and shuddered, 'No, it was a good old-fashioned hangover, Smudge.'

'But you don't drink!'

'Didn't. After the concert – which was dire, by the way – we went to the pub. Roger asked me what I wanted and all I could think of that was half-way nice was cider. I don't know what sort it was, but after a glass of the stuff my head was swimming. And he kept buying me more. Oh, God, Smudge, it was awful. I couldn't ... I had to take my shoes off to get to the toilet. So embarrassing; I kept falling off the stilettos! They were all laughing at me. And then, when I was practically senseless, he took me home through the park. I was so sick ...' she almost smiled, 'in the goldfish pond. God, they'll all be dead by now, poor things.' She closed her eyes. 'And then he took me in the rhododendrons ... we went in the ...' She stopped. Swallowed. Trapped her hands between her legs and hunched her shoulders. While the blood beat in my ears. 'My first time, Smudge. First ... ' She frowned and bit her lip. 'I don't remember much about it, to be honest. Except it hurt like hell. Like burning.' She rubbed hard at her forehead as if trying to erase an image. 'Christ.' She looked at me and her eyes were full of hurt. 'It was horrible, Smudge, horrible. I felt so ill, and I knew, *knew* it was wrong, that I should stop him, but I couldn't.'

'But ... I mean, do you, you know, love Roger?'

'God, I don't know. I thought I did. He's nice-looking. Just had to smile and my insides'd turn to mush. And when he said those things, that I was beautiful, sexy (whatever that means), when he nibbled my ear, kissed my neck ...' Then her eyes hardened. 'But last night ... He didn't have to do that to me, get me drunk. If he'd waited ...' She shook her head. 'He was like an animal, a pig, Smudge. Gross. Grunting, pushing. He didn't care that it hurt, that I wasn't ready, that I was feeling lousy. He didn't give a damn; not for *me*, Smudge. It could have been any old body with a warm hole in the middle. He was just interested in, you know, doing it.'

I couldn't help asking, 'What, what happened then? Afterwards?'

'I was sick some more.'

'Oh, Fen, you poor thing! Didn't he, you know, give you a cuddle? Try and cheer you up a bit?'

'Well, he helped me walk home. He had to, I was so wobbly. Thank goodness the parents had gone to bed. He hardly said anything. Except "It was great!"' She clenched her fists and there were tears in her voice again. She sniffed. 'Great, great, great!' And the grief bubbled up and brimmed over. 'What a stupid bloody word!' she sobbed. 'It doesn't *mean* anything!'

'Oh dear,' I said inadequately, 'I thought it was supposed to be gr ... a wonderful experience for the, for the girl, too.'

'That's the story they put about. Men. And D. H. bloody Lawrence. But you just end up feeling dirty and sore. And used. A lump of meat.'

I could see the others coming across the playground. Morning lessons must have ended. Maggie and Rosie put on a spurt when they saw us on the bench. Anna, seeing that Fen was in a state, tried to hold them back, but concern for their friend or curiosity about the exam drew them on. Jo was taking the day off.

I nudged Fen and she blew her nose, in time to give them a watery smile. 'Well,' she said, 'that's me up the Swanee. Roger got me drunk and raped me last night. Not much point in doing the theory paper now, is there? I'm probably pregnant.'

'You're joking!' Anna cried.

Rosie had to sit down. 'Jesus,' she was saying. 'Not Roger ...'

Maggie was the one to make the connection, to voice it.

'If you'd come out with us last night, this wouldn't have happened.'

'Don't, Mags,' I said, 'she doesn't need it.'

'If she'd come with us,' said Anna. 'If he hadn't got her drunk. If she hadn't given him the big come-on.'

'I *didn't*.'

'You did!'

'Oh, wonderful,' Fen snarled, 'so now you all think I'm some sort of floozie!'

Rosie said nothing but her expression made it clear what she thought: if the cap fits.

Anna said, slowly, 'You have been, um, flaunting yourself a bit.'

'Flaunting? What does that mean, flaunting? I've only been making the best of what I've got. Like you do. Like you all do.'

Rosie's voice was bitter. 'You couldn't bloody leave him alone, could you? Every opportunity, you've been all over him, touching, teasing him. You knew I liked him.'

Anna said, 'I wouldn't have thought Roger was the sort ...'

'Oh, they're all the sort, given the chance.'

'And you're the one to give them the chance, eh, Fen? God, getting yourself paralytic! What were you thinking of? You were asking for it!'

'I don't know why you're on your high horse, Rosie Woodhouse,' said Fen, 'Roger wasn't your one and only, was he? Last Sunday at the Whistle-Stop you had Monk down your throat.' My heart stopped.

She had the grace to blush. 'And Caesar's Gallic Wars coming out of my ears. I needed a break. So I went to the Whistle-Stop hoping Roger would be there.'

'And you found Monk instead.'

'So what, Fen? So bloody what? I like Roger. I can talk to him. He wasn't around and Monk was. Okay so I kissed him a bit. I soon stopped. I don't lead boys on. I know if I'd gone to the concert with Roger, the idea of rape wouldn't have entered his head.'

'Well, let's face it, Rosie. You just aren't that sexy.'

For some reason, they both exploded. Peals of laughter that broke the tension and ended with them both hugging each other.

I wasn't laughing. I was angry. With men who fell for pretty faces. 'For God's sake, you two. Fen's in, Fen's in terrible trouble. What are we going to do about, about Roger?'

Maggie said quietly, 'I don't think he could help it.'

'Course he could help it,' Rosie said, now on Fen's side, 'he planned it, didn't he? Rotten sod. Saw his chance and took it!'

'There were other forces at work,' said Maggie, darkly.

'Oh, here we go!' Anna rolled her eyes. 'What was it, Maggie, Venus in opposition to Saturn?'

'It was the pact, you know it was.' Maggie's eyes were wide and green. If she'd been a cat, her ears would have been pricked back. But her little voice was level, determined. 'She should have come with us last night. That's why everything went wrong. It was Fate.'

I shivered. 'That's what I thought, too. That's why I had to, had to run. I didn't want to be late.'

'Poor old Smudge. You were scared shitless,' said Anna.

'Me, too,' said Rosie, and she laughed again. 'The relief when I saw you coming down the road! Ridiculous, really. Because it's all in the mind, isn't it?'

'Exactly, we make our own Fate.' Was Anna quoting someone famous?

'So maybe we made a Fate that punished Fen for breaking the pact.' And a shadow passed across the sun. I looked up but no one was there.

I heard Anna breathe, 'For God's sake, Maggie! No one would wish this on Fen. We're her friends.'

Fen reached out and patted Maggie's arm, smiling still, if grimly.

'And what are friends for, eh, Mags?'

Maggie stiffened, staring at Fen's hand, at the blood oozing through the plaster.

I rubbed my thumb in sympathy. I still had a scar from last summer. We all did.

CHAPTER THREE

Jo in June, 1966

'Jo,' he said, 'look, Jo. Here's a letter from Rosie. I'll read it to you, shall I?'

'Oh, Rob,' I thought, 'I don't want no letters. Leave me be, there's a love. Give us a bit of peace. And quiet. Let me just slip away somewhere quiet.' But he wasn't having that, the bully. Just kept rattling on, about this and that and nothing at all, to keep what was left of my brain ticking over, I suppose. Never give up was his motto in those days, not while there was still a flicker of hope.

'"*Dear Jo*,"' he read, like he thought I was listening, '"*are you OK? I was worried when we didn't see you at the Tate last night.*"'

Last week, she meant, didn't she? When my brain had snarled into a tangle of spaghetti. No, perhaps she was right. Last week, last night … a letter takes time … I shook my head to clear it, but nothing happened; the spaghetti just slumped from one side of the pan to the other.

Triggering panic.

Heart banging around like a moth in a lampshade. Banging. Stop, stop, stop. Calm down. Work it out. You forgot, that's all. Muscles don't respond automatically, not these days. Unlike panic. These days it's a matter of shifting stiff, protesting gears. Mind over muscle.

Try again; turn to the right, slowly, feeling the pillow on your cheek, feeling the cool, sterile hospital pillow, warp and weft, your cheek touching. Got it? Right, remember what it's like, now to the left, to the left. Oh shit, are we there yet? And breathe, you better breathe, girl.

'What is it, Jo?' He was peering into my eyes anxiously, as if to read my thoughts. I wish he could. 'Shall I stop?'

Nodding was harder and by the time I'd got there he was back at the letter.

'"*The date with Fate – you didn't forget, did you?*"' Forget? Never in a hundred years.

His voice was rasping, sore. 'Why didn't he pack it in and let me go? I knew why. 'Drink some water,' I willed. He did.

'"*Six, six, sixty-six. Jack says it sounds like the clatter of cloven hoofs. Scoff, scoff! He regards our blood pact as some sort of bizarre female thing, like a D and C. Messy but fairly harmless. But after what happened to Fen last time I'm not so sure.*"'

Nor was I, Rosie, not now.

*　　*　　*

Fen strode into my mind on long Bahama-brown legs, bold and blonde. Undefeated champion in raspberry silk chain-mail, with satin trimmings. Very expensive, very glam. And she was smiling. Perfect teeth in a perfect smile, perfectly confident; her eyes, quietly challenging 'judge me if you dare,' under that heavy fringe, under that huge, floppy hat. Another new man on her arm. Something in films, she'd said. Or publishing? Or was this the rock star? I couldn't bloody remember. Not that it mattered; he wouldn't last.

Where was this? A party? It was like trying to tune in one of those old crystal sets that Gramps used to make. A barrage of babble and bleeps, a few snatches of sense and then more gibberish. How many loose wires *were* there? Grey stone steps, I got that much, and the dark curve of a doorway. A church, it must have been. Sun warming the bricks. And we were all there. Rosie, tall and dark and pregnant, in something loose and lime-green, and carrying her little boy. Anna, in a skimpy turquoise number; dark-skinned children round her knees; heavy hair wound with ribbons like a ... like that painting, the one by ... Oh, shit. Come on, girl. Orange tree in the background. *You* know. No, it had gone. Let it go. So who else had been there? Smudge, joyously bursting from creamy sprigged cotton, like a chubby butterfly emerging from its pod, her hair long and loose and burnished chestnut. And there was Maggie, smiling through a gauzy white veil, dressed up like a little fairy doll. Maggie's wedding day, that was it. Maggie and ... Oh, here we go ... Stephen? Sean? Some such. He never called her Maggie, though. 'Margaret.' 'Margaret, won't you introduce me to your friends?' Very cut-glass and family silver. He thought I was very quaint with me dropped aitches and me double negatives. When? It had been warm still. Hot in the marquee. Leaves trespassing on the lawn.

52

September. The last time I'd seen Fen. Flirty Gertie. Dancing too close in the smoochy numbers, showing too much leg and tit in the jive. Drinking too much, laughing too loud, trying too hard. Rob playing up to her. And the others. But we all knew, well, we hoped, they were safe with her. It was a game they all played, a kind of joke. A rehearsal for when the big fish swam into her net, the one with influence, who would take her to the top.

She'd slunk around even the bridegroom, the cat, curling his tie through her fingers. 'Sly old Maggie,' she'd purred, 'keeping you all to herself ... A lord, even. But then, who could blame her?' And she'd walked her raspberry nails up his frilly shirt front. 'Men like you are so ha-ard to come by ...' lifting her eyebrows to make sure he got the joke, and laughing in that husky way of hers. Rosie had told her off. 'This is Maggie's day,' she'd said. 'Lay off, tart.' But she'd not said it unkindly. You weren't unkind to Fen, not after what she'd been through.

What she'd been through ... Hang on to that. My brain buzzed and squealed as I reached further back. Crackling scraps of memory faded in and out. Think. Blimey, it was like trying to find Luxembourg on a stormy night. Here was something. School. Our corner of the classroom. Maggie, Anna, Smudge, Rosie. Fen was somewhere else. I'd missed something, out of circulation, they were filling me in on the story. Fen's cooking exam had gone all wrong. But that couldn't be it. She was always failing exams. Didn't she have to take Art twice, as well? And R.E.? No, there was something worse, something really bad ...

I could see them clearly now. Maggie's face, earnest, a frown creasing her forehead, as she told me about Fen and Roger. Each girl chipping in with her two penn'orth. Jazz, drink, the park, the sex. Oh, yeah ... And Maggie trying to read something sinister into it. Twit! Anna had no time for her cranky ideas, just got cross. She got cross with everyone except Rosie. Rosie could do no wrong.

Smudge, I remember, was trying not to cry. She felt so bad. So she should. You couldn't get eighty-seven per cent in a cookery exam, for God's sake! Not when we had you down as a non-achiever. It wasn't nice.

Rosie was suspicious of Fen's mood swings, the highs and lows, remorse to rage to self-mockery. Anna thought she might do something silly. Not Fen, I thought. Fen loved Fen too much. Rosie said it was all an act, not that she gave a damn really.

And what had I *really* felt? Shock? At first. Curiosity? Oh, yes. But there was another response, somewhere secret and dark, that shivered in delight, that got off on it, somehow.

A few weeks after that three of them left school, didn't they? Maggie to work in her mum's posh dress shop; Smudge to the Tec to do catering; and Fen. If I squeezed my eyes tight I could see her standing proud, among the snivel and blotch of the last Assembly. *'Oh God our Father / Who dost make us one ...'* milked to the very last drop of sentiment. *'Heart bound to heart ...'* Oh God, the pain, the pain! Soggy hankies all round. *'Now as we part/ And go our several ways ...'* Voices broke under the strain. We could do it to order. But Fen's eyes were dry, her mouth a thin, hard line, her neck long and pale against the white of her blouse as she tossed her honey-blonde hair.

'I'm tired of tears. Waste of time.'

* * *

She was right there.

I headed off through the crackling and whistling in search of another memory.

It was February and freezing when Anna and I had gone to see her. We had walked from the train, up the hill to where the big Victorian houses sat brooding like maiden aunts at a shotgun marriage. Smudge had drawn us a map.

'Oh, you can't see her now,' snapped the door-keeper, taking in our youth and sex and finding us wanting. I felt we should have given a password or Dorothy's ruby slippers, at least.

'We don't mind waiting,' said Anna, 'we've come a long way.'

'Visitors from three o'clock in the afternoon.'

'Three o'clock! But we thought we could take her out to lunch!'

'No. Fenella will be lunching in. She has things to do.' And the door clicked shut, very politely, but with military precision.

The cold was stinging my nostrils now we had stopped moving. My cheeks ached. I wanted to be somewhere warm, where there was food. I suggested going back to the town centre.

'Hang on,' said Anna, 'she might be around. God, this place is a mausoleum,' craning her neck for the full grim frontal. 'Poor old Fen, she might as well be in prison.'

The house was on a corner and so we prowled around, looking up at the dark windows for a friendly face. Anna was singing loudly, 'We looked for the Queen but she never came, well God take care of her all the same.' Some gave us a grin, some two fingers and some signed 'Clear off!' but none was Fen. And then we heard voices on the other side of a wall, and we jumped up to see.

There in the garden were long lines of laundry, unmoving, freezing where they hung in the sub-zero temperature, and pegging out the clothes, like the maid in the song, was Fen. Her breath was steaming but her long, tapering fingers looked sore and her pert little nose was red and runny with cold. Even a hungry blackbird would have thought twice.

On our next jump we levered ourselves across the top of the wall and hung there like those jointed wooden clowns that somersault between parallel bars.

'Hey, Fen!' we shouted.

Although her face beamed when she saw us, her finger was on her lips, hushing, and she peered over her shoulder anxiously. Using drooping sheets as cover she edged a bit closer and whispered,

'Anna! Jo! What are you doing *here*?'

'Come to see you, take you to lunch, but the old bag said you weren't allowed.'

'Got to finish my chores,' she said.

'Do you have to do what they say, then, Fen?'

She nodded and her mouth twisted. 'Tell you later. You are coming back, aren't you?'

At five past three, we were perched on a settee before a dirty coke fire. It was a vast, stale room, smelling of cigarettes and dinner, crowded with big-bottomed furniture and perching girls, some about our age, lots younger, and visitors, parents, friends and a few weedy youths, also perching, lost and unhappy. A radio up on a shelf beside the fire was yammering out Saturday football for the comfort of men.

We'd been whispering self-consciously, trying to appear non-residential, when the door smacked open and Fen came in.

'You must be sick to death of hanging about,' she said, plonking herself down between us. She hugged me, awkwardly, as if she hurt, and tits like torpedoes dug into mine. And I noticed the stale smell of her. Boiled laundry, fried food and nicotine.

55

And BO and dirty hair and an indefinable cheesy smell to do with babies. The shampoo and perfume breeze of the schoolgirl was long gone.

'Little sod takes forever with her feed,' she said, 'keeps dozing off and you have to flick her feet to wake her up again.'

I stared at my hands, thinking of tiny feet, a tiny body, cradling a tiny head against my breast, a tiny mouth sucking. Before, I'd never been able to imagine any of us as mothers, but now I could. It was real and Fen was metamorphosized. Irreversibly, like tadpole to frog. It wasn't just the smoker's pallor that was new and the heavily plucked eyebrows; it wasn't the matronly bosom and the fluffy slippers; it was more subtle than that. Her skin seemed to ooze smugness. I guessed it was something to do with her hormones, but Anna said, afterwards, that it was a barrier, a 'Fen and us'-ness, like she was getting ready to repel knocks and snide remarks. I don't know. No doubt if Maggie had been there she'd have gone for auras. And Rosie would have said she was posing. Rosie always thought Fen was posing.

She was chirpy, Fen, full of chat. I suppose I'd expected to find her diminished in some way, taken down a few pegs, and was almost disappointed to find her in a new knitted jumper and a skirt instead of sackcloth and ashes.

Her voice, rustling with silk and cashmere, seemed out of kilter with the situation, rising above it. 'See that girl over there? Not all the ticket, poor thing. Her dad put her in the family way. Isn't that awful? The baby's got a club foot. And that girl sitting by the fire? Her baby was born on the same day as mine. Little girl: Tracey. Guess how old she is? Twelve. Her boyfriend's the same age. Eleven when she conceived, can you imagine? But her mother's going to pretend the baby's hers, so she can keep it. Be funny, being your own baby's sister. That girl, by the window, the pretty one with the black hair? She's quite old, twenty-three or -four. Ever so rich, got her own house and everything, she says, so I don't know why she chose to come here. She hasn't had her baby yet, expecting it any minute. You'd never even know she was pregnant, would you? Not like me. Side of a house.'

'Hand-ball! Was that a hand-ball? The London crowd is sure it was but the referee says 'Play on!' And it's young Dennis Law now with the ball. Just out of school, he really is unstoppable ...'

The men's ears twitched and, though they nodded their heads dutifully at the women's talk, you could see where their interest lay, which side they really supported. Subtle shadows flitted across their brows as the players kicked the ball down the field towards the Spurs goal.

She still spoke of Roger with loathing. She'd seen him once or twice, 'Just to get things straight in my mind,' she said, and from total denial he'd come round to talk of love and marriage.

'But I just can't bear to look at him. He makes me squirm, he really does.'

'Oh, poor Rodge!' said Anna.

'Poor Rodge, nothing. That's what Mother keeps saying, Poor Roger. She thinks he's wonderful, with his three A-levels and his goo-goo eyes. She forgets he raped me.'

'She's seen him then?'

'Oh, yes. He's been crawling round them for this address. He wants to come and see the baby, but I'm not having him here, I've told them. Don't you go telling him where I am, will you?'

''Course not. Haven't seen him in ages, nor any of the others. We don't go to the coffee-bar any more ... I gave up my job.'

'Oh ... Good. Don't know what I'd do if he turned up. It's bad enough when the parents come, nagging me to death. They were fine before Bridget was born. It was all arranged, I was to have her adopted and then get started on a secretarial course. Forget this whole damned business. But now Mother's seen her and fallen in love with her, she's desperate for me to keep her. Keeps coming up with all sorts of plans. For me and Roger to marry, mostly.'

'And you don't want to?'

'No, I don't. I'm never getting married. This place has cured me of all that. Babies and shitty nappies and drudgery and having to run around after some man? No sodding fear!' The swear-word sounded strange. It wasn't one that we used.

'*Here's Law pounding down on the right wing, beating Norman and finding space to pass to Charlton. Charlton with the ball now, with a clear shot at goal, but Blanchflower's there with a beautiful tackle ...*'

'Don't you feel nothing for the baby?' I asked.

''Course I do. She's a pretty little thing.' Thinking I detected a tremble in her voice I took her hand. The skin was dry and chapped and there was no response to my squeeze. 'But I'm not getting married just so's I can keep her. Certainly not to Roger.'

'*And Charlton passes to nineteen-year-old Duncan Edwards, who heads a **beautiful** ball. Just beating Brown as it clips the bar. And it's a goal! One-nil to United!*' The crowd was roaring. The commentator could hardly make himself heard. Three of the men in the room groaned and buried their heads in their hands. Three girls twisted their hands and bit their lips, despairing of Daddy's forgiveness. The other men were United fans, wreathed in smiles in spite of everything.

'Do you want to see her?' It was expected.

We followed her down the passage to a large modern room, a recent extension to the house, jutting out into the lifeless garden where Fen's washing hung, ramrod stiff. The room was light and warm, lined with alternate cribs and low armless chairs. One of the unglazed walls was hung with a flowery curtain which was caught back over a trolley to reveal shelf upon shelf of bed-linen and nappies and baby clothes. And against the other wall was a large formica-topped table where a baby lay squalling and kicking tiny red legs while an exhausted-looking woman folded a nappy beside it.

'Hi Kath,' said Fen. 'Brought my friends to see Bridget.'

'Mind Matron doesn't catch you,' glowered Kath. 'You know what she's like about bringing germs into the nursery.'

'She's in the office with some parents,' said Fen. 'And they're only going to have a quick look.'

Kath said, 'This child is going to have a hernia if he keeps this up. He's not stopped since the ten o'clock feed. Don't know what's the matter with him.'

Tiptoeing, despite the racket the kid was making, we followed Fen to a cradle in the corner where her baby was sleeping soundly. There wasn't much to see, just a downy head that would fit the palm of your hand and a porcelain profile. I looked at this little girl who had come from Fen's insides and thought, 'How could you give that away?'

'Fen, she's beautiful,' I said, meaning it, and saw that Anna's eyes were all doey and soft.

'She looks like him, doesn't she?' she said.

Fen nodded, blankly. Then her face changed, became animated again, as she whispered, greedily, 'She's got grown-up kids, Kath. Thought she was safely past babies, at forty-four. Had a bit of a fling while her husband was abroad and got lumbered. He doesn't even know about the baby!'

Anna looked at me and raised an eyebrow. There was something wrong here, something wanting. I shrugged. I'd never been one for dolls, myself, but my kid sister had shown more fondness for her old Raggedy Rose than Fen seemed to feel for her little daughter. Maybe she was trying to keep it in check, harden her heart against the time when the baby would be taken from her. She was doing a good job. We were hustled back to the lounge, where the match was still prattling on.

'There's no way you can keep her then?'

'Not without a wedding ring. The parents would throw me out and I'd have no money to look after her. I ... I couldn't cope with people treating me like scum.' There was a look of real pain in her eyes. 'I wasn't meant for that. And as for that poor little bastard ... she'll be far better off being adopted.'

'Mmm, 'spose you're right.' Though I had my doubts.

'Well, it's nearly over now,' Anna said, brightly.

'When they letting you out?'

'In four weeks.'

'Four weeks! Gawd, they get their money's worth, don't they?'

'I've never heard of anything so cruel,' said Anna. 'You just get to love her and they take her off you.'

'It's as though they're punishing you. Like you've committed some crime, or something!'

'That's not the half of it. You have to go and get "churched" before they let you go.'

'Churched?'

'Well, you're unclean, aren't you? All that giving birth makes you dirty in God's sight. The priest has to come and make you clean again.'

'Bloody cheek!' said Anna. 'I bet some man thought that one up.'

'Why don't they rope in a witch-doctor and be done with it?'

'... *Really exciting first half. One-nil, Peter. Looks like Spurs are in for a battle royal against Matt Busby's young team. What do you think, Peter? Will the Babes win the day?*'

* * *

She was right, she *hadn't* been meant for that. No more than I'd been meant for paralysis. What had we done to deserve such a rotten deal? We weren't bad girls. Quite the opposite; our lack of worldly wisdom was painful. For all Fen's pouting and posing she'd been a virgin when she was raped, and I had saved myself, as they say, for Rob. So, *what*?

Then I knew. The rush of realization tore my breath to shreds, pulsed in my veins with absolute certainty. I knew what it was. What Fen and I had in common was not turning up for the Tate.

Maggie'd been right all along.

And I'd known. 'Course I had. I'd pulled out all the stops to keep that appointment, God knows.

But what had God to do with it? This was the other side of the coin. This was the hand of Fate and Fate was a cheat.

*　　*　　*

Rob was there at the end of the tunnel, always there, as I struggled out through a web of deep unconsciousness. His voice could arouse me, melt my insides, but right now it grated, teasing my nerve-endings, like dirty fingers tormenting a snail, and I couldn't move, too weak even to draw in my horns.

'Put a sock in it, for Christ's sake!' I snapped, but he couldn't hear me.

He'd been staring out of the window, airing his ideas for the next production. An undersea fantasy. As he mopped up my dribble, musing on mermaids and fishes, I was forced to listen to his plans. And I realized they wouldn't work. Limbs on strings jerk and twitch. There would be no way of conveying ebb and flow or sinewy, swishy movements. Unless ... How about lots of tapering segments? They might make a fish-tail look like it was rippling. And to make the seaweed flow you could have it attached by strings to a gently rocking beam overhead. Or an electric fan, off in the wings, to blow hair and filmy garments ... Oh what! I was teeming with ideas. We could do it; I could picture it in my mind. I could *picture* it!

When it first happened, when blood filled my brain, when ego and id went fizzling off like spit on a hot iron, when no one was me, all I had was numbers. I came round after the operation and I was counting: counting heartbeats, the rings on the curtain, the liquid dripping down the tube, thirty-two, thirty-three, thirty-four, straight to my stomach. I had no gag reflex, they told me, so I couldn't swallow, not even saliva, which piddled incontinently from my palsied mouth. Thirty-five, thirty-six. The beds in the ward, sixteen, seventeen. The buttons on a white coat, four, five, six. I've always been good at numbers and that was where my safety lay now. I began adding and subtracting, multiplying, dividing, and here I was, a week later, planning our next production. Problem-solving, creating.

Excited, I opened my mouth to tell him and gagged on my own dysphasia, the utterance a groan, jaw-trembling and hopeless. I'd forgotten I'd forgotten how to speak. Whoops! Down I slid, arse over tit, down the slope of despair. All the things I might have been, and here I was cursed by childish meddling to be a-drool-ing-mute-a-prisoner-to-the-slow-drip-drip-torture-of-his-voice-doomed-to-listen-never-to-reply-never-to-do-anything-for-my-self-not-wipe-my-own-mouth-nor-any-of-the-other-dribbling-orifices-and-I'd-end-up-hating-him ...

As I opened my eyes my nostrils filled with the smell of ether. He was holding my hand, making a stroking motion with the fingers but I couldn't feel them. Idly I noticed that there was a fresh plaster around my thumb. They'd been taking blood again. Always the same thumb. It had to be that one, of course, the blood-pact one. When had he stopped talking? The underwater play? Time seemed to have passed without my noticing. Lights were on that had been off before.

'Hi, beautiful,' he said, brightly, 'you've been asleep.' So much for black despair. And as for beautiful! They were trying to protect me from mirrors and shiny surfaces, but I guessed they'd shaved off my hair; they'd have had to. Beneath the bandages there were excavations, bore-holes, drilled to syphon off the haemorrhage. And I knew what Gramps had looked like. Twisted mouth, droopy eye, slack, useless muscles down one side of his face. And that's me now, I thought. That's my fate. Beautiful? Well, Rob was just being kind. He loved me, 'course he did. He smothered me with love. Look at him now, so concerned, his hair, tousled like a haystack in the wind and his eyes shadowed even greyer with worry. God, I was an ungrateful cow. A hot tear squeezed onto my right cheek. There might've been one on my left, too, but I couldn't tell.

'Oh, baby, don't cry,' he said. 'You *are* beautiful.' And his lips pressed mine in a long, numb kiss, reminding me of dentists and cocaine. I couldn't even feel the gap in my tooth. If I had teeth.

The nurse ripped away the curtains, exposing us cruelly. 'And how are we this morning?' she breezed.

'Just fine,' said Rob, sitting up abruptly and wiping my saliva from his mouth. Just fine? What did he know?

'Uhuh!' said the nurse, absently, lifting my tongue to slide in a thermometer and settling down with my left arm to take a pulse. I mourned the loss of my arm even more than my leg. It was there, lying beside me, clothed in summer freckles, but it was dead, quite dead. Soon it would start rotting. What could you do with one arm?

'And what have we been doing to get ourselves in this state, I wonder!' She tutted suggestively, busily shaking down the mercury. 'Can't leave you two love-birds alone for five minutes, can we?' And laughed at her little joke. Rob blushed as only he could, a throbbing crimson that left his eyebrows white.

She prattled on as she took my blood pressure, Rob mouthing 'Silly cow,' over her head. But I wasn't attending. I was far too excited. As the band round my arm had tightened, as she'd squeezed the bulb of air, I had felt something. No more than a far-away tingle, the barest pinprick of light glimpsed out to sea on a foggy night, but something! Oh, God, oh, God, thank you, thank you.

Days later, when I could swallow again and move my head without trying, when my lips were only drunk-numb and there were aches in my arm and leg twice a day, after they'd been 'passively activated' by the physiotherapist, I remembered the letter. It was on the side-locker, gathering dust, among cards and chocolates. He seemed to think it was the cards I wanted to see. He read them like the best man at a wedding.

'Love you always, from Paul, Roz, Zach, little Joe and Anna.'

Anna. She had scribbled cartoons under the kisses. The puppets, the ones she knew, were cheering so hard their hats, hair, heads even, were flying in the air and in the centre, in a raised boxing ring, a skinny contestant with criss-cross plasters on her plucked head, with a black eye and a broken-toothed grin had her foot planted squarely on a flat-out cut out of Muhammad Ali. Her gloved fists pumped the air for victory beneath the caption which Rob had to read: 'Keep fightin', gel, we're rootin' for yer!' Anna had always seen me as some sort of thug! And that was supposed to be the way I spoke, broad Warfamstow. Well, she drove me to it with her new plummy accent.

They'd all sent cards, except Smudge. Rob said he'd rung round.

Rosie's went: 'Don't _do_ this to me, Jo. I need you. Get better soon.'

Fen's: 'Tight schedule – will come at earliest, bringing some really snazzy wigs. Hang on in there!'

Maggie's: *'That's the worst over, sweetie. Star signs positive. Here's to a bright future.'* And a drawing of two champagne glasses chinking, 'Cheers!' She'd signed it *'Simon and Margaret.'* Simon, yes, of course. Not Sean. *Lord* Simon. And if she expected me to call her 'Margaret', she had another think coming. I could no more do that than call Smudge 'Sandra'.

Oh, Smudge. Why hadn't *she* got in touch? I hadn't heard from her in months, not since the postcard from Tel Aviv. Still, she'd 've had to come back for the reunion. Rosie must have news of her. In the letter.

The cards were never-ending: from his Mum, his sister, other relations, neighbours, Tim-at-the-theatre and Joyce-and-all-the-girls at Fantabricosy in Penzance, where I bought my materials. People from school. He even had to read the card from Mum and Dad, which they'd left the day before along with flowers and chocolates, a new nightie and a bottle of Lucozade. Poor things, they'd tried to act so cheerful, jawing on about some old chiffonier Dad was fixing up for a customer. Anything to fill in the silences. Half the time they forgot I was there and talked to each other about the garden and a curtain material Mum had her eye on. Rob had seized the chance to get some fresh air. But here he was now and when was he going to get back to the letter? I needed to know how Smudge was. I flapped my right hand, pointed. He understood. Made a face.

'Rosie's letter? Why don't we leave it until you're feeling better?' What was the matter with him?

I insisted, 'Now!' But my mouth still wouldn't behave and my tongue was too big to cope. He held out until he saw hate in my eyes.

'Where were we? Um ... see, you dropped off halfway through. Start again, shall I? Are you sitting comfortably ...?'

I'd rather have read it myself but words seem to swim around the page too quickly, slipping past my eyes like tiddlers through your fingers. In any case he'd got into the way of doing things for me.

'I warn you, you won't want to hear this.' So I listened all the harder. Nothing in the first paragraph. Next.

'"Yesterday was an eventful day all round. I guess you heard that the US got an unmanned spacecraft on the moon."'

On the *moon!* But he was using my amazement to scan the lines. He was planning to leave something out. 'I really don't know if

I should read you this, Jo. It's very sad ...' I swiped at him with my good right fist. 'Okay, okay ...'

'"Well, something even more important happened, yesterday afternoon. My nan died."'

The old woman lowered herself and her rheumatism carefully into the armchair of my mind. She had changed into a clean dress of cornflower-blue, home-made to fit her plumpness, and she had brushed her short white curls so they shone. Her fingers drummed the arm of the chair in restless spasms as she took us along the ride of her memories. And there was Rosie, telling me she was dead?

'"My Dad phoned to tell me before I left for London. She died at home, in his arms, quite peacefully. I told you she was ill, didn't I? Cancer, poor old thing. I'll miss her dreadfully. Expect you will, too. Amazing to think that when she was born transport was horse-drawn and now we're exploring space. Do you remember that time we first went to stay with her? It seemed to rain non-stop, didn't it? And she let us loose on her rag bag. All the scraps from all the shirts and dresses she'd ever made. And she sat and told us all about the people she'd made them for and their weddings and dances and dinner parties. And we started that patchwork. I found it really fiddly, all those tiny little stitches, but you were well away, stitching like you'd been born to it. I've often thought that that might have started you off with the puppets. All those beautiful stuffs that you dress them in. Each one's a creation, and when they all come together in one of your fantasies, Jo, it's magical. A hundred times more fulfilling than teaching, I'm sure. Still, needs must, eh?

"You know she turned it into a bedspread? It was over her when I saw her two weeks ago. The drugs kept her drifting in and out of reality, but she was able to ask how you were getting on. I didn't know she'd sent you a load of scraps to help you get started. That was kind, Jo, to include her in your project. She made me cry, you know; said she'd try and get down to Newlyn, when she was better, to see what you had done with them."'

Rob kept mopping my tears, asking whether I wanted him to stop reading. No. I could shake my head properly now, though it made rocks rumble behind my eyes. No.

'"Jack had the children while I went down there. Oh, God, what a performance that was! When I got back, feeling bloody depressed, Jude was roaring. Poor Jack was at his wits' end. He'd been walking the floor with her all day, couldn't get her to feed from a bottle. Tom was dragging around the flat in a stinking nappy, though Jack swears he changed *him off and on. I don't think. Well, last night I stuffed her full of Farley's at tea-time, intending to feed her again when I came home, but she slept right through 'til six o'clock this morning. Worn out! Just as well, because I couldn't not go. Unlike some! I'm just too superstitious. Silly, I know. Anna said I should have taken Jude with me; fed her on the steps of the Tate. Don't know if I'm quite that liberated yet.*

"Anyway, although it was lovely to see everyone, I couldn't really relax, what with worrying about Jude and then 'absent friends'. Oh, yes, we toasted you. Several times!

"So where were you and Smudge? We waited until half-past, in case you'd both been held up."'

Rob grunted, and flicked the paper nervously. There it was, my worst fear. Oh, God, I wailed inside, not Smudge, too. She'd been through enough. What treat had Fate reserved for her? Rob was reading again. I'd missed a bit.

"'… is a bit far to come, even for an old girls' reunion! But what about you? Last I heard you were on your way. Maggie was having kittens, of course, you know what she's like. Well, we all were. Did you miss your train or what?"'

'You could say that!' muttered Rob. He looked up. I glared at him and he went on.

"'Anna and Fen were footsore and fed-up, having walked around the gallery all afternoon, so we got a taxi to the Aldwych. I enjoyed the play but I don't think Fen was all that struck. She'd wanted to see 'Loot'. We'd tried to get tickets but they were sold out. So we chose 'A Midsummer Night's Dream' as we'd done it at school. Remember trying to get Smudge to open her fingers for the chink in the wall? She wouldn't do it, would she? Thought it was rude. So it was, the way we wanted her to do it. That was the whole point. Anyway, you'd have enjoyed it; very pretty, with all the fairies flitting about on wires like your puppets. I'd forgotten it was so plot-ridden, though. You lose track of all the ins and outs. Juliet Mills was lovely as Titania. Not as fey as Anna was, then she's that way naturally. And no one could equal your Bottom!

"Maggie came down on Friday, slumming it. She thought you were coming, too. It would have been nice."'

'See,' said Rob, 'someone's got sense. I said you should have gone up to stay with her when she asked you, but you know so much better, don't you?'

What! Just who was he kidding? Did he think I was daft as well as brain-dead? I could remember exactly how it had been.

* * *

We had been in the yard, re-painting the flats for the cave scene; Rob's sun-bleached hair fell over his eyes, shielding them from mine. He was sulking.

'It's ridiculous,' he'd muttered, his teeth clamped on a paint-brush while he used a sponge to stipple the green. The boards wobbled against the wall as he dabbed away. 'They'll all be down in the next few weeks anyway, for their free holiday by the sea.'

'That's not fair, Rob, they all chip in. And we're always welcome at theirs.'

'You might be. They put up with me.'

'Oh, don't be pathetic, Rob – this is one of the few times we can all get together.'

'You're always getting together, weddings, christenings, and each time it costs me money ...'

And me, I might have said. But arguing about money was pointless. We were never likely to have enough. Everything we earned from our part-time teaching jobs was eaten up by the cottage and running expenses. Everything we earned from the theatre was ploughed back into the theatre. We had the van but no luxuries. We were poor but happy. As a rule.

'Why are you being such a sod, Rob? I told you about this months ago. It's once every eleven years, for God's sake. It's important. Sue says she'll stand in for me; she's looking forward to it.' Sue taught drama at the school where I taught maths. She was a great actress, with a range of voices, male and female. She was utterly reliable.

'You *didn't* tell me months ago.'

'Did, did, hundred times did. God, you've got *such* a conveni-ent memory, Rob. Don't you remember having a go about the train fare? You said we should arrange the reunion for August so Fen could give me a lift to London.'

'Well, why not? That's a bloody good idea. And Fen could hardly charge you petrol when she's been freeloading.'

'I told you, August's no use. It has to be June, the sixth month.'

His hair fell back as he raised imploring hands to the sun. He had a black streak across his forehead. 'You're nuts, the lot of you.'

He stepped back for a good look at his work, wiping his fingers on his jeans. With the lights out the new luminous paint would look weird and creepy. The kids would love it.

'So, that's all right, is it?' I said at last. 'Sue's agreed to cover for me from Friday night so I can make a long weekend of it. I'll go over the script with her and she'll be word-perfect by Friday, I promise. I'll try and get back for Tuesday night. You'll have to phone in sick for me.'

'Tuesday night!' he squawked. 'That's seven shows, with the weekend matinées, Jo! I can't pay Sue for seven bloody shows!'

But it wasn't just the money that was bothering him. There wasn't much room backstage of our puppet theatre and Sue was a big girl, bigger than Rob. So, naturally, she couldn't duck and weave round him like me. Last time he complained of being compromised in the crossover! If I was there chaperoning, he was much happier, and when we did our epics with a cast of dozens, there might be three or more of us black gods, pulling the strings in our seven-by-four heaven, and never a cross word.

In the end, I let him talk me into going early on Monday morning. He'd do a one-man show on Monday night and leave Sue out of it.

If I'd known a duff blood vessel was lurking somewhere over my right temple, I wouldn't have given in so easily. I'd have gone on Friday as planned and stayed with Rosie. Then I wouldn't have been in such a tearing bloody rush that Monday morning, wouldn't have sat there stewing while he drove the hundred blind bends into Penzance, wouldn't have tumbled onto the platform, frantic that the porter had slammed the last carriage door. Wouldn't have got my blood pressure up. I might even have caught the train if I hadn't looked up to check the clock, to find that there were still a few minutes before departure time. Instead I saw the hand clunk on to six o'clock. And I blacked out.

But there had been no way of knowing, no warning. They reckoned it could have happened anytime. A congenital weakness. But Rob blamed himself, of course.

What nobody had known was that it was timed to a T. The Fate of the Tate would've got me one way or other at six o'clock on the sixth. It just happened to have been a cerebral haemorrhage. And it was my turn. Because of the blood pact.

*   *   *

'Jo, it's going to be all right,' he was saying, relief colouring his voice, and when I opened my eyes this time I saw that his pale lashes were wet. And my heart melted. Oh what a soft thing I had become. I reached over and smeared a tear across his cheek-

67

bone with my thumb, my good thumb. Next thing he was all over me, kissing my face, my neck, my hands.

'They moved, Jo. You were dreaming and your fingers moved. Your left hand.'

Strange how remote I felt from his joy. I regarded him curiously, mildly surprised that he cared so much. He's shared it all, I remember thinking as his eyes closed and he grew heavier and heavier. Poor old thing, he's exhausted.

We lay like that, him sprawled across me until the nurse came in with the tea and rescued me. As he heaved himself off I realized, with joy, that my left leg was pins and needles where he had been lying.

'Goodness me, you two!' twitted the nurse. 'We've not been exciting the patient again, have we?'

I nodded, 'Yes', and gave Rob half a smile.

After that I put everything I'd got into the physio sessions. No longer passive, no longer hopeless, I squeezed and flexed, pulled, pushed and lifted my legs, little by little. It was exhausting but I was desperate. I had to get well, and quickly. Every day there was some tiny triumph. Left-handed, *left-handed*, I could pull myself up on a hoist. They were worried about my foot; said the tendons had been stretched, that there might be permanent foot-drop. No way, I thought. I'm not having that. Every spare minute, I'd be pointing toes, rotating ankles.

When they took off the turban my head felt small and sandpapery, like Dad's weekend chin, and tender in places, as if I'd crowned myself on the corners of a few windows. Anna's cartoon had just about got it right. The stubble seemed darker than I remembered, though Rob swore it had a copper sheen. I sent him to buy a headscarf and tied it gypsy-fashion at the back. It looked stupid but it kept out the draught.

I might have been able to move but talking was still beyond me. Not because of palsy any more, but because what I wanted to say came out in Jabberwocky. They gave me a scribble-pad and a pencil to see if the words would come that way. But I never was much cop at spelling. I nearly threw in the towel one day, when I wrote what I thought was 'drink' and they pulled the curtains to and brought me a bedpan!

And I couldn't read, which really bugged me. When you come to it late, you've got so much catching up to do. Out on the dunes with the sun and Thomas Hardy, that's what summer mornings were for. Not stuck in a noisy hospital ward, twiddling my toes. Rob read me the rest of Rosie's letter, close-written blue scrawl, impossible for me. I guessed she'd nicked the typing paper from Jack's study. Jack wrote children's books which Rosie illustrated, in between feeds. Rob didn't like Jack much. Jack's last book, about children who fell down a well into an under-ground world of rivers and caves and magical cities, was so much like our play, 'The Legend of Tomakin's Well', it was a joke. Rosie said that she felt they'd both been inspired by the well on her dad's allotment, but I thought, pull the other one, girl. Jack didn't get on with Anna's husband, either. Paul lectured in physics. Said he found Jack patronizing. Paul came from Barbados.

'"It would have been nice ..."' Rob recapped. '"So we left Jack with the children and took a wander down Oxford Street on Saturday, Mags with her notebook, poaching ideas for the shop, and me with my eye on the remnants. I found some pretty bits that you might find useful. I'll bring them when I come. I bought some dear little dress patterns for Jude. Ahead of myself, I know, but it'll probably take me until next year to make them. Maggie showed me how to put zips in, so now I can make some little trousers for Tom. She sat him on her lap yesterday, and distracted him with books and nursery rhymes while I cut his hair. He looks like a little Beatle now. Tom adores her, almost as much as his Auntie Jo. He insisted on going round to the station with Jack to see her off, which is how come this letter is so long. She's going to make a lovely mum. You did know she's expecting a baby in Sept-ember? Says they planned it that way so that it can get the best shot at education. Seems a bit cold-blooded; still I wish I'd thought of it. August babies always get a raw deal. Hopefully, being a little Leo, Tom will have other strengths to compensate. You're a September babe, aren't you? The oldest of us. Do you feel advantaged? You should. Just think, a few days earlier and you'd have missed knowing us, been in the year above! What was that? 'Curses!' did you say? I've just realized that the day we meet in 1999 will be your birthday. Guess you've thought of that already. Not the best day for suicide!"'

Rob frowned.

'Whoops, Rosie!' I thought.

'"God, what a stupid idea that was! Hard to believe we were ever so naïve. In three years we'll be thirty, half-way there, and I haven't lived yet. Sixty is no age at all. I mean, my nan was eighty-six when she died. If she'd popped off at sixty I'd never have known her, and nor would you."'

'What's she on about, Jo?'

I blinked my eyes and shrugged. Sometimes not being able to talk has its advantages. In fact, I agreed with her. And I, for one, was going to hang on to life by my back teeth if necessary.

'"I think Anna's having a tough time reconciling her Socialist- stroke-egalitarian principles with her life in Reading. She says Paul is a firm believer in the Division of Labour. Don't ask. It certainly doesn't mean equal shares, because Anna does the cleaning, the shopping, the cooking, the mending, the gardening, looks after the kids, throws dinner parties for influential profs and toffs and does cartoons for magazines to keep him in the middle-class manner to which he's fast becoming accustomed. He does his research and the occasional lecture, hangs around the college bar and cleans the car on Sundays. She's Mrs Doormat. But that's love, I suppose.

"Did you see that one in Modern Woman? *No, I don't suppose you did, not your thing. First picture: sweet young girl picking petals off a daisy going, 'He loves me, he loves me not'. Second picture: same plus heap of petals. Sweet young girl going, 'Best of three!' Well, I thought it was funny. She wants to get herself a 'proper job', in the Probation Service, just as soon as (wait for it!) as soon as she can find a decent nanny for the kids! A nanny, for God's sake! How the other half lives, eh?*

"Fen has a new job, secretary at the BBC. 'A job with prospects,' she says, wink, wink. I guess someone must have said, 'Play your cards right, girl, dot, dot, dot.' And we all know what that means. Working flat out. (Flat on your back, I mean!)"'

'Bit of a bitch, your Rosie,' commented Rob.

She only puts into words what everyone else is thinking, I thought, and Fen'll tell you she's no stranger to the casting couch. Thank God for the Pill, she says. The letter went on:

'"She finished with that photographer, by the way. He wanted her to do some really awful things. She says that even she had to draw the line. Now she's with a footballer, Don Hagerty. I've never heard of him but Jack says he's quite famous. Plays for Arsenal. A-a-and ... is in the England Reserve side! So we might be seeing him at Wembley next month."'

'Wonder if she could get us tickets?' There was a spark in Rob's eye for the first time in over a fortnight. 'Bet old Jack's thought of that. I might just ring him up, Jo. You wouldn't mind if I popped up to London next month, would you? Get your mother down for the weekend.'

God, I thought, let's get our priorities right, shall we?

'Don Hagerty, eh?' He cleared his throat, thoughtfully. There was a long pause until I kick-started him. 'Er ... um ...'

"Fen and I had a row, as usual. I can hear you groaning. I do try to be nice to her but she manages to rub me up the wrong way, every time. She's such a stupid bitch. I won't bother you with the details. All too trivial. Oh, go on, then, twist my arm! She started it, Miss. Said she wasn't surprised Smudge couldn't hang on to her man, the way she looked. She'd really 'let herself go', she said. Apparently, Fen had invited her to a Christmas lunch at some posh restaurant in Knightsbridge and Smudge turned up in cowboy boots and a poncho.

"Fen was really shocked. 'I mean, there's no excuse for looking like a beatnik on a teacher's salary,' she said. 'Oh, she's a mess, Rosie; she must have put on about a stone, and her hair was all over the place, looked like she hadn't washed it in weeks. She had no make-up on, and this horrible old sweater. God, I felt ashamed of her. I mean, God!' You know how she talks.

"Well, I wasn't standing for that. I think Smudge is lovely and she's had more to think about than how she looks. Unlike some! Don't know quite all the ins and outs of the Monk business, but she's taken some pretty hard knocks, seems to me. What did happen, do you know? When we saw her at Maggie's wedding she was so happy, full of plans for her bistro, happy in her relationship with Monk, and then suddenly it's all off and she's doing volunteer work in Israel. Maggie reckons Julia wouldn't give him a divorce after all. Terrible shame, just when things were going her way at last. Though as Anna says, anybody else would have buggered off at twenty-one, clutching their cooking diploma in their hot little hands. But she's not like that, is she? Couldn't bring herself to leave Liz and Derek to cope with Gregory on their own.

"Did you know she found Liz cowering in the corner one day and Gregory kicking shit out of her? Didn't like the TV programme apparently. He's frightening, isn't he? Over six foot and so strong! Smudge is the only one who can manage him. Only comes up to his shoulder but she can deck him, no sweat. Wouldn't like to meet her on a dark night! Still, it's as well they got him into that residential place last year. Not before time, and all. So then she was free; she had her savings and her plans, and her man, and what happened?"

'She doesn't know?' asked Rob.

I shook my head. No, we were the only ones.

*   *   *

71

We never expected a visitor, not on a night like that. The old army blanket across the door fought an ongoing battle with draught, and Rob and I huddled into our wing chairs close to the fire. I was sewing sequins onto a fairy costume for our Christmas show and listening to the Third Programme. Rob was marking essays, in between conducting Shostakovitch's Fifth with his red marker pen. Out in the bay, the sea had its own per-cussion section, crashing down onto the rocks and sliding, suck-ing back, breathing deep, holding it, holding it and crashing down in another mighty crescendo.

'No-o!' Rob would roar, snaking his pen in four-four time, through a faulty passage of script, and 'Yessss!' he would spray, ticking triumphantly, and the sea would echo, 'Yessss!'

In the middle of all this magnificent noise and tumult there was this faint tap, tap at the window.

That was how she came to us last winter. The orphan of the storm. We'd thought the tears in her eyes were from the wind.

'Can you, can you put me up for a while? I ... I had to get away.'

'Oh, good,' said Rob, jovially, 'decent food for a change!'

But when she took off her coat and gloves I could see why she needed time to sort herself out. Her wrists were bound up with dirty bandages.

'Wicked, wicked thing to do,' she admitted, sipping hot tomato soup, smiling ruefully. 'Don't know what I was thinking of.' But as the wind in her cheeks faded and grey weariness showed through, tears slid again down her nose. She took off her glasses to wipe them away.

'I'm sure he loved me. I'm sure he did. But you know what he's like. Bit of a dreamer.'

'Wanker,' corrected Rob.

'Rob!'

'No, you're right. While Greg, while Greg was at home, while Mummy and Daddy needed me there, he was safe. He could, he could fantasize, make promises, have his cake and eat it. And it could have gone on indefinitely. Indefinitely. A once-a-week affair. Just, just so long as Julia believed he was off playing bridge, and they, and they kept our room free at The Post House. And then when Greg went into the home, I suppose, I suppose I assumed too much; came on, came on too strong. When it came to the crunch he couldn't bring himself to hurt

Julia and the kids, so, so, so it was me he dumped. My own fault; I pushed him, pushed him too hard.'

The sea hissed and roared in the silence. Rob and I looked at each other and Rob rolled up his eyes.

We put her in the back bedroom, where the cast of 'The Toy-maker' hung round the walls in a state of near-nudity, waiting to be fitted with costumes. There was more room to manoeuvre here than in the box-room, which had been turned into room-length storage for marionettes. There they hung in splendour from racks behind a curtain, leaving just a narrow corridor to the sewing machine under the window. Elbow room was at a premium.

She said she didn't object to the wooden nudes, when I offered to transfer them from her picture rail to ours.

'No, don't, don't do that,' she said.

'They'll give you nightmares,' I said, regarding Tink and the other gnomes doubtfully. Their papier-mâché faces were pretty gruesome, really. I'd worked out some of my deepest inhibitions on them.

'If kids can stand them, I'm sure I can,' she said. 'Besides, they'll, they'll remind me of Monk!'

Had I heard aright?

'Oh, yes,' she said, 'I'm under no illusions. He's a pig of the deepest shit. The deepest. But I need to keep reminding myself, so, so, so I can learn to hate him. Ten years of thinking of him as a lovable rogue is sort of, sort of hard to shake. But I'll get there.'

'Oh, Smudge,' I said, hugging her, 'I do love you.' Then, 'Look, I really ought to take them out, else I'm going to keep coming in and disturbing you, taking measurements and pinning up hems.'

She told me to do just that. She would welcome the disturbance.

'Thought you might want to be alone ...'

'I wouldn't have come here if, if I'd wanted that.'

She'd brought hardly any luggage; a rucksack and a guitar, which she stowed on top of the wardrobe. I guessed she couldn't carry anything heavy, not with those wrists. She didn't intend to stop long, she said, just until the confusion cleared.

She wasn't any trouble. Though she had every reason to 'let herself go' as Fen put it, she never did, not as I recall. We'd drive off of a morning, and she'd be up, washed and dressed, in a jumper and jeans or a long skirt, sitting in Gramps' rocking chair, elbows on the window-sill, hair coiled high and neatly pinned. And I don't think she was all that overweight, either. She wasn't thin, but then, she never had been. More like Fen was the one with the problem. Fen never moved without a ton of make-up on her pussy-cat face. Smudge would wave us off and then resume her vigil at the window. I know, 'cause I came back one day, for a poster or something, and there she was, gazing out over the harbour, like she might be able to read some clear strategy in those far distances, might hear a call to action in the gulls' cry. When we came home, the fire was laid, the room tidied, a bit of washing was hanging in the yard or airing in the scullery, and something wonderful would be cooking on the range. It was great. Like having a wife, I'd imagine. I'd've been happy for her to stay for ever.

The rocking chair became Smudge's chair, even after she was gone. On those evenings we weren't at the theatre she'd pull it closer to the fire, and if Rob wasn't marking essays she'd play her guitar. She had an extraordinary voice, deep and mellow like Helen Shapiro's. She preferred folk to pop, and moody love songs to the rollicking sort, but she wouldn't sing them as they made her cry. So we had rousing choruses of 'Jug of Punch' and 'The Wild Rover' and a snatch or two of 'Love Me Do' and 'Glad All Over'. Until the night, at the end of term, when we sank a couple of bottles of cider donated by a grateful parent, and Smudge's fingers rippled out a D-minor chord, gradually leading her into the first bars of 'She Moved Through The Fair'. She stopped, hesitated and started again. Her voice, smooth and round and rich like cream, lilted on the grace notes and swelled with the music. Rob and I were spellbound, but she choked up on that bit 'It will not be long, love, til our wedding day' and we all ended up in tears.

Sometimes if we were listening to the radio, music or a play, she'd forget we were there. She'd lean forward, like she was gripped by pain, and rock for minutes on end, her eyes tight closed, her face stern, her hands clasped in her lap; that same keening movement that her brother used when he switched off the world. Like it gave her some comfort.

'It's as if someone's dead,' whispered Rob into the back of my neck as we lay listening to the creak, creak, creak of the chair below.

'Yeah, she's grieving,' I said. 'It'll take her a long while to get over him. She stopped at home for his sake.'

'I thought she stayed to help with her brother.'

'Nope,' I said, turning over to face him. 'She wasn't that happy at home.'

'Who would be, with him around?'

'It wasn't him she was afraid of, it was dear Daddy.'

I told him how Derek used to lash out when things got too hectic. Half the bruises we'd seen, that she'd said were run-ins with Greg, were actually her dad's handiwork. Rob was astounded.

'*Derek* ...?' His face contorted with disbelief.

'Ssshh!'

'But he's such a weed,' he hissed, 'with his "tash" and his pretensions. And he always seems so fond of the boy.'

'A front, like everything else.' I'd never heard a whisper of it from Smudge herself, but seemingly. Liz, Smudge's mum, had blurted it all out one day to Pat, Rosie's mum, and Rosie had told me. Greg was a holy horror and threw furniture out of the window, pulled light fittings out of their sockets, that sort of thing, and it was understandable, I suppose, for Derek to lose his rag from time to time. But he would have murdered Greg if Liz or Smudge hadn't waded in. And then he took his frustration out on them. He was always ever so sorry, when the red faded from his eyes and he was able to see what he'd done. But it never stopped him next time. Liz told Pat she would have left him long ago but for Greg. She could never have managed him alone.

'Bloody hell,' said Rob, cupping my breast and stroking the nipple with his thumb. And then, 'And there but for the grace of God go I or you or anyone at all. Poor Smudge. Poor Derek.'

'Poor Greg,' I said, nudging my bum into his belly. 'He can't help being damaged.'

One Sunday night we were sitting round the fire, sharing a pint of winkles Rob had brought in. It was a fiddly business, removing their front doors and curling them out with a pin.

Rob began to laugh. 'If you could see yourselves! So deadly serious. Really concentrating.'

'It's a serious business,' Smudge said. 'You can't, you can't let them break mid-twiddle or you lose, you lose the best bit.'

'A dying art, twiddling winkles!' I said.

'Chance'd be a fine thing,' snorted Smudge. When we'd finished hooting and choking and banging each other on the back it occurred to me that she was on the mend.

But she'd still go off by herself during the afternoon for long walks over the cliff path to Mousehole in one direction, or Penzance in the other, her hands thrust deep into her pockets, her duffle hood pulled up to keep out the wind. Or I'd see her leaning on the harbour wall, a gusty statue against the rocking fishing boats. She'd come in smelling of cold and salt air, stamping the sand from her boots, bringing in a newspaper or some fresh-caught mackerel. Gradually the pale cheeks darkened and she grew strong.

She said one day, after one of these walks, 'Don't you ever feel you need to get right away from this little island? See something of the world?'

'Nope.'

'Mmm. I suppose it doesn't help being cooped up with a psychotic for twenty-six years.'

So I wasn't surprised when, just before Christmas, she told us she was leaving.

'I'm not going home,' she said. 'I couldn't, I just couldn't take it again. Mummy and Daddy going around all tight-lipped as if I'd done it to spite them or something. I don't know what disgusted them more, my sleeping with a married man or trying, trying to commit suicide. It doesn't, it doesn't go down well in the staff-room, does it? "Oh, by the way, my Sandra, the one, the one with the first-class diploma in Cookery, youngest head of D.S. at St Winnie's, my pride and joy, in lieu of the son I never, never mention, well, she slashed her wrists last month because her fancy man went back, went back to his wife!" Not something you can boast about.'

'So where will you go?'

'Israel. To work on a kibbutz.'

*　　*　　*

Rosie's letter went on.

'"What's wrong with cowboy boots, I'd like to know? Anyway, I got a bit heated and I think I might have asked Fen just who she thought she was, the bloody Queen of Sheba? Don't know quite what made me go for a Biblical reference. There was more along those lines and Fen got huffy and I shall have to apologize sometime, 'cos we mustn't be nasty to Fen, must we? The cow.

"Better go, I've been all morning at this. It's turned into a bit of a tome. Perhaps I should actually write a book one day, instead of just drawing the pictures. Jude will be waking up soon for her lunch, and Jack and Tom will be in wanting theirs. Trains always give them an appetite. Hope Tom's not going to become a spotter in an anorak.

"Fingers crossed that nothing has happened to you. Do write soon and put us out of our misery. Or _phone_! Yes, yes, yes, it's true. Coppermill 6254. Jack's finally relented and had us wired up to the rest of civilization. I realize that doesn't include you. I tried phoning that number you gave me and Mrs Whatsit said she couldn't leave the shop as it was pension day but she'd send 'Orace up the road for you, soon as he came back off the milking! I thought, it's quicker to send a letter. Love you lots,

Rosie et al"'

So she'd had no word from Smudge. What the hell had happened to her? Something dreadful, bound to be. You don't not turn up at the Tate and get away with it. And she was suffering, all alone, out there in some strange country. Oh, why was I such a useless bloody lump?

Then we got the telegram:

'GUESS WHAT STOP SMUDGE MARRIES BOY NEXT DOOR STOP SIXTH JUNE EINDOR STOP WISH US LUCK STOP ALL LOVE SANDRA AND DAVID'

CHAPTER FOUR

Anna in July, 1977

'Rosie, it's me. Look, love, there's no way I'm going to be able to make it tonight.'

I flinched, hearing her suck in anger and spit out, 'Shit!' Not that I'd expected her to take it well.

'Can't help it.' I was trying not to whinge. 'We've got a runner.'

'You're doing this on purpose, aren't you? Proving a point.' My ear registered her bone-white grip on the phone.

'Not this time. Not when it means so much to you.'

'Then why?' she demanded.

Breathing was difficult; air heavy with rush-hour lead thudded through the open windows into the office. I pushed weary fingers through the damp hair at the back of my neck. It had been a long, hot day.

'It's this kid ...'

'It's always some fucking kid.' So I had driven her to swearing.

'Please, Rose. He's dangerous.'

'I don't give a shit. Let the night shift deal with it.'

'I am the night shift. I'll carry the can if someone gets hurt.'

'*You'll* get hurt if you don't come to the Tate. Fen was and Jo was. You'll be next.'

'Rosie, that's nonsense.'

'You're so much wiser than the rest of us, aren't you?' she sneered. 'We're just superstitious fools, thinking there just might be something bigger than us out there, waiting for someone to miss a reunion. Anyone with any sense knows that it's pure coincidence when them as don't turn up get dumped on. Well, I may be a fool, Anna, but I'd sooner not take the risk. No need to worry about you, of course ...' and the curl of her lip was audible, 'you're immune, aren't you? God's bloody elect, or something.'

'We make our own fate,' I said, wincing. I recognized a pompous platitude when I heard it. 'I ... I just don't go for this "Woe betide" business.'

'No, of course, Jo wished that stroke on herself, and Fen ...'

'Oh, for …! Rosie, we've been over and over this! Yes, I think fear has a lot to do with it. Faith, fear, they're two sides of a coin; they can both make things happen. You believe you can walk on water, you'll walk on water. You think something awful's going to happen if you don't go to the Tate, it'll happen. Smudge wasn't afraid and nothing happened to her, did it? *I'm* not afraid.'

'*I am*,' she muttered into a pause. Her sigh blew against my ear. 'Please come, Anna.' The husky murmur was hard to resist.

'I … would if I could.' My voice was wobbling stupidly. I cleared my throat. 'Look, I'll try and get along for Act Two, but don't count on it. I'm really, really sorry, Rose. I was looking forward to seeing everyone again.' I swallowed as the words threatened to dry again. 'Haven't seen Maggie or Smudge for yonks. Or Fen, come to that … Oh, what can I say? Stopping here, waiting for this damn kid to phone in is the last thing I wanted. But he's likely to do something stupid, unless … Well, I'm the only one he'll talk to.'

'Naturally!' Her voice crawled along the line, heavy with sarcasm. 'They all take a shine to you, all the nasty little thugs. You're such an extraordinary person, Anna, so full of warmth and understanding. Pity you can't spare some of it for your friends.'

'Rosie …' I protested.

'Get stuffed.' She hung up.

Thanks, I thought, that really helps. Sweaty fingerprints dried on the bakelite and I wiped my palms on my trousers. Bloody woman. I lit a cigarette and dragged down the smoke as the memory played itself back.

'*Please come, Anna.*'

There was no intention to seduce, of course, no notion of the effect on me, the heart-flip that always surprised me. Thank God. I'd never risk telling her.

'You still here?' Victor stuck his head round the door. He was flabby with heat, his tie undone, his jacket hooked over his shoulder. 'Thought it was the girls' night out.'

'Billy Riley,' I explained. 'Broke probation.'

'They told me.' Victor worked in the next room, a bearded, burly man, with a bite worse than his bark. I'd hear the gentle rumble of his voice through the partition, putting his clients at ease, getting them to talk. Some made the mistake of thinking him a pushover, but he was shrewd, summed them up in an instant and stood no nonsense. He'd taken it upon himself to show me the ropes when I came to the job, six years before, with a late starter's self-doubt and a divorcée's inhibitions. Trouble was, he couldn't let go; and there's nothing so maddening as an unwanted agony uncle. I was a grown woman – thirty-eight years old, for heavens' sake; I could blunder along quite happily now under my own steam. He came in, leaving the door to his office ajar, and regarded me over the top of his glasses.

'No need for you to hang around, though. Good God, girl, if we all ... Look, you've done the best you can. Kid's a nutter. No one could have foreseen that he'd ... that she was in danger. It's out of your hands, Anna. Matter for the police now. You push off to your reunion. I'll be here for a bit.'

I shook my head. Rosie reckoned I should tell him what to do with his wise pearls, one by one, but she didn't have to work with the man. Besides, it was too hot to argue. 'He won't talk to any-one else, Vic,' I said. 'He's got to ring.'

Victor considered this, clammily. He had been out all afternoon, at court, missing the action.

I threw him a sop. 'Never expected him to turn on his gran, though. He was fond of her.'

'Oh, right; that's what you do when you're fond of someone, is it? Beat them up when they catch you with your fingers in the cookie jar?'

'It's that damned temper of his,' I explained. 'Doesn't know what he's doing. He'll be abject when he cools down.' Why was I defending the little sod? Except he wasn't so little any more.

'Abject!' squawked Victor. 'You bet he'll be abject! He was sit-ting pretty so long as he stayed out of trouble. Granny-bashing, nicking the holiday money, they'll throw the book at him. And for what? A few lousy quid! She didn't deserve that. Breda Riley may be an old bag but she gave him a home when he needed it, and a job.' He sat down in the visitors' chair, wearily shaking his head. 'How *do* their ungrateful little minds work?' He pulled at an ear-lobe. 'She gonna croak?'

'Can't say. Head injuries and a couple of broken ribs; some internal damage. They're operating now. She made out she trip-ped on the carpet, and that she *gave* him the money, but the neigh-bours heard it all. They've got thin walls in Tiverton Road.'

He leaned forward and poured himself a glass of water. 'And you're going to be his friend, eh? Rather you than me. What makes you think he'll call here? Last place I'd ...'

81

'He already did.' I enjoyed the way his beard drooped. 'To find out how Breda was.'

'Oh?'

'He was in a bit of a state; thought he might have killed her.'

'Touching!' He seemed mildly surprised beneath the sarcasm. 'Hope you put his mind at rest.'

'I told him she wasn't dead. That he should give himself up, hand back the money. Usual things.'

'The police know all this?'

'Of course.'

Victor shrugged. 'Well, you did right. But there's no point in hanging on here.'

'He said he would phone again. See how the operation went.'

'Let him stew.' He eased himself out of the chair and headed for the door. 'You're his PO, not his flaming mother. Go home.'

But I didn't.

I phoned to tell them I'd be late. It was ten to five.

'Look,' I said to Roz, 'you'll have to cook the tea. You can manage that, can't you? There are fish fingers in the top of the fridge and frozen chips and things and you can open a tin of fruit for dessert.'

'Oh, Mum,' she whined, 'I was going out. Can't Zac do it?'

'You're *not* going out, Roz. I told you that this morning. I want you to stay in and mind the fort, please. I'm not having the boys left on their own.'

'Why can't Grandma come round?'

'It's her typing class. Where were you going anyway? It's not youth club night.'

'Up town. Late-night shopping with Lisa.'

'No, dear, sorry.' Why hadn't she mentioned this before? 'I thought you didn't have any money.'

'Dad sent some. Ten quid.'

'Ten! What, each?'

'Yep. Good, eh? Thought I'd get some shoes. Letter was on the mat when I got in. Wait 'til you hear this!'

'Do I have to?'

She ignored my reluctance and I heard the rustle of air-mail paper. 'He's in Florida. Says it's too hot to stay in Boston.' I listened in spite of my sudden nausea. I suppose you can't help but be slightly interested in the comings and goings, mostly goings, of the man who fathered your children. His voice, coffee-brown,

82

percolated the written words, stuff about end-of-term exhaustion and how much he missed his little family. I could see the tip of his tongue licking his lip, pink against brown, as he composed the lies. No, that was unfair and I crossed through the ugly caricature I had been scribbling on the blotter. Roz adored him, despite the casual way he had ditched us when the Harvard appointment came up. She excused him on the grounds that this was how men were taught to behave in Afro-Caribbean matriarchal society. Very O-level Sociology. Even I couldn't get my head round that one, not when the man in question had a first in Physics from Cambridge. There were no excuses.

She'd have been nine, getting on for ten, that Open Evening. I'd sat at her desk in a room full of parents, waiting for my turn with the teacher. Her News Folder was open in front of me. Riveting stuff. Every Monday she'd written an account of how she'd spent her weekend.

'On Saturday Daddy came into my bedroom and said, ' "It's a lovely day today. Why don't we all go to the seaside?" Then Zac and little Joe didn't want to come, so Mummy stayed with them. Then Daddy and me went off in the car. It was a long way in the car, about two hours. We sang songs all the way to the seaside. Then we came to the sea. Then Daddy took me swimming in the sea. Daddy gave me rides on his back and ducked me in the water. Then we played cricket on the beach. I scored twenty runs. Then we had an ice-cream. Then we went to the fair and Daddy and me had rides on the big wheel.' Then, then, then … Page after page of fun-packed activity. She'd even drawn pictures to prove what a whale of a time she'd had. Daddy and me in the car. A lumpy-looking limo with two currant-bun faces looking out. Daddy and me in the sea, at the zoo, at the pictures, at the Tower of London. What a happy pair!

'She's a quiet little girl.' Then the teacher, a knitted tea-cosy sort of woman, began to gush. 'But she has such a happy home life and a wonderful relationship with her father!'

That's when I choked up. I had to tell her. 'Roz hasn't seen her father in six months. He left us just before Christmas. He hasn't written or phoned; didn't even remember her birthday!' What a to-do there was then! Roz Griffiths's mum, queen of the PA, who should certainly have known better, crashing through the classroom, blind with tears, knocking over chairs and upsetting the Nature Table, her sobs echoing back down the corridor, and then, and then … foul curses, as she lashed out at the headmaster, who had only tried to put his arm round her. But, of course, you could expect no more of a woman who married a black man.

The letter to the principal at Harvard was a touch below the belt perhaps, but how else was I going to get Paul to face up to his responsibilities? And things did improve, after that, at home and at school, if you don't count the anorexia. Now he sent money on a fairly irregular basis and American Football posters for the boys. They wrote to him and sent him photos. But I would never forgive him.

Not that it hadn't had its good side. We had scraped Reading off our boots and moved back to Walthamstow. A smaller, humbler dwelling, without Paul's money to bolster us, but now the kids had grandparents again, the East End had a brilliant new probation officer and my life was my own. More to the point, Rosie lived close by in Woodford, she upwardly mobile now that their books were so popular, me backing onto the railway.

I was doodling. Equidistant, parallel lines. Join them up to make …? Steps. One, two, three, four …? Seven. Yes. And then the figures. Strange, lost little figures. An Afro-frizz perm and cheesecloth for Rosie. Flowing hair and flower-power for Smudge. Fen? Something smart. Trouser suit. Yes. Jo, skirt and skinny top. Maggie? God knows, I hadn't seen her in yonks. Something haute couture from one of her shops. And a hat.

'So, what do you think?' She had come to the end of the letter. 'Can we go?'

'No, Roz, I already told you. I want you home tonight.' Where I know you'll be safe, I might have added. But it wasn't that I was afraid, it wasn't.

'To Florida, Mum,' she said patiently. 'You switched off, didn't you? Dad wants us to go for August. He's sent three tickets. TWA.'

'We're going to Jo's,' I said, knowing full well that they'd be going to Florida and I'd be going to Cornwall on my own.

After Roz had been bribed to stay home with the promise that I'd think about the Florida visit, I tried phoning Rosie again. Maybe if she let me explain … Tom answered, his gruff adolescent voice contrasting with the bright burble of *The Magic Roundabout*.

'Sorry, Anna, Mum's just gone. Auntie Jo and another lady came for her in Jo's new VW. A 'Herbie', like in the film. Oh, Anna, can you ask Joey if he wants to come to a party next month? My birthday. Zac can come, too, if he likes. Do you want to talk to Dad?' I declined politely and put down the phone. I didn't want to talk to Jack. Now or ever.

Who was the other lady, I wondered? Smudge or Maggie or Fen? Damn. A longing, a sort of loneliness was gnawing away under my ribs. It was really happening, this reunion, and I was missing out! For what? A poxy sense of duty. Who was I hoping to impress? My colleagues? My friends? Billy Riley?

His file lay open on the desk, thin and pathetic like the photo of him, taken at his referral and stapled to the inside cover. It showed a raw fifteen-year-old, somewhat phased by the enormity of his first offence. First and last, I had thought. The file recorded colourless, run-of-the-mill interviews, but even brief notes flesh out over two years, just as he had built up muscle and sinew with daily workouts at the gym. He had lost the sharp cheekbones and the long, greasy locks. Now he was a punk. Dandelion hair at his last visit, and an anarchic white face, a coat from Oxfam, fastened with safety pins, jeans torn at the knee, white socks and pointy black shoes. Zac had an identical wardrobe at home. I didn't like Billy, particularly, but probation officers are not required to like their clients. My business was to be impartial, official. Most of them were villains, dyed in the wool or embryonic, and it didn't do to get too close. But a few passed through for whom it was possible to feel, if not liking, then a sort of sympathy. There was the guy who had helped his aged mother out of a demented world with an aspirin overdose, and the destitute mother of six, driven to holding up the post office with her small son's toy pistol. I had to ask myself what I would have done in such extremes. Then there were the protesters, the CND sit-downers and the anti-apartheid lot, with whom I identified only too closely.

'Ban the Bomb!' I had yelled on the march to Aldermaston. 'We shall not be moved!' as they hefted my limp body into the Black Maria. 'Where have all the flowers gone?' Sweet singing in the police cells, but I had left quietly enough when my long-suffering Daddy came to bail me out. So I didn't get to spend the night with the drunks and the prossies. I didn't go before the magistrate next morning and I didn't end up with a criminal record. Others did. I picketed South Africa House. Ditto. I subscribed to Amnesty International. I married a black man. My heart was in the right place but cushioned from the pain.

I felt sorry for Billy. The runt in a family of bully-boys, he was their natural victim. He had managed to survive by keeping out of their way as much as possible. While the rest of them sprawled round the front room watching telly, he would be along the passage in the bedroom, reading. While Colin and Chrissie and Danny and Mark were down the square, playing footie or fighting or thieving or tormenting cats, leaving the flat free for Mrs Riley's 'business', Billy would be sitting on the cold stairs, reading. He was not clever at school, but he could read and fantasize. The library was his refuge, and he would spend happy hours after school, swinging through jungles with Tarzan, fighting off Sioux with General Custer, and he'd limp home, mortally wounded, after battles with dinosaurs or merciless SS men, until the shrill voice of his mother would jolt him back to a different sort of struggle.

'Billy, where you bleeding been? I'll pay ya, you little sod, you come home this time again! We're all bleeding starving! Get round the chippie. Cod and chips six times, and get a bleeding move on!' The money would follow, winging down from the eighth floor in a brown-paper bag fastened with an elastic band. She didn't 'pay' him anything; she counted the change on his return, with a cuff round the ear for good measure.

So, to make a few bob, he sold cats' meat on his grandmother's stall in the Saturday market and helped with an early morning milk round in the flats, quickly converting cash into books before the brothers could take it off him. Then came a day in muddy November when he arrived home to find space under his bed where there had been reading matter before.

His brothers, Colin and Mark, smirked and nudged each other when he challenged them.

'What you lost, Bill? Pile of old books?'

'Oh, Gawd, they wasn't under the bed, was they?'

'Didn't fink you wanted them.'

'Give 'em to some kids, dincha, Col? Come round the door asking for stuff for the bonfire.'

'You never!' gasped Billy, his eyes big with loss.

'No, we never. We took 'em down the market and flogged 'em for a fiver. Wanna make sunning of it?'

When he thought of all the milk crates he had lugged up the stairs when the lifts were out of order, all the early mornings; when he thought of all the stiff yellow fat he had trimmed from the horse meat, all the rancid smells he had had to wash from his hands; when he thought of all the adventures, the ghost stories, the space sagas, the mysteries and thrillers that would now be read by someone else, he did want to make something of it. He couldn't help himself. All the rage that he had damped back over the years came flaring up and spewed from dragon lips.

'You fucking bleeders!' he cried and he put down his head and charged. But Colin sidestepped and Mark caught his arms and twisted them behind his back.

'Oh look, we missed one, Mark. What's it called, "Billy the Kid"? That 'im on the front? That cowboy? Giddyup, cowboy, come an' get your book! Yee-haw!' Colin jiggled the book before Billy's contorted face. Billy made to grab it but his brother held on tight.

'Doncha wannit, then? Nah, it's a crumby old book, innit? All the pages coming out, look.' Slowly and deliberately he yanked out a wad of pages and dropped them over the window ledge. They fluttered on the damp November air, down, down out of sight. 'Book ain't no good when 'alf the pages are missing.' He tore out some more. This was great; the kid was really blubbering now.

More pages followed and more, until there were none left. Fun over, they left the boy and sniggered off down the passage to the front door. They were starting down the stairs, the lift being out of order again, when there came a roaring behind them. They looked up too late. Like a whirlwind Billy charged, knocking both youths off balance. Down they went, crashing, tumbling down the stone steps, piling into the wall at the bottom of the flight, and Billy pounded on after, a kicking, screaming fury. Colin managed to stumble upright only to be ploughed down the next flight. When Billy came to himself, when he was pulled off the bleeding mess by a neighbour, Mark lay still on one landing and Colin lay still on the next. They were taken to hospital and Billy was nicked. Anyone in Billy's winklepickers would have done the same, as I told the magistrate.

So Billy went to live with his grandmother and came to see me once a week. And he booked in at the gym, to be ready when Colin and Mark came to do him over, but so far they had thought better of it.

I hadn't rated him as a recidivist, any more than I could see the man with the senile mother sending any other old woman to her Maker. The motivation was missing, the need. Billy seemed settled with his job on the cats' meat stall, his body-building, the occasional nervous girlfriend and his books. His bookshelves, like his biceps, were bulging. I gave him a greasy copy of *War and Peace* and a duplicate *I, Claudius* and he thanked me, though nothing like so effusively as when I handed over a mixed bag of kids' classics and Paul's Ian Flemings. Ah, I thought, and thereafter only passed on the lightweight stuff that came my way. In two years I must have given him forty or fifty books. Two unnecessary years, in my opinion. And then this. What had poor old Breda done to make her grandson turn violent?

It was so out of character. Or was it? Had I simply misread the signs? Had he let *me* down, or I him?

At five o'clock doors began to slam and feet clattered down the iron stairs. Young heels tip-tapping down the stone-flagged corridor; exit the girls from the typing pool. Then the clerks, plod, plod, the supervisors, strut, strut. They all left. Parting shots faded, the ironwork stairs quivered one last time and were quiet. Leaving me and Victor working late and the electric fan flapping tiredly at the flies.

There was plenty I could be doing; bringing case-notes up to date, writing up reports and home-visits, reading the latest interdepartmental bulletins. After five minutes I flung down my pen. This was crazy. Vic was right, as always. This was a job for the police. I closed the file, put it in the 'Pending' tray and cleared my desk.

Maybe I'd just telephone the hospital for an update on Breda's condition before I went. A ruptured spleen, they said. But she was a game old girl; she should pull through.

Good news. I'd just hang on 'til half-past for Billy. If he thought his gran was out of danger ... And there'd still be time to get to the Tate. Make Rosie's day.

'She out?'
    'Billy, it might be best if you phoned the hospital yourself.'
'Went okay, did it?'
    'Billy ...'
'She ain't dead? She's all right?'
    'She's holding her own, they said.'
'Oh,' he muttered. 'Right.' There was a deep shuddering sigh of relief. I wished I could see his face.
    'Give yourself up,' I prompted.

'Like hell.'

'Be better in the long run, Billy. You must have had a reason to go for your gran like that. They'll take that into account. What was it, an accident, something like that? Self-defence?'

'Nah.'

'You're not on something? Drugs or ...?'

'Nah.'

I couldn't keep the squeak out of my voice. 'Then why the hell did you *do* it?'

'You'll see.'

'I don't understand, Billy.'

'Nah, you don't, do ya? Nor did me Nan. I says to her, like, "Today's the day, see. All the lucky sevens, innit?"' And there must be thousands, I thought, with the same idea. Auspicious day: give up smoking, get married, meet your friends at the Tate, beat up your granny. He went on, 'I says to her, "Bleeding cats' meat pisses me off, gel. I can do better'n this. Give us a sub, like, and I'll be on me way." But she reckons she don't owe me nothing. So I, like, twists her arm a bit 'til she coughs up, old slag.'

'What? You mean you deliberately ...?'

'Yeah.'

He needed treatment. Tra, la, la, down the road to seek his fortune, with his knapsack on his back, leaving Grandma for dead. It wasn't on.

'Look, Billy, I really think you should go to the nearest police station and ...'

'Oh, I ain't done yet, not be a long chalk. That was just for starters. See, Mrs Griffiths,' he pronounced it Griffiffs, 'I know how I can get me hands on real dosh, big dosh.'

'Why are you telling me all this?'

'You're 'ave ta wait and see, woncha?'

'Billy, I'm not staying here to play games. Let me give you the hospital phone number.'

'Nah. You gotta stay put, that's part of it, see. You gotta be there to pick up the phone when I call.'

'Well let *me* call you. I have to go now ...'

'Fucking stay put!' The phone snarled and went dead.

I sat, attaching strings to the five little people on the seventh step of my blotter, turning them into marionettes, and then I knocked on Victor's door.

'Sounds like he's really flipped,' he said, pulling at his beard. 'He fancies you, of course; that's why he needs you to listen to his drivel. POs and shrinks, it's par for the course. And God knows he needs a mother figure. Can't blame the lad for that. Wouldn't say no to a spot of mothering myself if Mummy looked like you ...'

Why did he do it? I shook my head in despair. He *knew* how it wound me up; he just didn't seem able to help himself. But I didn't have the energy for a fight. Besides, I needed his help.

Victor was a local boy; he'd sparred with the likes of Terry Downs in Solly's Gym, and had a broken nose to prove it. He had even been on nodding terms with the Kray twins. Nodding and forelock tugging, if you ask me. But he knew these East End kids, what made them tick, so he was more than useful in that way. The problem was that Riley and his mates identified with the King's Road and the seventies, not Cable Street and the fifties.

'Well, what if I wasn't here when he phoned, would he feel betrayed? Be more likely to hurt someone else? And if I stayed, would I stand a chance of talking him round, bringing him in?'

'Your guess is as good as mine, girl. See, it could easily work the other way. He might see you as the fair damsel who's going to be won by his brave deeds.'

(Hardly, I thought. I'd seen Riley's 'fair damsels' waiting for him in the corridor, panda-eyed, tattooed ladies, spitting out their nails. But I wasn't going to disillusion Victor.)

'If you buggered off,' he went on, 'he'd have no one to impress. And the whole shebang, the lucky day, the fortune, the whole castle of dreams would come tumbling down. He'd come to his senses and walk into the nearest nick. And that's,' he grinned sheepishly, 'about as much wishful thinking as you'll hear in a month of Sundays. No, the only thing I can say with any certainty is that whatever your decision it's bound to be the wrong one.'

'Oh.'

'Did he say where he was calling from? I mean, could the police pick him up? Could they trace him?'

I shrugged, 'He was in a call-box.'

'He wasn't making threats?'

I considered this. 'Well, no, not really, though I felt threatened.'

'Mmm. And I suppose if you went off gallivanting you wouldn't be able to enjoy yourself, thinking about Sonny Jim ...'

'Exactly.'

'Well, suppose it takes all night? What about your kids?'

'They're not babies, Victor; Joey's thirteen, for goodness' sake, and Roz is sixteen. They're very sensible. They ...'

The phone began to ring in my office.

A clatter of coins and then, 'Anna? Hello. Voice from the past!' I knew it, knew her, knew those rich, warm tones, the slightly sibilant 's', the trace of East London twang, the hint of humour. But I had to think back a few years before I found the face to fit.

'Smudge?'

'Not bad, not bad! Look, I can't talk long; I'm in a phone box ... Rosie says you aren't coming tonight.'

'I can't. There's this maniac ...'

'Yes, she said. She *said*.'

I'd forgotten how nervous she was. I knew she'd be twisting her hair or nibbling her nails. Now her voice had picked up a hesitant tick. Was it me she was frightened of, after all these years? Me that made her consider her words so carefully? Was I so awesome?

'Anna, Rosie also said ...' she paused, 'she said the reason you weren't afraid was that *I* hadn't turned up in sixty-six and nothing had happened to me ...'

'Not only that, Smudge. But, well, getting married's hardly a misfortune ...'

'But it *was* a misfortune, Anna, of the very worst kind. The very worst.'

'Oh, no! Don't any of our marriages work? And you were so happy, you two, when we saw you that summer at Jo's; all over each other!'

'Hard to believe. Hard to ... My marriage was a disaster, Anna, the pits, from start to finish.'

'Finish?'

'Oh yes, I'm out of it now. Out, out, out. Lucky to escape with my life.'

'Your life! That's a bit strong ...'

'Well, if it hadn't been for the people at Chiswick ...'

'Chiswick?'

'The Refuge, you know?'

Refuge? My mind buzzed around pubs and churches. But I only knew one Refuge in Chiswick, and she couldn't mean that.

'Erin Pizzey's place,' she confirmed.

'Really? What were you doing there?' Because it still didn't reg-

91

ister. She couldn't have been a refugee. My friends didn't batter each other.

'They had to get the police out to restrain him. He nearly, *nearly*, had the door down. See, he became so possessive, David. Jealous of anyone close to me, Greg, Mummy.' She repeated, 'Even Mummy,' as if she had just realized how preposterous this sounded. 'At the end, if he caught her giving me a hug, just a hug, he'd stand there scowling and when she'd gone he'd ... 'punish' me. I had to stop them coming over. Had to.'

'Oh, Smudge! Why did you stay with him?'

'Well, it's quite flattering, being worshipped and adored. And ... and when they're so protective that they won't hear of you getting a job, you think they're being ... kind; when they give you the third degree about where you've been ... where you've been and who you've seen, you think it's, well, charming and rather sweet. I suppose. I told myself, this man loves me *so* much. Once he realizes he can trust me, he'll ease up. I thought I could change him. Change him ...' Her voice tailed off. Was she nodding to herself? She took a breath. 'But he got worse. He began to, began to insist on meeting me ... whenever I – I went up to town, or he set me time limits. Or, or he found reasons why I should stay at home. Shouldn't go out. I could have my friends come home to see me, he said; he didn't like to think of me travelling on the Tube late at night, and when I suggested learning to drive, he just shook his head. Shook his head. So I mouldered away at home. I thought it would be different, might be different, if we had children. He didn't want them, though, couldn't relate to them. I thought, I thought, if it were *fait accompli* he would have to change his mind. But he pushed ... pushed me down the stairs when I told him I was pregnant.'

'No! *David*?' As if she must have meant someone else. 'But he wasn't the violent sort ... We used to play with him, for goodness' sake. Monopoly. And he always let you win. He was barmy about you.'

'Besotted,' she said wearily. 'He said I'd stumbled and he'd tried to stop me falling. But there was no mistaking that shove in the back.'

'But why? God, pushed you down the stairs? I can't believe it.'

'Rage. Blind, blind rage. He'd got it into his head that it was, it was some other man's child. I miscarried and just as well. Just as well. I couldn't bring a baby into that house. There was no

92

love, no real love, no trust. After that he never let me go out on my own, not even shopping. If he couldn't come with me, he had the shop deliver. As for friends, my friends, well, didn't you wonder why I sank without trace?'

'Yes, of course, I thought that … when you didn't answer my letters I thought you couldn't be bothered with us any more. People drift apart.'

'He destroyed all my letters, Anna. Tore them up before I could read them.' Her voice caught on a sob, 'Sorry, I …I didn't mean to let that happen.' I could hear her blowing her nose.

'Smudge, you poor thing! Couldn't you, I don't know, talk to him, get him to see reason?'

'You think I didn't try? He wouldn't listen. Wouldn't listen. Said awful things, that I was meeting men on the quiet. Monk, mostly. He had a thing about Monk. And he began to slap me about a bit. And then more than a bit. I had to go to hospital a few times, for repairs; told them I'd walked into a lamp-post, fallen down the cellar steps, that sort of thing. That … sort of thing …' Her voice turned away from the phone, and returned, 'And when I came out he'd slap me about some more.' She dropped a few more coins into the slot.

I said, 'But, Smudge, you can floor Gregory on a bad day. Didn't you hit him back?'

'I couldn't, Anna. I … somehow I thought I deserved it. He could twist things, you see. Make out I was incompetent. Defective. I was a nervous wreck. A nervous … If I cooked a meal he didn't like, if I broke anything, left a ring round the bath, he'd say I was trying to make him angry. He didn't want to be angry; it was *my* fault.'

'Mmm, I've come across that. Some of my clients have been wife-beaters. Bloody manipulative bastards. Even had *me* feeling guilty.'

'He wanted me totally dependent on him, body and soul; started locking me in, whenever he left the house, front and back, and he nailed all the windows shut. Nailed them shut. I got so frightened with nothing to do all day but worry about what sort of mood he was going to come home in. Then I heard about the Women's Refuge on the radio. It was like the answer to a prayer. Somewhere to run to. So I did. I broke out and they took me in. They took me in. And thank God.'

'When was this?'

'Two years ... just over two years ago.'

'Two years! And you didn't try and get in touch with us?'

'Anna, I was ashamed. I wanted to crawl into a hole and hide. The Refuge arranged counselling and stuff but it's taken a long time to sort myself out. So don't, don't go thinking I didn't get my come-uppance, eleven years ago. I did, with a vengeance, just like Jo, just like Fen. The other two who defied the allotment thing. Three out of three.'

'Shit,' I said. There didn't seem much else to say.

'So will you come tonight? Please. I'm frightened for you.'

As I left the washroom the telephone began to ring. I had put on fresh lipstick, brushed my hair and scrubbed at a biro scrawl across my Indian smock-top with Government-issue soap. It looked like a breast leakage and stank of raw cotton but it would soon dry in the heat. The ringing was insistent. I thought Victor might pick it up but his office was an arid wasteland through frosty glass; he would have gone home, of course, knowing it was now safe to do so, that I'd abandoned my watch. He didn't like my setting precedents. Good old Uncle Vic.

It was Billy Riley.

'Mrs Griffiffs,' he crooned, 'Anna ...' I frowned at the familiarity. 'Someone 'ere wants a word ...'

A whimper. Then, 'Mum?'

I tried to make the connection. Roz and Billy Riley? What had she to do with him? The shock, when it came, jolted through me in spasms.

'Mrs Griffiths? You still there?'

I held on tight to the desk to keep from sinking beneath the waves of black oblivion. I was drenched in sweat and the smell of raw cotton was sickening. 'Don't hurt her,' I croaked. 'Don't, please don't hurt her.'

'Course not, Mrs Anna. Wouldn't dream of hurting your nigger brats, not one frizzy black hair on their heads, not if you're sensible.'

Of course, he would have them all. They had been together, at home, grilling fish fingers when ... He was in my *home!*

'Joey? Zac?' Their names squeezed, breathless, past the tight panic in my chest. 'Are you all right? Roz?' Why couldn't they speak to me? Animal sounds, dredged up from somewhere primal and deep, making my throat ache, snarled through my teeth, 'What have you done to them, you bastard?' and I let go of the table the better to rip and tear the flesh from his body. But I dropped the receiver and found my hands clawing at empty air. My helplessness erupted in an impotent sob. Only words were any use and I didn't know the magic ones that would save them.

I reached again for the phone; it was heavy, slippery. It took two hands to hold it steady. 'Billy,' I gritted my teeth, 'what's got into you? You're not like this. Where's it all going to get you?'

'Rich, Mrs Anna Poncy Griffiths. Stinking bloody rich.'

'But I don't have any money.'

'Yeah? So, bell your old man, your tame nig-nog. I want money, loadsa lovely dosh. What do you reckon they're worth then, your kids? Ten grand? Yeah, reckon a Yank professor can lay his hands on a measly ten grand. He'll 'ave to phone it through so's you can pick it up from the bank tomorrer morning. You can get ten grand in that briefcase of yourn, easy well. Used fivers, right?'

'I can't!' I wailed. 'We're divorced. He could be anywhere. And he doesn't support us. He doesn't give a damn about us, not really.'

'Well, someone's gonna have to find some dosh, and sharp-ish, else it'll be the worse for your kiddiwinks.'

'Oh, don't ...' I sobbed. This was a nightmare. What could I say that would make it all right? 'Your nan will get well, Billy. She won't press charges. You'll be in the clear and all this for nothing.'

'Know what?' he said, as if it were some juicy piece of gossip, 'there was this kid, yeah? Snatched be a gang, year or two back, made all the papers? And his grandad, right, this rich geezer, wouldn't cough up, so they chopped the kid's ear off and sent it to his mum in a box.'

'You wouldn't ...'

A schoolboy's snigger and then a voice edged with pure malice. 'You better come up with the readies then, encha?'

'Oh God. I don't know where ... I can't ...'

'Or fingers. Yeah, nice choccy fingers ...'

'Uh ...!' I heard myself groan from a long way off. No, don't faint, don't faint! I dashed the water from my eyes. 'You can't hope to get away with this. All on your own. The police ...'

'I cetch one whiff of the filth, that's it. Chop, chop!'

There was something I'd forgotten. I shivered with the effort of remembering; my teeth were beginning to chatter. Yes. 'There's a letter,' I said. 'Came today. A number to phone, in Florida. Roz'll know where it is.'

95

A clunk as the receiver was laid aside, and I could hear him relaying what I had just said. Then she spoke. Her voice was shaky but clear. She told him that the letter was upstairs on her dressing-table. We all waited as he pounded up the stairs. Springy steps.

'Mum,' her whisper, close to the phone, came as a surprise. 'Do as he says. Please. He's got the carving kife. Don't talk, he's coming.'

I took down the Florida phone number with a pencil that shook and slipped and eventually broke. 'And tell your old man no cops, right? Or yer kids get it.' Substitute 'the dame' for 'kids' and what he said could have been lifted straight from a Mickey Spillane. He was acting out a part, a fantasy. There was no reaching him. He said he would phone later with further instructions.

'So don't fink of going nowhere!' he said. Then he hung up.

I spent precious minutes just staring at the phone. What to do? What to do? My head was spinning. Oh, my babies. What if he ...? I massaged my temples, twisted my wedding ring, lit a cigarette. Got up, sat down. I had to be there, of course, be with them, even if ... My car was downstairs, in the car park. Yes, yes, go home. Then what? Kill him, kill him! Oh yes. How? He was strong. And he had that knife, Granny's knife, its long, bendy blade worn razor-thin and shiny by years of Sunday sharpening on the back step. Ears and fingers. It was a family joke, how he'd been stealing currants, my dad, naughty boy, while she was making cakes, and she'd picked up the first thing to hand to swipe at him. Chopped his finger clean off. They'd fastened it back with bandage and Germolene and it had grown again leaving a raised white scar all round his finger: a ring of proof. Oh, God, let Paul be there!

It was early morning in Florida and he was mumbly with sleep.

'Anna, hi!' Even his yawn was well-heeled. 'Kids coming for the vacation, are they? Fantastic! Say, why don't you come, too? Trudy'll be glad to put you up, won't you, honey?' Silence. I could imagine Trudy frantically flapping, 'No, no!' on the other side of the bed.

'No Paul, I ... Paul, I'm sorry. Terrible things are happening.'

He was shaken, of course he was, but that didn't stop him blaming me. Just as he had always done. It had been my fault that he had been trapped into an early marriage and fatherhood, my fault that we had been estranged from his family and mine, my fault that he had been forced to leave the job at Reading. Oh yes, if I had been able to satisfy him he would not have sought the comfort of Trudy's arms.

Now I was an irresponsible bitch who couldn't be trusted with the care of his kids. When this was over he would make damn sure the custody order was changed. He'd bring them to America where they'd be properly looked after.

'For God's sake, Paul, you're the one who abandoned them!'

'I'd have thought this situation called for more than petty recriminations, Anna.'

Bastard! I'd forgotten how he could deflect guilt.

'How soon can you send the money, Paul?'

'Oh now, this needs some thought, Anna.' Why? And why this new note of cunning in his voice? 'I'm not sending off ten thousand bucks into the pale blue ...'

'Pounds, Paul, not dollars, *pounds*! Sterling.'

'No, no. I need the cops to tell me it's on the level. Otherwise, how do I know this isn't another of your lowdown tricks to get your hands on my money?'

'Don't be so bloody ridiculous!'

'See, Anna, you've kicked me in the balls before.' (That letter to his principal.) 'How do I know you're not in cahoots with this scum? He seems to know all about us. Knows about the kids, where you live, when to find them home. Knows that I'm good for a few grand. Now how would he know all that unless you'd told him? Huh? You screwing him, Anna? That it? Never could resist a good cause, could you, Anna? Come one, come all to my milk-white breast, huh? And let's face it, my dear, you've screwed a black, so one cheap hood, more or less ...'

I couldn't listen to this; took the phone from my ear, mystified by the odious matter leaking from it. My head thumped. I needed to howl and hammer my fists on the desk but first I had to make him see reason.

'Paul, please, this is stupid. I may have done some pretty dreadful things but I wouldn't do that to you, and you know it. I'm not a cheat, am I? Think. And risk my job, too? No.'

I told him that everyone knew I had children. Their photo was on the desk. I was looking at it now. Taken on Newlyn beach last summer. And they were beautiful. All willowy, like him in his youth, fine bones, eyes to drown in, smiles to break your heart. Though not Riley's clearly. How he had known my address was a mystery to me. He had no car to follow me home, though I suppose hiring a taxi to 'Follow that Mini and damn the expense' might have appealed to the adventurer in him. Maybe I'd left my diary out on the desk or ... and, like a comic lightbulb flashing beside my head, blink, blink, I knew the answer, could even see the labels, enlivened with scrolls and curlicues, that Roz, the little bureaucrat, had stuck in all her books, one wet weekend about five years ago:

> *If this book should chance to roam*
> *Smack its bum and send it home*
> *To Roz Griffiths*
> *38 Oliver Road,*
> *Walthamstow,*
> *London, E17.*

All her books, that I'd so grandly given to Billy Riley! Including such gems as *William, the Outlaw* and *Kidnapped*. Ironic, if you could remember how to smile. But he must have realized as soon as he discovered that Oliver Road was a seedy terrace of railway 'villas', cast from the same mould as Tiverton Road, E7, that I was as poor as a church mouse. I didn't know how he had found out about Paul and his money. Didn't know, couldn't think. But he did know, and now he wanted a share, in exchange for the lives of our children.

'Paul, you *must* send the money, soon as the banks open! Phone it through to Barclays, Aldgate branch, because I can't leave here. Tell them I'll pick it up around ten. No, don't argue any more. Just do it, Paul, please!'

His voice was kinder. 'Talk to the police, Anna. Then I'll maybe think about it. They'll know what to do, and he needn't suspect they're involved until the last minute. The guy's an amateur, a kid working on his own; the cops'll make mincemeat of him. Jump him while he's checking out the saddle-bags, that sort of thing. And I'll bet they'll want to use Monopoly money. They don't go for pay-offs, the cops. It encourages copycats. So sending the real stuff'll be a waste of time.'

'I can't, Paul,' I wailed, 'he'll cut them, mutilate them, like that Getty kid, couple of years ago. Paul, he's got Granny's carving knife!'

'Get the cops, Anna. If you don't, I will. Phone me when they're there.' There was a click.

'Paul?' No answer. Fear stabbed me. 'Paul?' But my cry was met by four thousand miles of mechanical indifference.

I was alone in the building, apart from Gilbert, the night porter, who gave me a direct line when he'd had enough of ringing my home number and finding it engaged. Riley must have left the phone off the hook.

Seven o'clock came and went with the cleaners, who dusted around me, incuriously. I'd watched the clock hand move past the twelve, expecting to die. Or the phone to ring with Riley cackling over some atrocity he had wreaked on the children. He wouldn't kill them: the ransom depended on their remaining alive. Unless ... but that was a thought to send me mad. I was already on the edge. It occurred to me, fleetingly, in between wild thoughts of robbing banks and throwing myself on the mercy of millionaires, that if Rosie was right, if Fate had chosen me as Miss-Fortune 1977, it had done so long before the appointed hour, making pretty damn sure that I would not go to the Ball. Riley must have hatched his nasty little plot months or even years before. The thing was rigged.

A fly landed on my blotter but I was too busy to swat it. Doing my sums.

Where else could I get ten thousand pounds?

I had about two hundred in the bank, after the mortgage and the regular bills had been paid. Mum and Dad had their savings but they wouldn't amount to a hill of beans and, in any case, they'd insist I went to the police. Phil, my brother, might help out; though he probably thought he'd done me enough favours over the last six years. My other siblings were far-flung and poor, and anyway, their addresses were at home. My only rich friends were consorting with Fate and wouldn't leave until the theatres closed.

So much money, twice what I'd paid for the house. Not the sort you kept lying about in a current account. I doubted that Fen and Maggie would be able to raise the sum between them. And suppose they did have it, how would I ever pay them back? Rosie would be no help. Jack gave her an allowance from their joint earnings and she put up with it.

Oh shit, oh God, oh, what was I going to do? I blew at the fly, foraging among the sun-bleached hairs on my arm, and found I'd been drawing bundles of banknotes on the memo pad. What would ten thousand pounds look like? In fivers? In bundles of fifty fivers? When you opened a briefcase? The fly took off as I scrabbled for my purse, germs of an idea dividing and multiplying. I'd withdrawn thirty pounds from the bank at lunchtime, ready for the spree tonight. The six five pound notes trembled as I laid them, side by side, on top of the papers in my briefcase. What luck, (hollow laugh) they just fitted! That's all he would see as he opened the case: six blue notes with the Queen smiling up at him. He'd never guess if each was fastened with an elastic band to forty-nine sheets of bumff. How many bundles? Ten thousand, divided by five, divided by fifty? Forty. Forty bundles with a real fiver on top of each. Two hundred pounds; my bank balance, give or take the weekend Tesco bill. More luck. And should he turn over a bundle, any bundle, on the top layer, to check that the words went right through the middle, he would see there another fiver, one of the thirty pounds' 'spree' money. I swiped at a tickle on my ankle, and squished the fly stone dead.

'Yes,' I said, lying only a little. 'I got through. The money will be in the bank when it opens.'

'Better be.' The voice, slipping now between London's East End and Chicago's gangland, would have been pathetic if it hadn't curled with hate. 'Okay ... So this is the deal. You get the money in your bag, yeah? Your briefcase, like I said. Used fivers, right? Now ...' and I got the feeling that he was reading from a script, 'you cetch the train from Stratford, the over'ead to Chingford. Ten forty-seven. Got that? End carriage. Right? And when it goes past your back yard you, like, chuck the bag out the window. Right? And that's it. You come 'ome, I'll be gone. And you and the kids can have a knees up. But no funny business, right? Else you'll be getting your kids back bit by bit.'

Simple. Easy peasy. That's what the children had said about clambering over the back fence, down the embankment, to rescue an injured fox or, before I caught them at it, to flatten pennies on the line. Pennies! A bit different from ten thousand pounds.

Even as I gave him my assurances I knew, with a sinking heart, that two hundred and thirty pounds, thinly spread, wouldn't fool him for a minute. Maybe a few seconds though. A few vital seconds when I could get into the house with a policeman, free the children and be ready for him when he came in, raging. Because, of course, I'd get someone else to drop the case off the train. Rosie or Victor or ...

No. He was well versed in trickery. He'd been swindled all his life. He'd even be ready for Paul's 'Monopoly money.' He'd probably send Zac or Joey down to pick up the bag, while he held the knife at their sister's throat. And when he discovered the hoax, he'd want to hurt …

Oh, why couldn't it be real money? I'd gladly have given ten thousand, ten times over, to see Billy Riley scuttling away down the railway line, out of our lives.

If only I could see them. Make sure they were all right.

'Billy, look, you'll get your money, you know that, it's all arranged. Could I … I suppose I couldn't speak to my children, just to satisfy myself that they're all right?'

'You what? You ain't got the hang of this yet, have you, slag? You ain't bleeding talking to no one. Only me. Got it? And if I bell you again and get 'engaged' it's chop, chop. Right?'

'But suppose my husband …' I squeaked.

'Right?' he barked and I knew he meant it.

'Yes,' I said hurriedly.

'Good gel!' His bad guy turned greasy. 'Gonna be a long night, babe. Cetch you later.'

Beside the guillotine was a growing pile of the thinnest sky-blue air-mail paper filched from the typing room, cut neatly and precisely to banknote size, and arranged in stacks of forty-nine sheets. I spun round violently, knocking the fake money off the desk, when I heard heels clanging on the stairs and someone calling my name, and blue confetti was still fluttering down around me, caught in the fan's desultory thermals, as I flew in utter joy to the door.

'If the mountain won't come to Mohammed …' said Rosie, and staggered beneath a torrent of such fierce sobbing I thought I would turn myself inside out.

'I think, I think she's pleased to see us,' said Smudge, though neither she nor Jo were smiling, seeing no pleasure to respond to.

Rosie held me to her, murmuring, 'Sshh, sshh, it's all right …' as to a child, offering comfort first, without criticism or question. But then, when I was able to shape the horror into words, she cried with me; they all did.

And they all agreed that we should manage this alone. No husbands or police. For what could they do? And how might their egos get in the way? It was a pity I'd had to alert Paul. When, if, he phoned again, I should tell him it was sorted. Panic over. Put him off the scent, somehow.

The murder in their souls cried out to get Riley now! Sod the money. Free the kids tonight. There was no knowing what he might be doing to them, what he might have done already. He wouldn't have to cut them to scar them for life.

'No!' I panicked. 'We can't just go barging in. He's deranged; he'll kill someone! And what if he phones here after we've left and finds me gone? He'll know to expect trouble. He'll be waiting for us.'

'You stop 'ere then and *we'll* do it,' said Jo.

But that was too hard; I couldn't leave the fate of my children to someone else. Could not.

We had to plan this carefully.

Riley phoned back just before ten, and though everyone froze, I was sure he'd know I had company, from the seething of underwear against shaven legs, from the fretting of lacquered fingernails on the desktop, from the blazing of red hair. I had to remind myself that he couldn't smell the fumes of anger, that he couldn't see the glittering eyes. We'd done this before, two or three of us squashed together into a telephone box, luring likely lads to assignations, giving unlikely ones the brush-off. Then we'd had to swallow giggles, not rage, and stifle squeaks, not curses, while the protagonist performed. Now it was my turn. Nervous as a first-nighter, I took a deep breath and went into overdrive.

'You've killed them, haven't you?' I shrieked down the phone. Rosie smiled encouragement, her dark eyebrows lost under her frizzy fringe. Jo held onto her blazing hair with freckled hands and sucked agony through her chipped tooth. Smudge sat on the edge of the chair, her hands imprisoned between plump knees. 'Go on, go on,' she mouthed. The slats of the blind cast stripes of orange sky across her pale and puffy face. I took a breath for momentum.

'That's what you've done, you bastard! That's why you won't let me speak to them. Because they're dead, aren't they? Lying on the floor with their throats cut.' Through streaming eyes I noted the shock on the faces before me. Part of me wasn't acting. 'My poor babies! You didn't have to kill them, you madman! You monster!' I gave him the benefit of a few racking sobs

102

before I took a deep breath and hissed, 'Well, don't think you're going to get away with it. They'll send you down, boy, and they'll throw away the key! As for your wretched ten thousand pounds, you can just whistle!' I crossed my fingers. 'Just fucking whistle!' and I slammed down the phone.

'An-na!' winced Jo. 'A bit OTT, duck …'

They were all staring at me, aghast. Smudge was biting her nail.

'Oh, shit!' said Rosie, a caricature of agony. 'You've been and gone and done it, now!'

We waited, listening to the pulsing of the fan and feeling its echo in our temples.

When the phone chirruped, we rolled our eyes to thank God. He'd fallen for it. Give the girl an Oscar!

'For fuck's sake, you stupid cow, they ain't dead!'

'They are, they must be!' I sobbed, 'if they were alive, you'd let me talk to them.'

A long, long pause, a scrabble with the receiver and then, the sweetest sound in all the world.

'Mum, it's me.'

'Joey!'

Then Riley was back. 'Satisfied?'

'Oh, please, let me talk to him. Is he all right?'

'Tell her you're all right. Go on, tell 'er.'

'I'm all right, Mum.'

'She can't hear ya. Louder.'

'I'm all right!'

'Louder!'

His shouting, screaming, '*All right!*' stretched every nerve … And was suddenly stifled.

'Now you, nig-nog.'

'We're okay, Mum.' A surly monotone, on the growling edge of tears. Poor Zac; being a man was so hard. Riley was close beside him, prompting, with a hiss like icicles plunged into fire, and Zac obeyed. 'He wants his money … The arrangement stands … The 10.47 from Stratford. Aagh!' My hand flew to my mouth; Riley was hurting him. And Zac couldn't fight back; his hands must be tied.

I whimpered, 'Leave him alone!' But what was the good?

More sizzling ice. 'He … he says if you want … aagh!' He was breathing hard, then moaning with pain. I tasted blood as I chewed the inside of my mouth. He gasped and said, quickly, 'Nice one, Mum, you had him going there! Uh, you bast ...! No! Christ!'

'Stop it! Stop it!' I moaned, 'Oh, Zac!'

'He says ... he says, "If you want ..."' He stopped and the pause shuddered and yelped. I cradled the pain in my heart until, at last, he told me, '... if you want Roz to get the same ... to have her nipples twisted, too, you can talk to her next.'

'No, Jo,' Smudge called out, 'not yet!' Jo looked back, surprised to see that we weren't following her out of the door. 'That's what he wants, don't you see? To make her mad, so she'll get straight in the car and head for home. He'll give her enough time to get started, ten minutes or so, and then he'll phone back. When she doesn't answer it'll be the excuse he needs to use the knife, and it'll be her fault, not his. He's made these rules and he'll stick to them. He's like David.'

It was more like fifteen minutes, in fact, before he phoned, and he did sound disappointed to find me still at my post.

'Where did you expect me to be?' I snapped. 'I want to find my kids in one piece when I come home tomorrow. If they're OK I won't need to get the posse out after you, will I?'

When he rang off I turned to Gilbert, in whose evil-smelling booth I had taken the call. 'Sure you know what to do?' The old man nodded a wink, flattered to be included in the complicity. 'If he phones again, stall him. Likewise any calls from America. Say I must be in the loo or asleep or something, and ask them to hang on while you go and investigate. Leave them hanging on. Whatever happens, you're quite, quite sure I haven't left the building. Do a good job, Gilbert, and there's thirty quid in it for you.' I blew him a kiss as we stepped into the dark; a lot depended on him.

We drove the VW slowly past the house towards the main road, but there was nothing to see. The curtains downstairs and up were drawn and the lights were off. There were no windows open; they must be stifling inside. Jo stopped the car at the end of the road, took off her shoes and crept back to listen at the front door, but she could only report the radio burbling in the back room; some night-watchman DJ playing lullaby pop, inviting a restless audience to believe at eleven twenty on a sticky Thursday night that all was right with the world.

Back in the car she turned left into the main road and parked behind my Mini, well out of sight of the houses in Oliver Road. We left the car and ambled along to where the road bridged the railway. On either side of the bridge was an impregnable, cast-iron wall, pimpled with rivets, designed to keep pedestrians from throwing themselves or other missiles at the trains, but before that, on our side, on the incline, there was a brick wall, a découpage of ragged posters and graffiti. Taking care that no one was watching, Jo looped her skirts into her waistband and put her dainty foot into Smudge's cupped hands for a 'leg up'. I heard her land, lightly, on the other side and then I followed, rather less gracefully, with a good deal of huffing and shoving from the other two. Then I too landed, heavily but full of hope.

I'd not done this before but Zac had assured me it had been a doddle, one winter's night when he had locked himself out. You clambered along the bank holding on to back fences until you came to ours, then over into the garden, up onto the roof of the outside loo and in through the bathroom window. Easy peasy!

Smudge and Rosie watched us slither down, soundlessly, between fences and walls, creeping across unnameable rotting and rusting things that hardly flumped or squished or clanked at all as we picked our way onto the narrow embankment.

Slap into an angry bed of whiskery old nettles! Presumably nettles hadn't figured in Zac's midwinter adventure.

Our squeals of pain stung the silence and, when we looked back, the bridge under the street-lamp was empty. We froze as our skin throbbed, expecting sleepers to wake and make for their open windows, for rude voices to demand that we clear off, or worse. But nothing happened. Maybe they thought it was cats.

When we were sure we hadn't been rumbled, we slid down the steep cutting and limped along the track, rubbing our pain and trying not to scrunch gravel. The only other problem, apart from irrational fears of electrocution and/or being flattened by trains, was that, down here, I couldn't tell where I was. Black banks rose up on either side, taller than trenches, unbroken terraces of grim-backed, unlit houses reared up above them, silhouetted against a starless, moonless, red-black sky; dark on dark on outer-London dark. Like walking through a tunnel. Our house was towards the end of the street, past the bend. From the bottom of our garden you couldn't see the bridge at all. So I kept turning, stumbling over Jo, who kept up very close, to see whether the bridge was still visible behind. When it disappeared, eaten by the curve, I guessed we must be nearly there and climbed up the bank to have a look.

Two houses short; maybe twenty yards, choked by brambles and nettles. We would have to walk along the line some more to where it seemed to be clear, at the bottom of my garden. What a stroke of luck that the brambles should end just there! Particularly if someone wanted to get down to the line quickly to fetch something, a briefcase, for example ... Could he, could he possibly have been working on it, quietly grubbing out that lil' ole briar patch during the day while we had been out? Dressed as a railway worker, perhaps. And when we reached a neat set of dirt steps heeled out of the turfy bank I knew exactly where they led. Billy *had* been busy! We sat on the steps, thinking, as a train approached on the up line, the last stopping train to Liverpool Street. Maybe he also knew about the broken catch on the bathroom window. Maybe he'd been in and out of the house at will, sorting through our things, through our drawers, handling our clothes, our private papers. Maybe that was how he had found out about Paul and his money. By the time the train had passed with a squeal of sparks, iron on iron, braking for the station on the far side of the bridge, there were no more maybes. I was sure.

The lights were on in the back room and we could see him through the nets, hunched over the table with his back to the open window as he waited for a fortune to roll neatly into his lap. We took off our shoes in the garden and I padded across the lawn to see whether the children were in there with him. They weren't. The kitchen was in darkness.

I tried the back door without much hope, grasping the handle firmly and turning it slowly and silently, willing it not to spring back, but the door didn't budge. It was locked and probably bolted, too. I'd have done the same if I had been Riley. So we lifted the dustbin from beside the door and heaved it round the side of the outside lavatory onto the flower bed, trampling lavender and stocks, and wedging it against the sweet peas which had been doing so well against the sunny wall, screening it beautifully from interested commuters. When Jo stood on the bin and found the sill of the window with her toe, she paused before pushing herself up onto the roof to bury her face in the blooms, closing her eyes in rapture like a Bisto kid. So did I. Breathing in beauty helped a bit, to still chattering teeth and brace wobbly knees and we even managed a grin at the idea of two grown

106

women, dressed to kill, prowling about like burglars. Up on the tiled slope, on all fours, Jo inched towards the bathroom window, a flap of dull glass which appeared to be closed.

All our other windows were the original sash type, impossible to open in the winter when the wood swelled with damp, and having to be propped up in the summer to stop them smashing down on your fingers. But the bathroom had been fitted in the sixties as part of a government modernisation plan. Everyone in the street had had to move out while the builders were in. The old girl next door grumbled; not only had it made the back bedroom smaller but she missed the camaraderie of the High Street slipper baths. She and her cronies used to relish their monthly soak and chat before the torture of the hairdresser, over the road. It was a treat, a nice change from the usual scullery scrub-a-dub, in water heated in the brick copper. (After three-bathroom luxury in Reading, I don't think I could have faced either prospect. A bathroom was a must. It was the only place in our house you could hope for a little privacy.) But new fittings on old wood meant that the bathroom window, in our house and others, had never fastened properly. The frame dropped below the sill, leaving a draughty gap where fingers could creep. An owl hooted somewhere and bats flitted across the gardens. But that wasn't why I shivered.

We imagined we heard it before we did. A faint clatter and clicking that moved the still night air, disappeared and reappeared, a little louder, a little nearer. We waited. Now there was no mistaking it; a goods train was coming down the line. 'The Midnight Special', the kids called it: a long and motley collection of trucks and containers of all shapes and sizes, it rattled through the night, every night, non-stop to London, a clanking, squealing dissonance of heaving metal and diesel roar.

Jo took her signal from me and rose up to lift the window then, supple and slick as a fish, she slipped inside. There was no point in my attempting the same thing. She was fit as I would never be. Every day she was swimming, surfing or sailing and had acquired all sorts of footpad skills backstage of the darkened puppet theatre. The hardest part was to come, creeping along the landing and down the stairs, through the passage, past the room where he was sitting over some book, no doubt, and through the kitchen, but the train provided noisy cover, as we had anticipated, not to mention Capitol Radio's raucous punk.

By the time it was thundering past the back fence, shaking the worms back down their holes and rattling the windows, she was at the back door, turning the key from inside and drawing back the bolts to let me in. And he, none the wiser. Smudge and Rosie, meanwhile, had taken their cue and were ringing the door-bell. Would he hear it? Would he answer it if he did? We needed to get him into the hallway.

No.

But Plan B had the desired effect. As they let themselves in with my key, we heard a chair move in the next room and heavy boots pad across the rush matting. The door banged wide to let out the sound. He flicked on the light and through the reeded glass of the kitchen door we saw him emerge in quadruplicate, dandelion head thrust forward from a black T-shirt and, as he rocked on his heels in the hall, the glint of an old carving knife held behind his back was vertically sliced a hundred times. And there were Smudge and Rosie, playing innocent, battering him with questions.

'Who's this, the boyfriend?' Rosie shut the front door and plonked herself firmly in front of it.

'Where's Anna?' asked Smudge. 'She was … um … supposed to meet, to meet us tonight. Wondered where she'd, where she'd … um … got to. Is she all right? Is Roz around or the boys?'

'Ro-oz!' Rosie shouted up the stairs, 'It's Rosie! Where's your mum, dear?'

'And the boys, where are they? Oh, God, I bet, I bet I know what's happened, Rosie. She's been taken ill, hasn't she? She's ill and they're all round the hospital. Where've they taken her? Whipps Cross, is it …?'

Giving Jo and me time to get out into the passage. Two abreast was a tighter squeeze than I'd bargained for. But Jo leapt straight at him, a wildcat, grabbing him round the neck, and pushing his arm high up his back with her left hand, so that the knife lay flat against his neck. And the Sex Pistols were screaming, 'God save the Queen and the Fascist regime …' while I worked on his hand. The fist was tight, the fingers tattooed with H-A-T-E. I pulled back on E, the little finger, as Smudge had told me to, back, back until, sure enough, something snapped and the knife slid from his grasp. He was roaring and kicking and grabbing at me so, while his attention was elsewhere, Smudge gave him a mighty kick in the crotch and, with an agonized cry, he sank to his knees. My head was thumping with the driving rhythm.

'*No future, no future, no future for you!*'

I was astonished at how easily it had been accomplished, how quickly the monster had been unmanned. His fear smelled like old shoes. His head was bowed, wholly absorbed with his pain and, as his back arched and writhed like a dancer's, I studied, with a sort of interest, the dirty pores on the back of his neck, the dandruff on the seams of the black T-shirt, the single loop of gold in that grubby ear-lobe.

And I picked up the knife from the floor.

'*When there's no future how can there be sin?*

We are the flowers in the dustbin ...'

I felt a driving thirst but my mouth watered with a rush of pure venom. I could as easily have sunk my teeth into the taut muscles of his neck, or buried the blade in the darker black stain between the shoulder-blades. Instead I took the ear between my fingers, marvelling at its smooth intricacy, its naked warmth, that of a tiny new-born mammal, and I lined up the blade with that moist and tender crease ...

'*We are the poison in the machine ...*'

'No!' cried Jo, grabbing my wrist and holding on tight as I hacked the futile air above his head, moaning my frustration. He jerked around in time to see the hate in my eyes and Smudge's toe, in her new stacked shoes, swung up and cracked his jaw.

When he was quiet and the song had ended, when the rasping of our breath had eased, we were able to hear the thud, thud, thud against the door under the stairs. They were there, packed into that dark cupboard with the wellies and the skateboards and the spiders and the mice. I opened the door and Roz was blinking at me, her dark eyes screaming what her mouth, sealed by brown sticky tape, could not. She was trussed into a sitting position, her hands taped together under her knees, her calves down to her toes wound about like a mummy's, but still she had managed to tap on the cupboard door. Zac was further back, against the wall, and Joey was lying on the floor, stuffed into the wedge of the stairs like a bundle of old newspapers. And suddenly I was weak as water. I found myself on the floor, on all fours, retching and heaving emptily.

They were all right.

There was blood on Roz's dress but, though I ran my hands

over her poor, bruised body, I could find no open wound. Nor on Joey nor Zac. He had hit them, they said, out of curiosity, simply to see whether the bruises showed up on their black nigger skin. And then I wept, for the cruelty of ignorance. Sticks and stones may break my bones, but words, the weapons against mind and spirit, can hurt beyond healing.

The blood was mine; already another dark red gobbet was blooming on the ball of my thumb. The carving knife must have touched it during the struggle.

Jo stared, white-faced, and Smudge said, 'I cut mine on my wedding day. On a broken wineglass. I should have known.'

I turned to where Riley lay, still unconscious on the ground. He had pissed on my Habitat rug, the filthy sod! I can almost remember sitting astride his shoulders, grabbing his matted yellow hair and smashing his face into the floor, again and again, but I might have imagined it. And, though I don't remember when or how, I must have kicked him, too. I know because my toes were bruised for weeks afterwards, and the toe-nail came off. My shoes were still in the garden. Rosie told me I was shrieking like a mad-woman, and that it was all they could do to drag me off.

We sat around the front room, drinking, not being up to sitting at the table where he had sat, reading Roz's *Seventeen* magazine. Gin trickled into my veins and I stopped shaking. I smoked a cigarette and was gradually able to think other thoughts than that my children were safe. Alive, whole, and safe. They had been warmed into a semblance of life with food and love and promises: one, that they would spend August with their father, and the second, that Riley would be gone by morning. I would have promised them anything, given them anything. I was determined to make it up to them. It was my fault. All my fault. I, who should have been their protector, had led Riley to them. Some-how I would salve the hurt.

They had gone to bed then.

We left the radio wittering quietly to itself as we talked. We didn't want to be overheard.

What were we going to do about him? Phone the police now and subject the children to further trauma, or deal with it our-selves? The through train from Liverpool Street was due in twenty minutes.

CHAPTER FIVE

Anna in August

If anyone was in trauma it was me; the kids were having a
whale of a time. Buoyed up on decibels, they were on a con-
tinual high. Punk rock howled under doors, through the floor-
boards, around the crannies of my skull, and the house, its found-
ations already loosened by regular pummeling from the trains,
threatened to shimmy into the dust. Young boots pounded the
stairs from bedroom to larder and back again, and back again,
and back again, and the ceiling-lights bounced to the bass beat.
I told myself that high spirits were only natural after what they
had been through. They had just escaped death, for heavens'
sake; life was a celebration and I was inclined to indulge them.
But as July wore on and rhythmic flakes of plaster continued
to float down into my coffee, I decided it was time to wind
down.

Easier said than done. Reared on extended speech, the kids
had always been amenable to reason; no need for threats or
violence, or a man, come to that. Now suddenly, they wouldn't
listen. Who was I to stop them having a good time? They were
famous and in demand! Ah.

They were pressed for every sickening detail by media and
friend alike and, being well brought up, could do no more than
apologize ('Sorry, no!') that nothing more dreadful, more titil-
lating could be squeezed from the story; could only apologize,
for God's sake, for the lack of blood, rape and murder!

Still, their friends conceded, it must have been scary. Look at
the torn clothing, look at the bruises on Zac's chest, look at the
chafing on wrists and arms and legs, at Joey's black eye, at the
fingermarks on Roz's shoulder where he had gripped her to
hold the knife to her throat. But when the crocodile tears were
dry ('Vile man, vicious man!'), their eyes gleamed greedily.
('Was he good-looking? Did he try anything?')

So the hard face of the truth was lost in the telling. Fine, if soft-
ening the edges enabled them to cope, but when cruelty and

111

violence were embellished into something almost glamorous, almost alluring, that troubled me.

What troubled them was the completely crap rescue. No cops, no megaphones, no 'Come out slowly with your hands up!', no breaking down doors, no hunky heroes. Just four housewives swinging their handbags. And to have to admit to your mates that one of them was your Mum ... God! I mean, it didn't do much for your image, did it?

I always got it wrong. But this was worse than buying them sensible shoes or Clothkit trousers, worse even than blindly grabbing their hands to cross the road. They never truly forgave me.

And the police were tight-lipped too, because I had deprived them of a victim. They went sulking to the papers.

'Look what happens when Joe Public "has a go"! "Chummy" is cornered, panics and takes off down the railway track. A messy outcome, in every sense of the word. Far better to leave these things to the authorities.'

I couldn't feel any guilt. Not consciously.

But down in my subconscious ... now that was something else! Every night for weeks I would lurch from a precipice high over a stinking pit of blood, where ears floated and fingers beckoned, where Riley's face appeared briefly, smiling, and went under. At my back a yawning tunnel, roaring, smoking, rumbling with the unstoppable train. The scree beneath my feet began to shift and slide. Bits of rock shook free and plummeted down. I had no choice but to ... jump ...

The lurch woke me, to find my heart racing and black spectres racketing across the moonlit curtains. Tight as a ball, I stopped my ears and shuddered cold spasms of terror. Only when the through train had sunk into the quiet quilt of the night could I begin to breathe again, dare to untangle myself from my damp and clammy sheet.

I bought ear-plugs and a blindfold, slept with the window shut and kept the whisky by the bed, but the dream continued to haunt me. And what was it but guilt?

Time is a healer, Jo reassured me. Give it time.

Sex is a healer, promised Rosie. Get yourself a man.

New interests, said Smudge. You're too close to it. Move house, change your job, take up photography.

But they all agreed that he was better dead. Alive, albeit behind bars, he would have allowed no one to sleep and all our days would have been waking nightmares.

The wind shifted, blowing thistledown up from the embankment and sending tremors through the baby lettuces. Indoors, excitement was mounting as suitcases were packed and repacked with suncream and hot-pants, hair lacquer and snorkels. Thunder and departure and the Banshees hung in the air and my head ached. The mortar, dry and crumbling, sifting from between the bricks, was borne away on a chilly gust.

Take-off was delayed by a cloudburst, but at last the plane roared into a blue sky, next stop Florida, where they wouldn't need their parkas. I worried that they would lose them, leave them on the plane, leave their passports or their tickets in the pockets, and the wet road home from Heathrow dazzled my eyes. Oliver Road steamed like smoke and the basket over the porch dripped geranium tears as I let myself in, alone. There was silence. Whole roomfuls of it. Even the trains went by on tiptoe. My nerves crept out of their shells, tested the air and sighed, spreading fatly in the sun.

I made myself a salad lunch instead of the interminable beef-burgers or hot dogs. I switched on the radio and tuned it to 'Woman's Hour', put my feet up and did the crossword. And I didn't want to clean their rooms and cope with the stains and dog-ends of teenage defiance. I didn't even want to finish the crossword. So I didn't.

I went in the garden and lay on the wet grass, like a snake that has sloughed its too-tight skin, not minding the home-heading commuters tut-tutting from the train windows as I wriggled in glistening and lazy joy. When it started to rain again I went inside and switched on the telly. But I was too early for the News.

It was a documentary about hard times and the upper crust; how the nobility were having to admit the hoi-polloi into their marble halls, in order to meet crippling maintenance bills. (Oh, tough luck, old bean!) Some capitalized on their collections of antique motor cars, some were forced to turn their grounds into wildlife parks or fun-fairs. 'A pretty pass,' the voice-over commiserated, with as little sincerity as she could muster, 'when an Englishman's castle is no longer his home but his livelihood.' Good girl. Who was she? I knew the voice. Seen her somewhere. In a play? A sitcom?

Why was I watching this stuff, anyway? I couldn't be bored, could I? Already? Missing the kids?

I was about to switch off, I swear, when the god took over the machine. The voice took on flesh. There she was, driving along a leafy lane in an open sports car, and even before she took off her sunglasses I realized why she had sounded like an old friend. She was. Fen Swinton in all her glory! Only subtly changed in however many years. Wider-eyed without liner and false lashes, blonder, more streamlined, but no older. Even in the black and white of telly, no laughter lines. I pulled the chair closer.

She drew up in front of an impressive pair of wrought iron gates. 'Stately homes *per se*,' she admitted, 'leave me frigid. Trudging round after a guide, looking at old masters and mistresses ...' and she yawned elaborately behind heavily varnished fingernails. The camera panned up stone pillars and rampant lions. 'Between you, me and the gate-post,' her eyes twinkling, her voice breathy with conspiracy, 'history was never my bag. Couldn't tell my Walter Raleigh from my Waterloo.' Just a smidgin of a pause. And then, 'Time-travel has changed all that!'

The camera whizzed back to her face for a double-take. She gave a broad wink and the camera followed her gaze to a banner stretched above the gates, announcing,

'PIGDON 1677 – HISTORICAL RE-CREATION'

With a gothic squeal, the gates swung open slowly, and the car slid through into a poplar-lined avenue. Fen parked between the trees and stretched long, leopard-skinned legs towards the grass. The camera trailed after her, tongue lolling, as she strolled towards a toll-booth where there sat a small woman in Laura Ashley maternity wear, her pointy face framed by a headscarf, tied gypsy style at the back under long dark hair. I gaped.

'Hi,' said Fen, in a most familiar way, as well she might, for the woman in the booth was Maggie. Maggie Willis, as was. I wanted to share this with someone. 'Hey!' I wanted to shout, 'Quick, come and look, kids. There's Fen and Maggie on the telly!' I would have to get used to living alone. Hardly taking my eyes from the screen, I reached for the telephone and dialled Rosie's number.

'Lord Foxwell,' Fen was telling her audience, 'came into his inheritance six years ago when Pigdon Hall was in danger of falling into disrepair. He and his wife sold off the larger part of their holdings in the dress chain Willis Fashions, and, with hard work and a little help from two hundred local craftsmen and actors, turned Pigdon into a living, breathing Restoration manor house. Lady Foxwell, perhaps you would like to ...'

Rosie answered as the camera moved in for a close-up of Maggie. There were crinkles around her startled fawn eyes and a worried crease between fly-away eyebrows.

'It's me,' I said, 'turn the telly on. ITV.'

'What? Anna, I'm in the middle of frying sausages ...'

'Just do it, Rose.'

Maggie was speaking. I turned up the volume. She seemed to find the plum in her mouth a mite restrictive. '... Back to the year 1677. You will find yourself in rooms and grounds designed and furnished in the Restoration manner and occupied by people from the reign of Charles the Second. The third Lord Brackley,' she pronounced it Breckley, 'is entertaining guests from Court in his private rooms, but elsewhere, you will be able to talk to other members of the family and their retainers, and to commoners, too.' The speech over, she smiled nervously at Fen for approval.

'Can't wait,' said Fen, waggling her eyebrows. 'Off we go then, back through the years to the Restoration ... The Common-wealth is at an end and the people of Merrie England are just that. Ooh, it's dark and sca-ary ...' She dissolved into squiggles and the pulsing of time machines, stolen from the soundtrack of 'Doctor Who'.

It was fairly convincing. She emerged from a black-painted plywood tunnel onto the grassy skirts of a manor house and a scene of rustic tranquility. Barefoot shepherds and their flock sheltered from the noonday sun beneath a spreading oak. A rag-ged goose-girl bid her good-morrow and scolded the geese, which were stretching inquisitive necks towards the leopard-skin trousers. Fen yelped and hurried towards the drawbridge, passing haymakers, to her left, scything the long grass, foresters to her right, pollarding trees, and motley tinkers, tailors, beggar-men and thieves in between. A fiddler, inspired by the cameras no doubt, struck up a merry reel, which seemed to be the cue for everyone to drop whatever they were doing and drag poor Fen into a wild and clumsy dance. All unrehearsed, of course. Dizzy but undaunted, she continued, only stopping to handle the rough pottery and leather goods offered for sale along the moat bank. After a verbal tussle with three burly retainers, she was allowed across the drawbridge and into the house, where she encountered a whole spectrum of actors and students doing their bit for history. You name it, there were common drudges and scullions, craftsmen, scholars, butchers and bakers and candle-stick-makers, lords a-leaping and ladies dancing.

'Three hundred years have dropped away,' Fen's voice-over commented dreamily, 'thanks to two hundred volunteers.' Her voice hardened. 'And that's about all they get. Thanks. And work experience. And for that they do a full working day, performing non-stop for a staggered audience of up to four hundred during term-time, bussed in from schools, more at the weekend and in the school holidays. "Hands-on education" they call it, and it sure is a winner. At two pounds fifty a head, half-price for kids ... Well you work it out.'

I wouldn't have invited her to dine after that little disloyalty. But I guessed the Foxwells were not privy to the script, for there she was at the groaning board, quaffing her ale and flirting with the third Lord Brackley (aka Simon, Lord Foxwell, be-wigged and over-acting), while his good lady, swamped now in the frills and ribbons of Restoration maternity wear, picked at her lample pie and chatted nervously to her guests. The talk, the snatches you could hear over the jangling of a spinet, concerned the court at Whitehall and good king Charles, the re-building of the London churches after the Fire, and suchlike well-researched topics of the day. Fen's chit-chat looked rather more consequential; oh, to be able to lip-read.

During dessert the camera nipped out through the casement windows across the lawns, to eavesdrop on the paying public as they were scurried from one historical craft to another, from charcoal burner to potter, from wheelwright to lace-maker. And somehow Fen was there, too, taking an impromptu fencing lesson, joshing with a lecherous gardener, peering through rhododendron blooms to watch a shrouded bee-keeper at work.

'And if you want to take some honey home for Mother,' she twinkled, 'you can buy it, in authentic little hand-thrown pots, along with lots and lots of other useful and expensive souvenirs from the past, when you get back on the other side of the time-tunnel. Oh, go on then. Beam me up, Scotty!'

And back in the marquee, beside the overflow car-park, twentieth century cash-tills were ringing with a ferocity seldom heard this side of Sainsburys on Saturday morning.

The telephone cut through the credits.

'Well, well,' Rosie commented, drily, 'life goes on!'

'Let's hope so,' I said. 'The rhododendrons were out, did you see? That film was made in late May or June. She must have had the baby by now. Around the seventh of July, I wouldn't mind betting.'

But that wasn't the way it worked. The baby was fine. A sweet little thing, with dainty features and a mewing cry, unlike any newborn in my experience, all of whom had lungs like traction-engines. Her name was Daisy because, Simon said, the lawns from the bedroom window had been awash with the flowers the morning she had been born, the twenty-third of June, a week after the programme had been made and two weeks before the seventh. The lawns were still awash, though not with daisies. Rain fell steadily and only puddles danced.

'Lucky you don't have a lawn like mine,' I joked, 'full of dan-delions!' A wet peacock wailed sadly, and Rosie's pained look was discouraging. The two little boys regarded me solemnly and Simon raised a weary eyebrow. He had deflated since his television appearance, his pomposity punctured by events, no doubt. His green velvet jacket and his yellow waistcoat seemed to belong to a larger, more imposing man. He had lost his dash, his swank and swagger, his wig and moustache. Only the mother-in-law, the dowager Lady Helen, a tall, thin woman in a stiff grey perm and a cashmere cardigan, threw me a puzzled smile. She remembered me from somewhere. I reminded her that we had met at the wedding, twelve years before. We were Margaret's friends from school though we hadn't seen her for six years.

'Somehow,' explained Rosie, 'we seem to have lost touch. You know how it is.' She didn't say that the newly elevated lady of the manor had neglected to inform her old friends of the change of address. Even Christmas cards had been returned to sender. It looked as though she hadn't wanted to be reminded of her East London roots. Fair enough. But missing a reunion was dire. We couldn't let her suffer alone. That was part of the deal.

They weren't expecting us and we were relieved when the gates eventually folded back on well-oiled hinges to let us through. Rosie ducked back into the car, water staining her dress and drip-ping from her fringe and eyelashes.

'Bloody stupid intercom,' she snapped, 'I'm soaked. Took Simon ages to answer. Where's all the hired help?'

'Perhaps they've got the day off in view of the weather. Won't be many customers today.'

'Mmm, he sounded a bit pissed off. But he bucked up when he knew it was us. He's such a prick, Simon! Thinks he's God's gift. "Rosie! Anna! Greetings, gentle ladies!"' She mimicked the high-born accents of Maggie's tubby lordling and as water dripped from the end of her nose I could visualize his corrugated curls and self-important smirk.

The rain swept us up the long drive, through ruts and puddles and animal dung, but I could see no other evidence of Stuart occupation. Washed out good and proper, I thought. After two good years, this summer must be disappointing, money-wise.

The time-tunnel was in sections under the dripping trees and the marquee sagged in the mud. We drove past bedraggled sheep, past abandoned carts and rickety barrows, crossed the drawbridge and parked the Mini on a paved forecourt before the great front door without being accosted by beggars or tinkers, or challenged by armed retainers, for which I was grateful. No one likes the wet.

They had put Maggie in a room at the back of the house, out of sound of the baby, out of sight of the customers. Best to keep her quiet. 'Don't say or do *anything* that might worry her,' they warned us, 'and if she seems confused, humour her.'

'I won't come in,' whispered Simon from the corridor, 'I seem to upset her.'

She looked a mess, puffy and unkempt in a man's shirt and jeans; there were bruises on her forehead and on her pointy chin, and her hand was in a flesh-coloured canvas splint. Yet she was sewing, still sewing, ruffles onto a silky shirt, which she flung aside like dross when she saw who her visitors were, and she hugged us, each in turn.

'Oh, but this is wonderful!' she cried, 'I can't believe it. All this way and on such a dreadful ... You caught the programme, did you? After all the excitement I missed it, would you ...? Oh, it's very nice to see you both, very nice!' And she pressed us to her all over again. She had an unwashed, stale smell.

We told her we would have come before had we known where to find her.

'Oh, I know, I ...' she fluttered, 'wasn't I silly? I didn't want you to think ... All this ...' The compass of her arms went beyond the barred windows of the old nursery, to include wealth and privilege in general. 'You would never have approved, Anna. And then I regretted not telling you but by then I was too ...' She made a face. Rosie raised a curious eyebrow. Maggie took a breath and grinned, 'Never mind, never mind, you're here now and you don't think too badly of me, do you? How are you? How is Walthamstow?' But she hardly cared. Her face was animated but her eyes were flickering, as if her brain were sending messages too fast for transmission.

'Are your books still selling well, Rosie? Jamie's getting a bit old for them now but Perry wants me to read them over and ... He likes the pictures best, of course ... Oh, there's so much news to ... Have you seen the others? Fen was here ...' But the thought was trapped by a frown, and the words by her lips biting sharply together. Then she laughed, hooking her long black hair behind her ears. 'You'll stay, won't you? We've acres of room. And you can join in. Yes, that's it. Oh, it'll be such fun.' And on and on she prattled, hardly pausing for breath, her hands flying about like little birds, one brown and one prosthetic pink. She was flushed and delighted with her idea, 'You must be ladies-in-waiting, no, no, neighbouring gentry, and then you can dance and play music and talk to me ... Otherwise it's all a bit like hard ... And you have to speak in character all the time, "Egad" and "Forsooth" and "Stap me vitals". It's a hoot!' But a cloud cut across the giggles. 'There can't be any slip-ups or asides, though, or you'll spoil the ... The children are the worst; they love to catch you out.'

A bosomy, bustling woman brought us tea and cakes on a trolley, and a couple of pills for Maggie.

'Thank you, Mrs Turpin,' said Maggie.

'I'm to watch you take them, madam,' the woman insisted and stood over her, relishing the small reversal of power. When she had gone Maggie frowned.

'Tell me, do I seem hyper to you?' She didn't wait for a reply. 'They say that I am, that without the drugs I'd go ...' She circled her finger at her temple and made a face. She explained, 'It's a post-natal thing, a psychosis, to do with the rush of hormones. I'm manic. Only temporarily, of course.'

'Manic? What's that?'

'Is it to do with post-natal *depression*? I've heard of that.'

'Depression? Oh, I'm not depressed, not in the ... The very opposite. Do I seem depressed to you?'

We had to admit that, though she was a bit bashed about and nervous, she seemed remarkably chirpy. Despite not turning up at the Tate. Perhaps she had got away with it. Perhaps she had been so spaced out that the seventh had passed her by, confirming my theory that we created the evil out of our own fear. Which was comforting, in a way. I didn't want to believe in devils.

Maggie was exploring the bruise on her forehead gingerly with her splinted hand. She caught my concern and laughed, wryly.

'Trophy of war,' she said.

'What do you mean?'

'Windows and mirrors and ... so they tell me. Thought I could walk through them. Nuts!' she giggled. 'Mad as a ...! A week after Daisy was born I was so happy, apparently, I went dancing down the village street, starkers, dears. Luckily I can't remember ...'

Rosie and I goggled at her. Sweet little Margaret, Lady Foxwell, so prim and proper? Dancing naked in the street?

'That's why they won't let me look after the baby, in case I squeeze her to death or throw her out of the window to see if she'll fly or ... Of course, I wouldn't ...' She spread her palms, helplessly, and looked about to cry.

Rosie frowned. 'But you weren't like this when you had the boys, were you? I saw you after Jamie and Perry were born and you were sober as a judge.'

'Mixture of things ... the fact that she's a girl, that I'm getting on. Oh yes ...' She saw us exchange frowns. 'Thirty-eight is an advanced age, practically senile in maternity terms. And I was working of course. Up to the last ... They kept telling me to rest but I just love it so much, it's not like work ... directing and performing, you're on a constant high. Things are going so well now. The house is paying for itself and more. Plus all the excitement of the television thing, working with ... and, when that was over,' she flashed us an empty smile, 'there was the reunion to look forward to, in July ...' A small frown creased her forehead. 'And when that was over ...' She paused, frowned and tried again. 'When that was over ... I mean ...' She looked from me to Rosie, tried to shake some intrusive thought from her head. Sweat started on her forehead and her breath came faster. Then she was sucking back her eyeballs behind long lids as if to scour her memory, but when they opened she had only found fear. She was very pale. She begged, 'I did get there, didn't I? To the Tate? Just that I can't ...' and she began to rap her poor bruised forehead with her knuckles. Rapping the bone. Hard. Then her chin, groaning with some inner pain.

'Maggie ... Margaret! Don't, love, don't, you'll hurt yourself!'

'Out!' said Simon, appearing from nowhere. 'Quickly, outside!'

When she saw her husband her expression changed to one of sheer hatred and she growled, like a dog, as she bit into her hand, the one with the splint.

'Sorry, sorry, sorry,' said Simon, shepherding us back to the polished calm of the sitting-room, leaving Mrs Turpin and another nurse to wrestle with the patient. The heavy, panelled door gently shut out her screams. 'I thought I'd take the chance as you'd come all this way and she's been so keen to see you. She was looking better today, more her old self.'

His mother was perched on the edge of a chaise longue, twisting her papery hands. 'You see how it is, she can be quite lucid, quite coherent and then, suddenly, her mind can't cope.'

Rosie was white and shaking as she folded down next to her. 'It was the talk about the Tate,' she stammered. 'Something awful must have happened.'

Simon glanced quickly at his mother. 'My fault,' he admitted, with a sigh. 'I didn't realize how important it was to her.' There was a moment's silence as we watched his fingers making steeples against his lips and his busy eyes working out how much we needed to know. At last he sniffed decisively and leaned over his clasped hands, staring moodily at dragons on the Chinese rug.

'She was dead set on getting to London. Wouldn't listen to reason. Just laughed, as if I was the one being ridiculous. But she was in no fit state,' he pleaded, 'I mean, hell, if you'd seen her ... She'd just had the baby, high as a bloody kite ... Singing, laughing, drunk on bloody hormones.' He shrugged helplessly and Lady Helen chipped in, shaking her grey head at the memory,

'She went dancing down the street, you know, wearing nothing but a crown of weeds.'

I said, 'Oh shit!' and Rosie's hand flew to her mouth.

Naked is as naked does, but a crown of weeds is something else. Enough to convince us that, even in her confusion, Maggie

121

had remembered the seventh. She, for whom touching wood and avoiding ladders was a way of life, who would beg a magpie out on his own to give her regards to his wife, who would take to her bed on Friday the thirteenth, would have moved heaven and earth and the creatures under the earth to keep the date with Fate. And if she were prevented from doing so ...

Simon continued his defence, 'So there was no way I was going to let her travel on her own and frankly, I couldn't spare anyone from here to go with her. This is our peak time you understand. We have to take advantage of every fine day.' We all stared gloomily at the water rippling down the casement windows. Two hundred volunteers and not one to spare.

'I had to lock her in her room,' he mumbled.

No wonder she gnawed her hand when she saw him, spat hate at him. He had tipped her over the edge, into a pit of fear. But his sad, lost eyes and his stubbly chin told me that he had acted for the best. Let's be generous, I told myself, he wasn't to know that he was just a tool of Fate.

'And,' reasoned Rosie, 'I suppose if she was likely to freak out like that ...'

'Self-mutilate,' I said.

'Oh no,' piped up Maggie's mother-in-law, 'that came later, after the accident.'

We blinked. 'Accident?'

Simon stretched his lips but his eyes were unsmiling. 'Gee, thanks, Ma,' they were saying.

'She got out.' He hung his head. 'Tried to drive.' He cracked his knuckles and when he raised his eyes there were tears in them. 'But she was out of her skull. Lost control of the car and rammed a tree. Car's a write-off.'

'Jesus! She's not hurt?'

He shook his head to reassure us but, by avoiding his mother's eyes, gave us more to worry about. 'She was so bloody desperate to see you. I didn't realize.'

'She wasn't desperate to see us,' I told him. 'She managed without us for six years. She thought she'd be cursed if she didn't keep the appointment. Bad cess. You know how superstitious she is.'

'She was scared witless,' said Rosie.

We declined Simon's offer of a grand tour. It didn't seem right, not with Maggie gibbering away upstairs. We made our excuses and prepared to leave. There was nothing more we could do for Maggie and we had another call to make. As we were being bustled out into the wet, Rosie had a thought:

'Oh, Simon, could you let us have Fen's address? Save us going to Tees Valley TV.'

'Sorry, no, I don't know where she is,' he said. Lying toad!

'She wouldn't have written in your visitors' book?'

'No.'

'Could we...?'

'Ask Maggie? I don't think that's a good idea, do you?' That wasn't what I had had in mind but I wasn't going to pursue it.

'Why is he being so totally unhelpful?' I demanded, under cover of starting the car, which wouldn't. 'Are we such pariahs?'

'That's not it,' said Rosie, turning to wave farewell to our host. But he had already closed the door, politely but firmly. 'They're hiding something.'

The windscreen misted with damp and heavy breathing. 'Come on!' I urged the motor. I wanted to be away from that sad place but the car had never liked starting up again after a long journey, particularly in the wet. Coughs became splutters, told me I was getting there and at last the engine fired, the wipers swung into action and, as I mopped the inside of the glass with a tissue, I was surprised to see Maggie's mother-in-law hurrying towards us, jiggling an umbrella up and down to catch our attention. Her other hand was hooked onto something silky. A scarf? We hadn't forgotten it. As I wound down the window to deny ownership she thrust her face and the scarf through the gap.

'Take it; he's watching,' she hissed through neat plastic teeth. It was a pretext. What she wanted was for us to meet her in the village tea-shop in twenty minutes. She had something to tell us.

'Told you,' said Rosie, as we bumped across the drawbridge. 'It's about Fen. Has to be.'

'Simon is afraid the scandal will be bad for business,' whispered her ladyship between sips of hot tea. We leaned closer, unable to believe our ears. Lipstick was bleeding into the string-purse lines of her mouth. She had put on make-up for her outing: pink powder that argued with the yellow of her neck, and brown eyebrow pencil.

'What scandal?' Rosie demanded, angrily. 'Maggie is ill, for heaven's sake! It's nothing to be ashamed of.'

I was about to add my two penn'orth when Lady Helen patted Rosie's hand.

'No, indeed,' she said, her finely-honed consonants cutting through the steamy fug and clatter of the shop, 'of course she can't help it. In any case the doctors have assured us that she will recover, just as soon as the hormones right themselves.'

'Really?' I had my doubts.

'Oh *yes*! But once word gets out it'll be all over the North-East, and you know how the media twist things. She's so well known on the television. Oh, she is up here,' she said, seeing our mystified looks. 'She presents that children's programme, "Northern Highlights" on Tees Valley TV.'

It dawned on me, at last, that she wasn't talking about Maggie.

'What's she been up to then, Fen?' I asked. As if I couldn't guess. Some peccadillo with his lordship? It had to be. She had always fancied him.

But that wasn't the way of it. The old lady was adamant. Fen had been a regular visitor to Pigdon Hall since the Foxwells had moved in, and to their home in Gosforth before that. When Fen had worked in London, at Bush House, the Foxwells had both travelled down to stay with her. When she landed the job with TVTV and came north, they put her up until she found a place of her own.

'Fenella is Margaret's best friend,' the dowager assured us. 'I am quite sure neither woman would want to compromise that friendship.'

I lit a cigarette to cover my scepticism. Rosie cut her caramel slice into very small pieces, as a way to avoid meeting my eyes.

Lady Helen filled us in on events. 'Baron Stonybroke', Simon's father, had died in 1971, leaving them nothing but dry rot, woodworm and noisy plumbing. Simon's own small savings from his firm of accountants were swallowed up in death duties. If it hadn't been for the popular retail chain Willis Fashions, left to Maggie by her mother, they would have been forced to give up Pigdon Hall. Maggie sold off a substantial part of her stock in order to restore the family home to something like its former glory, insisting that thereafter the place must pay for itself. So Simon gave up his work and Pigdon Hall Enterprises was born. Together they had tried out various ideas, letting the place for courses and conferences, holding fashion shows and mediaeval feasts in the banqueting hall, running ghost-hunting holidays, and finally hitting on the idea of historical re-creations.

'It has brought them closer, pooling ideas, sharing the work,' said Lady Helen, smugly. 'He will whisk her around the country "trawling", finding students to work at Pigdon. They found a lovely young girl at Leicester recently, who makes shoes. Such clever hands. She's turned out some beautiful period footwear, for the lords and ladies, at discount rates. And a chap who works in gold leaf, illuminating pictures and writing, just as they did in the monasteries. I didn't realize there were such people about, did you? Margaret made him a monk's habit, but he provides his own materials.' She tittered.

'Or,' she said, warming to her subject, 'they'll be together in the kitchen, cooking up some concoction to sell in the shop, oatmeal soap or tallow candles or some vile herbal cure. And the number of times one has been left to entertain visitors, dealers or actors and the like, while they have been messing about outside, clearing cow-sheds, dredging wells, building those, whatnots, those pottery oven things ...?' She clicked her fingers for the answer. 'Kilns, thank you. Out of solid clay. Filthy, horrible jobs. When they come in they are quite exhausted and trailing unbelievable muck ... and yet, they are so very, very pleased with themselves ... one could fancy that they had been building their relationship rather than the business.' She paused and set down her empty cup precisely into its saucer. It fitted. So much else did not. I played with my cigarette, not wanting the lighting of it to distract her ladyship. She said, quietly, 'They were so looking forward to the baby.'

'Poor things,' I said. Rosie was drawing with her knife on the tablecloth.

The older woman sucked in her breath.

'One has no proof, of course, but I believe that my son has always been completely faithful to Margaret. He adores her, is quite captivated by her. She's such a sparky little thing, fizzing with business ideas, and she's a wonderful wife and mother. He couldn't do without her.'

Or her money, I thought. What a nasty, suspicious person I am.

'Fenella has always been a good friend to Margaret. Even though she plays at flirting with Simon, I can assure you there has never been *any* impropriety. Besides, Fenella is a career girl who has worked her way up the ladder.' She arched one of her pencilled eyebrows above a gleaming grey eye. 'Whenever she visits the Hall she invariably has someone in tow, someone who can help her along the way, a director or a newsreader or someone.'

'Well, it's paid off,' said Rosie. 'She got to make her own programme.'

Her ladyship was tutting and shaking her head. The permed curls, stiff as wire wool, did not move despite her agitation.

'You saw it, the programme? Oh dear. What did you think of it? Do tell me.'

'Very good. Well-made and ... informative,' said Rosie, politely.

'It was how we knew that Maggie ... Margaret, and Fen, were still in circulation.'

'But didn't you think it showed us in a very bad light?'

I squirmed under her scrutiny. How to be tactful?

'I, um, I was a bit surprised that Fen chose to take that particular slant.'

'Why did she do it, do you know? Say those beastly things? All these years one thought of her as a friend, batting for one's team, so to speak. She was at school with Margaret, you know.' We smiled. We did know. 'And after sitting at one's table, sleeping under one's roof, to imply that one is exploiting these people ...! What made her do such a thing?'

'Probably got a bee in her bonnet,' I said, thinking that it was more likely that she'd got off with one of the students and was making up to him.

'But we don't exploit them. Pigdon is a showcase for them. And they sell their work.'

'Not in the rain, evidently,' murmured Rosie, earning herself a kick from me and a sharp look from the older woman.

'Of course, one didn't know at the time how she intended to use the film, use us, what nasty things she would say ...'

I was getting impatient. When was one going to get to the juicy bit, the scandal?

'... Until we saw the film two nights ago. We were shocked. And hurt. One can only be grateful that poor Margaret was unaware of her friend's treachery.'

'Why didn't she see it?'

'Simon thought it best in the circumstances. It might have been upsetting for her.'

'But she was happy about the film. You all were.'

126

Lady Helen stretched her stringy neck and screwed her lips into a crimson ink blot. I felt one might be getting to the point at last. 'Seeing Fenella on the television would have reminded her ...'

'Of what?'

She lowered her voice. 'That she had almost killed her.'

That was it, then. Some scandal, eh? Maggie, in her madness, had tried to murder Fen. Fen must have been asking for it. Must have been bedding my lord while my lady was in an interesting condition, despite Lady Helen's assurances to the contrary. We knew Fen and that was about her level. I'd have murdered her, too, if I'd been Maggie and had the excuse of diminished responsibility. No point in wasting a good mania. How had she done it, I wondered? A knife? Suffocation? Poison?

'The car,' said Lady Helen.

Oh, right, she'd tampered with Fen's car, had she? Removed the brake cable, possibly. Though she'd have needed her wits about her to do that.

'Nothing of the sort!' snapped her ladyship, horrified at my suggestion. 'Margaret wouldn't harm a fly, not intentionally. Fenella is her friend. She wouldn't want her dead.'

'But you said?'

'There was no deliberate intent, my dear. None at all. Margaret is not herself ...'

'But I thought ...'

'In spite of the television thing, which was quite beyond the pale, one has to acknowledge that Fenella was kindness itself to Margaret. One can only suppose that she meant well, letting Margaret out of her locked room.'

'*Fen* let her out?'

'Oh, yes. She had been sitting up with Margaret, trying to keep her calm. It was very early in the morning, five or six. I must have woken when I heard them moving about. I looked out when I heard Fenella's car starting up. It's a sports car, you know, an MG. Distinctive sound. Well, I wondered where she was off to. Imagine how surprised I was to see Margaret sitting in the passenger seat.'

I took back almost every rotten thought I had ever had about Fen. She had turned up trumps, after all, doing her best to ensure that Maggie kept her appointment with Fate.

But they had not arrived.

'I watched them go over the drawbridge, and then I lost sight of them for a while, the wall, you see,' said Lady H, 'but I could hear them, and the car was roaring away down the drive, very fast. One can only suppose that Fenella had opened the main gates on the time-switch and wanted to be through them before anyone tried to stop her. The time-tunnel doesn't go across the middle gates until nine o'clock when the programme starts, so they had a clear passage. But something must have frightened poor Margaret because she seized the wheel, causing the car to crash into the tree. The car is not fitted with seat-belts and Fenella went through the windscreen. Margaret, thankfully, was unmarked. Physically, that is. But I'm afraid Fenella's injuries are rather more far-reaching.'

It was a private hospital, sworn to secrecy. Without Lady Helen's card instructing them to '*Admit the Bearers* ...' we'd have been turned away. Instead, we were whisked down a bright, lino-tiled corridor by a swift, rubber-soled nurse. Rosie dragged her feet: she had never had much time for Fen. She wanted to wait in the car but I needed moral support. The nurse squeaked to a halt, knocked smartly on a door, leaned her wasp-waist this way to listen, that way to beckon, and we were in.

It was a lovely room, for a hospital, furnished as you would wish your own bedroom to be furnished if you had the money. *En suite* shower, pedestal hand-basin with roses worked into the china and gold taps, a gold-framed mirror above with a towel draped across it. The bed was spread with a white satin quilt and curtained like a four-poster with drapes in a tiny Laura Ashley rose print. The same print was used for curtains and cushions and to cover chair seats and stools. Around the walls were white fitted cupboards, glass-topped, and more mirrors, designed in threes with the outer two on hinges like an old-fashioned dressing-table. Two things struck me as strange. That there were no flowers, anywhere, at all, and that the mirrors had been turned in on themselves and fastened with huge bulldog clips.

She was on the verandah. Poor Fen. By her legs we knew her; long and burnished against the white towelling bathrobe, stretched out to catch the watery sun. Her face was anybody's guess; eyes still swollen with bruising after a good three weeks of treatment, her left eyelid heavy with black stitchery ants

crawling down from her eyebrow *en route* to her ear. A second
battalion marched from the broken bridge of her nose, packed
with dressing, down its left side, emerging, whiskery, from her
nostril before diving for cover between her lips. A tentative
seam of cut tacking reappeared to spill over her lower lip, dribble down her chin and along her jaw. And still a third contin-
gent was grouped on her forehead. When she caught us peering
round the french windows she cried, 'Oh bloody hell!' through
uncomic gaps in her teeth, and put her hand up to her face to
hide. 'I might have guessed you two would turn up. Bring on
the ghouls, eh?'

I just caught the muttered 'Blow you, then!' as Rosie turned
on her heel.

'Rosie!' I growled, 'For God's sake! She's hurting.' I managed
to haul her back through the door. 'We haven't come to stare, Fen,
or to gloat or anything. We're just so sorry to see you like this.'

'Not half as sorry as me.' She spoke with a nasal lisp and
stitches dragging at her lips. 'Who told you I was here? Foxy,
was it, the rat? Simon? Sensitive as a ten-ton truck. Or was he paying me back for my little piece of treachery? Saw the programme,
did you? Wasn't I lovely? Oh, don't look so pitiful. I'm just sorry
for myself. Oh, sit down, sit down, for Christ's sake.'

She took her hand away momentarily to flap at a couple of
stacking chairs. Her right arm was in a sling, the thumb, protrud-
ing from plaster, bearing the tell-tale badge of the sisterhood:
two lone outriders, neatly stitched.

'You have come from Pigdon, haven't you? How's her ladyship? Killed anyone yet?' She sounded bitter, as well she might.

'Haven't they been to see you?'

'What do you think? Out of sight, out of mind.' She rummaged
on the floor among books and towels and bottles of lotion for
her sunglasses. To spare our pain or hers.

'Oh no,' I said, 'not out of mind, not by a long way. They're
just paralysed with shock.'

'I'll bet,' she said, relaxing a little. 'Wetting their knickers for
fear I'll spill the beans about mad Maggie. Wouldn't make for a
happy public, would it, knowing there was a maniac on the loose
aboot the hoose?'

'Will you?' asked Rosie. 'Spill the beans?'

She had to ask. Now, she had to. In the past it would have
been unthinkable that Fen would betray Maggie. That bond had

been sacred. The last time I had seen her, at my divorce party six years ago, she had deflected all broadsides against her ladyship, who had not even replied to the invitation. Fen was not one for permanent ties, a 'lone shark' Rosie had once described her, but Maggie's friendship was important to her. Nevertheless, her public criticism of the Foxwells' recruitment policies raised the question. And here she was, sighing, hesitating even.

'I ought to. Why should they get away scot-free, while I get my face sliced off by Lottie?'

'Lottie?'

'Oh,' she waved her hand, 'some nonsense of Margaret's. Thought you knew. The genie of the allotment now has a name. It was going to be Lotto. A numbers game? Or Otto, a palindrome. But it has to be female, don't you think? Spiteful, mischievous, doesn't play by the rules ...?'

I smiled, despite myself. 'Lottie. Short for Lottery. Why not?' Giving it a name, even one as silly as Lottie, helped to pin it down. Like naming God, or Satan. For this was no nebulous creature of our own fear, as I had thought. This was real. A maleficence that had taken on our case and hit each of us where it hurt most. Me with the kids, Fen with her looks, Jo, Maggie, Smudge ... It had a mind of its own; cold, calculating and evil. This was no capricious Lady Luck. This was Lottie, an old bag of a hag. I could almost visualize it. Her.

'She talks to her, I discovered. Mad Maggie. It was Lottie's fault she grabbed the wheel and slung me through the windscreen. Wot larks, eh? But I don't recommend it as a pastime, folks. Plays havoc with your looks.'

'Oh, Fen!'

'I wouldn't mind, but we were on our way for God's sake! Five hours and we'd have been with you at the Tate.'

'Doesn't seem to work like that,' said Rosie.

'No, she's a bitch. Lottie, not Margaret. Poor Mag's just a victim.'

'So you're not going to tell the papers?'

'Oh, what could I say? Me and my loony friend were off to keep a date with destiny, when said crackpot gets the urge to play pinball with the trees? I mean, who's the loony? Margaret? Or me, for agreeing to take her?' Behind her sunglasses she squinted her eyes like a schoolgirl. 'Or Foxy for asking me?'

Rosie and I hunched forward.

'Simon asked you to take her?'

'When he knew that's where I was headed. He begged me.'
She frowned, her head on one side. 'Why, what did you think?'

'Simon's mum said it was your idea. That you'd been sitting up
with Maggie and in the morning whisked her away in your car.'

'How sweet. No, it was his idea. The screaming was getting
him down. Said taking her to London would calm her down.'

'She should have been in hospital,' said Rosie, 'with proper
nursing care. She's dangerous.'

'You don't know the half of it.'

'What?'

'I was coming round afterwards, cross-eyed, whirling stars,
birds tweeting, the lot, and there's Lady M standing over me,
about to sever my jugular with a piece of glass.'

'Jesus!'

'"Your poor face,"' she mimicked, in a syrup-sweet, dreamy,
little girl voice, '"It would destroy you, Fen; you couldn't take
it. Better this way, Lottie says. You do understand, don't you?
Why I had to kill you." I guess she thought she was doing me a
favour, like I was an injured animal, to be put out of its misery.
Foxy reached us just in time.'

'Oh Fen, how dreadful!'

She nodded, her eyes heavy with the memory. 'Yep,' was all
she said. Then, 'I sometimes wish she'd succeeded.'

In the silence that followed I tried to imagine how it had been.
The open-topped MG bumping over the drawbridge, the roar of
the engine, the wheels spitting gravel. And then swerving out of
control, hitting the oak tree, glass splintering.

'What was it that scared her?'

'When?'

'What made her grab the wheel?'

'Lottie. I told you. Mags suddenly started jumping about and
squealing – "No, Lottie! Not that!" As if she could see something
in the time tunnel. The future. She swung the wheel to avoid it.'

'Oh no!'

'God, I mean God, she was *beside* herself, rolling up her eyes,
scratching me, yelling, trying to climb over the back of the seat!
Then she was wrestling me for the wheel. You wouldn't believe
how strong she was ...'

An auxiliary, a handsome young black guy, came in with a
tray of food for Fen, fresh salmon and a tossed salad and bread

131

and butter, and looked rather put out to find us there. Fen sent him back for two more trays, and a bottle of wine.

'I declare!' said Rosie, as the door closed. 'This is an improvement on the National Health! I should have come here for me varicose veins.'

'Money talks,' laughed Fen. 'That's the only voice in my head. And I love it.'

'Does he come with the room?'

Her coy giggle told us all we wanted to know. 'And,' she added, rolling her eyes, 'discretion is all part of the service.'

'So nobody knows you're here?'

'Nobody but us chickens. The hospital only knows that I was involved in a car crash, not the whys and wherefores.'

'But the police must know. Aren't they bringing charges?'

'What police, Rosie?'

'Simon didn't report the accident ...?'

'No. For some reason he doesn't want it known that Lady Foxwell is off her trolley, or that she tried to kill a famous TV personality. That he's to blame. Oh, he is. What did he think he was doing, locking her up? She worked herself up into a terrible state that night. She was okay before that. Round the bend but amenable. No, he made her into a monster. Me, too, when you think about it. Which is why, if they take the stitches out and I still look like a horror movie, I shall sue him 'til he squeaks.'

She explained that she, too, wanted to avoid publicity.

'Don't want it to get back to my bosses that the lovely Fen is no more. They employ me to be a face,' she said. 'No face, no job.'

'That's discrimination,' I protested. 'If you were a man a few scars wouldn't make any difference.'

'TVTV like their ladies to be flawless. Mustn't scare the kiddies. And flaws there are likely to be. After I busted the windscreen I slid sideways before I fell back. Nearly sliced my nose off. Seems my face was hanging off in strips when they brought me in ...'

We winced.

'But they've done a great job, don't you think? Poking bits back, tacking bits on. It *could* all work. Wouldn't do to be premature. Ever the optimist, that's me. You never know, with plastic teeth and Polyfilla, I might come out of this new and improved.'

It was a joke and we smiled encouragement, trying to imagine the damage made good, trying desperately to think of something hopeful to say.

132

Which is why I came up with the following little gem:

'And even if you're not ... new and improved ... it doesn't have to be destructive, Fen. Seems to me anyone who's had a run in with, er, Lottie,' feeble grin, 'has got over it eventually. Picked up the pieces and put their lives together again.' Too late I saw her lip curling over the clichés.

She snorted, 'Picked up the pieces! Wonderful! Brush yourself off and start all over again. All good character-building stuff, isn't it, Pollyanna? A patchwork face, an illegitimate kid, a rape: I feel like a fucking Aunt Sally! I've been knocked down so many times ... It doesn't seem entirely fair.'

Me and my big feet. I tried to apologize, but she turned away.

'Oh, piss off!' She took off her sunglasses to stare over the flower-beds, over the lawns, to a place beyond hurt, where the sun was lowering behind the cedar trees. The back of her head gave no clue to the front, the thick, iron-straight hair, perfectly cut, perfectly blonde. 'You have no idea what I went through!' She turned back and her ravaged face was a shock, all over again.

'Fen, don't ...'

'It was hell having that baby. I've never got over it. Twenty-two years ago a life was destroyed. Not the one I gave birth to. Mine! My innocence, my expectations, people's good opinion of me, the sweet, soft part. Utterly destroyed. No bloody pieces left to pick up. Just a dirty shell ...'

'Oh very graphic,' Rosie said in disgust. 'Sounds like it could be a television script. What you going to do, turn it into a documentary? "Forged in the Furnace of Life" or some such crap?'

'You're so bloody clever, aren't you, Woodlouse?' (Name-calling from way, way back. Their antagonism went deep.) 'You haven't got a clue, have you? You've done it all by the book. A nice man, nice marriage, nice kids. So *nice* you couldn't soil your hands coming to see me in the Home. You're like everyone else. They treated us like dirt, all the girls, tarred with the same brush like we were all cheap tarts or something. You lose all respect for yourself. They tell you you've thrown away your life, that no 'nice' man will ever look at you, and you're young enough to believe it, to be formed by it, coarsened. You toughen up. You don't become a better person, you become more efficient, do things that you find hard, things that you're squeamish about, because you've got to prove them wrong.'

'Like slagging off Maggie and Simon on the telly ...?'

133

'Okay, yes, when it came to a choice between my career and my friends there *was* no choice. Pig-selfish, me. I admit it. I couldn't have the viewers remembering Pigdon Hall and forgetting Fen Swinton, now could I? If I have to show up Mr Fox and his fine lady for the pair of shysters they are, then fine. I can do that. I probably couldn't if I'd still been sweet and soft.'

'Sweet and soft!' Rosie was breathing hard, colour high in her cheeks. 'You were *never* sweet and soft. Sweet and soft people stay sweet and soft. Okay, you've had a really tough deal, but you're a tough cookie. You can take it. And being raped and having a child is no excuse for shafting other people, for God's sake. You've always used people; you were born using people, that's your talent. You used Roger, truth be told, but it misfired. You've never given a toss for anyone. Not even Maggie. How come you've not bothered to ask how she is? She could be in a padded cell for all you know. Anna's had a bad time, too, since the Tate. And Smudge. But it never occurred to you to ask, did it?'

'No, Rosie,' she said, quietly, 'it didn't. And would you have thought of tracing me or Maggie if you hadn't seen us on the telly? I don't think so.'

She had a point.

Thunder rumbled in the hills and the sky was dark as we three sat brooding. I could see Rosie's eyebrows working on her next cutting remark but her lips were pinched too tight to let the words out.

The door opened and the guy came in with our trays. No-body felt in the least like food. There was a bad flavour in everybody's mouth. Fen's dish lay untouched beside her.

'Thanks, Josh,' she said and waved him away with long fingers. 'Um ...' she arched her eyebrows, 'see you later?'

'All three of you,' said the guy, hopefully.

'You should be so lucky!' They both laughed as he went out.

She turned to us, 'Oh, come on, let's stop fighting. We all agree Fen's a bitch. What does it matter how or when or why? What did we used to say? Make up?' and held out her little finger. It was a silly gesture but irresistible. The playground oath rang in my memory.

Make up, make up, never do it again.
If you do you'll die in pain.

Utterly, utterly binding.

134

So I linked my finger with hers and she pulled me to her, brushed my cheek lightly with her damaged one. The stitches tickled.

'Sorry,' she whispered, 'I'm just feeling a bit touchy. I ... It was good of you both to come all this way. Hey, Rosie, how about it, kiss and make up?'

Rosie shook her head, like a wilful child.

'Hey, come on, Rose. I promise you won't have to put up with me again for another eleven years. I'll just be a little ole bad dream.'

Rosie rolled her eyes and shook her head again, this time in exasperation. She took Fen's face between her hands and planted a kiss on her forehead. 'I'll hold you to that,' she grinned.

It was all over.

So what happened to you, Anna?'

'Forget it.' My problems were pale beside hers.

'Oh, come on,' she said, 'let's not be coy, I'm dying to hear your news. Whatever it was, you're looking well on it.'

It began to rain again and we had to bring the chairs and trays inside. My story went down better with food and wine and we even managed to laugh. I went to find Josh for a second bottle.

When I came back, Fen was sitting on a long stool before the mirror, studying her scars. I sat down beside her.

'You're good for me,' she said. 'I couldn't look before.' She traced the line down the side of her nose. 'Maybe it's not so bad. You can do wonders with make-up, these days, can't you? There's this really heavy-duty prosthetic stuff to cover birth marks and things.'

Rosie came to join us, leaning over Fen's shoulder. I thought we'd all improved with age: Rosie, a smouldering brunette, her Afro-frizz making her face less stern, more animated; me, bottled auburn, my hair piled up, hopefully emphasizing a long neck, and eyes, blue-lined to bring out the colour, though there were smoke-shadows beneath that I really ought to do something about. And Fen.

'You won't need that stuff, Fen. Even with scarring, you'll still be better-looking than nine-tenths of women our age.'

She ignored me. She was studying us carefully. Reading our thoughts. Reading the envy. We had our looks, our 'nice people' auras, our IQs, our families, our friends. What could we possibly envy about this sexy woman with half a face?

'Might even put in for a chin-tuck while I'm here, since Foxy's paying. What do you think?'

'Simon?'

'Don't you think he should?'

'I thought you must have some sort of insurance,' I said. 'An occupational scheme or something.'

'I have. Name of Simon Foxwell. Best hospital, best plastic surgeon. New car in the offing. Only the best. He can afford it, or rather she can. And he owes me. All these years, playing second fiddle to her ladyship ...'

The rain had stopped. The sky, marbled pink and purple, was reflected behind us. Across the lawn from Fen's verandah a spent cone dropped through the branches of a stately cedar, landing softly on a cushion of needles. And a blackbird chittered in fright.

'Didn't you know?' she said.

CHAPTER SIX

Fen in August 1988

Nice one, Rosie. I stared at the page until the words blurred and I was breathing hard, trying not to scream or to jump up and down on the book, yelling obscenities. It wouldn't help. It would get us thrown out of the gallery, but it wouldn't help at all. No matter if I shredded the pages, burned them, flung the ashes into the Thames, it would still be there, in every bookshop in the country; and in every town, people would be going 'Aha!' and 'Oho!', over their coffee and cream doughnuts, as my affair with Foxy was dragged, naked and wriggling, onto the printed page. And all the while, Rosie was sitting on her advances, licking her fat-cat chops.

No doubt she was feeling very happy. 'Fulfilled' was probably a better word. Her novel, the one she'd been on about for years, finally written and published.

And the rest of us could go screw ourselves. No longer useful. Ever since we'd known her she must have been dropping our fruity bits into that crock of distilled vitriol she called her creative side, until, after nearly forty years, it had brimmed over, stinking, festering, to cover us all in shit. Not just me. That wouldn't have been so remarkable: she'd always had a down on me. Everyone had been dropped in it. Everyone. Even the beloved.

Moe had taken the message from the answerphone. She reminded me after the run-through.

'*What* friend?'

'Anna Griffiths. It's on the pad. She said it was urgent.'

'Anna? Oh, she'll just be reminding me about a meeting tomorrow. Sort of school reunion thing.'

'It's the Awards Dinner, tomorrow night.'

'I know, I *know!*' Why did Moe always assume I was on some other planet? 'So long as I'm at the Tate for eight ... I'll be back in time for the ceremony.'

Moe looked askance. 'Why don't I just phone her and say you can't make it?'

'Don't you dare! I can manage both, easy well.'

'So will you phone her or shall I?'

'God, Moe, I mean *God*, just stop hassling ...' I stopped myself; I shouldn't snap at her. It was her job to hassle me. 'I'll do it later, shall I, Moe? I do have one or two other things on my plate just now. Like an interview with a child abuser in half an hour?'

'She was quite insistent. Said you'd want to know. And could you make it before nine?'

Like *now*, in other words. I sighed.

So, Anna wasn't staying in to watch the programme. And it had had excellent reviews. I was surprised at how miffed I felt.

'She sounded anxious.'

'Moe, not another word!' She opened her mouth. 'Not one!' She closed it again. I picked up the phone, hesitated and gave in. 'Oh, for God's sake, what's the number?' I found I knew it, give or take a code or so. Anna was still living in Oliver Road. So much for beauty and university degrees! We bears of little brain, who lived by our wits, had posh flats in Hampstead and cottages in the country.

She answered at the second ring.

'It's Rosie,' she said, sounding depressed.

'She's not dead, is she?' I found I wasn't terribly bothered. Surprised, yes. Rosie had always seemed remarkably robust to me, physically and mentally. No problems with periods, pregnancies, menopause, stomach of cast-iron, nerves of steel, that sort. But I wasn't unduly concerned.

'She's written this book. Out tomorrow.'

'Oh, yeah? She writes a lot of books, doesn't she?'

'Children's books. She illustrates them for Jack. This is the first she's written herself. Not for children.'

'Great.' What did I care about Rosie's scribbling? I really couldn't see that it merited a phone call, with a show to do in ... shit, twenty minutes! We were going to see her tomorrow, for God's sake. Did Anna want me to chip in for a bouquet or champagne or something?

'Anna, look, I really must ...'

'It's about us, the book. You and me, Jo, Smudge, Mags ... You must read it.'

'Yes, of course. What's it call ...?

'You really need to get hold of a copy, Fen.'

'Tonight? I'm a bit pushed for ...'

'I've only flicked through it but there seems to be a lot of stuff about you and Simon. Could get you into trouble.'

'What!'

'She's changed the names but anyone with any sense will know who she's writing about.'

'What does she say?'

'You name it. Your worst fears. Sorry, I don't have time to go into it now, Fen; I'm expecting a call from Boston. Look, what I suggested to the others was that we meet up at the Tate tomorrow, early, say eight o'clock, on the steps, and we can decide what to do. It would fulfil the other thing, too. Buy the book on the way. *Friends for Life* it's called, by Rosemary Woodhouse. She's using her single name. Okay? Sorry to cut you short. Oh, by the way, it's probably best not to tell Maggie. What the eye doesn't see ...'

Wouldn't kill her. Or him. She trod a fine line between fruitcake and bananas as it was. Finding out that I had been Foxy's bit-on-the-side since whenever would put her in a strait-jacket. And the Swinton connection wouldn't do a lot for Foxy's standing in the Lords, I wouldn't have thought. It might even jeopardize his place on the Hunt Committee, think of that! Not to mention the dozens of Boards he was on. And his London club.

My own street cred would plummet, what was more. If Swinton's heart was not made of gold, after all, if she could treat a friend so shabbily, *if she was so good in bed*, she was clearly not the sort of person you wanted to run the 'Safe Travel for Women' campaign or to interview rent boys. That last torrid scene had been little short of a plain man's guide to sex, all slippery tongues and pricks; and not a single euphemism in sight. It rang all sorts of bells! God, I mean, God, it wasn't on!

I didn't need to lick my thumb to turn the page: it was already damp. I noticed that the nail-varnish was chipped, that the veins were swollen with the heat; there were too many rings, all solid silver, making my fingers heavy ... What was the time? My watch had slipped round on its slim silver bracelet.

Twenty to ten.

Come on, Fenella, no more delaying tactics. Now read on. I sighed. It was the sort of book I usually liked: juicy eye-openers about people I knew. If only it had been about somebody else.

139

'"Over here! Look this way!"
"Miss Winters, please!"
"Your guest tonight, is she ...?"
"Our readers want to know ...?"
"The viewers ..."
Flash, flash, flash! Cameras popping off like the fourth of July. Instinctively I throw up my arm to protect my eyes, and microphones bristle in my face. Biros, scribbling lies in shorthand, opt for the soft underbelly.'

And what she doesn't know about soft underbellies ...! I mean, Fay Winters, queen of the chat-shows? Who could that be, I wonder? And Liz, the teacher with a dark secret. And Sally, the golden-haired puppeteer, betrayed by a near-fatal disease, and poor old Phyllis, running her bakery at Brighton and getting fat, nay obese, on the proceeds. And Olly and Nina, la crème de la clotted crème: she, into tarot cards and cranial osteopathy, and he heavily into the queen of the chat-shows.

My mind raced around, trying to find an objective angle. Why shouldn't her readers take it that the couple cavorting on the monogrammed silk sheets were figments of Rosie's fevered imagination? Would they really have me sussed, straight away, as the fictional Ms Winters? Wasn't it more likely to be some vague tip-of-the-tongue, can't-put-your-finger-on-it feeling of having seen her somewhere before? Of knowing the type? But what if their suspicions were stronger? One thing was sure, if I so much as squeaked, they'd make the connection straight away and jump to all the right conclusions. I'd be cutting my own throat and Foxy's. Rosie would have known that. Her publishers, Briggs and Holman, would have known that. They'd have done their homework.

'Out of the taxi to an empty forecourt, through the revolving doors, and wham, bam into an ambush. My poor heart's flip-flopping like a pair of rubber sandals. God, they're lethal, this lot. Back off, why don't you? But smile, keep smiling. Any hint of irritation and they'll have you down as "hollow-eyed" and "dishevelled" and start checking on your age. At least the camera can lie. Say so myself I look pretty damn good. Work-out fit, honed hard, past the burn. Buy the video! The silk trouser suit, fresh off the catwalk and hanging like a green waterfall, the Italian shoes, hand-made to prettify feet, the marigold hair, shaggy-cut this morning by Vidal, himself. The face, invisibly-mended ...'

Oh great. I reckoned that was the clincher. The marigold hair might have kept them guessing: I've never been anything but blonde – going on platinum these days, with the occasional spray of electric blue or hot pink for a party. But, apart from the odd coma case, there could be no one in Britain who wouldn't instantly recognize me from that description. Instinctively I ran my finger down the side of my nose to feel the tiny ridge of hard tissue. It had faded in eleven years but still showed up white under a tan.

'The face, invisibly-mended, is bright and pretty as a doll's. I flash them another smile.

"Okay, fellers! Don't get your tights in a tangle, you'll get your story." I bat my lashes and sidle, so surreptitiously, over to the lifts where Stan, the doorman, has already pressed the button. They follow, scribbling madly:

"Anything to say..?"

"Who is it tonight?"

"This woman from your past ... have you seen her, spoken to her?"

The lift has arrived, the doors are open, about to close. And good old Stan leaps between them and holds them apart like Samson. I duck under his armpit to safety and kiss his leathery cheek.

"Thanks, sweetie!" I coo, digging my chin into his epaulette, smiling wider as the gap narrows on the brothers and sisters. 'Watch the show, suckers!' I mutter as the lift takes off.

"Get onto Vinny!" I dump my bag on Doris's desk. "He'll have to bring her in the back way. There's a lynch-mob down there!"

"All taken care of honey," she soothes, handing me the message-pad in answer to my clicked fingers. "Take it easy ..." Her voice is malt-rich, brown, sweet and revitalizing, like a chocolate advert. She waddles over to the drinks machine and pours me a coffee.'

"Waddles!" My rude laughter earned me a glare from the gallery-guide, squatting like a toad in the doorway. I glared back and his face lit up with recognition. He smiled and nodded. I expected him, any minute, to be over for the autograph.

"She's even got poor old Moe in this!" I nudged Smudge, who looked up without seeing. She had been brooding over her bit for well over twenty minutes. I had skipped a lot of that, but I got the impression that Smudge (Phyllis, in the Woodlouse version) had only herself to blame, that she had known of her husband's violent tendencies before she married him. The others didn't stir, too entrenched in their own misery. I hadn't really wanted an answer, just a breathing space. Yoghurt in a hot curry. I couldn't wait to get back to the chat-show presenter. This story of Rosie's was a real page-turner.

'"*Who's been feeding the hounds?*" *I look round the office for someone to blame. Innocent eyes blink back at me.*

"*It won't do us any harm, Fay.*" *Clyde unwinds from his clip-board, the thick stripes of his shirt hanging from clothes-hanger shoulders like streamers.* "*Could even push up the ratings.*"

"**You** *told them? Shit, Clyde, I thought we agreed ...*"

"*Not me, Fay,*" *he swears, showing me a long clean palm.* "*They were here when I checked in. They don't really have much. Just that tonight's guest is someone from way back. And that it's a woman.*"

Doris pushes coffee at me. I try and shake sense into my head. No, Clyde won't have told them. He values the frisson of surprise as much as I do. Who, then? The research team has been shooting pretty much in the dark. Doris is too attached to her kneecaps. Which leaves our guest. She won't have said anything. Now that tells you something, doesn't it? Me thinking I know how her mind works. And I've never even spoken to the girl. But she's agreed to be on the show and, to me, that says it all.

Not that I haven't already decided to "come clean". Milk it for all it's worth. Great publicity. But I have to be the one, otherwise... No, it won't look good.

I've got it all worked out, what leads to give her, what to say. Don't get me wrong, it's not scripted; no idiot boards, not on my show. That's the beauty of it: you never know how it's going to take off. But you can't sit there in front of five million viewers, yakking on about the weather. You have to have some idea. Some juicy morsel about their love life or their latest political gaffe or something nasty in their woodshed. Exposure makes the world go round. Tread on their corns and they might take a pop at you, or the viewers might complain, you never know your luck. No news is bad news in my book. Only this time the corns are on the other foot.

I've never felt this nervous before a show – because it's personal, I guess, me in the spotlight. Paula, the make-up girl, fluffs more powder onto my nose and chin, a matte skin being less ageing than a shiny one.'

'Exposure makes the world go round?'
I scanned the next few pages with mounting panic; my heart

flipped as I turned them and the sound was loud in the hushed grand hall. She had turned my story into a pantomime, with me playing Widow Twankey! It was coarse, clownish and cruel. And her timing was spot on. Today of all days! Though she *couldn't* have known about the Awards Ceremony when she wrote it, couldn't have foreseen that 'Six Weeks' Wonder' would be nominated as an 'outstanding piece of television journalism; a brave and sensitive disclosure.' Could she? I had my acceptance speech all ready. 'On behalf of the production team, of whom I am but one…' The usual thing. But nobody would be in any doubt as to whose inside knowledge, whose special handling had made the work extraordinary. Who better to recall the two-faced fifties, the censure, the heart-break decisions? I had been so careful to get it right, filming the flash-backs of school and home-sweet-home in black and white, letting bigots and chauvinists talk themselves into corners, doing the interviews myself, gently sifting through cruelty and pain until the wriggling nerve-endings were exposed for all to see. Brilliant, if I say so myself.

And here was Rosie giving it the chat-show treatment. No controls, not even a script; except her own, of course. She could make me say and do anything she liked. Pulling my strings, or rather Fay's, like Jo and her puppets. She had me at her mercy. Head-first down a well.

'Clyde comes in, his Navaho cheekbones raw with excitement. She's arrived. He wants to tell me about her but I won't let him, not even a hint. The surprise must look real. This high on adrenalin maybe I can even manage to cry a little. Not too much. Tears reveal scars. I tease a few wispy curls over the temples and around the ears. They're no secret, the scars, not since the piece we did on plastic surgery, in '81. But you don't have to flaunt them.

Doris is complaining, not unusually, about my jumble sale fashion sense. She approves the frothy black lace skirt and the matching tights, the court shoes and the wide choker of rhinestones but not the heavy white T-shirt from Quant.

"On anyone else it would look ridiculous," she grumbles.

"And on me?"

"Fabulous," she concedes, reluctantly.'

I heard a sniff and leaned forward to see Anna, on the end of the seat, with a wad of tissue pressed to her nose. Tears dribbled over the laughter-lines, magnified to white quilting by her reading glasses. She smeared them with smoke-dried fingertips. She was taking it hard. Meeting my eyes, she shook her head, in sorrow or denial, I couldn't tell, and got up quickly, leaving her jacket but taking her bag. And the book. I could see her in the entrance hall, explaining to the man at the counter that she would be coming back. I guessed she needed a fag.

Jo had turned away, at her end, resting a thin elbow on her knee. Her hair, arranged in aggressive little spikes, moved down and up as she massaged her forehead. Her neck, freckled with splashes like gold paint and curved over the book on her lap, stiffened, straightened over some printed horror and the hand moved to her mouth.

Smudge sat quite still, next to me, holding her copy open with both dimpled hands, her Princess Di fringe veiling her eyes from me as she read. The small muscles of her lips twitched. It was a vulnerable little mouth in a face that had grown too large.

'The audience is restive, aware that tonight's show is going to be different. A little hype goes a long way, as Clyde foresaw.

The lights dim and there is a hush, a cough or two. Then the set is bathed in blue light and Vivaldi ripples round the studio. I step out of the darkness briskly, and skip down the steps. I wait, smiling patiently, in my cosy set of white leather settees. They've put lilies on the coffee table. That's me. Pure, white, honest.

'Welcome, everyone to "Winters Here" ...'

Didn't quite have the ring of 'The Questing Mole'. Chalk and cheese, in fact. Or a TVTV prime-time chat-show and one of my late-night, in-depth, cutting-edge investigations. But the difference really didn't matter. Fay was me and the veil was so thin it was transparent. Rosie wasn't trying at all.

As if she were daring me to sue. I could just see the headlines:

'MOLE SKINNED FOR LIBEL SUIT!'
'TRICKY CAN OF WORMS FOR QUESTING MOLE!'

I was beginning to wish she had dropped me down that damned well when she had the chance.

'"Tonight," I tell them, "I'm turning the tables. Tonight, I'm the one with the past. My guest is someone I have been avoiding for thirty-two

years. *She had to come looking for me! And to be honest ..."* I confide nervously to my friends, my fans, my audience, *"I wish, now, that we'd rehearsed this. My knees are like jelly, I kid you not. Ladies and gentlemen, a first for me, for you and for television ... please welcome Louise Talbot, my daughter!"'*

My knees were trembling. This was everything I detested about pulp television: the ballyhoo, the crude sensationalism. I would no more have subjected myself or Bridget to a live public reunion than fly in the air. And Rosie knew it.

So she thought my lovely film was crap, little more than a cheap publicity stunt? Good old Rosie, she had that way with her. Saying nothing and then tipping you arse-over-tit down a well, or latterly, dropping unsubtle tablets of stone on your foot, to cripple you. And why? It couldn't be simply that she objected to my making capital out of personal tragedy. Everyone did that. Library shelves were full of books, archives full of films, papers full of stories by people who had done exactly that. They called it autobiography. Perfectly respectable.

And if I hadn't done it quickly, there'd have been some sleaze-happy journalist doing it for me. Or a Woodlouse.

'The clapping is sporadic at first, as they digest what I said. Forewarned, the camera picks up on the raised eyebrows, the bewildered looks, the mouthed "who?"s and "what?"s and "oohs" and "ahs". Then, as the warm-up man windmills for 'More!' and the fanfare sounds, and this tall, long-limbed creature steps into the spotlight, the patter of applause becomes thunderous.

My slim figure, I observe. My genes! My nose prickles with sentiment, of all things, and rogue muscles twitch all over my face. A red electronic eye studies the phenomenon of Winters in tears and I struggle to get a hold. She is careful down the steps. A curtain of brown hair, thick and heavy as mine, hangs over her face until she reaches me but when she swings it back, when she raises her eyes to mine they are the clearest blue, like mountain pools. Deep and cold. She's prettier than me. Brighter, I suspect. More difficult. In fact, there is nothing in that face to tell me she is mine. The cheekbones are too high, the chin too square, the eyes too wide, too searching. But it is a face I know. It looms over me from the dark, jaws stretched by orgasm, by a cry almost of pain.

I swallow something in my throat, that isn't tears at all. This girl, this daughter of mine, is no longer a voice from the blue, brought to me by some earnest social worker, no longer just a great idea for a stunt.

*She's flesh and blood and she's here and she's no pushover. She's going
to want to know the truth. All the ins and outs. Ha! She'll ask me, and
the eyes will narrow to a laser probe, "**Did** he rape you, my dad? Did
he **really** get you drunk? Didn't you lead him on? Just a bit?"*

And the audience will hold its breath waiting for my answer.

Can I, dare I, lie to her, too?'

The book had fallen to the floor. Somehow I seemed to be folded
over my knees, staring at my 'Truly Plum' toe-nails. Saliva was
seeping into my jaws and I was shivering. I wanted to get up from
this ridiculous position, recover my dignity, but Smudge was
pressing down on my shoulders.

Jo's voice, far off on the other side of a rushing river, told me
to keep my head down, told me that Rosie was a vindictive cow
and that I should take no notice of her lies.

'I think she's coming out of it.'

'It's all right, Fen! It's okay ...'

But I knew it wasn't. Not now that Rosie knew the truth. Perhaps she had always known. Maybe that was why she had always
despised me. *I* could see Roger, now, dark curls fallen across his
brow, eyes squeezed shut to hold onto the moment, glistening
skin stretched soft over the ridge of his throat, that quivered with
his coming. And me smiling in delight. *Me*, hugging myself. I
had him. In *me*. Dishy Roger, the one they'd all wanted. The one
clever, pretty Rosie had wanted. I had him first. I'd won. And I
said it was rape.

But if she thought she was going to get me to confess, she could
think again.

As I shook off Smudge's arm, I looked up to meet a hundred
painted eyes, united in condemnation. All Rosetti's stern women
with their curled red lips, *Monna Vanna*, the rich bitch, *Beata
Beatrix*, looking terribly pious, even poor old *Thoughts of the Past*,
caught with her hair down. Sad, disappointed faces, looking
down from the walls. Like my mother's, my father's, Mrs Mountjoy's at school, the social worker's. Shame, they said. Shame on
her.

Afterwards we sat in the restaurant. I sipped clinking ice-water
while Smudge and Jo talked over their carrot cake and coffee.

'Why'd she do it?'

'Menopause, I should think. Mid-life crisis.'

'Wanting to make her mark before it's too late?'

146

'Has to be something like that! Has to be.'

'But why take it out on us? We're her friends.'

'It's as though she hated us. Hated us!'

'And she's never said a word! That's what I can't get over.'

'When we see her we'll tell her.'

'And what?'

'Well, maybe she'll withdraw it. Maybe.'

'Some hopes!' Anna had been gazing sightlessly at the queue along the food counter, like some pale Greek statue, her tawny hair wound up in a complicated knot, its weight tilting back her head and arching her white neck. Now she turned her eyes upon us, dead eyes, and in a voice rasping with smoke and despair she said, 'You don't know her. She's changed. Things have happened. Right this minute she's at a book-signing in Charing Cross Road – loving every minute, I expect. She won't withdraw it.'

'You've seen her?'

'Not for some time. She wrote to me.'

There was a pause as Anna's remark was weighed and found wanting.

Smudge prompted gently, 'What she, um, suggested ... in the book, about you ... that was uncalled for, Anna ...' and took a last mouthful of cake.

'Libellous,' Jo said, hopefully. My ears pricked up. I was suddenly feeling better. I hadn't got as far as Anna's story, yet; I've always been a slow reader. But Anna's thin lips were letting nothing slip.

Smudge tried another tack. 'So can't we get it banned?' in a voice muffled in crumbs.

'Well not if it's in the shops already, you wally.'

'They can withdraw it.'

'Why would they? I mean who're we when we're at 'ome?'

'Not even if we won a libel case? If we won?'

'We wouldn't win,' Anna grunted.

I agreed. I was feeling stronger but no happier. 'Libel is only libel if it's lies.'

'It *is* lies, innit?' Jo's frown swept around the table, from me to Smudge to Anna. 'Most of it ...' She had to be joking. Or fishing.

I shrugged ignorance while Anna dragged on her cigarette and blew out a sigh. She looked so tired; her eyes glittered blue on sleep-starved saucers. What on earth had Rosie got on her?

Success had gone to Smudge's shoulders. Forget Dallas.

American football was nearer the mark. She could barely raise her chins above the purple pads. The colour did nothing for her, either, clashing with her rosy pinkness.

'Of course it's lies! What I did, Phyllis did … she had no choice. It was either that or …' She glanced at me and her voice tailed off, 'Well, it wasn't like that at all.'

There was a silence as we all thought our thoughts. I felt the others knew something I didn't.

Then Smudge tried again. 'And she's got it all wrong about David and me.' Her fierce little eyes dared us to think otherwise. 'I *did* love him and he loved me. He did. He was really sweet at first, that time in Israel, really sweet … on that kibbutz at Eindor; he'd come all that way, all that way…' She pushed her plate away and swept invisible crumbs off the table, again and again, as she dusted off the memory. Her eyes focused on the fork, and she pushed it to a perfect six o'clock on the empty plate. 'I'd just finished with Monk, d'you remember? And he was so understanding, so understanding. He didn't blame me for, you know, the suicide attempt. He even shed a few tears. A few *tears*.' She nodded in emphasis and lifted her arm to pull at her fringe. The massed gold bangles slipped far enough down the thickening arm to reveal the single fishbone scar. Visual aid to a memory jog. We saw again the girl in cheesecloth and love beads, hand in hand with the man who said he loved her and later, beat her.

'He kissed them, kissed my wrists,' she said simply, staring at the scar, surprised to find herself talking about it and her voice steady. She continued, nodding as the picture came into view. 'We'd come outside to cool off after the dancing.' She paused, distracted by remembered music and laughter. 'What did they call it, that dance? That Jewish dance where everyone, kids and old dears and everyone, all get into a long line, arms round each other's shoulders, two or three steps forward, one back, getting faster and wilder?'

Anna didn't know.

'Zorba's Dance,' offered Jo. She stretched her arm across my shoulders, humming the monotonous tune, 'Dah-dumm … dah-dummm … diddly-dummm … dah-dummm …' tapping out the rhythm with her boot, somewhere under her slim maxi-skirt. So I swayed with her, sideways and back, glad of the diversion. Smudge was unconvinced.

'No, that's Greek,' said Anna, irritably.

'The Yugoslavs have a dance like that,' I said, seizing the chance to get the subject back to me. 'We did it last year by the lake. Everyone was tiddly on juniper gin and the waiters led us in this dance along the shore ...'

'Horah,' interrupted Anna, rudely and triumphantly.

For a moment I thought she meant me.

'That's it,' said Smudge. 'The Horah.' She nodded, hooking it into her mind, and her eyes took on a cosy look. 'That night we'd had stuffed vine leaves and a wonderful garlic sauce.' Food was her comfort in memory, too. 'And so much wine. They lay on quite a spread, the kibbutzniks. Well, it was our last night, the volunteers. They'd want to give us a good send-off. Propaganda, I suppose: life was good; the cause was good. But we didn't need telling. We didn't. We thought everything was just great, the caring and sharing ...' She sighed deeply, 'Great. And after the dance we came out to the pool. Not to swim, just to lie on the stones – they were still warm – and we looked up at the sky. It was so huge, *so intimate*, as though we'd been trapped like two bugs under a bowl. With a million holes to let the brightness through. You've never seen so many stars!' She twitched her fringe away for a better look. 'So big you could pick them out of the sky, like apples, and hold them in your hand. And shooting stars ... like a trick of the light. Look again and they'd be gone. Gone.' Blunt fingers slid back and forth along the table's formica edge, recalling the night by friction. 'Frogs were croaking and there were those insects ... not crickets ... they make this shrill sort of purring. ...?'

'Cicadas?'

'Cicadas. And there was a scent of warm fruit. Spicy. You could almost taste it. Wherever you looked there were fruit trees. Oranges, peaches – not just in the orchards where we worked: in the gardens, along the paths, up against the houses. I remember David picked me a pomegranate that night. From just above his head. You could just reach out and pick them. Nobody minded. What you wanted you took. And he broke it open and fed me the seeds. Red and sweet and juicy. Pushing them into my mouth with his thumb.' She flushed. 'And when he asked me to marry him, I thought, "Forget Monk. This is David. He'll look after me for the rest of my life. The rest of my life."' She hiccuped on a dry sob. 'It was the most romantic thing that had ever happened to me. The most romantic ... And we wandered off, arms round

149

each other ...' She frowned. 'A guard shouted at us to get back. We'd got too near the perimeter fence. They were expecting an attack ... He had this huge repeater rifle slung on his arm.'

And the cosiness had quite left her face when she turned to us again.

'I'm not having Rosie making out I'm some sort of sado-masochist... that I married David because he was violent! I'm not having it! It wasn't like that at all. At first I had no idea, no idea.

'And that terrible stuff she wrote about Mummy and Daddy! How could she? Lies, from start to finish. Have you read it?' She dragged the book from her big soft leather bag. Gold clasps. Gold rings on her fingers and bells on her toes. The label poking out of the neck of her stylish two-piece spoke of success and money. But there was a crumb on her lip and already the book had a dog-eared look. She banged it on the table like a piece of raw steak, and it fell open at the page where she had broken its spine. 'Where is it?' She zigzagged her finger through the words, reading, '... *subconsciously repeating the family dramas of her youth. Of her youth* ...' I mean, can you believe this? This is supposed to be our house ...

'*It was a small room, a vile room, testimony to violence. The wall-paper was torn back to the plaster, the chest of drawers, scratched and scored with years of rough treatment, the wardrobe door hung askew. And now a new indignity. He had smeared excrement over the wall, the sheets, the pillow. The bed was sodden and semen dripped down the mirror. Phyllis clawed at her father, screaming at him to stop! stop! as the arm swung back to club again the hated thing on the bed, the incubus that occupied the flesh of his flesh. But he was strong, powered by rage, driven beyond reason – You damned moron, damned filthy pervert –*'

She looked up, her eyes pleading for help. I noticed, as she swept back her perfectly-cut fringe, deep frown-lines etched into her forehead. She had grown very plain.

'He never said that, would never have done that to my brother. My dad was a gentle man, a civilized man. Well, you knew him. He was kindness itself to Gregory.'

Indeed. From what I remembered, Derek had been a mild-mannered, inoffensive little chap. But their Gregory had certainly had his moments. I'd seen him peeing out of the bedroom window. Enough to try a saint. How had they dealt with him? Maybe I could make a film ... Get on to The Autistic Society ...

'God, I mean, God, what's she playing at.' I was full of sympathy. (What could I call it? 'Blessed Fools'?)

'There's this theory,' said Anna, wearily, 'that women brought up with violence unconsciously seek the same thing in marriage.'

'But I had a peaceful, utterly non-violent childhood. She was there, for Christ's sake. She knew that.'

'Gordon Bennet, Smudge,' said Jo, in desperation, 'it's not meant to be *you*, you wally. This is a *novel*, for Chrissakes. She's taken your situation, that's all, the family with an autistic son and gone "What if ...?" Twisted it a bit.'

'Twisted!' I squealed, and again, 'Twisted!' I leaned over Smudge's shoulder and the words of rage and fear leapt out at me. *'She remembers her father's face, distorted, ugly. How he had pushed her from him, struck her across the mouth, – Stupid little bitch! This is all he understands! If it was a mad dog, you'd have it put down! – Then the boy on the bed screeched with a harsh, adolescent animal voice and bared his teeth in a snarl. In an instant he had his father's hand in his mouth and was biting to the bone ...'*

Smudge shook her head, 'She didn't think I might be upset by that? Having other people read that?' Her hands opened on the table, in a beseeching gesture.

Jo was patient. 'They're fictitious, the characters. Look.' She thumbed to the front of her copy. 'See, "Any resemblance to real persons, living or dead, is purely coincidental."'

I couldn't see why Jo was so keen to exonerate Rosie, sucking her fork, thinking the best of the bitch. Jo was usually the first to call a spade a shovel. There was still a wodge of cake on her plate. She was taking an age to eat it. Slow eaters stay slimmest, they say. Not as slim as me, though, whose sweet tooth had been drawn long ago.

Smudge, on the other hand, had spotted a few crumbs she had overlooked. She wet her finger to trap them and popped it between her lips.

Jo said, 'That puppeteer woman, I, well, I suppose she's like me in some ways, but in others ... well, nothing like me at all, really.'

Well, no. Not really.

'That puppeteer woman', Sally, had had a small theatre in Bethnal Green, near the Museum of Childhood. Sally had been married, happily, she thought, to Steve, an accountant, for twenty-four of her forty-one years, when she was taken into hospital for a lumpectomy. When she came round she found she was missing a breast. During the ensuing chemotherapy, when she lost all her hair and felt sick most of the time, Steve was a great comfort, working late and disappearing at the weekends. But he left it until Christmas, decent chap, when her hair had grown back and she was feeling stronger, when their two daughters were home for the holidays, when the in-laws were safely gathered round the television, sleeping off the turkey-dinner-with-all-the-trimmings, until *Christmas*! to take her into the kitchen and break the news that he was leaving.

Big of him.

He dried the dishes while he explained to her. Calmly, in an adult manner. He said he had always regretted their early marriage, the twins who had made it necessary. Sally, the woman who had 'ensnared' him with her beauty, was no longer attractive to him. He felt he was free to find someone else. And had done so. Out of the goodness of his heart, he said, he wouldn't ask her to give up the puppet theatre or the house. She could sell him his half. He was surprised when she picked up a jug, a precious bone-china hand-me-down containing half-a-pint of brandy cream, and flung it at his head.

During the next few months she lost all the weight that she had put on over Christmas, and more. The girls took it in turns to look after her but she was afraid for their studies. One was a medical student in her final year, one training to be a clinical psychologist. She sent them away.

And then, standing at the back door one March morning, she felt the wind change. She filled her lungs with spring, with the perfume of sweet violet and narcissus and, on an out breath, went back into the house and made a few telephone calls.

The Sue Ryder van was there within the hour and, within the hour, she had stripped the cupboards of his clothes, the shelves of his books, his records, tapes and discs, the garage of his weights, his wine-making gear, his bike and fishing rods. (He had taken his golf clubs and had promised to return for the rest of his gear when he and the new woman moved into their new house). She took down pictures she had always hated, dragged out furniture she could never stand, and when the van drove away, she looked around at the empty spaces and drew strength from them. She had a bath and then took herself off to the hairdressers'.

The spiky punk style suited her and the yolk-yellow dye made her eyes even bigger and more luminous. She bought shirts and long skirts and leggings and Doc Martens boots.

On the way home she called in at the theatre and sorted through her puppets. Out into the yard went all the Steve look-alikes, every one, carried out on their strings like those little spiders you eject from the kitchen. But these were less than spiders, these erstwhile heroes of her folk-tales and fantasies. Some were dark, some fair, some were clothed in velvet, some in rags, but they were all clones of her perfect man, her husband. Never mind that the parts could be recycled, never mind that the costumes could be fitted to understudies. She shrank from them, could hardly bear to touch them as she dropped them one by one, a higgledy-piggle of loose-jointed wooden limbs, clatter-clatter, into the wire-framed incinerator and put a match to them. She even found herself doing a little hip-hop of triumph as the flames leapt higher, as tiny carved fingers clutched at the smoke, as nylon hair frizzed and bodies arched and joints twitched and smouldered.

Back home Sally rolled up her sleeves, weighed out the clay and wedged it thoroughly, driving out all the air bubbles, all her old misery. She worked from photos for accuracy, although she hardly needed to refer to them at all. The faces were grafted onto her mind.

When each bald head was as perfect as she could make it, she sliced it through with her cheese-wire, behind the hairline and down through the neck, and took plaster-of-Paris casts of each half. Carefully, carefully the clay came out leaving a clean white mould ready for the mastic to be poured in. She let them dry, then glued them together and painted them, miniature portraits, matching skin tone and eye colour exactly. When they were finished, with hair and eyebrows – even eyelashes – in place, she had six quarter-size heads on her dining table, characters in search of their bodies. So lifelike were they that she would talk to them. As if they were old friends. She couldn't wait to dress them, to write their parts.

Apart from the location and other small details, like the sex and age of Jo's children, it was her story exactly. As she said, you don't have to miss a date at the Tate to get shat on.

I had been there, the Christmas of '81, when Rob walked out. He'd had a full house but no applause. Two sets of in-laws, the boys, their girlfriends from college, and me. Jo had plenty of room

153

for guests now that they had extended into the cottage next door. Most of us were 'Scrabble'-ing round the table when the china crashed against the kitchen door. The tiles went skidding in all directions, triple-word-scores wiped out, 'Q's and 'Z's and blanks alike, lost forever between the skirting board and the stained boards of the floor. Rob hurtled through from the kitchen, closely followed by the turkey carcass and the brussels sprouts, which would never now make Boxing Day bubble-and-squeak.

He bounded upstairs and we heard him banging about while I plied a white-faced Jo with apricot brandy, and the two mothers went to clear up the mess and to speculate on the cause of the row. Rob's father went up after him and came down again with a flea in his ear, shaking his sad old head with its festive paper hat still in place.

A few minutes later Rob was barging out of Christmas to the front door with a loaded suitcase, pulling on his coat and trailing party-popper streamers. The door slammed. The car boot slammed. The car door slammed and the engine started. And stopped again. He came back in with a sheepish look on his face.

'Thank God,' said his mother. 'He's changed his mind!'

But Rob had only returned to claim his love, his stacking system. We watched in silence as he trudged through the wreckage of lives with his tape deck, his radio, his turntable and his graphic equalizer.

Later that summer I was down there again, researching a piece for BBC 2. Ben Nicholson had recently died and there was a lot of media interest in all the Cornish artists: Hepworth, Leach, Lanyon and the rest. Newlyn and St Ives were the places to be. There was even talk about building another Tate Gallery at St Ives. Just to confuse the issue.

I knew Jo was feeling better long before I reached the cottage. Every town, every village I drove through from Taunton down was splashed pink with her handiwork. Posters announcing the reopening of Carter's Little Theatre, marvellous new premises, a completely new cast, a completely new programme. A feminist programme. *'And why not book a meal at Le Bistro to complete your evening's pleasure?'*

I was intrigued.

The food, of course, was delicious. My order was taken by Madame Sandra herself, who recommended the *pôtage aux legumes* with a girlish giggle, and who sat down with me at the gingham and lace-covered table to drink a celebratory glass of champers while it was being prepared.

'Smudge,' I said, 'what a great idea! Wonderful food and then theatre. It's the ideal partnership.'

'A captive clientele,' she smirked. 'And those who haven't made a booking are welcome to have a coffee or a beer before the show or in the interval.'

'And French cuisine, in Cornwall, that's really special.'

'It was Jo's idea. She'd had to borrow madly to buy Rob's share of the mortgage, from her dad and her sister as well as the bank. She'd taken in a lodger and there was nothing else she could do to save the theatre. And then she had this idea.' She waved her hand around the old barn, where every table was occupied, every customer munching happily on *poisson* or *mouton* or *canard* or *l'agneau*, and quaffing wine, with a blissful look on their faces.

'Well, Jo and I had always got on so I thought I'd risk it. Don't you love the tables?'

'Très joli,' I said. They were. A vase of fresh flowers on each, candles, baskets of bread, bottles of wine. And, beneath the long tablecloths, distinctive black-painted wrought iron legs.

'Sewing machines,' she said.

'Quoi?'

'I saw one in a junk shop in Polperro and the idea came to me. Two put together to make a square. And so heavy that they can go outside and not get knocked over or knocked off. Every dealer in Cornwall had one. At least one. They practically gave them away. And bentwood chairs. Have you any idea how many bentwood chairs there are in the south of England? The kids painted them black for us and Rosie and Anna made the tie-on cushions.'

'Kids?'

'Anna's boys were down with their girlfriends, and Tom and Jude, and Jo's two. Spent their Easter holidays up to their armpits in black gloss.'

It had been a co-operative effort, then. I suddenly felt quite out of it. A stranger coming in at the tail end. Why had no one told me? I could have helped. I had money.

'Oh, we had plenty of help, Fen. Didn't think you'd want to be bothered. You're always so busy.'

Jo made sure I had a seat in the front. It was important, she said, that I saw the puppets clearly. And then, giving me her Dennis

155

the Menace grin – she'd never had her tooth fixed – she handed me the programme and whisked behind the curtain. Each of the protagonists, in each of the little playlets, was female. The programme read: 'Anna, the Resourceful Wife', 'Fenella Crackernuts', 'Red Rosie and the Crock of Gold', 'Mad Mags, the Cat-Witch' and 'Sandra's Search for Luck'. The Mistress of Ceremonies was, of course, Josephine, the Liberated Woman.

The puppets were delightful, instantly recognizable, and I loved the fact that they always came out on top. Fenella Crackernuts won her prince by cunning and daring, rolling nuts to the fairy baby so that it would toddle after her and drop the magic wand. She took the wand home and waved it over the prince and he was hers for ever more. Quite right, too. In fact, I used my namesake as a trademark for the series I did for the Beeb. She was sploshing paint onto a seascape à la Lanyon as the titles came up: 'Britain's Artists By the Sea'.

Rosie, of course, had Jo, in the guise of Sally, masterminding some sort of puppets' coven. Using our likenesses for occult purposes. Acting out little scenes of retribution, to bring bad cess to her five blood sisters.

'It's a shame,' Jo said, mildly. 'She coulda written sun-thing wonderful and we'd all've been proud, instead she's gone for Jack's sad old trick.'

'What's that?'

'He was always nicking our ideas.'

'That's not nice!'

'No, that's plagiarism.'

'She's not only nicked our ideas,' I said, 'she's nicked our love-lives, our problems …'

'Why, though? That's what I don't get,' said Smudge. 'She's not like that. Oh I know she gets by on being sweet and soft and that underneath she's granite, but she wouldn't hurt us, we're her friends.'

(Not the best judge of character, our Smudge. Take David and Monk, for instance. I rest my case.)

She was nodding again. 'It's as if she's deliberately made everything so much worse than it is.'

'Dramatic licence,' said Jo.

'And don't you mind? She's made you out to be some sort of a witch!'

Jo shrugged. 'So long as you don't go believin' her ...? No? Well, she can say what she likes, then, no skin off my nose. Might even be good for business. Mind you, I might try sticking pins in Red Rosie, see if her namesake hollers!'

Smudge was clearly unhappy that Jo was so laid back. 'She's made your Alistair out to be a money-grubbing gigolo ...'

'Well, he is, isn't he?' Jo grinned. 'Thank Gawd! He'd never've give me a second look if I hadn't had the wherewithal. When he puts his strong young arms around me and gives me that "take-me-to-bed" smile I often think, "Now you're only hoping I'll burst another blood vessel so's you can cash in my chips!"'

'Jo!'

'No, I'm joking, aren't I? He's a love. I'm just so lucky to have met him. For some reason he seems to think I'm something special. Fusses over me like a bleeding mother hen. Rob was never like that.'

'Well, be careful.'

'Oh, I am, he keeps me on me toes. But I haven't any illusions. He's young and attractive and I'm fast becoming an old hag. So I'd better make hay while the HRT shines, eh? You haven't met him yet, have you, Fen?'

She fished out a photo of a beach party. Sun and sea and Alistair. What a dish! He looked hardly older than Chris and Martin, Jo's boys, and very dark against Chris's blondness and Martin's red hair. He went abroad a lot, she said, to Saudi and Dubai, as some sort of an agent for Jessops, the oil people. All expenses paid. First class travel and accommodation. They thought the world of him.

So he wasn't short of a few bob. Rosie had got that quite wrong.

'And look what she's done with Fen's rape!'

I stiffened. What corns was Smudge going to step on now?

'According to Rosie, Fen made the whole thing up! Got herself pregnant to get off school or something. As if. And all that stuff about Olly and Fay, all that sex ... That's just silly. People don't do things like that to each other ...'

With a sort of fascination I watched the double chin slowly sag as she read the truth in my eyes. I sighed, feeling suddenly much older than any of them. ''Fraid they do, Smudge. Rosie's been unnervingly accurate, in fact, give or take an orgy or two.'

Jo's fork hung on 'Pause' before her open lips. She had saved the butter icing until last. Waiting for the moment. To float the sweetness over every last taste-bud before swallowing.

I smiled. 'She was spot-on in that scene with the aerosol of dairy cream. Except that we didn't do it on the floor. Ever tried getting cream out of a shag-pile? At least you can pop sheets straight in the washing machine. 'Cause it goes everywhere! Places you wouldn't dream of. You think you've licked it all off and you find there's more lurking in some secret corner of his anatomy. The last snow on the mountain. There's a lot more squirt in one of those cans than you'd think.' I closed my eyes, licking my lips like a smug cat. I couldn't help a grin, 'I do recommend it! Not much good for your waistline but it does the rest of you a power of good.'

Anna smiled wanly. She seemed to be cheering up, thank God.

Jo looked at her empty fork in dismay. She had eaten the icing without noticing.

But Smudge wasn't laughing; she was shaking her head, not knowing the words to ask. 'You mean ... you've been Simon's ... Simon's ... Under Maggie's nose? But there were all those other men! How long. ...? I'm ...' She gave up in the end and snapped, 'God, you certainly kept that dark!' She turned accusing eyes on Jo. 'You knew about this, did you? Am I the last to know? I mean apart from poor Maggie ...'

Jo admitted that she had known. Well, she had guessed. She was pretty cute, old Jo. Too clever by half. Wasted in the puppet business.

'Oh, Fen!' said Smudge, 'How could you? Your best friend!'

How could I? How could I not? Forbidden fruit is the sweetest, after all. Irresistible for someone with my appetite. What other thrill could match waking on a summer night to find this dangerous man, this somebody else's husband, nuzzling between your legs? There's no turn-on like illicit sex, whether it's a quick grope in the linen cupboard or a more prolonged coupling on damp leaves in the woods.

In the winter we'd take Maggie and the dogs, the children if they were home from school, and any other ambulant houseguests like my latest toy-boy for blistering hikes over to windy Housesteads or icy Cragside and return, as the daylight faded, to the boot room, muddy and sore with exertion. We'd slough off our rucksacks, kick off our wet boots and gaiters and pad in our thick socks up the back stairs to the bathroom of our choice. Some wonderfully sensible forefather of Foxy's had equipped each of the five bathrooms, long ago, with king-size, claw-footed baths. Wide-mouthed brass taps gushed piping hot water so deep that only your nose need show above the steaming bubbles as you soaked away your aches and sweaty grime. With a shower-head the size of a soup plate you could wash your hair and wallow at the same time. Sheer bloody heaven.

Add to that a six-foot hunk of rampant aristocracy, pot-belly not withstanding, massaging your back for starters in all the right erogenous zones, soaping your breasts, working around the slippery nipples with fingers and tongue. And leaving one to bob, rosily, in the suds, begging for more, while he delved deep down to do the twiddly bits before lifting you onto his lap and delving deeper. Oh Eureka!

Explaining to concerned enquirers beyond the locked door that the grunts and groans were to do with chilblains and aching joints, that the wild thrashing of water was an attempt to find the soap, only added a certain piquancy to the experience.

While I had their attention, I told them that my 'best friend', as Smudge put it, darling Mags who had done her best to slit my gizzard, was only still counted among the living because she was my ticket to the best damned sex this side of the Kama Sutra.

Foxy made noises now and again about leaving Maggie but he never would. And thank the Lord for that, sir. I had my career to think of; I certainly didn't want to be tied down to any man, especially one with a peerage, a moathouse and three kids. Maggie was welcome to all that. And he needed her, oh, he did. Her business acumen, her enthusiasm, her money. He also needed her to be Margaret, the gracious Lady Foxwell, mistress of his household. And she could still do that: shake hands with royalty in soft kid gloves, make pretty speeches at fêtes and prizegivings, organize the Re-creations down to the last scullery maid and souvenir soap-ball. She knew who she was when she was acting a part. She was only weird off-duty. Like Hamlet, when the wind was southerly she knew a hawk from a handsaw. But boy, nor'-nor'-west was a scary place to be! That was when she communed with Lottie.

Smudge had never witnessed Maggie in delirium.

We all had stories to tell. Whenever Anna's kids came back from Pigdon – they used to 'help out' with the Historical Re-creation, i.e. they worked their socks off for their bed and board, playing at musicians and swineherds – they would regale her with

Maggie's latest lunacies. She had long since waived her right to sit in the withdrawing room playing Elizabeth, Lady Brackley, holding court among her ladies, for the meatier role of 'apothecary'. They set her up in a sunny, timbered room over the old stables and hung bundles of herbs from the rafters. The walls were lined with shelves of leather-bound books, of measuring jugs and jars and retorts, of all the misshapes from the pottery, turned best-side-out and containing her ingredients, her snips and snails and powdered rhino horn, her cure-alls and quack remedies, labelled convincingly in old-fashioned script. Swallows nested under the beams and the parent birds flitted in and out through the ever-open window fetching flies and titbits for their greedy babies while Maggie, enveloped in no-nonsense brown linen, aproned and capped in white cotton for tidiness, was in her element. The public, filing up through the trap door and encountering a woman muttering over smelly pots of 'simples' on a charcoal burner, progressed nervously along the edge of the room, behind their cordon, reassuring each other that Mistress Hapgood was an actress like all the rest. One agitated fourth-former, however, remained unconvinced when Joey ('apprenticed' to Maggie in the mornings, master fletcher after lunch) told her she was mistaken if she thought she had seen his mistress popping something live and wriggling into her pot. Maggie was a herbalist, and a vegetarian to boot. Nevertheless, when Joey checked, there was one baby swallow missing from the nest. Coincidence, surely?

To an outsider she would certainly appear to be muttering spells but Joey said she seemed to be talking to someone.

'What did she say?' asked Smudge.

'Oh, she just seemed irritated, he said; kept telling Lottie to shut up and go away, as if the voice in her head were a nuisance, a naughty child. "Not now, Lottie, I'll talk to you later." Once, apparently, there was a "Piss off, Lottie, go and boil your head."'

'Glory be!' said Smudge in despair. 'She's round the flipping bend.'

'Not necessarily,' said Anna. 'People hear God talking to them and that's perfectly acceptable.'

I said, 'Foxy says it's just that she's highly sensitive, that her unconscious somehow leaks into her conscious mind. It happens to artists all the time: Dickens used to have great conversations with Martin Chuzzlewit!'

'When I was a kid,' said Smudge, 'I used to talk to an imaginary friend. Mum used to have to lay a place at the table for her.'

Anna said, 'When I was a kid, I used to talk to Rosie. She lived up the road and we'd natter away, though she was half a mile away. One night she told me there was treasure under her bed and I was to come and help her look for it – she was afraid of the goblins who guarded it, or something. I got in terrible trouble when I did!'

We somehow didn't find this hard to believe.

'But you grow out of it ...' said Smudge.

'Sadly,' said Anna. 'Of course, Maggie may just be a junkie. Have you considered that?'

She told us that Roz had been in the woods with her boyfriend Gary, when they had heard Maggie nattering away on the other side of a rhododendron bush. 'All right, all right,' she was saying, 'these are them, right? These tiny white ones with the nipple on top? Yes, yes, I heard, if the underside is white they're the wrong sort. Well, these are black ... Okay?' They didn't dare move. I gather they were *in flagrante*, though Anna didn't say. They could hear the dry scuff of leaves, which was Maggie shifting position, and plastic rustling as a carrier bag was filled with whatever it was. A dank and fungal redolence told them what she was about. After a while, they heard her moving away towards the lane, cracking small twigs with her small feet and, when they dared to look, there was no one with her. Roz and Gary found some magic mushrooms that she had missed and fried them with bacon that evening.

'When was this?' I asked.

'Oh, ages ago. Roz was eighteen or nineteen. No, she didn't meet Gary until she was at university, and she'd had that year out ... She must have gone up to Pigdon for the vac, I don't know, summer of eighty-one, was it?'

'The selfish cow!' I said.

'Roz?' said Anna, about to get on her high horse.

'Maggie. She's been treating herself to whacky mushrooms for seven years, near enough, and she's never, ever offered me any, or Foxy, as far as I know! Mind you,' and I supposed I ought to tell him, 'it explains why she's away with the fairies most of the time.'

I told them I'd known about Lottie for years, since before Daisy was born, but then it had just been Maggie's shorthand for the allotment thing. If you didn't keep the date at the Tate Lottie would get you. I didn't realize Maggie had internalized the demon until she tried to kill me. Even then I'd thought it only a temporary madness.

She had the 'flu' one Easter when I was at Anna's, and after I'd cheered Foxy up with one of my special Dial-a-Cheap-Thrill phone-calls that had Anna and her kids in stitches, I asked him to switch me through to Margaret. That's when he told me that he'd had the phone taken out of her room at her request, when they'd changed over to digital dialling. She had trouble enough sleeping, she'd said, and it was no help to have 'blips' waking her whenever anyone else in the house picked up the receiver or put it down. Now I had passed her room on a few occasions, on the way to or from Foxy's bed, and heard her nattering away to someone. Since it was a one-way conversation, I'd assumed she was on the telephone – none of my business. But of course, next time I was up there and heard the murmur of her voice at half-past one in the morning, I listened at the door.

She was trying to wheedle out of Lottie whether or not Willis Fashions should risk putting in for one of the lots in the swish new shopping mall proposed for Northumberland Street, Newcastle.

Lottie must have given her sound advice, because when Eldon Square opened later in the year, to a fanfare of brass, Willis Fashions was *in situ* and all set to thrive.

'Aha!' Smudge sat up. I almost expected her to yatter, like a cat that's spotted something feathery in a tree. 'Maybe *she* could tell me whether to buy up that greasy spoon in Polperro – my accountant is being very silly.' She was only half joking.

'Or which draws to do on the Pools,' said Jo. 'Now if old Lottie could put a bit of good luck our way to make up for the bad ...'

'Don't ...' I wanted to touch wood or cross my fingers, as you do when you tempt Fate.

'For God's sake!' said Anna, 'It's a figment. Lottie's not real. Just a voice Maggie imagines she hears.'

'Real enough to her,' I said, 'specially when she's on magic mushrooms.'

'Maybe they weren't for her ... or just a one-off. I shouldn't think she'd have found many more once the students got to know about them.'

'She shouldn't be making decisions about the shops, should she,

I mean, *should* she? Not if she's off her head?' Smudge seemed quite concerned.

'Why not?' I said. 'She's not put a foot wrong yet.'

Anna sighed and explained for the benefit of we mortals, 'See, when she's talking to Lottie, she's really just thinking aloud, calling on her intuition.'

'Her judgement's perfectly sound,' I had to admit. 'In the business department, anyway.'

Smudge looked as if she didn't think that was altogether fair.

'You'd think,' said Jo, to change the subject, 'with all her what-d'you call it? Her clairvoyance, she'd have some idea of your goings-on with Simon, wouldn't you?'

'It's not clairvoyancy,' said Anna. 'Schizos only hear things that are already in their heads, different aspects of themselves. If she doesn't suspect Simon and Fen she won't put ideas into her own head.'

'The only thing that'll do that is the book, and then watch out! You ever seen Maggie lose her rag? God, I mean, God! Quelle Spitfire! And with Lottie behind her the only thing to do is run for your lives!'

'Well, you'll just have to stop her reading the book, somehow.'

Easier said than done.

CHAPTER SEVEN

Fen again

'*Ccrrrackkk! The sound snaps the jaw like a wishbone. None of us knows the mechanics of it, what connects to what. Science is not our thing. But we aren't surprised when he topples forward and lies still at our feet, a dark trickle seeping from his ear. Phyllis removes her shoe and stands stork-like to stare at it in the dim forty-watts of the hall bulb. As if this inanimate thing had propelled itself. She runs her thumb along the sole's edge, and it is only wood. An inch and a half thick but only wood. It's hard to believe that a kick in the right place can bring a man down. A splinter comes away, and sticks in her thumb.*

I don't know how long we stand there, staring at her, at him, staring at the awesome shoe, as the punk on the radio rasps out a requiem – "no future, no future, no future for you." Long enough for the record to die and for the DJ to say a few last words. I can hear teeth chattering. Sally is shivering, her nerves shot. My arms wrap round, trying to warm her, to warm me, on this hot, sultry night as she clings and sobs.

I pat the wings of her shoulders as I would my own child. My own children. Where are they? It's not finished yet, is it? There's something else I must do.

I have to … I can't … Suppose …?

I find myself kissing her, thinking "I must find her something warm to put on." Kissing her wet eyes, her cheeks, her neck, her mouth. Her trembling mouth. Knowing this is not a child. Holding her face in my hands. Don't cry, love, it's over now. All the climbing over walls, through windows, risking knives, violence, death. No wonder she's shaking. I hold her close and feel her softness shuddering against me, sending ripples along my nerves, sending me forbidden messages …'

My eyes whizzed backwards over the words. Could that have happened? Anna and Jo? Dear oh dear, Rosie was paying off some old scores and no mistake. And with such soft words. Doing more damage than any old carving knife. Between the ribs and twisted …

Rosie at her nastiest. No wonder Anna was in such a state.

The possibility that Anna might be gay was, well, something one or two of us might have discussed over supper, turned over with the grilled trout, tossed about with the salad, and flushed away with the washing up water. I mean, here was this beautiful woman, divorcing a great-looking bloke and thereafter repelling all boarders. Anyone would mull it over, wouldn't they?

But you just couldn't picture Anna doing anything like that. She wasn't the sort. In fact, I'm pretty sure she'd have told us if she was homosexual. And everybody else, in all likelihood. I couldn't imagine her being a closet anything. No, no, she was so straight she squeaked.

She just liked her freedom, let's face it. Don't we all? And now that her kids were off her hands she was very much her own woman. She had her job and her voluntary work; she went on her marches, attended council meetings, popped down to Greenham Common at the weekend or visited her kids and their broods, or her endless brothers and sisters and cousins and aunts, or her friends. She knew interesting people, and I'll say this for her, she didn't give a toss who they were, union leaders, Labour peers, actors, lady TV presenters, she'd invite them round to her poky little place, give them dinner, even get them to stay. And she'd throw great parties. In between times she'd send off her daft cartoons to *Private Eye* and *Spare Rib*. She just didn't have time for a man.

When you think about it, Rosie could have done her a lot of damage, 'outing' her like that.

And why pick on poor old Jo, when she, Rosie, was the most likely object of desire? They were the closest of us all. Bestest friends. I had Maggie but, because of my little secret, could never drop my guard entirely with her. Rosie and Anna never had secrets; they always seemed to know what the other was thinking. They were more like sisters than friends, twin souls. Not that they never had rows; they did, real beauts, but they always seemed to get over them. Though not this time, I suspected. Rosie had gone too far.

I had come out onto the steps to read the rest of the book. It would have been a wonderful morning, without that cloud on the horizon; more like June than August. Fresh and sunny. I needed to top up my tan for the Awards that evening, but I would have come out anyway. I'd had my fill of the Brotherhood and the hushed reverence of the grand hall. All those prissy, bored women, curling their lips. Why the others set such store by them, I failed to see. Give me a Lucien Freud or a fleshy Spencer, any time. I like art to turn me on, not wind me up.

I was feeling calmer. Everyone seemed in favour of a low profile and that suited me. I've always been of the opinion that if you ignore a problem it will eventually go away.

'*I raise my eyes to meet Katie's which are wide with hurt. Her painted lips move to shape my name.*

"Liz!"

She's shocked. We're all in a state of shock. Reduced to instincts. Lopsided Phyllis and Katie, the White-faced Clown, are instinctively cross that I am instinctively embracing my good friend, Sally, who is instinctively responding.

He, Bailey, is dead, I instinctively feel.

For some weird and entirely inappropriate reason, a bubble of laughter chooses this moment to free itself, like marsh gas, from some long-buried sense of the ridiculous.

I look at Sally and her sad, puckered face is ludicrous.

I snort.

Katie sinks to her knees.

I snigger.

The murder weapon, soled and heeled for Gary-Glitter-strutting, is bizarre, considered from any angle.

I begin to shake.

That Bailey should have imagined, even for a moment, that I, I, with three teenage children to feed and clothe and entertain, could somehow furnish him with £10,000 ...

That he should have imagined that I would sit calmly at my desk while he carved his graffiti into their flesh ...

That four women with silly shoes and handbags should gallop across London to the rescue ...

That fat Phyllis should brain the thug with a high kick to the jaw ...

All this ...

All this, is so unutterably absurd ...!

I giggle, I chortle, I close my eyes and I throw back my head and open my mouth wide and howl!

With laughter. Unmerry, but laughter, nevertheless!

Wonderful.

My sides ache, my eyes are streaming, I need to pee, and when I see

their solemn amazement, I roar again! Leaning on the wall for support.
Priceless! If they could see their faces ...

Then I wake up, sober again and yawning with exhaustion. What am
*I doing? I have responsibilities. I'm supposed to be **doing** something,*
looking for something. Something warm for Sally? Is that it? Under the
stairs will be coats. I move in slow motion, twist the catch and slowly
open the cupboard door.

Children in the way! My children.

Found objects.

Bound and gagged, stuffed into the cupboard like old boots.'

This wasn't quite the story Rosie and Anna had told me at the
nursing home. It was a distorted mirror held up to a skewed
world.

Subtle embellishments to turn truth into fiction.

They hadn't mentioned to me that Anna had had hysterics but
it was something that could easily have been true. She was highly
strung.

In fact, the entire episode could have been true. To an outsider it would have been convincing. If they hadn't spotted the
deliberate mistakes. Things that an editor should have picked
up on.

Think about it. If Smudge had kicked Riley in the jaw as hard
as Phyllis had kicked Bailey, he'd never have recovered enough
to make his escape while Anna and Smudge were seeing the kids
to bed. He'd never have been able to crawl along the passage,
let alone vault the back fence and run along the line to play with
the trains. It was a pretty naff thing to do anyway but if you've
just had your brains scrambled by a kick in the head, you might
think it was a good idea. Why he chose to go out the back door I
suppose we'll never know. Even in a blue panic, I think I'd have
chanced the front door, me, even if it had meant going past the
parlour where Jo and Rosie were swigging brandy.

Plus, in *Friends for Life*, Rosie had Phyllis kicking him in the
balls just before the left to the jaw. Now I've kicked a few balls
around in my time. Believe me, they don't bounce back.

'I hope he isn't dead already, because killing him is my job, my right.
An eye for an eye. I live by the old religion.

After sixteen years of nurturing my children, loving them, shaping
their minds, this fiend had come along and, in a night, undone all my

good work. Treated them like meat. Bruised them, cut them, trussed them and then shoved them into a suffocating, fearsome dark, into a mind-warping hell. He shouldn't have done that. He shouldn't have spoiled what was mine. He shouldn't have forced me to sit astride his shoulders and smash his face into the floor, with a sickening crunching and crushing of bones. Again and again and again. As the tears course down my face.

He shouldn't have pissed on my Habitat rug.'

Bloody hell. I remembered that Habitat rug. A beautiful creamy sheepskin affair. Anna had been so proud of it and it had looked great against the red tile-effect lino.

And just who was the fiend here? Wasn't it fiendish to allow the fictional mother to give vent to passions that Anna had managed to hold in check.

'We drape it over him so the kids won't have to look on their way to bed. Though they are so doped up with brandy, hot milk, and aspirin it hardly registers, this dead mutton in sheep's clothing.

Phyl and Katie mop up the worst of the blood, pop a Sainsburys bag over his head, in case he bleeds onto something else, while Sal and I hurry off to fetch the cars. Hooking his arms round us, we "assist" him to the Cortina and drive back round to the railway bridge.

The pubs have all turned out and locked up. There's not much doing on a Tuesday night, not in Walthamstow, with work in the morning. Even the dirty stop-outs are in bed, the last passenger trains are in the sidings. The night bus hasn't yet left the Balls Pond Road.

There's no one around.

With a heave and a shove the job is done. When we look over we can see him curled on the track with his bare head pillowed on the line, just as though he were asleep. The carving knife lies where we threw it, a little further on.

Back at Laurel Road I rinse the carrier bag, fill it with kitchen waste, potato peelings and beef dripping and tea-leaves, and put it outside in the bin. Then I telephone the police and tell them the story – the Revised Version.

I have to shout to make myself heard above the racket of the train.'

Laurel Road? Couldn't she have been a just a little more subtle? Here was another fine mess she'd gotten us into. This whole chapter was serious libel. Anna and Smudge wouldn't allow her to get away with this, surely? They couldn't. And my peccadillo would pop out rudely, in the confusion.

169

That was some chip she had on her shoulder. Or chips. Something for everyone. I may have my faults but I like to think I'm upfront about things. If someone's upset me I tell them; I don't clutch my grudges to me and brood, darkly and mysteriously, smiling nicely all the while, until they hatch out into character assassinations.

I turned to the inside cover for clues. There was a photo of her looking soulful. Still good-looking, I guess, if you go for that smooth dark Mediterranean type, though now there was a touch of grey in hair worn swept back off her forehead. She looked very different without her frizz and fringe, and a bit sort of spaced out around the eyes. It took me a while to realize I hadn't seen her without thick black eyeliner since school. She didn't appear to be wearing any make-up. Ye gods! For your publicity photo?

The blurb said she was no stranger to the literary world, having co-written the 'Country Bus' series for children, but that this was her first full-length novel, 'a nostalgic ride through friendship.' ('A trampling over' might be nearer the truth.) It went on to say that she was an active member of her church, worked as a volunteer for her local Women's Aid group and had camped on Greenham Common for three months. (Anna had roped her in, I remember. She'd tried to get me, too, but I wasn't up to anything so primitive. Chemical loos for heaven's sake!). Now she worked for the environmental organization, Greenpeace. Very worthy. Still it looked good on a CV. Whiter than white, wasn't she, the treacherous cow? Saint bloody Rosie.

'It's by way of expiation,' said Anna, when she came out to find me. 'Rosie's eaten up with guilt.'

'Guilt?'

'For her part in Riley's death. It's getting her down.'

'But it was an accident ...'

I couldn't believe it when Anna frowned and pressed her lips together.

'God, I mean ...' I breathed. There were only the two of us on the steps and yet I felt that the world was listening.

'She wrote it the way it happened,' Anna said quietly. The hairs on the back of my neck stirred with her breath.

And I realized it had always been there, the suspicion that Riley had been dead when he left Anna's house, that one of my friends was a killer.

170

But it must have occurred to the police. too. They don't just take people's word for it. Would they have had any proof though, or even cared that much? A nasty little shit had been disposed of. A murderer, to boot. (Breda Riley had taken a turn for the worse the next day and died, poor old soul.)

When you think, there but for Maggie's madness went I! If she'd kept her hands to herself and let me drive her to the Tate, we'd both have been party to it. Because we'd have colluded, sure as eggs, in concealing the evidence, disposing of the body. I was never able to hold out against peer pressure. Specially if they held me over wells. Though it would have been a railway bridge this time, in all probability.

Well, thanks for that, then, Maggie! What's a slashed face between friends? Or maybe it was Lottie I should be thanking. They say the Devil looks after her own.

So, there had been no escape over the back fence. No mad dash along the line. The train hadn't killed anyone, just squished a corpse to paté.

'Anna, why didn't you tell me?'

She shrugged, but I knew. I wouldn't have trusted me either. I am what I am. Media through and through. Even so my eyes smarted. I could imagine them discussing it, deciding which version to tell me. ('Not the truth; she'll blab to the world.') And they were all in on it, Smudge and Jo, too. And the kids. That hurt. I wondered why she was telling me now. I could still do quite a nasty little number on them if I put my mind to it. I had dirt of my own to dish.

And then she said, 'It wouldn't have been kind to saddle you with it, Fen. You had enough on your plate. We didn't tell Maggie, either.'

Really? I wanted to believe her. Well, if the worst came to the worst, with the right handling, they could even come up smelling of violets. I could do that for them, I supposed. What are friends for?

And I'd stand to make some goodly dosh if I could get the right people interested. On the down side, it might mean that Foxy and I would have to come clean. Fair's fair, you couldn't give prime time to Liz and Phyllis and the rest of the fictional gang and turn a blind eye to the frolics of Fay! How Maggie took it would be pretty crucial. If she had any sense she'd stand by her man, otherwise she might find herself out on her frosty little butt. Simon had a full kitty nowadays; he wouldn't need Willis money, and he could buy in managerial help until Jamie, their eldest, finished his business studies course. That young man was itching for a chance to prove what he could do.

But I doubted it would come to that. The business meant more to Mags than anything and she'd love forgiving Simon.

So I would lose a friend but I would have to bear that with fortitude. I wouldn't lose my lover, of that I was sure. Foxy and I would just have to be more devious than before, if that were possible. Could even add a certain *frisson* to the affair ...

Tell the truth and shame the devil has always been the Swinton way. And who could tell what we might salvage from the mess?

If it came to that.

'It was still an accident,' I said. 'Unpremeditated heat-of-the-moment stuff. Any mother would have done the same; it's the most basic of instincts. And any good friend would have helped. Even Buttercup the cow will kill to protect her calf.'

'But Buttercup the cow doesn't go slinging bodies under trains to cover her tracks.'

'She does if she has any sense. Rosie understood that eleven years ago. Why is she playing up now?'

Anna bit her lip. 'We fell out four years ago and I lost touch.' She said it quickly, like some people skim over death or divorce. Probe too deep and the wound will break open again. I knew she didn't see Rosie now. I didn't know how much it hurt.

'The letter she sent with the book didn't say a great deal but I gather she's well in with the church, and you know what they're like about sins and guilt, and confession being good for the soul ...'

'What did you do, Anna? To make her hate you?'

'Me? Nothing! She doesn't hate me.'

I looked at her sideways. Oh yes she did. Anna was lying her head off.

'No, honestly, Fen. Nothing.'

'You didn't try and make love to her?'

'What!'

'I mean you've always fancied her, haven't you?'

'Fen! I'm not ...' She lowered her voice, looking round furtively. 'For Christ's sake, Fen,' she hissed in my ear, 'it wasn't like that!'

172

No? Rosie seemed to have been right about most things, why not this?

We sank into a tight-mouthed silence, watching a pleasure cruiser chugging purposefully down the river, on the look-out for landmarks. There was only the Tate for the shutter-happy tourists to click at. Opposite was just dreary old Lambeth.

Rosie liked to make out that this was her favourite London skyline. The uncluttered sky reminded her of the left bank of the Seine, she said, talking out of her bottom.

Me, I love all the new London buildings, rearing up proud and phallic, jostling for room, glittering in the sun. It's exciting, busy, what a city is all about.

We were still wrapped in our thoughts when the gallery patrons started drifting out to eat their lunch. Lunch on the steps of the Tate, the stone sculpting them into Henry Moore figures with the sun shining through their heads. On a warm summer's day like many another. Incredible to think that the Chinese should have regarded the eighth of the eighth, eighty-eight, as a supremely lucky day.

The letter had been word-processed and edited, careful and tidy.

'*Dear Anna,*' it said,

'*What an age it is since I've seen you. Can't believe it's three years, or is it four? Thanks for your card from Boston last month (and for all the other correspondence that I haven't acknowledged – I'm not ungrateful, honestly). So Roz is lecturing out there now? Following in father's footsteps! Is it really twenty-seven years since we were wheeling her round Lloyd's Park in a pram? I'm pleased that you're getting on so much better with Paul and Trudy. She sounds our sort, though the brats don't. Good grief! Aren't you glad you live in England, with an ocean between you and the little demons?*

I expect you've gathered that I'm sitting here with a bundle of your letters and cards (of course I kept them!) wondering why I don't just pick up the phone and talk to you properly, or even pop round. I can't. I know I'd just love you to bits all over again and I can't be doing with all that. Not now.

The enclosed book, <u>Friends for Life</u> is out on Monday. It's about us. Well, they do tell you to write what you know! Initially it was meant as a sort of therapy, for private consumption only, to "find myself" as Jude puts it. A bit of a trendy teenage thing to want to do but I was so utterly confused, Anna, I thought I was going mad. Your fault! I had

173

*to do something to sort myself out, to get rid of a whole pile of **ghosts**. And nightmares, singular rather than plural, the same old one, over and over, and Jack, his usual understanding self.*

He was one of the things I had to sort out. And you. And the Riley fiasco; duty versus loyalty, the usual things. And the "Lottie" business.

Anna, that was so dangerous, like playing with a ouija board. It could have sent us all bonkers, not only poor suggestible Maggie. The mistake we made, of course, was to leave God out. That's why it went wrong, how evil crept in. Still, that's all behind me now. It took three years, and God's help, to exorcise all my devils (including you!). I nearly said "to get it down in black and white" but that wasn't the intention. It is fiction and only the "grey areas" as I saw them. The last thing I want is to get anyone into trouble. No one'll know it's you unless you tell them!

By the way, I won't be keeping the date at the Tate on Monday, not entirely from cowardice, (though I'm sure I'm the last person any of you will want to see. I rather think I've burned my bridges where our friendship is concerned). I'll be at Fitzells all day for the launch and then I have to travel up to Leeds for the northern bash. (Oh, the joys of having an agent!)

Look out for Lottie! You told me once that superstition was the religion of feeble minds. Hang on to that.

Have a good life and don't think too badly of me.

Love Rosie.'

'How long would it take to do an exorcism? Reckon they could fit us in this afternoon, or would we have to book?'

Anna ignored my flippancy. 'It's all a sham,' she said, 'all this piety tosh.'

'She sounds pretty convincing to me.'

'Possibly. Take it from me, she's as God-fearing as my big toe. Did you ever see *The Stepford Wives*? About women made into pretty robots to please their hubbies. That's Rosie. She's full of shit. Full of it.'

Anna's angst had been brewing for years.

She told me she had watched Rosie's marriage breaking down with mixed feelings. The man was a prick of the highest order but Rosie had never looked at anyone else. On good days she beat her breasts for wishing him out of her life on bad days.

'Leave him,' Anna had urged, whenever Rosie had come to her, still fuming over his public-school pomposity, his heavy handling of the children, his crass racism or his rudeness to her parents.

'How can I leave him?' she would snap, 'I'm bound hand and foot.'

'By love?' countered Anna.

Then one dewy morning in spring, Anna went on, she and Rosie had been walking Anna's dog on Chingford Plain, gulping down the sparkling air, getting high on catkin and blossom, throwing a ball for Gypsy to keep her mind off rabbits, and Rosie had sighed with pleasure.

'It's so good to be out of the house!' She had stretched her arms wide, turning slowly round and round, making a circle of green wellie prints on the silver grass. 'Wonderful to be free of Jack for a while.'

Anna had known better than to say anything.

'Sometimes, you know, I feel as if he's a great weight on my back, pressing down, stifling any sort of creativity. If only I could shut him up in a cupboard and bring him out when I wanted him.'

'When would that be?'

She had thought for a moment, and laughed, 'I don't know. When I wanted approval, that's pretty often. Or money. Or sex.'

'That's your order of priorities?'

'I suppose it is. It would be nice to have sex when *I* wanted it. On my terms.' She smiled, 'What a selfish cow!' and put on her Coronation Street voice, 'If only I'd known then what I know now ...! Ee, our Anna, I should never 'ave wed at all.' Then she'd sighed and said in Upper Walthamstow, 'I do envy you, you know.'

'Me?'

'You do what you want when you want. No man to intimidate you or criticize. Forever making demands and complaining.'

'It can get pretty lonely sometimes.'

'I crave loneliness! I'd give my eye-teeth for loneliness.'

Anna said for the umpteenth time, 'So leave him.'

'I can't.'

'I can't see any shackles.'

'Anna, there are a hundred things. The books ...'

'You can do the books on your own. Better. It doesn't take a genius to write kids' stories about a country bus, for God's sake.'

'There are contracts ...'

'There are ways round contracts. See a solicitor.'

'He needs me.'

'So what? He'll just have to find some other mug to draw the pictures. It might mean him having to dredge up some new ideas but that's his problem. It's time you did your own thing. You could write the stories *and* paint the pictures. You certainly don't need him. You were always a good writer. You could write for adults come to that.'

But Rosie was shaking her head.

'I couldn't do it to him.'

'*I* could. The man's a bloodsucker. He's using you.'

'He is, isn't he?'

'Come and live with me.'

Rosie had looked up then, startled, eyes wide with the idea.

'I ...' then she had frowned, and as Gypsy had come dancing, teasing them with the ball, grabbed it from her jaws and run ahead, flinging it high and far with all her strength. A skylark twittered madly.

'God!' she had screamed, punching the air, but whether in joy or anger, Anna, yards behind, had been unable to tell. When she turned again to Anna her expression was unreadable.

'I can't just leave him, Anna. That's the coward's way. You have to work at a marriage. I made vows.'

'Bollocks!'

The muscles in Rosie's jaw had bunched.

Anna said, 'If all that's holding you together is a vow, for God's sake, it's best to get out, isn't it?'

'How would I manage? I've no money of my own. We're paid jointly. He gives me housekeeping.'

'Sod that for a game of soldiers! Get shot of him. Do your own thing.'

'And what about the kids? I can't up and leave in the middle of Jude's A-levels. It would destroy her.'

'Let her finish them. What's that – two, three months? I don't mind waiting.'

But Rosie had no end of excuses: tender-hearted Tom and his traumas, her parents' disapproval, her sister's disapproval, her friends' disapproval, her children's disapproval, the gossip, the church.

'They don't believe in divorce ...'

'What do you care? You outgrew the church long ago. The only reason you went back was to keep him company. When are you going to start thinking for yourself? It's the church as much as anything that's made him the chauvinist charmer he is. He loves all that archaic claptrap. Boosts his wilting male ego.'

'I have a lot of friends there.'

'Try leaving Jack. That'll soon sort the friends from the goats.'

Rosie had been silent, chewing her lip and kicking savagely at a thick tuffet of grass.

'I suppose,' she said, at last, 'the top and bottom of it is, I'm afraid.'

'What of, Jack?'

'Not Jack.'

And Anna knew then. She was the one. Hot tears sprang to her eyes. 'Why, for God's sake? Why?'

'Oh, Anna, don't ... You see, well, I don't know what to think. You've got me all confused. I ... I'm scared I don't really know you. Do you ...?' She swallowed, shook her head, 'No, no, forget it.'

'What?'

'No.'

'For God's sake, Rosie, say what's on your mind.'

'Better not ...'

'Rosie ...!'

'Well, for you to ask me ... to suggest ... that I come and live with you ...'

'Seems the obvious solution.'

Rosie shook her head. Her cheeks were flushed. 'It's easy for you to say, you haven't really thought it through. What it implies.'

'Yes I have. You could have Roz's old room and we could take it in turns to do the cooking ...'

'It's what Jack would say in any divorce proceedings. He'd say we were lovers.'

'What!'

'People will think we're ... that I'm ...' She took a breath and tried again. 'I mean even putting it into words is like ... like ... God, I *wish* you hadn't asked me! It's giving you ideas, me ideas, spoiling what we've had, turning it into something dirty. And I'm not, Anna, I'm not like that ...'

'Like what?'

'Oh, don't act so fucking naïve ... I'm not gay, Anna.'

'Nor am I! I'm not!' she had protested.

Anna repeated her declaration to me now, less vehemently, less sure, 'I'm not ... I don't think so. Honestly, Fen, all I suggested was that, well, why shouldn't two friends live together if they want to? There doesn't have to be anything sexual, not unless you ... and there wasn't anything like that. She was my friend, for God's sake. I wouldn't have hurt her for the world.'

Rosie had been very quiet as they walked back to the car. She had hardly spoken as Anna dropped her off at her gate.

She had hardly spoken to her again, Anna said, end of story.

*   *   *

Fitzells was a new shop in Charing Cross Road, a glass-and-light temple to literature, its vaulted ceiling supported by great square pillars of shelves packed with books. Between the pillars were tables heaped with hardbacks (fiction), hardbacks (non-fiction), sports books, travel books, art books, music books. The paperbacks were racked round the edges of the shop, neatly and unobtrusively.

A display beside the children's section showed a dozen or so 'Country Bus' characters, gathered to goggle at a large smiling newsprint photograph of the Kellys, Jack, a stooping grey stick insect wearing specs and a cloth cap over his antennae, Rosie, tall but not as tall, nor nearly as old, as her husband, filling out prettily and looking rather butch in T-shirt and cords.

(School corridors all over Britain were lined with childish attempts to imitate Rosie's soft, watery style: it looked so easy. Deceptive, like the artist.) A few child-proof hardbacks stood about: *Country Bus Goes Missing*, *Country Bus Comes to Town*, *Country Bus in France*, bright full-frontals to remind customers of the new writer's credentials.

There was no sign of signing or signer as we rounded a central pillar and arrived in a sort of bookish grotto. Radiating like a sunburst over the wall, and stacked in swirled columns, were a few hundred pale yellow copies of the new publication. Free-standing on the other side of the table was (what else?) a card-board reproduction of the Burne-Jones *Golden Stairs* painting, showing the upper third of the enigmatic stairway and the last six of the graceful Greek maidens in their pleated silk nighties, stepping down from somewhere to somewhere.

178

I was familiar with the cover design, of course, having nursed the thing since early morning, but to see it now, a blaring fanfare to dénouement, to know that one of the troupe was me heading for a fall, actually made me blush. A phenomenon for someone whose greatest joy was to see herself in print.

I'd bought my copy at Victoria Station where the man at Smith's had to go hunting 'out-the-back'.

'Might've come in Sat'day. Hang on, Miss Swinton, I'll go have a looksee.' And after much ripping of cardboard he returned, bearing the yellow book like a golden offering, polystyrene curls still clinging to his sleeve. Amazing how a spot of fame improves the service. There was a queue of pin-stripes and skirts waiting to buy their FTs and *Playboys* and not a murmur of discontent among them. I signed a few autographs in appreciation before making off with my trophy.

'Where is she?'

'Miss Woodhouse will be back in about ten minutes.' The shop assistant wove towards us, pliant on champagne. Her empty glass leaned against the till.

'Where the fuck is she?' Jo was in no mood for pleasantries, having lost her cool over the exorbitant taxi fare from Pimlico. She hadn't wanted to come in the first place. Was it likely, she argued, that Rosie would listen to reason when she had some sort of a grudge against Anna, she despised me, she thought Smudge was pathetic and she was jealous of Jo?

'Pardon me?'

Anna took over. She always did.

'We need to see Miss Woodhouse urgently. We're friends of hers.'

'I'm afraid she's at lunch. The book-launch lunch ...' The poor girl could hardly get her tongue round it. Her glassy eyes strayed towards the ceiling and gave us the clue we needed.

'Yes, yes, we're supposed to be there, too,' I lied. (I'm not a journalist for nothing.) 'Rosie invited us. We're rather late, I'm afraid, the traffic on the motorway ...'

'They've already started the speeches ...'

'That's all right, dear. These the stairs?' I heard a ripple of clapping coming from above.

We squashed in at the back of the room behind a crowd of well-wishers, so many and so eager that we could not see a thing.

The platform party were over by the far wall but the platform wasn't high enough for us to glimpse more than the top of the speaker's head. It was a woman with a rather quiet voice. We could only catch the occasional word whenever she could bear to look away from the star of the show – Rosie, presumably. Words like '... multi-talented' and 'honest' and something about the pen being mightier than the paintbrush.

Who were all these people? The Kelly network, presumably. Publishers, editors, agents, writers. Names with itchy backs. Those nearest looked us over curiously and I could see my presence puzzled them. A media person at a literary function? What could it mean? Was I a useful connection? I returned a few tentative smiles and gave out my 'do not distract' signals.

I recognized Tom, who stood head and shoulders above everyone else. Unfortunately he had inherited Jack's stick insect looks rather than his mother's good bones. Definitely not my type. In fact I couldn't see anyone I fancied, which was a bore – chatting up has a bit more zing than speeches.

Anna found an ashtray and stood in the doorway, blowing smoke down the stairs. Smudge found the drinks tray, and she and I guzzled away, propping up the wall and trying to look as if we weren't working out ways and means of damaging the place. All these people, and they hadn't invited us, the famous five (if you counted Maggie), without whom none of this would have been possible.

Anna said, puffing smoke into an elderly gent's face, 'A bit of a do for a first book, isn't it?' I thought the old geezer looked familiar. It took a while for me to remember he was a producer of radio drama. Would we be serialized for 'Woman's Hour' or adapted for 'Saturday Night Theatre'? If we were abridged, my bit would be the first to go. And I would be sorry, I had to admit.

Smudge disappeared into the crush in search of food and Jo turned towards me, eyebrows a-quiver, and said, *sotto voce*, 'I think we know some of this crowd. That bloke over by the window – the bald one with the cravat? Keeps looking at us. And that oily-looking prat with the lantern jaw. I've seen him before.'

A bray of laughter filtered across to us. Polite heartiness. The sort where you tuck in your chin and shake your shoulders with fake mirth, Edward Heath style, while your eyes concentrate on not slopping your drink. By their cravats and blazers ye shall know them. And the women by their unleavened plainness.

'Jesus!' Anna said, 'They're mob-handed. It's Rosie's lot from church. That's Geoff Singleton over there.'

'Which one?'

'The weedy looking runt with the bow tie.'

'The Groper! After all these years!'

'Ssshh!'

'D'you suppose he's read our book?'

'*Her* book.'

'Probably. If they're here, the support group, it must mean she's discussed it with them, got their approval. God on her side and all that.'

'Well, *they'll* know who's who, no probs.'

'Pointing us out to their mates ... "That's the battered wife, that's the killer, that's the whore ..."'

'Ssshhh!' A woman in front of us, whose pretty Indian drop ear-rings I had been deeply coveting, swung round with a withering scowl.

'So where *is* the victim of violence?' I whispered.

'God knows.'

'Ssshhh!'

The extract she read was Katie's dream.

'It is unmistakeable, that thud of footsteps on wooden stairs, horses' hooves on a dirt road, shouts of desperate people, "Fire! Fire!" Yet when I run out onto the step, people are quietly shopping as before. A young man, with his small son in tow, squeezes past me into the sweet shop and takes my place at the counter. But outside, over the diesel fumes, I can still smell sweet burning wood, over the traffic's rumbling I can still hear the roar of wind-blown flames, the crackling of burning timber. The young church along the street, all tinted windows and sculptured concrete, sleeps in the heat of noon, but the great glass door beckons and my dream-self slips inside ...

'... To stand, not gawping in horror, but mildly surprised as you are in dreams, to find that this is no bright modern hymn to God. Here are the embers of what must have been a raging hell. The fire is nearly out, though wisps of smoke still flutter around the blackened pillars like magician's hands passing over a crack that grows in the stone as I watch, lengthening, widening, travelling swiftly up and up, wriggling like a lightning bolt that will split the column in two.

'And I twitch with too much heat and wrinkle my nose as, with a roar, the splendid pillar topples away from me, down the length of the

181

church, breaking into a hundred useless fragments, crushing the last flames from burnt-out pews and brittle lecterns.

'And the roof falls in.

'As it settles itself down into the dust and ash and clinker I am alerted by some slighter sound up there to watch another of the stressed timbers, burned to the bone, falling mightily through the vaulting space, down into the glowing charcoal belly of the ancient church with a thunderous crashing and thrashing of sparks and cinders and splintering wood.

'My unconscious finds a path through the smouldering litter and when the smoke clears I find I am at the altar, where times have changed again and a bride in a long white gown and her groom, smeared and smudged with smoke and soot but otherwise unscathed, gyrate to pop music played on a cream-coloured radio set. They turn pale faces towards me, open their mouths and scream.'

No one sipped or swallowed. No one moved.

I knew what Anna and Jo were thinking, and Smudge, very likely, wherever she was. We had lived with that dream of Rosie's, or something very like it, since we had known her. For years she had bored the socks off us with tales of the ruined church, the wedding, the scream. We had offered her our diagnoses and our advice, our teddy bears and our sleeping pills.

Maggie reckoned it had something to do with her menstrual cycle. It was clearly a sexual thing. Too much or too little. Or hormones. They can be nasty little buggers when they're out of kilter. Foxy reckoned she ought to get herself a good man. What did he mean by good? I had asked, snuggling into his side. Good, as in 'good at tennis?' Not tennis, Foxy had said, though Jack wasn't built for tennis, either.

Not many people liked Jack.

When Rosie was at her most bitchy and foul, you could bet she'd had one of her dreams. That or PMT.

I've known her, when she was desperate, attempt to paint the dream out of her subconscious with brush and water-colours. Art therapy, she called it. Her dream, the original one, had an old woman in it, I remember, and that painting was haunting, a crone with hooded, hungry eyes, like you see in those drawings of the holocaust. The scream was just an open mouth, not very successful in my opinion, but she liked it. The couple getting married caused her the most trouble. She always ended up leaving the faces blank. Time and again she'd let the wash dry,

182

select her finest brush for the details, load it with pigment and then freeze. The water in her jam-jar would be thick as paint with the washing and re-washing of her reluctant brush. It was painful to watch.

'Go on,' we would urge her. 'Get on with it.'

'It's just an exercise,' she would say lamely, defensively, finally ripping the paper in two.

In my experience, if exercise doesn't hurt it's a waste of time.

'A hundred volts of fear jump-start my heart. The church shudders and I am thrown to the ground, spread-eagled before the altar, as falling chunks of scorched wood rain down on my back. A sudden draught fans the glowing embers around me and they burn red-hot. I shall burn with the church. We shall all burn ... so hot ... so frightened ...

'Richard is digging me in the back. He's cross. He's always cross. "You're dreaming again, old girl, jumping around!" Anyone would think I did it on purpose. "Kate! Wake up! Good Lord, woman, how can I sleep with you bucking like a jack-ass?"

'But he does, on the next out-breath, leaving me wide awake and with a heart that's scrabbling around my ribs like a cat in a cage.

'I'm wringing wet. Night sweats, hot flushes, all in one. And shivering. I have to get up. If I go back to sleep now I shall dream again; if I don't I shall kill him. And although that would be delightful and I should plead diminished responsibility while the balance of my mind was disturbed, I couldn't be sure of getting off with a warning.

'Oh, what a joy I shall be in the morning! Tired and jumpy. And Richard will sigh and tighten his lips in Christian forbearance. Such a godly man, a patient man, a pillar of the church.

'Yes, of course I know what my dream means. I've known for years. But knowing what ails you and taking the cure are different issues. This is not simply a matter of holding your nose and swallowing hard. There are painful side effects to be considered.'

Jo and I made 'Well, I never!' faces at each other. This extract was from the penultimate chapter, 'Katie's Story', and neither of us had read that far. So, Katie cum Rosie understood her dream now. Writing as a therapy must have done the trick. As far as I could remember, Rosie had never mentioned a cracked and collapsing 'pillar of the church' when describing her dream, nor had she attempted to paint it. It must have been buried deep.

She had paused for a sip of water and to offer a little smile of reassurance to her husband. I could imagine Jack sitting there, stiffly folded like an ironing board, with his insect smile, twitch, twitch. I wondered what he thought of all this. She had sailed close to the wind in the rest of the book, why should she change tack now? Richard was Jack, no mistake, and she hated him.

And what about the rest of it? Had she identified the bride and bridegroom? Or groombride, whichever applied these days. One of them was certainly Rosie, herself. But who, who, *who* was the other?

Now she looked up, smiling happily at her friends by the window, at her son. From the back of the room we could just see her face, flushed with nerves, framed by her short, straight hair. As she took off her reading glasses I noticed Anna slip out onto the landing. Jo ducked to avoid catching Rosie's eye and putting her off her stroke. Speeches were not Rosie's strong suit. We could all remember occasions at school, in debates and later at christenings and parties when she had dried completely, flushing deep red and gawping like a fish. Give her a part to learn for a play and she'd never fluff her lines, but ask her to be herself? Say a few words? Hopeless. I slid further down the wall until she was out of sight. We were all so thoughtful, weren't we? So considerate to this bloody woman who had betrayed us all. Willing her to do well.

And she did. No voice tremor, no stammering as she told us about her great new life as a writer. How she would miss illustrating 'Country Bus' books but that her old school motto had been 'Neglect not the Gift that is in Thee' and she thanked God, oh, how she thanked God for this gift, this opportunity!

Jo rolled her eyes, and vomiting noises came from the landing.

'There are a few other people I would like to thank. One, my daughter, Jude, who bullied me into writing the book ...'

Jude's smiling face popped up to her mother's left and three inches higher. A beanpole, poor kid. Why had neither of them taken after Rosie?

'And not forgetting my son, Tom, who has been a tower of strength, and I use the term advisedly ...'

Tom raised his hand and turned to acknowledge the laughter. Like a blonde lighthouse he beamed this way and that, his smile faltering only when he spotted Smudge in the corner by the sausage rolls. But she wasn't munching. That was the last thing on her mind. She was gassing, nineteen to the dozen, to some guy in a checked shirt. So excited, she was almost pretty. From the back he looked like an ageing pop star with his steel grey pony-tail. Was he someone I knew?

The 'few other people' Rosie had to thank turned into a dozen: her agent, her editor, the 'Country Bus' people who had been so understanding, the 'support group' from church, de dah, de dah, de dah.

'... And finally, I have to thank my husband for his encouragement and his love and for making sure I sleep soundly at night ...!' said with a giggle and a blush, and so she should.

The cravats jiggled and the blazer-shoulders heaved ...

And he rose up beside her then, taller than I remembered, black curls greying now and a little fuller in the face but still bloody good-looking and gazing at his adorable new wife with those ink-blue eyes.

Bloody Roger!

The chap in the corner spun round, as did everyone else in the room, to see who had squealed and, what do you think ...? The chap was none other than Rodge's good friend, Maurice, otherwise known as Monk. It's a small world, n'est-ce pas? Smudge thought so.

Well, Lottie had a field day.

The network tore apart down the middle of the room and there was Rosie, peering through the rags of disruption, clutching at Roger's arm, a smile wobbling on her lips, going, 'Fen ... Jo ... Are you all here? How nice ...'

I struggled to stop myself sliding down the wall, to stand up straight. Get my face in order. I was a journalist. This was good copy. I faced far wider, more critical audiences week after week. Jo yanked me up. Doc Martens hold the floor better than stilettos.

'Shit,' she was saying. 'Shit and derision!'

And then a screaming tornado blew in from the landing, knocking me aside. She pounded down the room, eyes blazing, hairpins flying, hands flexing and gripping, losing their hold on reality. The Red Sea parted even wider.

'Anna, no!' shrieked Jo, but she might have been talking to the wall, down which I was sliding again. She leapt after Anna and I hit the floor in a heap. Someone helped me up, someone familiar. (God, how much more of my past was in this room?) But as I found my feet the sound of an almighty slap sent shock-waves round the room.

Anna had nearly taken Rosie's head off.

'Hey, hey, hey, now come on!'

'I say, old girl!'

'No call for violence!'

The support group gave voice to their impotence. This most certainly wasn't cricket. Not true blue county cricket, cheps.

'Rotten, sodding, miserable, sneaky ...!'

'Bitch!'

'Tart! Cow!' were some of the lesser expletives to reach my ears as I barged through the mass of bodies that had now filled the breach.

Jo had given up the struggle to restrain Anna, who was now white with fury and spitting like a hell-cat, with her hands locked around Rosie's pretty throat. Rosie's face was turning purple and her eyes were bulging.

'Roger, please!' she croaked.

He was doing his best. Trying to unzip Anna's fingers and at the same time fend off Jo, who was bashing away with her Doc Martens at his shins. Meanwhile Jude had her hands twined in Anna's hair and was pulling her head back to breaking point. Something had to give.

Anna's grip.

Jude and Anna went flying backwards in a flurry of skirts and nails and hair and then, as Rosie lunged forward with a choking roar of revenge, she somehow connected with a right hook from me. Oh boy! That felt so, so good. I didn't actually knock her to the floor but I heard a crack as I spread her nose and then I fell on top of her among the chairs. She was kicking and biting and scratching. Whatever happened to 'turn the other cheek'? Then I got a good grip on her hair and ...

It was a bit confusing after that. At one point I was grappling with Bridget. My belated daughter! What was she doing there? Of course, Roger was her daddy, wasn't he? She was the one who had picked me up from the floor.

'Fen!' she was crying, tears streaming down her face as she attempted to pull me off. 'Don't. You can't get involved!'

Oh, couldn't I? I had a well-full of grudges against Woodlouse, going way, way back and I shook my daughter off my back, but it was too late: Rosie had rolled away out of my reach and into Jo's boots. Roger had hold of my wrists.

'The lovely Ms Swinton,' he purred through curling lips, pull-

186

ing me up and appraising my high colour and heaving breast. 'Lying, cheating, selfish, scheming ...'

'Ball-breaking?' I suggested, giving him the full benefit of my expertise. He doubled in pain.

'Get the police,' he moaned and, when nobody moved, he gathered up his strength and yelled, 'get the fucking police!'

A few people began to leave and I thought perhaps I wouldn't stick around either. Anna was rewinding her hair, having head-butted Jude and given her a fat lip. Rosie had been rescued from Jo by the mob, one or two of whom had been savaged in the attempt. Rosie was sitting down, nursing her nose, surrounded by hovering advisers and hankies full of ice from the champagne bucket. Beetling their pacifist eyebrows at us with something that couldn't be hate – could it? – they vented on us their spleen at a God who wouldn't allow them to fight even the good fight when women were involved. Meanwhile blood dripped onto Rosie's nice cream-coloured suit.

'No police,' she snuffled. 'No police!'

So that was all right.

Jo was rocking up and down on her boots, her hair spiky as a land-mine and steam issuing from her ears. Her long printed frock made her look like a bar-room floozie in a western, her fists balled for someone else to hit.

'Smudge,' I yelled, over their heads, 'are you coming?'

She had been a great help. With the end in sight she had been rummaging in her bag, the huge, soft, scrummy one, for her Filofax, making dates, writing names, telephone numbers. Now she was hunting again, this time for her purse, her huge, soft, scrummy purse. Come on, woman! Was she going to give him money, a recipe? Show him her knitting? No. Her blunt little fingers fumbled and fussed and, at last, extracted a card. Of course, her business card. She was going to see him again.

That night I accepted the trophy with my left hand, the other being bandaged to hide swollen and torn knuckles. I joked that I had slugged a rival in love, and they laughed. What a ridiculous idea!

Bridget was supposed to have been there, too, sitting by my side at the banqueting table, smiling and supportive, but she wasn't. Poor Bridget had too many mothers, too many loyalties, too soon. There was the woman who had brought her up, a Mrs

Duggan. There was me. Who had given her birth thirty-two years before and then abandoned her, but who hadn't batted a false eyelash when she had come knocking on my door, saying,

'Hi, I wonder if I could talk to you for a few minutes. My name is Bridget McKenny. I'm your daughter.'

I'd welcomed her in, made the best of it, hadn't I? And a lovely film to boot, an award-winning film.

And there was Rosie, the stepmother, who married Roger, the father. All very complicated. For her and for me.

Smudge filled me in over a late and drink-sodden lunch at La Belle Étoile. Monk had had all the gen. He had been Roger's best man six months before.

Bridget had traced me by her birth certificate and ebullient social workers. She had traced Roger by the same means but had somehow neglected to tell me this part. Dear old Rodge was over the moon to find his daughter after all this time. (His first marriage had been without issue, and his second. He hadn't bothered again.) Not only a daughter, but a barrister son-in-law and two lovely grandchildren, an entire family looking for genetic roots. Black curly roots and blue, blue eyes.

(Oh, didn't I say that I was a grannie, too? My cup runneth over ...)

It was while buying said sprogs a couple of books for Christmas that he discovered his beloved Rosie again.

'*Sadly,*' announced the blurb beneath the photo, '*Rosie and Jack Kelly were divorced earlier this year. So this will be the last "Country Bus" adventure to be illustrated in Rosie's inimitable manner.*'

Bridget had looked up Rosie's telephone number in my address book, devious little cow, and a meeting was set up. Bingo! Love at second sight. They had a white wedding.

They missed my film while they were in Kenya on honeymoon, but they all watched Bridget's video on their return and Rosie was able to write Chapter Six with Roger's help. So it all worked out rather nicely for them, didn't it?

When I think about it, I suppose that Woodlouse and I are now related in some dubious sort of way. When the sprogs are married we shall both turn up to the weddings and create merry hell.

There might be a story in it.

CHAPTER EIGHT

With Lottie in Mind

Smudge – 9/8/89

By the time his divorce came through, nine months after the book launch, she had lost over two stone and knew that, at nearly fifty, she had never looked better. Nor had her bank balance. She had everything he could wish for: a chain of restaurants scattered all over the West Country, television appearances, thanks to Fen, a series of cookery books embellished with Anna's dotty cartoons, and an occasional column in the London *Evening Standard*.

They moved into an old watermill near Polperro, and *Your Home* did a glossy, four-page feature on the conversion, using before-and-after photos that Monk had taken. Dark, satanic caves and cells became, when gutted and restructured, a bright, streamlined kitchen with studio and dark-room attached, where they could work, cook and 'develop' together. (His joke!) Upstairs was their music room, where Monk would play his jazz CDs while she lay in his arms and sang scat to entrance him. Up another set of stairs were light and airy bedrooms, where he would entrance her!

They had been in residence just three months and were planting spring bulbs, bluebells and crocuses and narcissi in the beds under the windows, and Solomon's Seal against the wall.

The wheel turned. The river ducked through the slats, chuckling.

The telephone rang.

She remembered running to answer it, stopping at the patio door to slip off her gardening shoes.

'Hi. Sandra Hodgekiss here,' she announced brightly. She *felt* bright. Confident.

The space of a heartbeat and then the breath was punched from her body.

She must have dropped the receiver, because that was the first thing Monk did when he came in. Replace it. No, first he listened to the throbbing silence, *then* he replaced it. Then he held her tight.

189

For some reason this made her shiver.

'*What?*' he demanded. 'Sweetheart, what is it? Is someone dead?'

'I … it's the book …' she stammered. Why couldn't she stop shaking? 'S … somebody knows. Knows m … me from Rosie, from Rosie's des … description and thinks … thinks I killed that boy.'

Her throat was tight. She wished he wasn't holding her. She needed to be free, to move about, to think. But he was being protective, alternating 'Bastard!' with wet kisses to her forehead, her cheeks, her nose, her eyes. She wiped them off on his shirt, leaving mascara smears and smudges of pink.

His arms were hot, clamped in place. Tears of frustration sprang to her eyes. Her teeth were chattering.

'Hey, hey, hey … Smudgie …' He tilted her chin to look at him. His eyes were kind. 'Don't let him get to you. He's a sad man, whoever he is, trying to cash in on our good fortune. I guess we're going to have to get used to this sort of thing, now we're in the public eye.'

He didn't understand.

'He …. he called me … he said, "M … *murderer!*"' She heard her voice spiralling upward away from reality, but she couldn't stop. 'He'll tell the police, Monk, and there'll be a trial and … and … photos and headlines and … Daddy will have to, will have to know, and oh, Monk, I'll go to *prison!*' Oh God, she could see how it would be. So clearly.

'Prison?' He was looking startled. She realized she'd said too much. 'Why should you go to *prison*? What Rosie wrote was fiction. A fucking fairy story! Sorry, I shouldn't swear.'

Why not? He was always 'fucking' this and that and then apologizing, as though she were some sensitive plant. He invested her with all sorts of qualities she didn't possess, some more useful than others. Like neurosis. Like now.

'You're getting it all out of proportion, silly girl. No one'll listen to a crank like that. Certainly not the police.' He pulled out an imaginary note pad. '"Where's your proof, Buster?"' And taking on the crank's role, he spread his hands in a weak gesture. '"Oh I read it in some novel." They're bound to take him seriously, aren't they?'

He was smiling. Kind, reasonable Monk. Pat, pat. Silly old Smudge, getting herself in a state over nothing.

She was breathing too hard to laugh.

'How much did he want?'

'What?' She blinked. Caught on the words. There had been no mention of money. Just the accusation which still rang in her ears.

'It wasn't Bailey, was it, Sandra? In the Woodhouse book? Billy Riley was his name and you killed him. Kicked him to death and shoved the poor bastard under a train. If I were you, I'd start cooking up a few good alibis. Murderer.'

It was out. Someone knew. But how? None of her friends would have told him. Nor Anna's children. Like everyone else, they thought their tormentor had been killed by the train.

Lottie.

Of course.

This was the ninth of the eighth eighty-nine, marked on her calendar with a red L for Lottie. Palindrome dates made her nervous, like other people were wary of Friday the thirteenth. And like them, she had remembered before breakfast and forgotten in the happiness of the day. But, of course, Lottie wouldn't stand for that. Lottie would see to it that she paid. Dearly.

Not a stroke this time, not madness nor disfiguration.

Disgrace this time. Public disgrace.

It fluttered in her heart, beat in her ears, that fear. Heavy and rhythmic like the beating of a swan's wings. *Lottie*. This was the day and this was the reckoning. If only she weren't so hot. So hot. She felt the sweat oozing through her pores, saliva in her jaws. Closed her eyes against the swimming of the room ...

'Head down, head down!'

... And found herself sitting on the floor, his hands forcing her head hard between her knees. She struggled but she couldn't move. It was one of the positions of restraint she used to use on Gregory.

'Don't ...' she breathed. She was looking into her own crotch.

'It's all right, love,' he was saying. 'You came over faint. Just relax. It'll be all right ...'

'No, *no!*' She hated this.

But her nemesis was whispering, '*Murderer!*'

What could she do? She was hog-tied and helpless. She had to let him humiliate her. Not for murder, of course, because he didn't know, but for the trouble she was giving him. For causing strange men to phone up out of the blue and accuse her of awful things. For jeopardizing his happiness.

191

His fingers were hurting her neck.

'*Murderer!*' was burning her ears.

The fight went out of her.

It had always been that way with men. She couldn't resist. They knew best. She was just a woman. Too weak. Too ugly. Too stupid. She upset them. Her fault.

So she let them punish her. Beat her, kill her baby.

Her eyes squeezed shut then, on images that couldn't be memories ... of events that couldn't have happened, not really.

And came upon a dim hallway, thumping with a heartbeat of ugly sound.

'*No future, no future, no future for you!*'

Four women and a whipping-boy.

She had heard herself whimpering. Salivating. It had to be her. They must let her do it. Oh, please. She needed this.

Retribution for the damage that didn't show, to the mind and spirit. More disfiguring than scars.

The cry she uttered had startled them all. The primitive roar that came from the womb. The raging war-cry as the blow found its mark.

So, so sweet, that soft yielding of the boneless flesh to the wood of her shoe. So cleansing, it had brought tears to her eyes.

The boy crumpled, a gargoyle of pain. Ugly. Repellent.

Then Anna had come at him with the knife raised. Avenging Greek goddess, pale as stone. Music pounded. Someone was weeping.

Anna would do it. Yes, it was her right. She was the mother. But Jo had stayed Anna's arm and it was left to Smudge to finish the job. This one for Gregory.

Monk heard her mumbling and let her up. She faced him, strong now. Triumphant.

'There was a crack, Monk, something broke in his head and he died! I killed him, Monk!'

He shook his head, a smile telling her that she was confused. That he understood. He probably thought that the shock of the phone call had scattered her wits.

She crowed, '*I ... killed ... him!*'

Her insides were melting. An orgasm. Now? Oh, wonderful! She began to laugh. Pummelled his chest, threw back her head and roared.

192

He caught her wrists.

'Stop it, Smudge! Stop it. It's not true.'

He shook her then by the shoulders, hard. And it was so funny that he didn't know. That it *was* true and her knickers were wet.

He shook her as though he were emptying a sack of compost; her head fell back and her laugh caught in her throat. When she looked back she saw he had mad eyes. Like David and Daddy and Billy Riley.

She tried to twist out of his grip. Found herself drawing up her bare feet, one at a time, like a cat.

'Smudge, stop this!'

'Let ... me ... go!'

Because she was now very strong her right hand catapaulted free. Forewarned by something in her eyes, Monk turned his head in time and her bunched fist slid off his cheekbone. As she came at him again, he blocked her arm with his left, and slapped her hard across the face with his right.

'Sorry, sorry ...' he said as she stared at him through the pain. 'You were hysterical, darling. Saying crazy things.'

Now she was supposed to cry, snuffle pathetically into his handkerchief. That was how they did it on the movies. Then he was supposed to put his arms round her, kiss the tears away and carry her off to bed. That was what he wanted.

But she shook him off. Continued to stare. Her cheek was throbbing. She nibbled at the ball of her thumb viciously, as though she had a thorn there, never taking her eyes from his.

He took it that she was ready to listen.

'Don't worry about that joker, sweetheart. If he calls again tell him – nice try but he's not getting a penny out of us. No – don't even speak to him. *We'll* tell the police. They know how to deal with nuisances like that. Whatever happens, don't let him put ideas in your head – muddle you.'

What did he take her for?

'You didn't kill anyone,' he insisted. 'You couldn't, sweetheart. You damaged Riley but it was in self-defence. You didn't kill him, love, you didn't.'

Yes, he really believed that.

'Think about it, darling. The guy was able to get himself over the back fence when you were busy with the children. He wasn't dead. He got *himself* run over by a train. Tough – but it wasn't your fault. Rosie made up the killing, darling. She has a nasty

193

imagination, and you ...' he kissed her nose fondly,'... are a suggestible little idiot. We'll tell the police and everything will be all right, I promise you. Trust me.'

'I can't do that, Monk.' A statement of fact. He missed the ambiguity.

She left him the mill-house but sold all her other interests, lock, stock and bistros. The money was transferred to a Swiss bank and where she went and who she became, nobody ever knew.

*   *   *

Jo – 2/9/92

Martin had assured her that, apart from standing together for the photographs and to receive the guests, there would be no need for contact. It would be a strain, thought Jo, and their combined presence would provide more tasty titbits than the buffet, but for Martin and Nicola's sake she was prepared to tough it out.

Rob seemed taller than she remembered, and had lost weight. It suited him. Toppered and tailed, he had looked so like the man she had married, so unlike the ogre she had divorced, she found herself watching the ceremony through a misty veil. She shook herself. Don't be so bloody soft, she told herself. This is the bastard who deserted you when you were getting over cancer for God's sake! For another woman!

She sneaked a glance during the prayers, and then a longer one. His eyes were tight shut. Hypocrite. His hair was thinner and no longer bright and the lines of laughter and sorrow were etched deep. But he sang, 'Love Divine, all loves excelling ...' with a voice that was still strong. Strong enough to move her. When he turned to give her his arm for the walk to the vestry, there was a slight furrow between his brows and his blue eyes were trying to tell her something. Her own face twitched. What is it, Rob? Before settling back into the mask.

He was an attentive, if unsmiling, escort, supporting her arm with fingers that had once been able to caress her very soul. But those same strong fingers had snapped in the face of her need, she reminded herself as she forced her flesh to become wooden.

So don't, don't succumb to sentiment. Or the music of the loins. You don't need a man. You don't need anyone. Who kept the

194

theatre going, single-handed, after he buggered off, after Smudge buggered off, after Alistair disappeared into the Gulf to be swallowed by oil and war? Jo Carter. On her bloody own.

Like a puppet, she performed her duties, shaking hands, with a painted smile. But when the formalities were done and the tables were pushed back to the edges of the hall, when the music began, she could feel his eyes following her, and then there he was, asking her to dance, and it felt so good. Like coming home.

'Jo.' She could hear the catch in his throat and could not trust herself to speak. She was very conscious of the warm hand on her back. 'You're looking good!'

Martin and Nicola danced by, she all frothy white, he proud and pink round the ears. A junior consultancy at the Royal London, a new wife ... To see his parents back together would just about complete his happiness. She felt tears threatening. Too much champagne! Her cheeks were hot, her temples throbbing.

She had forgotten his energy, his enthusiasm. He whisked her around the floor in a waltz that left her breathless and she felt her corsage slipping from her lacy lapel.

As Rob led her back to her seat, she grappled with the pin and, like the princess in one of her plays, pricked her thumb. But she hardly noticed. The orchid was back in its place and so was she. He whispered, 'We must talk,' and the sweet curve of his mouth made her heart turn over.

But it wasn't until later, when the disco beat was upped a few hundred decibels and hair was let down, when flickering strobes made concealment easy, that she could prise herself away from her nearest and dearest to sit with her ex-husband.

'What can I get you, Jo?'

She really didn't need any more alcohol. She was dizzy enough.

'Mineral water would be fine, thanks.'

But when she tasted it, in the dim light, it was champagne. To celebrate, he said, smiling happily.

'Is this seat taken?' asked a voice, so heavy with nicotine and age it creaked. A fat woman, sweating from exertion, placed a pudgy hand on the back of the chair beside Jo, as if to take it away.

'No, no,' they both said at once, anxious to be alone, 'that's all right.' And were nonplussed when the woman flopped down on it, between them. A squishy marshmallow face creased into a confidential grimace.

'Just 'til I get me breath back! Cor blimey, mate! Where do the youngsters find the energy? Bloody twist'll be the death of me!'

Damn, thought Jo. Couldn't she see that they wanted to talk? Nine years of silence and there was so much to say, to explain, forgive. Rob rolled his eyes. He shifted his stool round the corner of the table to come closer to Jo, as though driven by noise. He had to shout.

'It's going well, isn't it?' He was trying to cut the woman out, but her interest was undisguised.

'Surprisingly!' Jo turned towards him, trying to create intimacy.

'Why do you say that?'

'I think Martin was expecting us to, you know, play up.' Out of the corner of her eye, she could see the woman nodding agreement. It was inhibiting.

'I think we're behaving very well.'

'All things considered …' She glanced round at Squishy Face, who smiled and said:

'She looks a treat, your daughter.'

'My …? Oh, no, no … Caroline's the bride's mother. Over there. The woman in light blue, chatting up the vicar.' And seizing her chance, 'Shall I introduce you to her?'

'No mate, ta. Looks like she's got her hands full right now.'

So have we! screamed Jo silently.

'No, don't tell me … you're the *boy's* mum, ain't you? Same red hair, I can tell. Got his dad's eyes though, ain't he? Nice-looking young chap.'

Jo began to wonder who this old girl could be, if she didn't know Caroline. She certainly wasn't a Carter. In fact, she looked as though she might have come in off the street.

At that moment Rob's knee touched hers. She sprang away as if it had been red-hot. Oh wait, Rob, wait. She couldn't handle this much, this soon.

The pace was hotting up: Abba were getting an airing and the dancers were caught up in a rocking, bucking frenzy. The floor shook.

He looked hurt and she wanted to explain. She loved him so much; she had always loved him, but how could she trust him?

'Rob …' She moved her stool along to the corner of the table, so that she was shouting into his ear. 'What you did …' she hesitated, 'I have to know … how could you do it? Leave me, when I needed you most?'

'What? Can't hear!'

'Waterloo! Couldn't retreat if I wanted to ...!'

He shook his head, craned towards her, hopelessly.

'How can I forgive you?'

He shrugged incomprehension, before he yelled, 'I love you, Jo!'

'Was it the sickness you couldn't handle? The mortality?' She shook her head over his frailty. 'Will you be stronger next time?' Her eyes filled with tears. It was so important to know.

He grabbed her outstretched, imploring hands ...

'I need you to tell me you won't hurt me again.'

... And he buried a soft kiss in her right palm, then her left.

'Waterloo! Waterloo!'

'Ain't no good, mate, he can't hear a blessed word!' came a cracked voice close to her right ear.

'Jesus F. *Christ*! You nosey old cow!'

The woman chortled wheezily and dug Jo with a plump pink elbow. 'I'd just give him a kiss if I was you, mate. Do you both a power of good. Go on, gel. A nice big smacker!'

And because that was what Jo wanted to do more than anything, she did, and the questions went unanswered.

As he pulled her to him, whispering, 'I'm sorry, Jo, so sorry, Jo,' and finally gathered her to him, a cheer went up, a spotlight found them and there was no going back.

* * *

Maggie – 9/5/95

Margaret was glad to put VE Day, and duty, behind her. As she told her journal, she wasn't cut out to play Lady Bountiful to the oiks. Thankfully no one these days expected manorial largesse, and the veterans and the other celebrants of fifty years' Peace in our Time had paid their entrance fee, like anyone else, at the time-tunnel. Even so, the takings were down on a normal business day, heavily down.

She had hated having to turn the moathouse into a red, white and blue travesty, having to organize tables on the lawn and loudspeakers in the trees, so that Vera Lynn and the All Clear could be heard down in Pigdon itself. It was all so *tacky*. But since it was expected (the precedent having been set in 1918 by Simon's great-grandparents), she had gritted her teeth and got on with it, almost single-handed: brass bands and Union Jacks, balloons

197

and bouncy castles, races for the children, punts on the moat, the lot.

Simon was *such* a help! ('*Not*', as her daughter's friends were wont to say.) Margaret had simply asked him to mention to the actors that, although there would be no Re-creation on the Bank Holiday, there would be a bit of a back-hander for anyone who would agree to wait table, dressed in forties flannels or land-army jodpurs and turbans. The girls turned up in everything from Norman Hartnell foxfurs to Mrs Mopp overalls and the boys in brown, navy or airforce-blue or in 'Grandad's de-mob suit, your ladyship!' A shiny, double-breasted whistle-and-flute with pockets full of mothballs. Quite unsuitable for waiting table. And you can't slap Brylcreem on a pony-tail and hope to be convincing! Or a trilby. All but twelve had to be sent home again.

She still couldn't believe that her husband had actually put the Mother's Union hand-knits-and-crochet stall next to their own Restoration lacework! A text-book clanger! When people can't make up their minds between expensive, quality goods and cheaper but, by comparison, infinitely inferior products, they tend to buy neither. Even worse, he had allowed the Parish Council to set up their Tombola next to the Rotary Club's bottle stall. They would have come to blows if she hadn't sorted them out.

He was getting worse. Fen always said he couldn't organize a piss-up in a brothel, or a brewery, or was that a bunk-up? Whatever. He couldn't. Left to himself he would have sold out long ago to the National Trust and be living in some tax haven off the Adriatic coast. He had no killer instinct at all. Quite, quite hopeless.

It had been politic to delegate the catering to the WI, since they, and they *alone*, it seemed, were capable of turning out a decent poached salmon and sherry trifle! Let them, Margaret had thought, she had enough to do. But when they had wanted to have red, white and blue paper tablecloths, and napkins as well, she simply had to put her foot down. She had her standards.

In the end, of course, it had all rolled along on oiled wheels, from the drum majorettes to the Boys' Brigade march-past, to the tea-dance and the Glen Miller music, to the parachute jump and the Hurricanes and Spitfires, to the glittering climax of searchlights and fireworks, as those visitors still ambulant conga'd around the floodlit grounds. She had even found herself relaxing a little, joining in.

But, oh Lord, those dreadful old men and their interminable reminiscences! Reluctant to stir up painful memories, they said, but they did nevertheless, on and on and on. And you had to nod and look as if you were listening and not itching to say something to the young girl who was pouring far too much cream into their coffee and serving it from the right! You had to. Smile a little and nod, because it was their day. And all the while there was Lottie suggesting that you kick the chair from under the old fart.

She had been surprised and not a little dismayed at her own reactions. Goose-bumps at the All Clear, for goodness' sake! Shivers up her legs during 'We'll Meet Again', and real tears when the beacon was lit. Memories of that other VE day had come flooding back, when a tiny five-year-old had been more frightened by the strange man who had whisked her up onto his shoulders than by all the noise and racket of the war. Quite petrified, she had clung on for dear life, not daring to say a word, though her bare legs had chafed on his rough uniform, and the narrow terraces (those left standing) had stalked closer, with Union Jacks, great flapping monsters, strung between crumbling window ledges, and shadows of leaping, leering hobgoblins thrown onto the walls by the flames of the celebratory bonfire.

Despite the late night and the heavy drinking they were all up early the next morning, taking down the bunting and stacking the trestles where the supplier could collect them, out of the way of Pigdon 1677. Margaret was determined not to lose another day's business. Out by the tradesman's entrance, also, were bags of unsold jumble from the Scouts' stall, unsavoury old clothes and saucepans and boxes of books.

'Go and look,' suggested Lottie, with cunning. 'You might find something interesting. Get in before the dealer.'

Margaret argued, Lottie insisted.

So Margaret unlocked the cardboard flaps and ran a reluctant finger along the bruised spines. It was a waste of time; tattered cookery books, Latin primers, bundles of women's magazines, ageing classics that everyone had read over and over.

'Next box,' insisted Lottie. 'There might be something.'

There was. A sharp staple that snagged her thumb. As her hand flew to her mouth she noticed a sickly yellow paperback: *Friends for Life* by Rosemary Woodhouse. It couldn't be.

Lottie left her alone for the rest of the morning, to catch up.

But Simon bumbled in and out, hot and bothered in his Lord Brackley outfit, what was left of his crinkly hair plastered to his pink scalp. He had removed his wig and flapped it to cool it down.

'What do you want done with the marquee ...?'

'The chap from the Bull and Crown wants to know when he can collect the glasses ...'

'The old boy who lent us the tapes says Jack Payne's missing ...'

After the tenth interruption, she blew:

'For God's *sake*, Simon! I'm busy! Can't Elspeth help you? – *she's* the ruddy housekeeper. Better still, give Lord Brackley the day off and roll up your own ruddy shirtsleeves!'

Some instinct had made her cover the book with a folder when he knocked at the door and, as she read on, through the traumatic birth of baby Lily, through the post-natal madness, the gibbering, the voices, she began to suspect that the reason she hadn't come across the book before was that Simon had been keeping it from her. He had probably bribed Fourcross, the newsagent in the village, not to stock it.

He needn't have bothered; she couldn't remember the last time she had read a novel. Her book at bedtime for years had been the Pigdon accounts. Come to think of it, Simon had started his 'anti-paperback' campaign five or six years ago, or even seven. As a matter of interest ... She turned to the fly-leaf. Well, now, Lottie ... First published in hardback in 1988, the year of the reunion. Round about August, she wouldn't mind betting. Its paperback brother had been born the following year.

'Cheap and nasty!' his Lordship had objected, shaking, by its black and silver cover, some tale of abuse and horror that eleven-year-old Daisy had been about to stow in her holdall to lighten the journey back to boarding school. 'A book should be a lovely thing, properly bound, to feed the mind and the senses.' As he shook the offending tome, a lone, well-thumbed page fluttered down the stairwell. 'There!' he said, triumphantly, 'I'll have no more of this soft-back *garbage* in the house. If your allowance doesn't stretch to proper books, Daisy, you'll just have to make do with what we have here in the library!'

And Daisy had raised an eyebrow in utter contempt. She would continue doing just as she liked, knowing that Simon's pronouncements would only amount to anything if Margaret added her small weight, which she didn't this time. Nevertheless, paperbacks were rarely seen in the moathouse unless the students left them by mistake.

Now she came to think of it, when the papers came on Sundays he always insisted on reading the literary reviews before anyone else. He could have saved himself the trouble. She rarely read them. Sunday was their busiest day.

She was touched by his efforts. All this time he had been trying to protect her from Rosie's outpourings. And it was all so innocuous, really. So she heard voices? So had Joan of Arc, so had Doris Stokes. They hadn't been sectioned and neither was Margaret, Lady Foxwell. And she wasn't likely to throw her apron over her head and go into a decline just because Rosemary Woodhouse had pointed the finger. Didn't Simon realize, yet, that she was made of sterner stuff? Far from being upset she had found the book vastly entertaining, so far.

It was old news given a face-lift, and face-lifts are always interesting, especially when the subjects are known to you, tarted up and barely recognizable. Wonderful stuff.

Why hadn't Fen told her about it? Had Rosie disclosed some dreadful Swinton impropriety, perhaps? Or were they in it together, Fen and Simon? Was everyone in it, the children, her friends? Was that why she never saw them now? A conspiracy to keep her in ignorance, to protect her? Well, that was kind.

Poor Jo and Sandra, they wouldn't like having all their dirty washing hung out like that for public scrutiny! All their problems, all their failures.

Whatever had made Rosie do it? Silly girl. Her friends would not take kindly to that, that ... well, disloyalty was too mild a term.

And then there was this business with the young tearaway ... (What was his real name? Not Bailey, was it? No, it had gone.) Dreadful things to have written, implying that they had killed the man and then thrown his body onto the railway line: '*I have to shout to make myself heard above the racket of the train ...*' If that were true it would be cold-blooded ... Well, maybe not murder. Something unlawful, anyway.

(Oh she couldn't wait to discuss it with Fen tonight!)

It didn't appear to have done anyone harm, anyway, that was the main thing. They were all doing well now, so Fen said. Jo with her puppets, Sandra with her restaurants, Anna winning a seat on the council. And Rosie? Well, she could understand why Fen never had much to say about her. She had probably been steering well clear. What was not quite so understandable was Lottie's silence on the subject. She had a bone to pick with that particular entity.

So Rosie was a writer now. Did that mean she still illustrated the 'Country Bus' books for Jack? Fen used to buy them for the children when they were small. Ages ago. It was time Rosie made her own way. Like the rest of them.

Though it had taken a broken marriage, in each case, for Jo and Sandra and Anna to get started. Not so lucky in their choice of men as Rosie and herself. Well then, Simon, she said to the door, we seem to have done something right. She smiled a tender little smile. She was still quite fond of the old bore.

She turned the page. And it was 'Fay's Story'.

By lunchtime she was tearing fringes in the edges of the pages. She sat still and pale, just her fingers moving, hardly breathing, a tiny figure in an expensive green silk shirt and mink-brown Lycra leggings, greying hair neatly plaited French-style down her narrow back, eyes still huge, staring, not at the book, but at the panelled wall, at miniatures of the past occupants of Pigdon Hall. That long line of barons and their ladies and their children and their children's children, in lace cravats and periwigs, far-thingales and bonnets, flapper frocks and cloche hats, bell-bottoms and neckties. On horses with gun dogs, beside a Harley-Davidson with goggles, in ermine-trimmed robes of state. From the earliest Brackleys to the latest Foxwells.

The line, the line was all. That had been her function: to keep that line coming, child after child after child. Dutiful wife and mother. While he …

'While he fucked your best friend,' said Lottie, back again.

Margaret's busy little fingers, bent into claws, continued to rip the pages, tearing them right out of the book now, and across, and across again, as she stared straight ahead. Her thumb bled onto the torn paper piling up on the desk, spilling onto her lap, drifting to the floor like dirty confetti.

A tear, the first, clouded her green eye and brimmed over. Her nose reddened and a drip formed, suspended in mucus and fell, and not a muscle of her face moved.

'For thirty years,' said Lottie. 'Hard to believe, isn't it? With her pick of men, she had to have yours. That's friends for you.'

A tremor, starting from her knees, shook her slight frame, and she drew in a shuddering breath. The fingers jerked in spasms.

'You know he's used you?' said Lottie. 'They both have. Your money, your body, your drive, your ideas. They've fed on you. And while you've been knocking yourself out raising his children, building up his beloved Pigdon from a pile of shit to a thriving business, making him a millionaire, he's been fucking your so-called friend. Thoroughly. Night after night. Under this very roof. So much for love, so much for loyalty, so much for all those fine, noble virtues. He has deceived you, Margaret, lied to you all your married life.'

She cuffed her nose on her shirt sleeve and sniffed back the rest of the tears. Tears were a waste of time and energy. She had learned that, at least, from Fen, the cow, the unspeakable bitch.

'You should have killed her when you had the chance,' said Lottie.

Margaret spoke then, her eyes hard as marbles and her lips thin and white:

'Second time lucky.'

* * *

She awoke late on the morning of the eleventh of May and smiled.

Simon did not come down to breakfast, and neither did Fen. When, twenty minutes later, they were found not to be in their rooms nor anywhere on the premises, when the station wagon and Fenella's Porsche were found to be missing, it was presumed they had left early. Both had had pressing business engagements, Fen at TVTV and Simon all over the country. He was expected to be away for a day or two.

He had a bale of flax to collect from Essex. Pigdon liked to show the children the complete educational programme, from the soaking and stripping of the fibres to weaving and wearing. Margaret would have liked to have grown the pretty blue plant in their own fields but it would not tolerate the northern climate. He needed to be in London by the afternoon, to interview an hautboy player who was hoping to join their minstrels, and to visit his accountant. He would stay at his club overnight, and then on to the Royal Academy where Margaret had arranged for two dozen

203

of their miniatures to be cleaned and restored by experts. On his way home he would pick up some day-old chicks from a farmer in Suffolk, who specialized in old-fashioned breeds.

The Royal Academy telephoned the next day to ask why he had not arrived. Two dozen priceless miniatures should not go unaccounted for. But Margaret was less concerned about the paintings than the whereabouts of her husband. As she told the police, she discovered that he had not kept any of his appointments. Where could he be?

They had, she admitted, had a bit of a tiff on Tuesday night. She hoped that he had not done anything silly.

When TVTV also voiced concern over the disappearance of the usually reliable Ms Swinton, the police were the first to put two and two together.

They interviewed the Pigdon staff who, in fear for their jobs, all maintained that they had never been aware of any impropriety between his lordship and his wife's best friend. They interviewed the itinerant students who said, Good God, yes, they'd been at it like ferrets! In the stables, in the woodyard, in the bakehouse, nowhere was safe. Surprising behaviour, they ventured, in people of their age and standing. When they interviewed Margaret, in depth, it transpired that the 'tiff' had been rather more than that. She had confronted the two about their long-standing love affair and had stamped and raged and thrown things.

The tabloids were in their element:

'FOXY AND MOLE GO TO GROUND'
'HUNT IS ON FOR LORD FOXWELL AND FLOOZY FEN'

Their photographs were plastered across the front pages. There were plenty to choose from: holiday snaps, winter sports, parties, clubs, horse shows, going back years and years. And now she could see what must have been obvious to everyone else. To Rosie.

They were a match. No matter who else was in the picture, herself or the kids or Helen or her own parents, they all paled into the background. Together, they were in focus. Even in a photograph their chemistry was apparent. Why hadn't she seen it before? That look on his face when Fen was around? That vitality, that special brand of sexiness, that oozed from Fen in Simon's company. How had she been taken in?

How had they managed it?

They had been seen in Florida, on the Costa Brava, in Tenerife, all within the space of a week. Happy and in love, said the reports. They were having a high old time. Simon must have found a generous buyer for the miniatures.

The station wagon was found parked outside Newcastle Central Station and the Porsche, what was left of it, some streets away. Fen would be distraught when she came back for it. The wheels had been the first to go, then the doors and the seats. Eventually it was carted away for scrap, a chap came from the Hall to pick up the station wagon and the journalists found new stories to hype.

Margaret, meanwhile, was in a bad way. She raved and spat and pulled out her hair. Jamie, her son, felt that the time had come for her to receive proper treatment and she was admitted to a private clinic. Rest and drugs and counselling did their work, and in time, that other great healer, she was able to read again, paint a little, listen to music. She spent much of the day with the newspaper. Not reading the news so much as doing the crossword, spotting the ball, studying the runners and riders in the 2.30 at Newcastle. For she found that if she listened to that still small voice of hers, that had never betrayed her and would never desert her, she could be a winner every time. And the occasional flutter amused her. Nothing too big; she did not want to draw attention to herself. Time enough for that.

Jamie had been longing for the chance to get his hands on the reins. He fetched the flax and the day-old chicks, interviewed the hautboy player and decided at once that he would do nothing for the minstrels' gallery. But there was a pretty little flautist ... He went and saw the accountant, who was impressed by his grasp of things financial. Jamie had done business studies at Cambridge. They would make a good team.

It was a hot summer and there was a hose ban. In the gardens and animal yards discreet standpipes, hidden from the critical modern eye by upturned carts and stands of lupins, provided water to fill heavy cans, which were carried to thirsty plants and animals before breakfast by anyone who could be spared.

But during business hours it fell to the lot of one poor soul, a history student, to play the part of water carrier. He was given a small handcart on which was fixed an enormous barrel. This he filled at intervals with an authentic wooden bucket from the well in the walled garden. He would tour the grounds crying, 'Water, fresh water!' and dispensing drinks from a tin cup on a chain. There were complaints from the crew about the inadequacy of the system, not to mention the potential health hazard.

It was brought to Jamie's attention by concerned school-teachers that some credibility was lost when their ever-reliable charges spotted bottles of 'Evian' under bushes, and six-packs of lager piled up in the charcoal burner's shack. The water carrier, himself, was not happy. It was the devil's own job he said, to walk the paths of Pigdon balancing a lurching barrel of water. Not only was it dangerous but historically inaccurate, to boot. The water-seller, of old, would have found himself the shadiest spot in the market square, set up shop there and let thirsty customers come to him. Tough, said Jamie.

One day, teetering down the drive to refresh the peasants under the trees, he keeled over in front of forty interested five year-olds. The cart overturned, pitching the barrel sideways onto the parched earth. It smashed open like an egg, and released forty gallons of sploshing water for the babes to paddle in. Whether he had had too much sun or real ale, whether he had caught the wheel on a stone or lost his balance, or whether, as Jamie suspected, he had done it on purpose, he had made his point. Something had to be done.

Jamie recalled a similar dry spell in his childhood. He was sure there had been other wells around then, all over the estate. In fact he had a distinct memory of sitting in a meadow, watching his parents digging just such a well. He could almost smell the cool dankness of the buried water, could almost remember carrying away rocks and earth in his little wheelbarrow, could almost hear the laughter and shrieks as Father and Mother had leapt about, wetting each other with chilly splashes. There had been joy then. No madness, no anger, no Fen.

Those wells had to be around still. He had no intention of dirtying his own hands, but if he could find them, get them opened up, they would be the answer to his problem.

So one morning in August, early, before the gates opened to admit the masses, he went in search of the well that his parents had dug, equipped with a couple of crowbars. It had been a grassy place, with buttercups. (Mother had shone a buttercup torch under his chin and decided that he liked butter.) The meadow in front of the moathouse was a likely spot. Though why they should want to sink a well this far out, he could not imagine. It would have been of no use to house nor garden.

As he searched through the swishing grass (dry enough for hay and far too long; perhaps, today, mowing should be top of the agenda ...) he seemed to recall, in the days of ghost-busting weekends and mediaeval banquets, talk of building a gatehouse where the time-tunnel stood now. A gate-keeper's well would have been a necessity. And hadn't he seen something of the sort? A round lid, flush with the ground, embedded in bricks. He'd taken it for a manhole cover, access to a sewer or the mains water flow. It was the sort of thing you saw every day and never noticed. Come to think of it, weren't manholes straight-sided, as a general rule?

Now a well down by the time-tunnel would be a splendid thing. When the drought was at an end it could become a wishing-well, with a catch-penny tray to receive hopeful groats, no not groats, crowns and half-sovereigns ... That the punters would have stocked up with, in exchange for solid sterling, before making their trip through time! Yes, yes.

He was brimming with money-spinning ideas: cart-rides for the kiddies, up and down the gravel drive, a refreshment area under the trees, where authentic serving-wenches would provide honey cakes and elderflower cordial with a smile. Perhaps a few orange sellers could peddle their wares, à la Nell Gwyn. Should be able to make a tidy profit if he did a deal with the local greengrocer. And over there was a stretch of green that was ideal for a country fair, with period side-shows. Boot out the merry maypole dancers. Modern kids would be far more interested in boxing-booths and bearded ladies. There must be plenty of freaks around who would like to earn a few bob. And all in a good educational cause. He supposed dancing bears and cock-fighting were out. Still, there must be ways and means ...

He found it at last, screened by nettles and dock, a rusty iron lid, rather larger than he had remembered. He stamped down the nettles and brushed away a fly or two before settling down to investigate his find. He expected the lid to be rusted in, after twenty-odd years, but found to his delight that the crowbar slipped under the metal lip quite easily. He bore down on the lever and the heavy cover parted cleanly from its bed. Another crowbar at the adjacent side enabled him to lift it, and, if he braced himself, to shift it sideways for inspection. But as he did so an excruciating smell of putrefaction knocked him sideways, and he dropped the cover back in place. The flies buzzed inquisitively. Dear Lord, he gasped, desperately filling his lungs with clean air, it *was* a sewer, or a cess-pit. He should have guessed from the flies. Thoughts of a plague pit actually crossed his mind. No, he thought, getting to his feet, three-hundred-year-old corpses would not smell so bad. A pity. That would have really drawn the crowds.

He made his way over to the woods where a number of students were camped in covered wagons, playing at tinkers. Today they would earn their crust, lazy lot of skivers. Today they would be mowers and reapers, and scythe that meadow into some sort of shape. Very picturesque, with pitchforks and a haycart. He had better warn them to fetch pitchers of water from the house. It was likely to be hot, backbreaking work.

CHAPTER NINE

Anna, September 1999

The papers were full of it for days:

FOXY LADY MEETS HER WATERLOO

Mystery surrounds the death of Margaret, Lady Foxwell, aged 59, whose fully-clothed body was found washed up under Waterloo Bridge, London, early this morning. It is thought that Lady Foxwell, whose home, Pigdon Hall in Northumberland, was one of the first stately homes to be opened to the public as an Historical Re-creation, came to London to meet old friends. Instead, this wealthy woman (who also owned the exclusive Willis Fashion chain of shops), cut her throat and threw herself off Vauxhall Bridge. Lady Foxwell had a history of depression. The police do not suspect foul play.

I had that sinking sort of feeling that told me I should have known! She had always been a stupid cow. Not with regard to business; hot potatoes in that department, but superstitious to the nth degree. So some silly girls had told her, a long time ago, to meet them at the Tate on the ninth of the ninth of the ninety-ninth for a jolly suicide tryst? They hadn't turned up so she had done it anyway. *Crass!*

I telephoned Jamie, immediately, to offer my condolences. Poor chap, he was distraught. She had been so much better lately, he said. If it had happened four years ago he could have understood but since her spell in the 'happy farm' (his words) she had been leading a contented, if somewhat eccentric life. Her illness was not cured, but controlled, with drugs, and she had Lottie on a strict timetable. She would chat to her after lunch and before bed and refuse to speak to her at other times. It had worked with a fair degree of success.

He ran the business now, but his mother had had a useful part to play, as wardrobe mistress. Of course, she had missed Simon and Fen, and in fact, he thought privately that that had been her prime motive in going down to London, hoping that Fen might be there. She had felt the need of old friends, people of her own age with whom to compare notes on reaching the big six oh, the turn of the century, that sort of thing. To reminisce.

Of course she had, poor little thing. You do at our age. Well, some people do. The weight of guilt on my shoulders nearly floored me. It was my fault. I hadn't been to see her in a million years.

I'd hardly seen anyone.

Smudge had vanished off the face of the earth, Rosie was *persona non grata*, Fen was on some idyllic South Sea Island with fat Simon, living on coconuts and the proceeds of the sale of the miniatures. And nary a postcard in four years, mean cow.

I did see Jo from time to time. I scuttled off down to the sea like an arthritic crab, for the occasional long weekend, and she and Rob came up for the London scene, once in a blue moon, but now that I'd retired to do my comic strip for the *Observer*, the house had become a dumping ground for kids, Zac's and Joey's, and it was difficult to get shot of them.

And Newcastle was too far away for a flying visit. I'd have had to've stayed and spent an entire weekend or more, squirming around the subject of the runaways. Because although I had every sympathy with Mags, and thought they'd treated her atrociously, I wouldn't have been able to take her part against Fen. I knew she was a bitch of the deepest shit, but I liked Fen and I was glad someone, at least, had a satisfying love life.

To be honest, the Pigdon lifestyle didn't suit me. The champers and Pimms, and cherries out of season. Sitting in chairs that cost a month's salary, or three months' pension, as it was now. Pictures on the wall that would have paid my mortgage three times over. Frightened to move in case I broke something priceless. Minding my Ps and Qs. I was an inverted snob, I was well aware of that, and playing at lords and ladies was not my bag. I'd far rather have had a ding-dong with them across the council chamber.

It hadn't occurred to me that Maggie would keep the tryst. That anyone would. Jo was involved in a big family party that day, to celebrate her sixtieth birthday. She had invited me but there had been an important meeting of the Housing Committee that I wouldn't have missed for the world. A crafty move was afoot to build on Green Belt land and I wasn't having that.

Rosie wouldn't be there. Sunk without trace. Not so much as

a Christmas card in all these years. I looked for her on the book-shelves but either she was one of these one book wonders or she was writing under another name. So I had to make do with *Friends for Life*. I read it 'til I was cross-eyed, until I knew it inside out and backwards, re-living every moment with her, every emotion, scouring the bits about me for some echo of my own longing. I read between the lines, between the letters of the words, trying to burrow into her mind. I worried over her choice of words, her style, the unnecessary flowery bits, the despairing cadence of a phrase. Why had she chosen to be ironic here, senti-mental there? What was she thinking? What did she feel?

The pages fell out in protest. When I went to buy a new copy they told me it was out of print.

I'd lost her.

Smudge, too. Wherever she was I hoped they had newspapers there, that she would read the obituary columns and maybe come back for the funeral. She hadn't looked in at the reunion, clearly. I hadn't thought she would. Poor love. Spooked by a telephone call, Monk said. And things had been going so well. But a funeral ... Well, maybe she'd send flowers and some sort of clue as to her whereabouts. I couldn't believe that I'd never see her again.

Fen also had good reason to steer clear of the Tate.

And since Maggie, Lady Margaret, had missed the last two reunions, I'd felt sure she wouldn't bother with this one. The suicide one. If I'd known ...

She should have said something. She knew where to find me.

Or I should have got in touch with her. Told her, at least, that I wasn't going. As I told Jamie.

He said it was nobody's fault. His mother was perfectly cap-able of telephoning and checking for herself, and obviously hadn't. But that was typical of Maggie. She was always pleased to hear from us but incapable of picking up a phone or a pen her-self. Always too busy or shy or something. I understood. It takes effort to keep up friendships. Good intentions are not enough. Good intentions are lists of people you really need to talk to. What happens when you lose the lists? Other things crop up. The years come between you. And you lose touch.

So she had gone 'on spec'. Jamie said he couldn't understand why finding nobody there should make her suicidal. She was made of stronger stuff than that.

211

This being the 'silly season' newswise, the paparazzi were digging up interviews with all and sundry. Several people seemed to have noticed her sitting on the gallery steps:

'There were four of us ladies,' said Mrs Penelope Givens, aged 65. 'We were there when the doors opened. On the dot of nine. We were so looking forward to the exhibition. And this woman leapt up and practically threw herself at us. Well, it was a shock. We didn't know her from Adam. She was terribly apologetic afterwards, of course, said it was a case of mistaken identity. She was a nicely-spoken woman, expecting friends, she said, some of whom she hadn't seen for twenty-odd years, and was no longer sure what they looked like. Well, it was an easy mistake to make, I suppose.'

A young man said she had asked him to mind her step for her while she nipped to the Ladies. Since she and he were the only people sitting on the steps he had found her request somewhat perplexing. People in the queue for the Millennium Exhibition remembered her pushing past them, recalled other people complaining. The doorkeeper had remonstrated with her but she had given him a ten pound note and he had let her through. The lavatory attendant also reported an extravagant tip. In the gallery shop, an assistant remembered her clearly. A smartly-dressed woman, with well-cut grey hair, jumping the queue, waving a bundle of postcards under her nose. Arrogant cow!

'Miss!' she had demanded. But the assistant was used to 'her sort' and refused to be swayed, certainly not by someone calling her 'Miss'.

'Oh, please, young woman, don't be difficult. I am in a dreadful hurry.'

People were grumbling and making loud remarks about money and privilege. The woman promptly took out a handful of notes, laid them on the counter, crying, 'Keep the change,' and walked out of the shop with her purchases.

People had seen her at various times throughout the day, smoking, eating a Kit-Kat, writing postcards, muttering to herself. Some gave her a wide berth, thinking that she wasn't all there. Some thought differently:

Mr Ravin Singh, 37, a primary teacher from Bexley Heath, was surprised and delighted when a middle-aged woman approached him on the steps of the Tate Gallery and insisted on giving his group of twenty-five schoolchildren fifty pounds. Said Mr Singh, 'It was an unexpected and generous action. Why should such a lovely little lady take her own life?'

Well that's what we'd all like to know.

* * *

I was in bed by nine, after a long soak in the bath, ready for an early start next morning. The drive to Newcastle would take me a good five hours and the funeral was set for eleven o'clock.

I awoke, in the middle of the night, to pandemonium. The dog was trying to bring the house down with his barking – the front door, in particular, by flinging himself, body and soul, against it. Someone on the other side had their finger jammed on the bell. The cat tore up the stairs in a frenzy when I switched on the lights, thinking it was time for breakfast, and I had to kick her out from under my bare feet, yelling as I did so at who-ever it was to keep their hair on. I may have inserted a telling adjective. I almost fell as I attempted to throw my dressing-gown over my gross nudity and negotiate the stairs and grandchildren's Duplo bricks and the cat, all at the same time.

'Hang on!'

I grabbed Traveller, Gypsy's grandson, who was in danger of busting a gut, and slung him into the front room.

'Sweet Jesus,' I grumbled as I finally got to the door, 'this had better be important!'

She turned an anguished face towards the crack in the door, her hands twisting, uncertainly.

'Sorry,' she mouthed.

'Rosie?' I blinked. I might still have been asleep.

'Hi,' was all she said.

I began to close the door.

'Anna ... Please!' she begged.

'I'm taking the chain off, dope.'

But she stiffened when I tried to embrace her, as though she thought I might still try to wring her neck, or rape her. That hurt. And there was a lump in my throat like an ostrich egg.

'Rosie,' I croaked. 'Oh Rosie, *Rosie*! Oh, God, it's good to see

213

you!' I felt like a kid with the most wonderful surprise birthday present.

'Is it?'

'Of course it is!'

Her dark eyes raked mine for any hint of a lie and finding none dared to lower her defences, just a little.

'I ... I had to come.' She seemed to find the salt-dough frame of my hall mirror of extreme tactile interest, tracing the little brown leaves and figures with her finger. She must have seen it a hundred times before.

I regarded her reflection, suspiciously. There was something different about her face for which age alone could not account. Her eyes were deeper set, and the muscles of emotion were tugging the skin around them into permanent tucks and pleats. Her cheekbones were sharper and pink with stress and her lips more crumpled. But she was still a good-looker. Grey hair, curly again and cut to fit round her face, and a two-piece dress, loose and filmy to flatter her long bones.

'You had to come ...?' I prompted, gently.

She whirled around.

'Anna, how could I have done that to you? The book and ... everything.' She had always liked to come straight to the point had Rosie. 'No wonder you hated me.'

'I *loathed* you,' I said. 'But it wasn't the book. The book just hurt.'

Her eyes were too bright in the hall light.

'Oh now come on, come in the kitchen, I'll make us some tea.'

She didn't move.

'I'd better go ...'

'Don't you dare!' I filled the passage with my bulk, cutting off her retreat. 'Look, for God's sake, we've all done things we're ashamed of; wasn't that the point of your book? Even "nice" people ...? But it's in the past. All over. Anyway ...' I had had a long time to think about this. 'I suppose some of it was my fault. You wanted to get your own back on me.'

'Yes.' Her eyes were a challenge. She, too, had worked out where to lay the blame.

'I frightened Miss Muffet away, making improper sugges- tions. And, as little girls do, you ran away to hide in the skirts of Mummy church. And slung shit at me, which hurts a lot more than sticks and stones, let me tell you. And just to prove your nice heterosexuality to the world, but mostly me, you dumped poor old Jack in favour of pretty Roger. Naa na na na naa naa!'

I waggled my sixty-year old bum like a brat.

She bit back a smile.

'Roger and I didn't work ... it was too late. Wishful thinking.'

I knew it.

'And the book was a flop, too, even in paperback. The advances hardly paid for the nose-job.'

That was it! The nose. The kinks were all ironed out. I ran my finger down the elegant result of painful surgery.

'It's nice,' I said. 'Fen would be pleased ...'

She grasped my fingers then and brought them to her lips.

'Oh, Anna,' she moaned, 'how could I have been so bloody stupid?'

And at some point during the frantic hugging and kissing that followed, she breathed, 'God, I've missed you,' but I could tell. I've always been a great believer in body language. It says it all.

I couldn't believe she was real. Kept stroking her. But when we found ourselves in the kitchen I had to let her go, to fill the kettle. Old habits ... She sat at the table, with her long feet in their flatties neatly crossed under the chair, and it was as though it were yesterday that she had sat there last with the cat on her lap, leaning her chin on her hand, watching me swill the teapot and find clean cups.

'So why are you here?'

A shadow flickered across her eyes. But she wasn't quite ready to tell me. She forced a broad grin. 'I couldn't resist your siren call, you gorgeous creature!'

Nuts. And as for being gorgeous. Jesus. She'd got me out of bed and I looked a wreck, hair riddled with grey and tumbling down my back, old candlewick dressing gown covered with cats' hair and stained with bleach, bare feet misshapen with bunions. But had I been tarted up and raring to go I would still have felt fat and frumpy beside Rosie. It had always been that way.

I gave her a grateful kiss anyway, on her velvet cheek, and put tea-bags in the pot.

She beat around the bush, admiring little Hannah's painting of a toffee apple on legs labelled 'Granny' that I'd pinned to my notice-board, and Ben's fire-engine. He only painted fire-engines. There was a lentil and pasta party-plate face, and a sweetie-paper butterfly, a few photos and Josh's certificate for his sponsored swim. The treasures of my 'Gallery'. I filled her in briefly on events, the grandchildren, the job, aware that she wasn't listening.

'Anna ...' At last.

'Come and sit down,' patting the other kitchen chair.

I guessed it was bad news.

'Anna ... I'm sorry ... Fen's dead.'

No ... I kept shaking my head and saying 'No' as if reprimanding the dog. 'No' as if saying it firmly enough could undo the harm, make everything right.

Fen, that bright and shiny girl, who had never let anything stand in her way, had been stopped finally. Dead. When I'd thought she was safe on silver sands beside a blue lagoon, with flowers in her yellow hair and Simon beside her, like Oliver Reed in *Castaway*, she'd been getting herself killed. How? Sharks? A tidal wave? Something exotic?

'Maggie did it.'

Eh?

Maggie? Little Maggie? She couldn't. Not with her big green eyes and slight over-bite. She was kind and good. She wouldn't hurt a fly. But that was Maggie from long ago. Maggie in middle-age had had an errant husband and a flighty friend. She also had Lottie, and they'd already tried it once.

I could feel the blood leaving my head and the room going digital. Virtual unreality.

Rosie was leaping about, going, 'Oh no, oh no, don't faint, don't faint. Wait, let me pour you some tea. Anna, hold on, oh where's the fucking brandy?'

'Whisky ... sideboard,' I gasped, 'in the front room. And let the dog out while you're there.'

In my head Fen said, 'God, I mean, *God*! Not Maggie!'

When I was more myself, with Traveller settled at my feet, Rosie said, 'Sorry, I didn't handle that very well, did I?'

'Will you stop apologizing?'

'Right. You're sure you're okay? This is going to be pretty harrowing.'

'Fire away. Fen's dead and ... M-Maggie ...' I sniffed and sniffed again and my face twisted, all by itself, into an awful grimace of grief.

'Have another drink. Blow your nose.'

So, fortified with whisky chased with tea, and with a roll of kitchen towel, I learned how Maggie, sweet Maggie, had killed her best friend.

Rosie delved deep into her pocket and pulled out six picture postcards, the sort you get from galleries, and laid them, writing side up, on my kitchen table as though she were going to give me a tarot reading. Each was covered in tiny, precise script.

My heart gave a little lurch. These were the postcards the newspaper had mentioned, the ones she'd been writing on the steps of the Tate, the ones she had paid for so dearly.

'My communication from Maggie,' Rosie verified, 'postmarked the tenth.'

The tenth? The next day, after she'd ... This was so bizarre. And to add to the surreality of it, on the first postcard, depicting our friends on the *Golden Stairs*, she had written:

Wish you were here ...

And down the side of Rosie's address, somewhere in Islington, *Hope you like the piccies*! Could she really have been suicidal when she wrote that? Could she really have stuck on the stamps, dusted herself off, gone to find a post box and then cut her throat?

Sorry to burden you with this, Rosie – it was my intention to tell everyone in person, sort of death-bed confession, but I'm sure you'll pass it on. You can't keep much to yourself, can you? Whether you tell the police is up to you but poor Jamie will need to know, so he can inherit. I read your book, finally, Rosie. Found it in some garbage I'd put out for the bin men, after the VE Day celebs, 1995. Unputdownable – you should be proud! Though I prefer a happy ending, myself. Kill off the antagonists, I say. Cont'd ...

Rosie sighed as she placed the card back on the table.

'It's all my fault. If I hadn't ...'

'Look, Rose, someone commits a crime, a journalist writes about it. Someone breaks the seventh commandment, a novelist fictionalizes it. Who's the sinner? Certainly not the writer.'

'But there was no call to ... Why did I? They ... you were my friends ...!' she wailed.

'Fen would have done it – she would have made it into a documentary, warts and all, if she'd thought of it first. Though

217

she'd have made sure Maggie didn't see it. And who's to say Maggie wouldn't have found out sooner or later some other way. Fen and Simon were sailing pretty close to the wind, had been for years. We all knew. Any one of us could have let something slip. Or one of her kids or the students. It was always a risk.'

'But it was me.'

'Yeah. And it was deliberate. To get back at Fen for Roger. For all those boring years with Jack. For poor old Bridget. Well, that's cool, as my American grandchildren would say. Fen has a lot to answer for.'

'But I hurt a lot of other people in the process.'

'You sure did, hon. You let it all hang out, all your gripes and grudges. Against me. Against Smudge and Jo and Maggie for ... I dunno ... for being victims, letting themselves be used. All of us for involving you in a murder.'

'Manslaughter.'

'Whatever. You were on a roll, girl.'

She frowned.

'What do you want me to say, Rosie? You were. You couldn't stop. You'd been hurt and just wanted to hurt back. No matter who.'

She sighed.

'But I really don't think you should blame yourself for what Simon and Fen did to Maggie. Or vice versa. They have only themselves to blame.'

She was shaking her head, about to deny ...

'Oh yes, Maggie, too,' I said, pre-empting her. 'If she hadn't been so busy making money, if she'd paid a bit more attention to Simon, she'd have seen what was staring her and everyone else in the face. She might even have stopped it. You knew, I knew, years and years ago, why didn't she? Her own fault entirely.'

Rosie took a deep and hungry breath.

'I could do with a fag, Anna.'

'You don't smoke ...'

'I didn't.'

I had given up, in fact, on VE Day. The ninth of the fifth ninety five, four years before. It had seemed like a good day for it. It had been a miserable, gruelling withdrawal and I had put on two stone.

'Hang on,' I said.

Up in Joey's old room, now the guest room, in the bottom of the wardrobe were two hundred Bensons brought back duty-free from my last trip to Boston. I'd intended to give them to Zac next time I saw him. He could spare his old mother one pack, at least. And as I undid the golden box, like Pandora, I saw myself releasing a whole heap of trouble. But for Rosie, anything.

The bed was in a state of undress. I'd have to sort out some clean linen and a duvet cover if Rosie was going to stay over. Maybe I'd leave it awhile, see what transpired.

Which reminded me to collect my reading glasses from my room. I wanted to have a good look at those postcards.

So we puffed our way through the next card and the next, good old *Awakening Conscience* by Holman Hunt, with the kept woman leaping out of her lover's lap with a look of Ah me, I am undone, and Rossetti's '*Fazio's Mistress*', which also seemed fairly appropriate. And on the reverse of each:

Wednesday was the staff's night off, in lieu of the Bank Holiday. (We work weekends at Pigdon.) Fen was staying with us on Wednesday night – she'd been down in London, reporting an East End VE Day street party for TVTV. The boys were away and Daisy was at a barbecue in the woods, with the students. I had given her no argument, for once, as it meant that I would have Fen and Simon to myself. I cooked them tincture-of-henbane-stroganoff, a speciality of mine. Henbane, for the uninitiated, is a powerful narcotic. While they ate I worked the conversation round to Daisy and the students. I had found, I lied, nasty things … cont'd.

… in the woods, half-burnt crosses, bits of paper with cabbalistic signs, chicken bones, antlers, things that led me to suspect that they might be up to no good. I persuaded Simon, who was, by this time, nicely groggy, to come with me to catch the revellers red-handed. Off we went, avoiding the drive (crunchy gravel). Simon was clearly not at all sure what he was doing, creeping across the meadow in the dark. He didn't want to catch Daisy in some sexy ritual in the woods. He wanted to have his own sexy ritual in bed with Fen, if he could stay awake. Nevertheless, where I led, he followed – as always. Cont'd …

The next postcard was Ford Madox Brown's *The Hayfield*. Dark enough for night, it even looked as though a moon was shining. She had gone to a lot of trouble in choosing her cards, I thought. She must have spent hours poring over them. But as Rosie said,

Maggie was so organized, she probably had the names of the paintings written down ready. She wouldn't have wanted to spend too long away from the steps.

I stopped once or twice for him to catch up, and the third time he disappeared ... Poof! Just like that! Down a disused well near the time-tunnel. (I'd been out earlier to remove the lid.) Just like one of those old silent movies – the Keystone Cops or somesuch. It was so easy, I had to laugh. Lottie said it would be. Well, there wasn't a sound except a sort of distant splash. As he got his breath back to scream the water must have closed over his head.

You had to hand it to the girl. Mad as a hatter, but she was all there when it came to murder. Getting them to walk themselves to their final resting place was not only efficient, it was quite brilliant. She was so slight, of course, she would never have been able to dispose of Simon. He was over sixteen stone according to the papers. She was lucky his beer-gut hadn't wedged halfway. I never could see what either of them saw in him.

('You wouldn't,' said Rosie, 'not your type at all.' But then I reminded her that *she* had always referred to him as 'that prick Simon'. 'Exactly,' she said, with a strange sort of smile. What had she been up to?)

Fen's turn next.
(Oh, poor Fen ... poor Maggie. Fat tears plopped onto the blur of blue writing and Rosie moved it out of range. She read the next bit aloud, while I took off my specs to wipe my eyes.)
She was almost out on her feet and slumped against me all the way. No idea what was happening. Until she came to the brink (now this is interesting), and she saw the moonlight twinkling down there ... cont'd ...

I could almost guess what was coming next. Fen had had a nasty experience with a well once before. I put my specs back on. There was:
Dante's Vision of Rachel and Leah by Rossetti. Of course, the two biblical sisters, both wife to Jacob, standing contemplating a well. Both very different, Rachel the mystic, Leah the bright and bubbly busy bee.

She seemed to come to her senses then, and it was almost as though she recognized that this was her destiny, what she deserved – she stepped forward of her own volition, Rosie, I swear. I was ready to give her a helping shove, but she didn't need it. Didn't even cry out as she went down. I popped the lid back on ...

Christ, she was so cold, so matter of fact. How quickly love turns to hate!

... Came down later with the miniatures. They were a nice touch, don't you think? Certainly, they were no loss, ugly things – Simon was welcome to them. While everyone was still asleep, I drove the station wagon to Newcastle Central, and got a minicab back ... cont'd ...

'Three guesses?' quizzed Rosie, her hand over the last postcard. Of course it was. Maggie was not an original thinker. Poor old *Ophelia*, babbling downstream with her handful of weeds.

> *'Till that her garments, heavy with their drink,*
> *Pull'd the poor wretch from her melodious lay*
> *To muddy death.'*

I didn't quote aloud. I wasn't quite that crass. Rosie's lips were moving, though.

'There's rosemary ...' she was muttering, 'that's for remembrance ... Oh Mags.' She pressed her lips together as we both studied the picture. Then, 'Who's it meant to be, d'you suppose, Fen or Maggie herself?'

'Funny,' I said, 'I always used to think Ophelia looked so like Fen. But she doesn't at all, any more.'

'Well, Fen had her face rearranged a bit, don't forget.'

'It has to be Maggie now, doesn't it? It just shows you, she knew exactly what she was letting herself in for. Probably why she cut her throat first.'

Now Rosie was weeping.

'Poor, poor thing. She was such a sweet kid. Fate has been really unkind to her.'

'Lottie, you mean? Lottie stood by her when the rest of us forgot.'

Did the same with Fen's Porsche. A different minicab company this time for the return journey. They thought nothing of it. They're always bringing people back to Pigdon at odd hours. Lying to the police, next

day, was quite exhilarating. As Lottie says, when you've only four years
to live you can't be doing with people cluttering up your life with
adultery and what Jo calls 'how's your father'. Don't go blaming your-
self, Rosie. It was meant to be. Nemesis. I'm taking her with me, by the
way. A pity really; you'd have found Lottie a great help with business
ventures and suchlike. She has a good head for figures. Don't know the
correct form for signing off a suicide note. Can't remember ever having
seen it in any book on etiquette! See you. Margaret XXX

'Bye, Maggie,' I said. 'Poor cow.'

'Good riddance, *Lottie!*' Rosie was emphatic.

'Don't like the sound of that "See you", though.' I was only
half-joking.

'Let's hope she's at peace now.'

I crossed my fingers.

'You're *not* superstitious?' she jeered, grateful for the diversion.

'Insurance,' I said, 'just in case!'

'Liar! Next time you cut your thumb or have a puncture on
the M1, or arrive at the supermarket checkout with a trolleyful
of shopping and no purse, it'll be her fault. Lottie's. Specially if
it happens on a palindrome day.'

'Not at all,' knowing she was probably right.

'Poor old Lottie. She gets the blame for everything. Fen's little
romp with Roger, the Riley thing, Smudge and dastardly Dave,
my damn book ... no one's fault, nothing to do with bad judgement or greed, nothing like that. It's all Lottie's fault. Too damn
convenient, that's the trouble with Lottie.'

'In fact,' I said, 'she was probably a good old girl. Maggie
liked her. They were inseparable, in fact!' My hoot of laughter
sounded hollow even to my own ears.

'You know what I think?' said Rosie, propping up her chin to
look at the daddy-longlegs' refuge I was running on my ceiling.

'More or less ... though I'm a bit out of practice these days.'

She flashed me a sideways look under arching brows, and
pressed on. 'I think, when Maggie had her brainstorm, after
Daisy was born, I think she took Lottie unto herself ...'

'Well, of course she did. We all know that.'

'No, I mean, she took her off our backs. Sacrificed her sanity
for us.'

'You mean like Jesus took all our sins away? Oh, give over,
Rose; you've had too much dogma stuffed down your throat.'

222

'Think about it. We didn't go to the Tate last week, did we? and nothing's happened to us ...'

We both rapped furiously on the wooden table and burst out laughing.

'... So far so good, anyway. No, listen, Anna. Fen *was* there in eighty-eight, with the rest of you, and look what happened to her?'

'And you weren't and look what happened to you?'

'No, that was a good year. It was only later things got a bit fraught between Roger and me.'

'Was it?'

'Mmm.'

'So you're saying Lottie has nothing to do with our lives? Well, pardon me, but isn't that what I've said all along?'

She said, 'She kept you and me together for forty-odd years.'

'Give or take fifteen. Was that her? Couldn't we have managed that on our own?'

'You're saying the blood pact on the allotment made no difference to our lives at all?'

'Well, apart from us all having a fixation with dates and wells and curses ...'

Somehow, something, call it Fate, call it Lottie, call it Life, had brought us to this point: Rosie, leaning across my kitchen table to hold my hand, looking very pretty, very desirable.

'Here's to Lottie,' I said, raising my glass.

'Well, yes,' said Rosie, following my train of thought to the letter.

Later I re-read the cards, sighing and sucking regrets through my teeth, reliving my friend's last hours, before pinning them, finally, without any pricking of my thumbs despite the booze and the lack of sleep, to my cork-tile 'gallery'.

Great pictures. But none could hold a candle to little Hannah's portrait of Granny.

'So what shall we do?' Rosie asked, at last, draining her glass.

'About what?'

'Do we tell Jamie where to find Fen and Foxy or do we leave them in peace?'

'We ought to. Tell, I mean. There's poor old Jamie, not quite a lord, and thinking his dad's done a runner with the family miniatures. We ought to clear his name.'

'We ought indeed.' Rosie poured us both another drink.

'They'll want to bury him on the estate, next to Maggie.'

'Will they? Even though she killed him? She won't like that.'

'And he's tucked in so cosily with Fen.'

'It would be cruel to disturb them,' she agreed.

'They might eventually come to light.'

'If something goes wrong with the drains ...'

Later still, we took the bottle to bed and mulled over 'if onlys' and 'what ifs'. What if there had been no reunions?

Rosie thought she might have gone to the concert with Roger. In which case Fen wouldn't have got pregnant. She'd have grown up to marry some nice safe stockbroker ...

'And bonked the living daylights out of Simon the minute Maggie's back was turned!' I said.

'No,' said Rosie, with certainty, 'she'd have been too happy with her stockbroker.'

'Fen was destined to bonk the living daylights out of Simon. And you'd still have managed to get a book out of it.'

'Ah, well ...'

'What if I'd not had you lot to help me out with Riley?'

'Oh don't. A nightmare.' Then, 'Do you still have them? Those awful dreams about the train and the precipice?'

'Nah.'

'You cured them?'

'Yep.'

'How? Sex?'

'You've got a one-track mind. I went to the police.'

'*What!*'

So I told her how Jo and I had been plagued by some loony telephoning and threatening to tell the police how we had murdered Riley.

'He phoned me, too,' she said. 'Several times. And then he stopped. Hey!' She slopped her whisky, stuck out her tongue to lick a runnel from the glass, and remembered. 'You don't suppose he tried it on Smudge, too?'

'I think so. It was around that time. 1989.'

'Oh poor Smudge. She was such a wimp, she'd have run a mile.'

'More than that.'

'We'll have to find her, you know.'

I nodded. 'Bring her home. Where shall we start looking?'

'France. She always wanted to go to France.'

'It was dastardly Dave, you know. The phone calls. He ... um ... he said he'd read your book.'

'Oh,' they had said, chewing their pencil ends, 'Yes ... well. Um ... thank you, madam. That's very interesting. Mmm. Witnesses?' They wrote on their proforma, muttering:

Lost track of two witnesses.

Corpse?

Dead and gone these ... When did this happen, madam? 1977? *... these twelve years.*

Uhuh. Evidence?

Scrapped and replaced with new rolling stock.

'Oh, you still have the carving knife.' They wrote that down. 'Fine. And the children ...?

... and one in America.

'Yes. Right, madam, if you wouldn't mind taking a seat ...'

Poor things. The course of true justice never did run smooth. They do like things nice and tidy, the police. Very keen on clear-up rates. And they'd thought that the case against Chummy, a nasty mess on the railway lines at the time, had nevertheless been cleared up very satisfactorily. Until this bloody woman comes along, stirring it all up again.

They unearthed the file. Read what he'd done to the children, saw the photos of their injuries, the cupboard under the stairs, the piles of sticky tape. They studied our account of the rescue. How he had threatened us with the carving knife. How we had damaged him in self-defence. What they hadn't known was quite how extensive that damage had been. Nor that he hadn't actually taken himself down to the railway and run along the track.

So they arrested me, and charged me with 'the unlawful killing of William Riley' and for attempting to pervert the course of justice.

'Anna, that's awful. But why didn't they come for me? Or Smudge or Jo?'

'Smudge had already done a bunk, you were off in the wilds of Rwanda or Biafra or somewhere, doing good works, and Jo was on red alert.'

'She knew?'

'Oh yes.'

225

'So I might have been arrested for murder.'

'Mmm. Possibly.'

'Thanks, pal.'

I told her then that the police had made out a report, which they had sent to the Crown Prosecution Services, emphasizing that the kick to the jaw had been a spontaneous and understandable reaction under attack (self-defence), that the intention had not been to kill, that I had not struck the fatal blow, in any case, and that the disposal of the body had been an attempt further to protect the minors. (Who, incidentally, all added their two penn'orth, corroborating my story as far as they could.)

They recommended that it would *not* be in the interests of the CPS to proceed, the case was dropped, sleeping dogs were left to lie and I was sent home.

'Yahoo!' she cheered and threw her arms around me.

* * *

After finishing what was left of the whisky and sobbing and laughing for half the night, we were in no fit state to go to Maggie's funeral next morning. We telephoned our apologies and spent most of the day in bed. It wasn't worth making up the one in the spare room, we decided. Not now.

'Do you still have *your* dream?' I asked, during a wakeful period. 'The one about the faceless couple getting married in the bombed-out church?'

'Not since I found out who they were.'

'Oh, yeah, who?'

'Read my mind,' she said.

Jacqueline Jacques was born in Tŷ Croes, Anglesey in 1942, but moved to Walthamstow, north-east London, whence springs the 'Lottie' myth. She has a husband, Peter, two grown up children and two cats, and now lives in Buckhurst Hill, Essex.

After leaving school she spent three unsatisfying years working for the Civil Service, before escaping to Newcastle-on-Tyne, where she obtained a degree in Sociology and met her husband. On to Leicester, for a teaching qualification which in no way fitted her for a lifetime's career in primary schools – even less so in latter years, when she specialized in the learning difficulties of autistic children. She began writing creatively (apart from school reports) in 1989, and many of her short stories have won prizes or been published, including 'Lovey-Dovey Cats' Eyes' in *Luminous and Forlorn* (Honno, 1994). *Lottie* is her début novel, conceived during a stay at Tŷ Newydd Writers' Centre, Cricieth. In 1995 she quit the day job and is now working on her third novel.